REALM CRASHERS

AND THE
SHADOW
KING

D1531315

Cover Design by Hampton Lamoureux of TS95 Studios

Chapter graphic: Kevin David Pointon
Story break graphic: Gordon Dylan Johnson

ISBN 979-8-9872396-1-2 (paperback)
ISBN 979-8-9872396-2-9 (hardback)
ISBN 979-8-9872396-0-5 (ebook)

Published by Octavo Press

OCTAVO PRESS

REALM CRASHERS

AND THE

SHADOW KING

Nicole Cavey

To VW

who helped me start this adventure

Chapter 1

It was Alex's dreams that disturbed him the most. They weren't the normal dreams where a person would fantasize about flying or getting a dog; not even as unsettling as fears of being kidnapped or drowning taking physical form. No, it was much worse.

They were a plethora of terror and downright confusion. Alex was lucid in the dreams, but he had barely any control. He could never move, nor was able to from his original position. He was just a passenger, a prisoner, of his own mind. He only knew a few things about his dreams—his nightmares.

It was always the same scene. Alex was never able to fully see what was happening; it varied how much he could and couldn't see. In some instances, he was fully blind; in others, he could barely make out the terrain around him. And it was always the same voices screaming inside his head, in the same pitch, with the same duration of the sound, every time. They were extremely haunting and equally frustrating.

And then the burning would start. It started in his hands, snaking up his arms, and after that into his legs.

Once it reached his chest, he swore that he was dying. Pressure would begin to build in his skull, pressing against his cranium and brain. Just when he would begin to scream in pain, he would jerk awake, desperate for oxygen to enter his lungs like he was a drowning man.

For as long as he could remember, it had been his constant dread. It never bothered him enough, however, to affect him outside of closed doors. Alex never mentioned it to another soul about what happened in his mind when his guard was down at night.

As time passed, it became the norm of life. A little thing that happened only a few times a year, and it bothered him less. Alex became in tune with his nightmares. He was sure that everyone had something they wanted to hide. But his morale cracked because something had changed within six months. Now *every time* he closed his eyes he would dream.

Alex didn't hate school. He truly didn't, but it did exhaust him. His history teacher, Mrs. Holts, was droning on about classwork, trying her hardest to be engaging with her students, but it wasn't working. She soon gave up on talking and let them work in silence.

It was quite easy for him to slip into sleep during class. His work was finished and he was drained. Letting his pencil slip from his fingers and land on the desk, he pillowed his head on his arms, not fighting the urge to keep his eyes open. He couldn't hang on anymore.

In the thralls of darkness, dread filled him. He knew better than to believe he was *just* sleeping. Alex focused and prepared for the worst.

An ear-splitting scream echoed around him. He counted how long it lasted, trying to figure out if this dream was indeed the one that had been tormenting him for years. The scream lasted four seconds, then it stopped abruptly. Another one started; a different person, but Alex recognized the scream.

Still the same, he thought to himself. He was so exhausted from this.

Something brushed up against his hands, such a soft touch, and the burning sensation had begun. Alex tried to rub his hands against the grass beneath him to snuff it out as if there was visible fire, but his movements did nothing to stop it. The burning pain was at his elbows, burning deep into his muscles and bones. He tried to fight for *control*; control of his own body and mind to make the madness stop.

The fire was still spreading. The dream was disregarding his every attempt to knock himself out of it. Alex smelled smoke, and soot started attacking his throat, sticking to his esophagus.

A shove to his body made him reflexively jump, and he was blinded by bright, artificial light. The screaming abruptly stopped. His throat cleared up. He opened his eyes, and he was back to reality.

He squinted and peeked up. Light blinded him. Alex got his bearings as his eyes adjusted to his classroom lights.

Right. I'm in history class, Alex thought to himself, dragging a hand down his face.

A hand tapped his desk in front of him. Alex jumped and glanced up. A girl was looking at him, leading him to think she was the one to push him awake.

"Holts wants you. She just called you up after the phone rang," she said in a hushed tone, pointing to the back corner of the room where their teacher's desk resided. The girl promptly returned to scratching her pencil against the paper worksheet she was doing.

Alex pushed his chair backward, cringing at the loud scraping sound it produced. He could feel a few pairs of eyes land on him as he awkwardly crossed the room to reach his teacher. Mrs. Holts gave him a disapproving look as he stood in front of her.

He sheepishly scratched his neck. "Mrs. Holts, I'm sorry for falling asleep—"

Mrs. Holts held up a hand to ask for his silence, her expression melting into one of teasing. "I know you finished your work already, Alex. Just try not to make a habit of falling asleep in my class." She picked up a pen and began writing on a sticky note after pulling one off the pad. "Student services wants to speak with you. You're not in trouble, don't worry. Since class is almost over, I won't be seeing you until after the long weekend, so may the rest of your day be enjoyable, Alex."

Alex took the pass she handed to him, smiling at her. "Thank you." As he approached the door, he scooped his backpack up and slung it on his shoulder as he wrestled with the other strap to put it on fully.

He slinked through the open door of the classroom, eyes wandering across the posters tacked on the walls or the bulletin boards in boredom of walking through the halls alone. There wasn't much to look at. His school was quite bland.

He reached student services and strolled to the front desk.

"I was called down," he told the woman behind the desk.

She was an older woman with aged lines on her face along with white streaking through her hair. She looked at him over her dark purple glasses, scrutinizing him. She flipped a paper over and read it over.

"Are you Alexander O'Connor?" she snapped.

Alex tapped his leg anxiously. "Yes."

With the paper still in hand, she pointed to one of the many doors. "Mr. Hammond wants to talk about your class schedule and college plans if you're going." Her tone was dismissing.

Alex forced himself to walk to Mr. Hammond's office after he found the name above the door jamb. He was calmer now, the rampted beating of his heart dying down. He still hated the situation because the day of reckoning had finally come for him; the conversation of the upcoming senior year of high school, college, and what his future held.

Every kid he knew dreaded it because they were indecisive about what they wanted to do with their life, but that wasn't the reason for Alex's nervousness. He was jittery because he knew the path he wanted to go down, but he was unaware if it would pay off. If it didn't pay off, then everything he had worked for might fail, and if that happened—

Shaking his head, he knocked himself out of his spiraling thoughts. He walked through the door.

Mr. Hammond was a younger adult than the old bat he just talked to. He sat in a comfortable-looking chair, surrounded by scattered papers and folders. He spun in his chair and pulled a manila folder out of his filing cabinet. The counselor met eyes with him standing in his doorway, and Alex knew he looked lost.

"Alex! Come on in!" Mr. Hammond said loudly, a large cheery smile spreading across his face.

After bulking his movements, Alex felt his legs move him to the chair across from the man. Dropping his backpack to the floor with a dull thud and slumping into the seat, he knew that the upcoming conversation was going to be a drag for him.

Mr. Hammond clicked his tongue to a mindless rhythm as he flipped through the pages littered with black ink.

"Alright. You're here so that we can talk about your course schedule for next year, and we can take a look at your graduation requirements for senior year, as well. I know it's very early to pick classes, but it allows us counselors time to plan the schedules ahead of time." He tore his eyes away from Alex, typing and clicking on his computer a few times.

Alex's eyes wandered the room. He would rather be somewhere else, but he would listen to what the man had to say.

"Right now, you're taking mostly advanced classes, which you already know," Hammond said, then blinking at his computer screen. "Correction, you're taking all advanced classes. Every single one is an AP, and you have straight A's. These classes will look impressive on college applications, really any application if you choose to not go to college. Right now you're on track for your graduation requirements. Moving onto next year you will need..."

Mr. Hammond whizzed on about Alex's choices for next year even though he knew all the information beforehand and what classes he was picking next year. He'd been planning his life out since sixth grade, striving to *get away* from his town. This meeting was just a formality for him.

He had sought counsel from his teachers in middle school if he could find out the path he would need to take to get certain advanced classes he wanted in high school and college. He had remembered how his teachers were minutely concerned about why an eleven-year-old was worried about specific classes he would take in high school and college, but they had helped him without hesitation.

"Can I get financial aid for the SAT and ACT?" Alex cut in, feeling bored with the conversation; he hoped it didn't come across as rude as Alex sensed it was. He wasn't poor by any means but getting financial aid would be helpful.

Mr. Hammond blinked, shocked at being interrupted but nodded, reaching blindly behind himself, hands fluttering over the hundreds of papers spread around.

"Of course! Do you need any information about tutors

or the dates since it seems like you do want to take both?" He handed Alex a piece of paper.

Alex shook his head no and took the paper, folding it up. He didn't need any more help than what he requested. "Thank you. I've got everything I need. And I know what classes I'm doing next year." The last thing on his list was the tests colleges required, and he could finally breathe after that. Until college started in two years, he would just have to worry about applying to them.

Mr. Hammond smiled once again, leaning forward on the desk. "Sounds good! Now, you need to finalize your classes in two weeks, so don't forget to do that. Let me know if you have any problems!"

He gathered his things, slipping the paper he had been given into one of the pockets of his bag, and glanced back to Hammond. "Thank you."

"No problem, Alex," the man said in return, stacking Alex's folder on one side of the desk, among many others.

Alex wandered into the cafeteria, being a couple of minutes late. Instead of eating and talking to his friends, he pulled the financial aid form out of its prison in his bag along with a pen. He filled out the form with lightning speed.

As he reached the bottom, he saw a parent's signature was needed. He noted one of his friends was peeking at the paper, not snooping on the contents of the form but what he would do with the signature line. Alex forged his mother's signature instantly.

The friend, Eli, pursed his lips. "You sure you want to do that?"

Alex glared at him. "You know they won't sign it. And I've been forging their signatures since they adopted me. I won't get caught. The school probably doesn't even care about the signature, but they still have to require it."

The other boy shook his head. "If you're sure, Alex."

While muttering under his breath, Alex shoved the paper back into his bag where it wasn't visible and pulled out a book with a huff. He turned his brain off as he read, ignoring the world around him.

"Hey, Alex, I need your help," one of his other friends called from a few seats down. He put his book down and leaned on the table to look at her.

"What's up, Mary?"

"Remember that essay that was due at the beginning of the year in English when we did a speed-read of *How to Kill a Mockingbird*?" the girl asked.

Alex nodded. "Yes. You still haven't turned it in?"

She shook her head no.

He frowned, shocked. "Will he even accept it this late?"

Mary shrugged. "He said if I wrote it well, he would take only ten points off the starting total for it being late, but I can't remember anything in that book that I need and he took it back months ago. I have the chapters that I wrote down when we got the assignment, but I just can't remember what happened during them. Can you help me?"

He sighed at her untimely ways but nodded. "Yeah, give me the paper with the chapters you need, and I'll write some stuff down." Sometimes Alex wondered how he got coaxed into doing his friends' work for them. Maybe he was too nice sometimes.

Her grin was so wide Alex thought she might hurt herself. She ransacked her bag and passed the paper down with a pencil.

As he rearranged the paper in front of him, Alex spun the pencil in his finger as he read the chapters, and after less than a minute of thought, he began to write. He could perfectly remember every detail in the book from cover to cover, and what happened in every chapter. It was easy for him.

Six minutes later, his words filled the page to the bottom

and even spilled onto the back of it. His handwriting was neat in the beginning but slowly turned sloppy as he continued down the page, hand cramping at how tight he always gripped his pencil. It was still legible, so he gave it back to her after checking it over. Everyone around the table stared in disbelief at the sight of the plethora of words he was able to write down in such a short amount of time.

"Lex, dude, we haven't read that book in almost three months, and you gave a full synopsis of four chapters in like five minutes!" Another girl pointed out.

Alex tried not to smile. "I'm aware. Photographic memory, remember?"

A kid next to Eli whistled quietly. "No offense, but you're freaky."

Alex's friends always joked that he was strange.

Imagine if they found out about the dreams, Alex thought. *They would really have a field day.*

"Now you can go back to reading which is also weird, by the way. No one reads anymore." Eli winked at Alex teasingly.

"With pleasure," Alex replied and reopened his book without guilt.

The rest of the day was filled with busy work in his classes, which was acceptable to Alex. It was mind-numbingly tedious, but it took his mind off of reality. He needed it at the moment because it also kept him awake.

If he fell asleep, he would start dreaming. He couldn't let it happen again in case he made movements while sleeping that he wasn't aware of. It would be unfortunate for anyone to find out about his issue because he acted like a freak during class.

The bell rang, signaling the end of Alex's last class

period. He stepped out of the building. He usually walked home with one of his friends, Micheal, but today he was alone because Micheal was nowhere to be found. Alex didn't necessarily hate it. Being alone gave him time to think.

His neighborhood came into view, and he stopped in the road.

I could run away, and they would never know. Could crash at Eli's place or someone else's. That was a recurring thought Alex had, but he never went through with it. He continued to his house.

Slipping the key into the lock, he quickly ducked inside, keeping his head low as he tried to reach the squeaky stairs as fast as possible. But to do so, he had to navigate through the mess of the house, stepping around a rickety couch and a lamp lying on the floor that wasn't in that position that morning.

He ignored all of it, turning a corner to go upstairs. He chose his steps carefully, stepping on the panels of flooring that wouldn't creak under his weight, stepping on his toes and not his whole foot. As soon as his foot hit the first step of the stairs, a loud voice appeared out of nowhere.

"Alex!" A raspy female voice yelled.

He froze like a deer caught in headlights. *Maybe if I don't move, she'll forget I'm here.* It was wishful thinking.

"I know you hear me! You get back down here before I crack you a new one!"

Alex gritted his teeth, feeling rage bubble up in his chest. He swung himself back around and down the step, minding his speed to not sound like he was stomping. He dragged his feet into the kitchen where the woman called him if it could even be classified as a kitchen. It was a janky room that had a few cabinets, most of them skewed or crooked showing that the person who installed them was most likely drunk. The paint was chipping off the walls and countertop. The only thing that looked half decent was a small silver fridge at the end of the counter.

"Yes, Renee?" he huffed, taking in the thin, petite frame of his adoptive mother. Her hand was already closed around a beer, staring at the hundreds of papers on the counter, all of them with red brick lettering on the front of them.

"Drinking already?" He couldn't ignore the urge to keep his mouth shut. She glared at him, but then she smiled. It reminded Alex of a smile that a witch would make.

"Lex, sweetheart," she said, putting on her fake-nice voice, which he knew meant trouble, "we have some payments that are late. You know your father and I are trying to get some money in, but it's just too late for the next couple of weeks."

Alex smiled sardonically at her. "So you want *me* to give you money? That's what you're asking, right?" He had never hid the fact that he had a paying job to his mother, but he was regretting not doing so.

"Yes." Renee didn't stutter.

His anger stayed rooted in his chest, threatening to burst out, but he understood if he were to blow up at Renee, his adoptive father would not be happy with him.

"Renee, I don't make enough to cover all the bills. You know this. You could be at work right now, but you're the one that got fired and not making an effort to search for another job. You've had months to do so." Alex settled on with a calm voice that held passive-aggressiveness. Yelling never got him anywhere with her, even if it did make him feel better. His plans to use his paychecks for his tests couldn't be ruined by him running his mouth either.

As she slammed her hand down on the table in frustration, he didn't even blink. She took a quick drink of her beer as if it would calm her down, but then she started yelling again.

"You ungrateful brat! We work hard to provide for you!

We give you clothes and food, we let you go to school to get an education—"

"You *legally* have to send me to school." Alex butted in, staring right past her head to the wall. "You can't just decide that or not." He turned on his heel, stomping away from her.

"Don't you turn your back on me, Alex! I will kick you out of the house in one second!" She screamed at him, following him with her alcohol still in hand.

"Go ahead," he said calmly, heading upstairs. It was a common threat from her and his father, but they never did. It was pathetic.

Her footsteps thundered behind him, so he picked up the pace and ran into his room, locking the door behind him. His so-called mother slammed, kicked, and punched the wood, but she never attempted to enter his room past those extremes. He ignored her actions and yelling, moving his desk in front of the door so she would have a more difficult time getting into his room. Alex scrambled to grab a book from the bookshelf and shoved it under the doorknob to make it even harder to twist.

She better not break anything trying to get in.

He blocked out all the noise, pulling his homework out of his backpack. Renee would eventually walk away; she always did. As he was absorbed in his homework, he lost track of time. His mind became such a blend of physics, history, and English that the endless black ink was blurring together on the pages. Exhausted, he wanted to throw everything back into his bag and do nothing else for the rest of the night. His mind traveled back to his conversation with Mr. Hammond, and he started thinking about college. His anxiety from the academic pressure of getting good grades to get into college forced him to finish his work.

When he lazily gazed out of his window after his tasks were finished, it was dark out. Alex cursed under his breath, feeling like the days went by too fast. He shoved his work into his bag and very slowly moved the desk back after removing his book from its wedged position.

He returned the desk to its original, pristine condition, stacking papers where he wanted them, returning textbooks to the drawers, and supplies to other safe places. It was rare that he had to clean his room, it was always organized the exact way he liked, never deviating.

After his task was done, he jumped back on his bed, sighing. Staring at the ceiling, he finally felt at peace. He didn't have anyone yelling at him, telling him what to do, and he wasn't working; his brain could process his life and what he was doing with it. And at the moment, he wanted to do absolutely nothing. Peace and quiet were a formidable combination to come by in his hectic schedule.

A ping on the outside panels of the house pulled him out of his happy place. His eyes fluttered as he glared at the ceiling. He ignored the sound, hoping it was just a one-time disruption. Then there was another ping on the glass.

Alex rolled over and fixated his glare on the wall, not knowing what the noise was, but he was aware it was irritating him. Getting to his feet, he braced his hands on either side of the frame of his window and peered down at the ground.

A figure was beneath him with a small shadow figure sitting next to them. In the darkness, the person was unidentifiable, but Alex had a sneaky suspicion of who it was. There was only *one* person in the world who would show up unannounced underneath his window.

He yanked up on the plastic wedge on his window and repositioned his hands to get more leverage to lift the panes of glass. He leaned his elbows on the ledge of the opening and leaned his head out with a grin.

"Are you going to Romeo me? Because I'm sorry to say you aren't exactly my type."

The person chuckled. Alex perked up at the warm sound. He knew his hypothesis was correct just by the sound of it.

"Look who's the comedian now. You're so funny," the person in the shadows deadpanned.

Alex scoffed. "Of course I am, Micheal. Your life would be boring if I wasn't."

Micheal chuckled quietly. "I'm not admitting that. Now get down here."

The blond raised an eyebrow. "You want me to jump and break my legs?" Alex could sense the eye roll without being able to see his friend's face.

"No, you idiot. Go through the door. I'll meet you down here," Micheal instructed.

Alex tsked and looked back inside his room, straining his ears to pick up movement. He didn't. However, he didn't fully trust that his caretakers wouldn't stop him if they were awake. "I don't know, Micheal."

"Trust me," Micheal said persistently. "We've snuck out so many times that I can't keep count on all ten fingers. You're fine. So get down here, and let's go for a walk."

Alex closed the window, leaving it unlocked in case he would have to crawl back through it. He extracted his phone from his covers and threw a jacket over his head, putting it on in a rush. His hand touched the cold metal of the doorknob, and he mutely turned it to the left. Once he reached the limit he could turn, he pulled backward cautiously. The door opened with minimal creaks and groans which Alex was grateful for.

He tiptoed through his dark hallway, making his way around the banister, down the steps, and onto the ground level. He fished his keys from the hook, and he opened the front door. He stepped out onto the short patio, and he slipped the key in to secure both locks as he stepped outside. Afterward, he put the key in his jean pocket.

The crisp air was refreshing to him, better than his stuffy room, even if he was slightly cold. The streetlights provided a yellow glow to the night and the street beyond, allowing Alex to see Micheal better than his view from his room along with his Australian Shepherd perched at his feet.

"Hey, boy," Alex greeted the dog quietly, patting his leg. The dog padded over to Alex, wagging his tail. Alex scratched under the dog's chin and behind his ears. "You didn't have to do the whole rock and window thing, you know? I have a phone," Alex said in a form of greeting to Micheal, still petting the dog's soft fur.

Micheal took his phone out of his pocket and waved it in front of his eyes, strutting backward until Alex and his dog caught up to him.

"I tried that. You were MIA."

He shook his head, denying it. "No, you didn't." He hit the power button on his phone and there were ten messages from the other teen. He closed his jaw tightly and looked away. *I must not have heard my phone go off.*

Micheal giggled like a five-year-old and ruffled his hair.

"Told you so." He bumped arms with him, shooting him a grin. Alex didn't return it, still in a bitter mood from earlier. "Okay, sourpuss, what's wrong? Even Pirate can't cheer you up." Micheal broke the ice, and they began strolling farther down the street. "And Pirate is adorable."

Pirate gave a bark of agreement.

Alex shrugged dejectedly, kicking a rock in the road. "Renee being Renee."

Micheal hummed, voice dipping lower. "What did she do this time?" The tension used in his question didn't surprise Alex as Micheal looked down at him.

"Said she and Bradley didn't have money for the bills this month. Asked if I could pay them," he mumbled.

Micheal murmured certain choice words under his

breath. "I really hate her sometimes. Correction, I hate her most of the time. Those two have never done anything for you."

Alex huffed, shoving his hands in his pockets. "Let's drop it, please. We've talked about it enough times, and I don't feel like talking about it."

The conversation was extinguished there.

Taking in the scenery, Alex once again appreciated the change of pace from his previous home in Kansas to Pennsylvania.

When they were younger, Alex and Micheal lived in Kansas. It was where they became friends, and their families coincidentally moved to Pennsylvania at the same time. While Kansas had a lot of *nothing*, Pennsylvania had slightly more to offer to the eye. Both had their fair amount of farms and cornfields, but their most recent move had brought more trees and foliage into their lives. It just felt different to Alex. Micheal and Alex's families had both moved years ago but it never took away Alex's gratitude for something different.

"You're spacing out again, and that's my job. I'm the one with the attention deficit disorder." Micheal's voice startled him out of his thoughts.

He shook his head to clear it. "Sorry. Can't focus lately."

Micheal crossed his arms over his chest, side-eyeing him. "Is something else wrong?"

Alex was so tempted to tell him. It was on the tip of his tongue, but he paused. *I can't tell him about the dreams. I never have, and I can't break that rule now.* "Nothing in particular. Just can't sleep well," he deflected the topic, trying to hide the shake in his voice.

The brunet laughed. "Story of my life."

Alex stuffed his hands in his pockets.

"You ditched me today. Did you go somewhere?" He remembered that he had walked home by himself without

Micheal.

"I had to take a history test. I missed it the other day," Micheal responded.

They reached a familiar clearing on the outskirts of their neighborhood. It was their go-to place to visit. They had discovered it not long ago.

The two teenagers lay down on the ground and fixated their eyes on the starry night sky. Pirate huffed as he laid down, resting his head on Micheal's thigh.

The stars twinkled in their dark home in space. Alex scavenged the sky for dull constellations.

"Have teachers started talking about college and applications with you?" he asked curiously, needing something else to focus on.

Micheal gave him a weird look. "Dude, teachers have been talking about college since sophomore year. We have to start looking for colleges soon or plan on what we're doing after school. You already have everything planned out though."

Alex ripped a blade of grass out of the dirt and tore it into smaller pieces, staring at it. The repetitive motion put him at ease. "Have you thought about what you're doing?" He deflected, then thought better of it, saying, "Hammond talked to me today. I zoned out halfway through. It's the same stuff as last year."

Micheal tossed his arms up. "Yeah, my counselor talked to me the other day, and I don't think she liked that I didn't have a plan for college or anything. She should've expected that though, seeing as she's known me for two, going on three years now." He sighed. "Back to your original question, I'm pretty sure my parents want me in the military. They want me to follow in their footsteps or something like that."

A lump formed in Alex's throat. The thought of Micheal possibly being in a warzone, thousands of miles away from him, made him crave the chance to throw something. "Do you want that?"

The other boy looked away, stroking his dog's head. "I don't know. I've thought about it. There are decent benefits to it, but you get shot at if you're on the front lines. That's not exactly comforting. The only reason I would go would be to get out of here. I'll jump at any chance I get."

The blond chuckled darkly. "I forget sometimes that you hate it here just as much as I do."

Alex was a person of planning. He knew exactly what he wanted and how to get there. Micheal, on the other hand, was a person with a "going with the flow" mentality. Even if they had different strategies in life, they both wanted to leave.

Micheal dramatically sighed, turning to face his companion. "I had my parents growing up before they got deployed, but you didn't. My brothers are insufferable, sure, but you've got terrible parents. If anyone should hate this place, it's you."

Alex clammed up, voice going small. "It's not exactly their fault." A hand roughly grabbed him and flipped him around. Micheal had propped himself up on one arm and was glaring down at Alex. Pirate moved away from Micheal.

"Do not try to make excuses for them. They make their own decisions, and they decide to make your life miserable. Don't even try it with me, Alexander." Alex opened his mouth to argue but was cut off. "It's their responsibility to take care of you. They're not doing that."

The silence that was once peaceful became slightly awkward and hostile. Alex was quick to think on his emotions. He also knew Micheal was very protective. Those factors meant they were both argumentative people. Alex never liked to fight with his best friend, so he stayed quiet.

Micheal eventually released his friend and solemnly

rolled back into a stationary position. "Don't feel sorry for them," he whispered; it was his final words before he didn't talk the rest of the time.

Alex stared at the stars, watching them shine weakly in the sky. The wish to see the brightest stars the universe had to offer just once overwhelmed him whenever he looked up at the night sky.

Pirate came over to him and laid down next to him, sensing his sadness. Alex looked down and patted his head, letting him stay.

After an hour, Alex checked his phone for the first time. It was nearly ten o'clock, and if he stayed out too much longer Renee or Bradley might notice he was missing. He wordlessly stood up and held a hand out for the taller boy to grab onto. Micheal heaved himself up with the help of Alex and brushed off any grass or dirt that clung to him. A few of his joints cracked and popped with the vertical movement upward, and he didn't seem to care.

"You're getting old," Alex teased with a sly smirk.

Micheal just pushed his head away, ducking his chin to hide a grin.

The walk back was peaceful and quiet with nothing interrupting them. Pirate would sprint around for a few minutes and come back to the two boys. The breeze had picked up, and Alex burrowed further into his warm hoodie, making his friend chuckle at him.

Micheal scooped up a stick from the edge of the road and showed it to the dog. Pirate splayed his paws out, lowering his front side down, readying to spring into a run.

"Fetch, boy." Micheal threw it far down the stretch of the road. It clanked on the asphalt, the dull sound ripping through the peaceful silence. The Australian Shepherd raced after it, his nails raking against the road.

Alex chuckled at the dog's excited mood. "God, I need a dog."

Micheal held his hands out in a way to gesture to himself. "Luckily for you, your best friend can easily hook you up with a dog. We've got twenty-three at the shelter, and a couple more are coming this weekend. So you've got options if you really do want one."

Alex laughed and shook his head. "I'm just saying it would be nice to have a dog, but there's no way I can afford one. No one would probably even do business with me since I'm sixteen."

Pirate came running back up with the stick in his mouth, nudging Alex's leg, wanting him to throw it. Alex took the offered branch and ruffled the dog's ears.

"Besides, I've got Pirate to be *my* pseudo-dog for now. I just don't have to pay a penny," he said, throwing the branch again. Micheal shook his head but had a smile on his face.

The familiar streets of their neighborhood were ahead of them.

Alex's happy mood burst like a bubble when he stepped up to his front door, the light above the door flickering ominously. The air seemed to be plucked away from his lungs, and he could feel every beat his heart took.

"See you at school, Lex. try to get some sleep tonight because you're looking like a wreck," Micheal said, smirking.

Alex snorted. "Why thank you, Micheal, for that kind suggestion." He waved goodbye as Micheal continued one more house down and then across the street with Pirate on his heels. Alex said a small prayer that his parents would be asleep as he unlocked the door. He cursed in his head when the door hinges groaned.

The bitter, familiar stench of alcohol instantly hit him, and he fought to not gag. It was vile. Holding his breath, he quietly shut the door, being mindful that Bradley was passed out on the couch. Bradley must've moved during Alex's outing because he hadn't been there when Alex left.

He left the key on the hook exactly where he had taken it, hearing it chime once or twice before it stopped swaying. Quiet as a mouse, he retreated to his room, leaning his back against the door with a sigh before twisting the little button on the knob to lock it. It wouldn't do much, but it would bring him comfort. Staring at his ceiling and finding himself in this position once again, he let out one sentence. One plea to anyone in the universe that cared.

"Get me out of here."

Chapter 2

Alex sluggishly pulled himself out of bed at the blaring chime of his alarm, blearily looking around the room for his clock to make sure he did indeed have to get up. He fumbled a hand around to turn the alarm off. He flopped back onto the bed for just another minute. Another torturous night had occurred, and he hadn't gotten nearly as many hours of sleep as he needed to function. His nightmares had plagued him once again.

The sun was just starting to peek over the horizon and between the trees, the pillars of shining light casting an orange hue through his window. The sunlight helped wake him up a bit.

He forced himself out of bed to gather the things he needed, then took out items from his bag that he didn't need. He cringed at the strain in his wrist and arm that the weight caused as he moved to bring the bag over his shoulders. Surely, the massive amounts of binders and books would kill him one day.

He tiptoed downstairs, and he became wide awake when he came across his adoptive father.

Bradley Johnson was a fairly large and intimidating

man, multiple inches taller, which allowed him to tower over Alex and stare down at him with brown eyes. Alex went deathly still.

"Quit staring and get going." The man jerked a thumb to the door, his voice rough and gravelly.

Alex didn't trust him to not come back after him as soon as he started moving, so he stayed rooted in place.

"Go!" the man bellowed.

Alex gulped and ducked his head, heading for the door. He prayed that neither Renee nor Bradley would stop him again. He fled from the house while grabbing his house key, fighting the urge to look behind him.

Shutting the door, he released a trembling sigh. There was no use in dwelling on it so he did his best to march on and ignore what just happened.

The motor of a car startled him as he was just about to step out onto the road to begin his walk to school. Micheal's face appeared from the passenger side of the car that pulled to a stop next to him.

"Hop in."

Alex snickered at his blunt order but opened the back door to the car and slid into the seat behind Micheal. He closed the door and put his seatbelt on, looking at Micheal's brother in the driver's seat.

"Hey, Mark," he greeted politely as the car began to pull forward.

"Hi, Alex," Mark responded, keeping his eyes on the road with one hand on the steering wheel. Micheal got comfortable in his seat, throwing his legs up to rest on the dashboard of the car. Mark smacked his leg, making his brother yelp in pain.

"Dude!"

"You better get your feet off my dash." Mark yanked his leg down. "You weren't raised in a barn."

Micheal's smirk promised trouble. "We lived in Kansas

which is the closest you can get to a barn. And I drive this car as well for your information!"

"Are you driving it right now? No. Driver makes the rules. Don't scuff up the dashboard again."

Alex hid a snicker behind his hand. It was a nice change from their usual arguing, even if they were bickering. He had known both Mark and Micheal for as long as he could remember, having practically lived at Micheal's house when they were younger.

Alex had met their older brother only a few times, but the man was now in the military just like Micheal's parents. He had spent most of his childhood around the two other boys in the car. But Mark and Micheal were tenser these days, and Alex could only guess their parents being absent didn't help.

He stayed silent throughout the rest of the ride, the bickering just turning into a low buzz in his head. The car eventually stopped in the high school parking lot, and Alex jolted in his seat, fracturing his daydream.

"Alright, you two. Get out," Mark announced, unlocking the doors.

Alex shouldered his bag and stepped out of the car, seeing Micheal doing the same after smacking Mark upside the head. Mark reached over to do the same but missed and just gave him a rude gesture. Micheal scoffed and waved a hand theatrically, not offended by his brother.

Alex and Micheal didn't wait for Mark to drive away before marching into the building.

Alex aimed a smile at Micheal as they entered deeper into the school. "You two seem to be getting along."

Micheal had the opposite reaction of what Alex thought he would give. Micheal stared straight ahead, the muscle in his jaw tightening. "Just doing better than yesterday. I don't know if you would call that improvement."

Alex balked, looking concerningly at Micheal. "Is that

why you Romeo'd me last night? Because you two were fighting?"

"Yeah, something like that," Micheal said plainly, keeping his eyes away from Alex's. The bell chimed throughout the halls. "See you later." He dashed away quickly.

Alex sighed to himself, knowing that the conversation could've ended better. He shouldn't have brought it up because it was always a sore topic for Micheal.

"Bye, Micheal," he said, even though his friend was no longer within earshot.

He ducked his head as he strolled to his first class of the day, not in the mood to talk to anybody. He stepped into his class, saying hello to his teacher as he passed her desk. Sitting down quietly at his desk, he pulled out his work from yesterday and worked on it. He rubbed his eyes after a moment of staring at the paper, feeling sleepy already.

Please, let this day go by quickly.

Alex slumped into his chair, allowing his heavy backpack to crash onto the floor without care, finally reaching his last class. He rested his head on his desk, letting out a mix of a sigh and a groan. His sleep deprivation from the previous nights had caught up to him throughout the day. He had been close to sleep numerous times, but in fear of dreaming, he would snap awake.

Multiple teachers had asked him if he was feeling okay, and he was forced to say yes so he wouldn't sound like a crazy person. He couldn't exactly tell them that he had a perpetual dream about burning alive, strange sights, and screaming without being sent to see Mr. Hammond or the school psychologist.

But to answer their question, no. He was not okay.

A chair clanging on the metal legs of another desk in front of him jarred him from thought violently. Alex lifted his head and saw his friend, Eli, settling into his own seat, staring at Alex with a grimace.

"You look like crap, dude."

Alex smiled tiredly at him. "So I've been told. Multiple times actually." He could *feel* the dark shadows underneath his eyes, it wasn't necessary for others to point out the obvious.

Eli narrowed his eyes. "You sick or something?"

He shook his head. "No, I don't get sick."

"Everyone gets sick, Lex." The pity in his friend's voice made his stomach flip.

"Well, I don't often. Being sick, in my mind, is being down and out. Where you can barely move in bed and are suffering for at least three days. That hasn't happened to me in about six years. So, ha." He stuck his tongue out.

"Mature." Eli smirked.

"Howdy, y'all." A girl with a long braid over her shoulder sat down as well, barely making it in time for the bell to ring. It was Mary.

Alex snorted, staring at her. "'Howdy'? Since when did you become southern, Mary?"

"Since I felt like it," she said and smiled, scrunching her nose up. "Besides, you say things with a southern accent sometimes."

He smirked at her. "Only when I'm feeling sassy."

The teacher called for the student's attention, effectively having silence after a second or two. "I know you're all excited about the long weekend ahead of you, but we do indeed have work to do. I'll pass out the assignment, it shouldn't take long—my gift to you. Just a few comprehension questions. If you left your book at home, feel free to borrow one. You can work together in small groups if needed. No copying word-for-word." He finished his spiel and started passing out the papers.

Taking the paper, Alex immediately started working on it, blocking out the chatter from his friends. He didn't even need to take out the book from his backpack. The questions were fairly easy for such a hard class. Well, easy for him, at least.

He finished fifteen minutes later, and as he was getting up, his friends called out complaints.

"Are you really going to leave us high and dry?"

Alex didn't respond, fighting off a smirk.

"You, who pretend to be our friend, are making us fend for ourselves...for shame, Alexander."

Alex shrugged before heading to the teacher's desk. He dropped the paper on the corner of the desk and walked back to his seat. Exhaustion seeped deep into his bones, and he couldn't help but lay his head down on the desk. He had promised himself to not fall asleep, but luck wasn't on his side.

It was pitch black in his mind like an endless, bleak sea. But it didn't last for long. His vision filtered into tunnel vision where it eventually expanded out, but everything was blurry. Alex felt dread fill him. He didn't want to be here. He *hated* it here. The woman screamed, and everything went into chaos.

Alex strained his eyes to see anything he hadn't before, and he caught a glimpse of something new. Two blurry people were standing about thirty feet in front of him, slightly to his right, but he couldn't make out any specific details about them. Instantaneously, streaks of stormy gray and deep green appeared to be shooting through the air. The people hunkered down, holding their heads as the colors disappeared, but Alex couldn't tell why.

The fire started in his hands, and he tried to shake his hands but instead, his whole body shook. It didn't stop, and it got more persistent until someone shouted his name.

"Alex!"

He blinked and sloppily pushed his head off his desk. He rubbed his eyes, free of his dream. "Yeah, yeah. I'm awake."

Mary had her hands on her hips. "Well, I would hope so because class is about to end. You can sleep at home." Alex could see the concern in her eyes, and he was grateful she didn't say anything.

He ran a hand through his sandy blond hair, closing his eyes for just a second more. *Chill out. You're fine. Just the second day in a row that you've fallen asleep at school. Breathe.* His eyes fluttered, closing temporarily. He took in a deep breath and slowly let it out, his chest rising and falling dramatically. He forced a relaxed expression to mask his fear as the bell rang.

His classmates jumped out of their seats, most of them saying goodbye to their teacher before they joined the sea of students released into too-small hallways, buzzing with excitement and energy about the long weekend ahead of them.

As his classmates left the room, Alex moved to help his teacher stack books back on the shelf, engaging in polite conversation with him. He conversed with him for a few more minutes, then he left when it came to a polite end.

Students were still milling about inside, being in no rush to get home. He weaved in and out between them, avoiding being tackled when some boys started to play-fight. He shoved the heavy door open to be free of school. He ran his eyes over the front of the school, looking for one person in particular. He made his way over when he found him.

Micheal was sitting down on one of the benches provided by the school, messing with a loose thread in his black jeans. He rested the side of his head on his fist, dark gray sleeves pulled past his wrist to his mid-forearm. He had a lost look in his eyes which led Alex to believe he was once again in a bad mood.

Alex put a hand on his head, playfully tugging on one of the waves of his hair. "Are you ready to go?"

Micheal jumped up to his feet, nodding, and he started to lead them back home.

They strolled to the side of the school, passing by other students on the walkway, who were going in the opposite direction. They reached the main road that was blanketed by tall trees. For a main road, people rarely drove on it, so they trekked on the double yellow line. People tended to live closer to the other side of the school or most kids had already left in their cars.

The walk home for Alex and Micheal was rarely one of adventure. They just spent most of their time in silence or filled the quiet with conversation.

During the duration of their walk, Micheal jumped into an array of different conversations, always starting one topic, never finishing it because he would get distracted mid-story and launch into another one.

Halfway home when Micheal finally stopped to breathe. Alex asked mirthfully, "Did you forget to take your meds today? You've been talking nonstop for the past ten minutes."

Micheal raised his nose in the air. "Rude. I'm offended. And for your information, yes I did.... They just don't work sometimes." He had been taking medication for his ADHD for the past seven years, but since the beginning of high school, he hadn't reacted well with it.

The shorter boy laughed at Micheal's hesitation on the last part of his words. "Why don't you go to the doctor and get something different from what you're taking now? I'm sure there's something else that can help you."

Micheal pouted. "Because that means I have to go to a specialist, and that's not happening. But you shouldn't be talking."

Alex nearly stopped walking in shock. "Excuse me?"

"Oh, nothing," Micheal hummed, glancing anywhere else other than Alex.

Alex rolled his eyes at his reluctance to answer but didn't comment further on it. They ventured further down the empty road, still ambling on either side of the double yellow lines. Trees cradled the road on either side of them, the shadows of the branches streaking across the asphalt. Alex could feel the sun seeping through the gaps in the limbs of the trees.

He went deep into thought until he didn't feel Micheal alongside him by his elbow. He turned his head and saw Micheal walking toward the trees.

Alex stopped. Furrowing his brow, perplexed, he looked back at the road, then to his wandering friend.

"Earth to Micheal, the way home is *that* way," he stated. He jerked his arm out to point down the remaining stretch of the road to his friend who was still meandering toward the trees.

Micheal gestured with his head toward an opening in the woods. "Come on, I wanna go this way." He had an excited grin.

Alex frowned and stared down at the opening. The woods were thick with the leaves in a beautiful array of bronze and orange with only a few hints of green left as Pennsylvania entered the end of fall. A wise voice in the back of his head reminded him that the trees were dense, and it was easy to lose your way, especially since he hadn't bothered to learn the dense woods around his neighborhood.

"Do you even know the way home?" he asked.

"Shouldn't be hard. I went through one day about a mile down. Piece of cake."

Taking a glance back at the spot Micheal wanted to enter, he shook his head. He didn't trust it. "No, let's go home. That was most definitely not there yesterday. For someone who makes a lot of pop culture references, you never reference any horror movies that start like this. You don't enter the spooky-looking place because that's you asking to get slaughtered." Micheal was unimpressed, a brow raised. "I don't want to meet my maker after somebody kills me in there." Alex finished, keeping his voice level.

His parents had given him up when he was a baby, and he guessed they were either somewhere around the world or dead. And if they were dead, he wasn't ready to meet them if he was murdered.

Micheal rolled his eyes dramatically. "You're such a baby. Come on, Lex."

Alex turned to face him and crossed his arms defiantly over his chest. "No."

Micheal pouted and tugged on his friend's arm. "Please!"

"Absolutely not," Alex hissed.

"Please!" He shouted so loud it echoed across the open space and into the trees.

Alex debated before glaring at the barely taller boy. "...Fine. You better not get us lost or I'm leaving you."

Micheal jumped up and down, clapping his hands childishly. "Yay!"

Alex scoffed and stuffed his hands in his pockets. "You're such a child."

They hiked down the remote dirt path, taking in their surroundings. It looked like any normal part of the forest, but something put Alex on edge. He stepped into Micheal's space and stayed there as if his friend's larger frame and backpack would hide him from his fears.

As the trail was about to dip, Alex looked back to see the exit of the path, but when he turned it was just dense forest. He swallowed the lump in his throat and continued peeking over Micheal's shoulder. He hated this. He just wanted to go

31

home the easy way.

They trudged on for a couple of minutes, hearing nothing but their footsteps crunching on the occasional branch or leaf. They took a few twists and turns. Alex noticed Micheal's head whipping back and forth like he was looking for something, making the brown soft waves on his head move along with him.

The shorter boy hit his friend hard on the arm. As Micheal squawked, Alex chastised him, "We're lost, aren't we?!"

Micheal bit his lip and looked away. "Maybe?"

Alex tossed his hands up and groaned in frustration. "Great job, Mikey! Really great job. You said, 'oh it shouldn't be too hard', 'Don't be a baby, Alex', 'Piece of cake, Alex' and look where it got us!" He started to storm in the opposite direction, but a warm hand gripped his wrist.

"Come on, let's keep walking." Micheal negotiated. "We'll eventually reach the highway, and I'll get my brother to pick us up."

Alex, not wanting to leave his friend alone, nodded silently and continued to walk, taking the lead. He hated every minute of it. The highway didn't sound any better than being in the forest, but at least there were other people on the highway that could be there to assist them if needed.

His backpack began to hurt his back, making him slouch, but he straightened up to the best of his ability, not wanting to complain to Micheal. The teasing would never end if he did. The less ammo Alex gave him, the better his life would be in the long run.

Something odd caught his eye on the path, right in the middle of it, and Alex suddenly stopped, making Micheal jam into him. He winced a bit as Micheal's broad frame struck him.

"God, Lex, a little warning next time," Micheal complained, groaning and rubbing the place where he collided with his friend.

Alex slowly crouched and reached down to the ground with shaking fingers and picked up a three-pointed leaf no bigger than the palm of his hand. It would've been a normal leaf with the same structure and texture on his fingertips except for the fact that it was a mix of deep-sea blue and violet. It didn't look like any color of foliage they had seen before. Alex wordlessly raised the leaf up to show Micheal who blinked dumbfoundedly.

"I...don't think that is a color in the natural world. Or any kingdom of nature," was all Micheal could say, his voice light and airy with surprise.

A rush of fear, adrenaline, and curiosity raced through him. He could readily turn back, go the opposite direction, and forget this ever happened. He had other things to worry about. But...he was too curious to turn back. So he, possibly stupidly, continued down the path.

Micheal rushed to keep up, nearly jogging. "Alex, when you see something like that, that is when you leave the creepy forest with *dark blue leaves*. I've seen pink, red, orange, and brown leaves but not blue!" He rambled.

"This whole plan of walking through the woods was your idea, Micheal. Don't be a hypocrite." Alex dismissed his concern. He began to see more blue leaves, large and small, up ahead.

"I'm the impulsive one, not you!"

Alex ignored him as he started to step on said leaves. The forest ground became covered in them under their feet as they pressed on, painting them in blues and purples.

Alex had no plan whatsoever of where he was going. He only knew that he wanted to find the source of the mystical leaves. The bark of the hemlock and pine trees of the forest slowly changed, getting darker in color as Alex continued on his rampage.

An interlude in the trees came up on Alex's right,

leading to a strip of green grass, the sky finally visible once again. He staggered into the valley of sorts, head turning in every direction sporadically, and his jaw dropped. Micheal caught up to him, and just as he was about to say something his jaw seemed to be glued shut.

In front of them were two rows of cars, all rusted and broken down. The cars did not have a large variety, almost all of them the same car or a similar model. But they weren't modern cars; they were from the '50s and '60s, something Alex didn't see often. Vines crawled across and latched onto the metal panels of the exterior, forcing them to be one with the ground.

The field they were in seemed to stretch on for an eternity in both directions. Alex was positive that there had to be an end to the odd sight because the highway wasn't much farther ahead . The same bluish-purple trees cradled the tree line, the leaves falling delicately and slowly on the cars.

"What is this place?" Alex whispered.

Micheal slipped his hand into Alex's, squeezing once then letting go. "I don't know, but it looks mystical. I want to stay."

"Indecisive today, are we?"

"Whatever. Speak for yourself."

They slowly walked down the middle of the rows, having enough space to walk side by side, soaking in everything they saw. Alex felt strangely at peace, relaxing in the creepy forest. On a highway frozen in time. Micheal abruptly stopped, pulling on Alex's wrist. Alex flailed slightly, getting caught off balance.

"What?" he questioned.

The wavy-haired teenager pointed inside the car. "It's a doll." The statement was plain, but he got his message across to Alex, a smirk sliding on his face.

Alex shook his head vigorously and pulled himself out of

Micheal's grasp. "Nope, nope, nope. I don't do dolls."

Micheal laughed hard and slammed his sleeved elbow into the brittle window. As the glass shattered, Micheal shook out his arm, rubbing his elbow. The sound had forced Alex to cover his ears, the noise startling him.

"You idiot, why'd you do that?!" Alex shouted.

Micheal reached a hand into the car and pulled out the doll, grimacing at the way it looked. Alex didn't blame him; it resembled the creepiness of *Annabell.*

"Yeesh. Creepy," Micheal muttered as Alex let out a small scream. Micheal grabbed his bicep so he wouldn't rush off and shoved the doll in his face with a sinister smile.

"Get it away from me, right now, Micheal Logan Barnes! I'm not kidding!" Alex screamed.

Micheal cringed, stopping his advances on terrifying Alex. "Ugh, don't ever call me by my full name. You sound like my mother."

"I'll do what I want until you get that thing out of my face!"

Micheal paid his friend no mind as he observed the doll, rotating it in his hands as Alex continuously made an effort to get away from the doll. Both of them saw something hit the light just right to make it shine into Micheal's eyes. Alex's complaints died in his throat.

Micheal let go of Alex and reached for the doll, pulling two black leather strings from underneath its light pink shirt. Each string held a single gemstone that sparkled in the sunlight. Micheal mindlessly passed one to Alex as he stared at the one in the palm of his hand.

Alex didn't take it, not trusting it.

Micheal huffed. "Take the thing."

Alex grabbed it with one hand, holding it as far away from his body as he could, suspicious of it. Intrigued, he brought it closer and flipped it between his fingers a few times, vigilantly taking in the texture. It was smooth, a layer of glass covering it and formed a flat dome. The stone itself was a solid royal blue with hints of emerald green swoops, reminding him of the ocean.

He turned his head to Micheal and he was observing his stone as well. It was the same exact shape. The stone was speckled with what looked like iridescent foils inside the stone that sparkled in the light of the sun, with the stone being a deep red.

It's an opal.

"It matches your eyes," Micheal said, looking at the sapphire stone, snickering at the glare he received from Alex.

"Har har," Alex responded but didn't dispute the comment. He had completely forgotten about the doll held limply in Micheal's hand; it was no longer his concern. He flipped the stone over and saw a symbol engraved on the rock. He squinted, making out the shape of three spirals connected at the center.

"Hey, look at this." The blond boy nudged the brunet. "It looks like a triskelion."

Micheal frowned in concentration. "Isn't that Greek or something?"

"Celtic. But means 'power from the center,'" Alex rattled off.

The brunet grinned like a kid in a candy store. "Are you telling me that these stones are *magical?*"

Alex knew he was kidding, but at the same time, he wasn't sure himself. The stone seemed to be trembling in his hand as he got closer to Micheal.

Magic doesn't exist. Don't be ridiculous.

"Does yours have anything on it?"

Micheal turned his over and nodded. "Yeah, looks like the same thing, but yours is indented, mine is raised." He tossed the doll back into the car.

Alex delicately took Micheal's and compared both of the

symbols, feeling a magnetic pull on them. He handed it back and faced his triskelion toward Micheal. "Line them up."

They slipped the backs of the stones onto each other and waited. Nothing happened.

"Alex, what was the point of doing th—" Micheal was interrupted by a single light pulse coming from the connection point of both stones. Another flash. And then another. The light got brighter each time the light rippled and flared until the boys were blinded by the light.

Alex felt like the ground was ripped away from underneath his feet. His heart stopped for a moment as his stomach dropped. Wind rushed in his ears, knocking his locks of hair from side to side. The light was so bright. They suddenly rushed toward solid ground once again.

Alex had no time to scream before his feet made an impact with the ground, to his great relief, still alive. Miraculously, nothing felt broken or damaged. He struggled to his feet, but black spots danced in front of his eyes as a wave of dizziness hit him. He collapsed to the ground on his hands and knees, boneless, feeling his friend fall beside him. Alex groaned, unable to keep his eyes open anymore. The last thing he remembered was seeing light bounce off something metallic, and then the world went black.

Chapter 3

Everything was fuzzy and far away when Alex woke up again. He struggled to just pull his heavy eyes open. He found the strength to complete the action, and his eyes were met with a wood ceiling with rows of beams crossing over each side. He attempted to sit up but his body wouldn't cooperate, making him stay stationary against what he assumed was a bed. It felt soft underneath him, and was that a blanket on top of him?

He heard whispering to his left, but he couldn't make out any of the words. Alex finally gathered enough courage and strength to sit up, feeling his head spin as he did. *I feel like I've been hit by a truck.*

He jumped when he saw a woman staring directly at him, her gray eyes looking him up and down.

"How are ya, sweetheart?" She asked, a southern twang thick in her words.

"Um...h-hi," Alex said dumbly, looking around the room. He noticed that Micheal was absent. "Where's Micheal?" he asked her, anxiety rising inside of him.

"Oh, the other boy? He's downstairs talking to our lord. He got up before you did and he went down not too long ago," she explained. "Y'all made quite an entrance. A few guards found both of you passed out on the road."

Alex frowned, not understanding the word "lord" in the context of her statement. "I'm sorry, who is he talking to?"

Now she looked at him like he had three heads. "Our lord. Ya know the person that runs their village or city?"

Alex just dipped his chin in a nod and stood up from the bed. He felt something slightly warm against his wrist, and he pulled his long sleeves up further, noticing the gemstone bracelet was now on his wrist. He pushed his shirt sleeves back down, thinking that the woman just put it on thinking that it was his. Which it was now, technically speaking. It had been abandoned for years around that doll's neck.

The woman gestured for him to follow her down a set of stairs that creaked under his feet, making him fear that the whole staircase would collapse, but the woman in front of him practically skipped down the stairs.

She led him into what he guessed was the living room, but it looked old-timey to him; a working fireplace, actual wood floors—not like the types of vinyl like Alex normally saw in homes—furniture that just looked out of place for the 21st century. At least, he hoped he was still in the 21st century.

Alex's eyes fell on his best friend, who was sitting in a chair at a table, and he sighed in relief. A young woman was standing on the other side of the table, who Alex assumed to be the "lord".

She was shockingly somewhat around the age of Micheal and Alex, definitely around the age of nineteen or twenty. She was adorned in cargo-like pants and combat boots. The neckline of a dark-colored shirt poked out that Alex couldn't clearly see because it was covered by a dark leather suit and plates of metal armor that stretched across her forearms and down to her wrists and a plate that went across her chest.

Her deep brown eyes matched her hair that was tied back behind her neck, eyes holding suspicion but also curiosity. The sun broke through a window to highlight her beige skin. She was beautiful in a regal way.

"Hello...Alex, is it?" Her soft and gentle voice held power that washed over him.

"Yes, I'm Alex O'Connor," he responded. His eyes followed her hand that was resting on the hilt of something that Alex didn't expect. It was a sword. *Who still carries swords these days? Where are we?* Alex's brain ran rapidly.

"I'm Katelyn Garret. It is a pleasure to meet you," the girl greeted him with a soft smile.

"Where are we exactly, Katelyn? You didn't exactly answer my question when I asked earlier." Micheal spoke up, only lifting his eyes to stare at the girl.

She leaned her hands on the table as the first woman Alex came with crossed to stand at her side. "You are in the village of Phoenix in Zalrona."

Micheal frowned in concentration, brown hair falling across his eyes. "Like...Phoenix, Arizona?"

Katelyn looked totally perplexed. "Apologies, I do not know of the place you speak of."

Micheal and Alex both stared at each other, worry and dread starting to flood their chests. Alex had a feeling they weren't going to get home for a long time.

"If you do not mind me asking, where do both of you come from? We can take you back to your village or city if you require assistance," Katelyn offered, obviously feeling bad for their situation.

Alex shook his head, staring at the floorboards. "I....I don't think you can help us. We have never heard of 'villages' or 'lords.' We're from Pennsylvania. I don't even know if we're on Earth anymore."

The older woman shuffled her feet. "I have never heard of this 'Pennsylvania' you speak of, hon. At least not in our kingdom."

Katelyn thought for a moment, tapping a finger on the hilt of her sword. Alex and Micheal didn't move an inch, numb to the shocking discovery that they weren't exactly on their plane of existence anymore. More like their dimension or realm.

Alex couldn't understand it. How could two stones they found by chance solve the mysteries of science?

"I think I know someone who can help you," Katelyn suddenly said. She turned to the lady next to her. "Thank you, Maggie, for your hospitality. It's always a pleasure to see you."

The woman, Maggie, smiled. "The pleasure is mine, Lady Katelyn."

Katelyn addressed the two boys. "Come, I will take you to see Sabine. She is the only protective magic user I know who might be able to help you." She strutted out the door.

Alex blinked before racing after her. "I'm sorry. Did you just say magic?!" He nearly ran into someone. He jerked himself back.

Three men, all in their twenties, were waiting outside the door for their lord. They varied in height but they all could look down at Alex. They seemed to be guards or warriors because they were dressed in the same way as Katelyn. However, their leather suits and armor had slightly different designs and markings, mainly the sizes of their swords and positions they were put in. Two of them held their weapons at their waist, and the other had a sword across his back and on his left hip. The hilts glinted in the sunlight.

Alex stepped back, definitely not wanting to rumble with three men that looked like they could snap him like a twig or pin him to the ground in a matter of seconds.

The three men all slipped into defensive positions, hands pulling swords out of their scabbards.

Alex tensed up, eyes widening while Micheal stepped behind him cowardly, using him as a human shield if the men decided to attack them for chasing after Katelyn.

Katelyn smiled then laughed at the men's reaction. "Oh, come now. Be nice. These boys are our guests, and they will be treated as such. Swords down."

They reluctantly lowered their weapons, still glaring at the two trespassers. The one guard with dark blond hair that reached his brow turned to the young lady. "How do we know we can trust them? What if they are assassins? Or spies?"

Micheal raised an eyebrow and then gestured to his smaller body compared to the other man's. "Hey blondie, do I look like an assassin to you? Even if I was, you look like you could beat me to a pulp."

The man growled and pointed his sword again. "Do not test me with your disrespect, boy."

Micheal made a disgruntled sound of disbelief. Alex fixed his grip to hold his wrist as a warning to keep him from digging a deeper hole for himself.

"Boy? Really?" Micheal rasped, gesturing to himself before pointing at the guard. "You're only like ten years older than me!" Micheal argued, much to Alex's dismay. "Honestly, you should take it as a compliment you dumb—" The boy cut his sentence off and shut his mouth when the guard took a menacing step toward him, making Micheal scamper behind Alex again.

Katelyn pushed the guard back with a roll of her eyes. "Rex, enough. We must get moving." She beckoned the two boys closer. They gratefully accepted her protective coverage from her gruff guards that glared at them with promises of a painful death if they did anything suspicious.

As they left Maggie's house, Alex didn't expect to see the things he did. The trees around the village had leaves like any normal tree, but the colors were so vibrant, nearly blinding the two of them. Alex noted they were quite similar to the ones from the strange forest they entered that day. Some of the flowers in front of houses or on windowsills even sparkled.

The houses were small but seemed homey enough, and to Alex, they looked straight out of a medieval story. The walls were created with hundreds of stones stacked together with strips of wood crisscrossing over each other to keep the foundation stable. The windows were small with slightly cloudy glass. Some didn't have any glass at all, just wooden shutters that were currently open given it was around midday to let the sun shine through.

Children of all ages ran around with their parents or with other children chasing after them. Alex caught a peek inside the houses through open doors or windows to see more children helping their mothers or fathers around the house.

People dressed in similar attire to Katelyn, Rex, and the other two guards patrolled around, saying hello to the people or ruffling kids' hair. Swords were harnessed against their hips too, and Alex guessed that it was the weapon of choice in this town.

It's so different here, Alex internalized. The people around engaged with each other. They had meaningful conversations. He rarely ever talked to his neighbors, and if he did, it never lasted long. He assumed most of them thought he was just as drunk as his adoptive parents and avoided talking to him.

"Hey Alex, I don't think we're—" Micheal interrupted Alex's observations, leaning closer and smirking at his friend.

Alex held a hand up, refusing to look in his friend's direction. "Micheal, I swear to God if you make a Kansas joke, I will never talk to you again. You made enough of them when we actually lived in Kansas."

Micheal pouted. "That's not fair. It's also technically a *Wizard of Oz* joke, not a Kansas joke."

Alex rolled his eyes at his friend's way to try and weasel his way out of things. "Still, don't do it."

Micheal was silent for a moment before he said in a rush, "I have a feeling we're not in Kansas anymore."

Alex closed his eyes and sighed heavily. "I hate you. You're dead to me."

One of Katelyn's guards failed to stifle a chuckle at Alex's reaction, snapping his head away to eliminate the temptation to laugh. The warrior was pale compared to Rex who was a closer complexion to Katelyn.

"What is a Kansas?" Rex asked, looking to Katelyn for an explanation.

She shrugged. "It's where they are from. That is why I am taking them to see Sabine. They speak of a land I have never heard of before. She is our best option."

The third guard with warm dark skin and cornrows going across his scalp into a short, puffy ponytail grumbled, "Why Sabine? She hates me."

The pale man elbowed him in the ribs. "That's probably because you tried to slice her in half the first time you met her, Jesse."

The other man pouted. "I didn't mean to. She startled me." He fixed the blond guard with a pleading look. "Rex, back me up here."

Rex looked over his shoulder with a small smirk on his face. "Don't look at me like that. Eyes like that only work for my brother, not you. And besides, Hunter has a point. You were close to hurting her, even if you didn't mean it."

Jesse squawked as Hunter burst out cackling. Katelyn hid a giggle behind her hand, and even Alex laughed. On instinct, he glanced at Micheal to see his reaction, and it was more shocked than amusing, which Alex hadn't expected.

Micheal's jaw dropped, and it made Alex laugh again. "You almost cut someone in half?!"

Jesse shook his head but was sheepish. "No, Hunter's just dramatic. It would take quite the amount of force to cut somebody in half."

"How would you know that?" Micheal asked, his suspicion making an appearance in his voice.

"I haven't done it myself if that's what you're implying." The guard waved his hands in a way to dismiss his question. "But I did *almost* slice her good. She did not take kindly to that, to say the least. Thankfully, she didn't return the favor, but she hasn't let it go yet. Hunter hasn't either, it seems."

Before Alex could say anything else, the four Phoenix natives led them up to a house. It was quaint with two levels. Alex snooped through the windows, eyes catching lots of books and scattered objects.

Katelyn strolled forward and knocked on the door before stepping back.

The door swung open, and the first thing Alex saw was a young woman with snow-white hair, half of it delicately braided into small plaits that twisted around into a small crown around her head. Her fingernails were painted a deep red resembling blood, wrapping around the door. Simplistic silver rings glistened on her hand. And piercing dark blue eyes popped out from her ivory skin tone. They landed on Alex and Micheal.

Her head cocked toward the side, eyes narrowing. "You two are out of place. I can feel something radiating from you...." She trailed off. Something flashed inside her eyes as they bounded back and forth to Alex and then Micheal. "Very odd indeed."

Alex pulled a weird face. "Nice to meet you too?"

Katelyn side-eyed the two boys and then looked at the woman. "Sabine, can you help Alex and Micheal? They wish to go home to their land."

Sabine shrugged and twisted on her heel, going back into her home. "Oh, the things I do for you, Katelyn."

The younger woman scoffed. "Oh, as if I do not do things for you." She stepped into the house, Rex, Jesse, and Hunter following.

Alex hesitated at the door, his feet stuck to the ground. He didn't fully trust the people he was in the presence of, even if Micheal stepped inside without a second thought. He was too wary of them.

Jesse poked his head back out of the house, giving Alex a soft look of pity. "I know you're probably scared, but Sabine is the only one who can help you. We just want to get you home. We won't hurt you if that's what you're worried about."

Alex knew the man meant well, but it didn't ease his racing brain much. Nevertheless, he went up the small set of stairs, hoping Jesse's assurances were true.

The house was just as Alex thought it would be ever since he met Sabine thirty seconds ago. It was witchy and disheveled. It appeared as if the house was decked through every nook and cranny with thick books with weird symbols on them, some of them that didn't fit in the bookshelves were put into stacks at around three feet tall on the ground. Flowers glowed faintly in the sunlight pouring in from the windowsill. Empty vials of varying sizes were scattered around the tables and chairs, and other glass containers with solid and liquid materials were on shelves on the right side wall of the level.

"What realm do you come from?" Sabine asked, opening a book on top of her table covered with papers and other interesting objects, tracing a finger down the pages before flipping them.

Alex's brain short-circuited. "What exactly do you mean?" He'd never encountered that word in casual conversation before.

Sabine narrowed her eyes. "Realms are images of a natural twin reality. Mirror images if you will; just with different ways of life and magic. Some realms don't have magic or even have something called 'science' or 'technology.' Right now you're in Realm Six. So what is the number of your realm?"

Alex sheepishly looked away, Sabine's dark, intense eyes making him nervous. "We don't know of realms in our... realm. No one does. We're not aware of the existence of other words."

She sighed. "That makes my job slightly harder. What name do you use in place of a number?"

"...Planet Earth?" Micheal uttered, but it sounded more like a question.

She waved her hand in an impatient motion. "What do you call your land specifically?"

Alex answered this time. "North America?" He couldn't think of a better answer.

Sabine's eyes ran over the page before she gave a frustrated sigh and slammed the book closed. She then bustled around the house, flying up the stairs then back down, then across the ground-level floor sporadically. Her boots made heavy clanks on the wood.

Alex stared at her wild movements, barely seeing Micheal's exact expression of confusion in his peripheral vision. He rotated around to see if the others had seemed just as startled as he and Micheal were, but he found that the guards had made themselves at home, leaning against chairs or the wall, and Katelyn stood with her back straight, looking presentable as ever. Alex had a feeling that her position of being a lord never stopped.

"Aha!" Sabine exclaimed with a smile, bounding down the stairs into her original spot. "I found it! This book speaks of many realms; let us hope 'North America' is *somewhere* in here." She peeled open a book, eyes flying over the words. Her fingers flipped the pages until she finally stopped. Her smile dropped, and she flipped over to a new section.

Rex sighed. "Well, that doesn't look like a good sign."

She didn't respond, too occupied with reading. The guards leaned forward from their positions of sitting or leaning, intrigued by what was unfolding.

A tense minute passed. Sabine closed the book with hesitation after marking the page with a pen-like object, looking at Micheal and then at Alex. "Good news is, I know how to get you home. This specific way allows you to not require a certain realm, just what you picture in your head." She tried to sound reassuring.

Alex nodded slowly. "And the bad news?"

She fiddled with a small chunk of a red and blue gemstone around her neck, the tip of it grazing the collar of her flowing shirt. "Bad news is we have to go through the Inferno Realm in order for me to create a portal powerful enough to get you back. Your realm is...how do I put this? Since I can't find it in any of these books, it's leading me to believe it is far away from ours. Unknown and undiscovered. That's the best way I can describe it, and even then it's still confusing. This method will take more magic, and the Inferno Realm holds very powerful magic."

"I'm sorry, the what now?" Micheal blinked a few times, head swiveling around at the others in the room for an explanation of what he just heard. Alex shrugged; he didn't have a great understanding either.

Katelyn cleared her throat. "They are not familiar with magic. It might help to give them an explanation about the Inferno Realm."

The other woman's jaw dropped. "How have you lived in your realm?! I mean, not many people have magic anymore, but how have your people survived without magic?"

Micheal thought and then shrugged. "Guns?" Alex shoved him, hissing at him in warning. "What?! Am I wrong?" he exclaimed. Alex just shook his head in disappointment.

"The point is," Katelyn jumped in, seemingly not surprised by the information just given out, "we could get you home, but it will be difficult. That's what I'm gathering, correct?"

"You would be right," Sabine said.

Katleyn's eyes stayed glued to Sabine. "And you are sure it must be through the Inferno Realm?" Her speculation didn't put Alex in a state of ease and comfort.

A curt nod was her answer.

Katelyn took a breath like she was preparing herself. "Then we will guide Alex and Micheal into the Inferno Realm in order to give them safe passage home."

The three guards unexpectedly stood up, gawking at their lord.

"Lord Katelyn, it is too dangerous to enter the Inferno dimension," Rex raised his voice. "There is a reason it is forbidden. And besides, what do you owe them? You would be risking your life and the king's rage for people you just met!"

Alex pulled Micheal along to shuffle out of the middle of the argument, seeking cover from Sabine. The woman gave an amused smile but didn't comment.

Katelyn's soft, warm brown eyes suddenly became cold and narrowed as she addressed her guard. "I do not recall asking for any of your opinions. Especially yours, Rex."

The blond man fixed her a glare of his own. "You would do well to remember what happened the last time we entered that gods-forsaken realm, in case you've forgotten."

The younger girl stepped up to him, not at all intimidated by the size difference between the two. "Watch your tongue when you speak to me." Her voice dropped low, warning him to continue.

Sabine sighed heavily, looking at her nails. "Not that this isn't entertaining to watch, but shouldn't we start preparing if we're going to get these two home?"

Hunter raised an eyebrow, unconvinced. "*You're entering the Inferno Realm? You swore you would never go there.*"

She shrugged, a mischievous smile coming to her face. "What can I say? I like a little adventure. Even if that means risking death, one way or another." Her smile faded. "On the other hand, our dear Rex is somewhat right. It is forbidden to enter any realms. We'll have to work very hard to cover our tracks so the king doesn't find out about Alex and Micheal being here. He could imprison them, or he could execute them if he was in the mood, because they crossed into our realm. And he'll execute us since we are about to break the law by assisting them in realm jumping."

Alex gulped. "Why would he punish us? We haven't done anything wrong. We didn't ask to be here." The anxiety in his voice was evident, much to his displeasure.

Rex's face became stormy, glaring at the wall. "That's the King of Zalrona for you. He's a cruel man. He wants total control over everything, no matter how much carnage he leaves in his wake. The gods are the only ones allowed to travel through realms but that's because he can't stop them lest he wants to be vaporized."

"Gods?" Alex whispered. There were multiple, real gods now? He couldn't handle everything being thrown at him. He just wanted everything to be back to normal where he was in control.

Sabine addressed the boys with kind eyes. "I would be happy to explain everything at a later time if you would like that."

Katelyn straightened up, taking a few steps toward the door. She looked at Alex and Micheal. "I must be on my way. The woman from earlier, Maggie Bennett, has offered both of you a place to stay. For now, you can roam around, but I ask that you don't travel too far. Sabine, I'm trusting that you can find a way to enter the Inferno Realm?"

The snowy-haired woman tilted her gaze to her lord and nodded curtly. "I'll update you by the end of the day. Let's just hope that we won't be strung up in the gallows."

The guards began to follow their lord, and Alex followed them, planning to go to Maggie's place. He looked back and saw Micheal's interested gaze trailing through Sabine's house and figured he'd be more occupied there.

Alex had little confidence in them getting home. They would most likely die before they did. This Inferno Realm, it seemed to be the embodiment of Hell by the way the others spoke of it. The origins of nightmares in this realm. How were they supposed to survive *that?*

<hr/>

"Alex, wouldn't you want to do something else?" Maggie asked Alex from the kitchen as he was perched on her couch.

He lifted his head out of his book. He had scavenged through the woman's bookshelf, finding only one book that could possibly entertain him. Everything else was written in a language he didn't understand. There were no words in the book he picked, just colorful pictures that seemed to tell a story. Whether it was for children or someone of any age, Alex didn't care. It was something to distract him.

"No, I'm fine here," he answered with a smile.

The woman squinted. "You sure? Most older kids don't like reading books. They prefer to do something more hands-on."

He kept his smile. "I like to read. And I won't read for long, seeing as this is the only book I can look at."

She stopped fiddling with the dishes she was washing and poked her head out. "Really? You can't read Standard?"

Alex studied the other books that were close by and said, "Huh, so that's what it's called. Yeah, I can't read Standard. The language I read is English and most people speak and read it. Does everyone read or speak Standard here?"

Maggie stepped two feet into the living room. "It's the most common in our kingdom. Other kingdoms have their own languages as the main form of speaking and writing." She smiled at him. "Back to my point. If you *do* get bored before the sun starts to set, you can go down to the dock for a while. You'll be able to see a bit of the ocean from the bay."

He bit his lip, a habit that showed he was in contemplation. With a satisfied expression, he closed the book and put it on the top of the bookcase for later. "I'll take you up on that offer. How do I get there?" She rattled off specific directions and landmarks for him to look for.

He left the house, only needing to hear the directions once, and he was off on his objective of reaching the water. He leisurely took that path that was given to him, trying to memorize the different landmarks and buildings in the village for later use. It would be extremely embarrassing if he had gotten lost on the first day he was in the village.

The main gravel road broke off into a thinner dirt path. Alex took that path and entered a grove of trees. He could see birds calmly sitting high in the branches, some even singing. The trees were shorter than the trees Alex was familiar with but the colors were vibrant. One fluttered down and he plucked it out of the air, examining it with keen eyes as he walked.

The small road came to an end once he could see the blue sparkling water of the bay. The bay itself was surprisingly small, but he remembered that the village seemed to be small from what he had seen during the day.

Around the bank of the bay was a stretch of white sand that led into bright, green grass. He strained his eyes to see through the gaps in the trees and saw darker water past the strip of land on the other side of the bay.

That must be the ocean, he deduced. He got closer to the wooden dock, and he came to a stop. Another person was sitting on the pier. Micheal must've gotten insight on the location of the spot before him because he was the one down there already. Alex moved closer.

Micheal's feet were dangling over the short wooden pier, just the very tips of his toes tapping the water. Alex sat next to him, pulling one leg up to his chest, and glanced at Micheal.

The bright sunset was making his emerald eyes reflect and shimmer like a rare gem in its burning red and orange tones. His dark gray sleeves were pulled up to his elbows, and the sun also made the stone on his wrist sparkle.

"Any idea what these are?" Alex asked, tapping Micheal's wrist above the bend of the stone.

Micheal sighed and observed his new accessory with distaste. "I tried looking in a few books that were in English that Sabine let me borrow when you went back to Maggie's, but I found nada."

Alex gave him a quizzical expression. "Since when do you read?"

Micheal held a hand up. "Hush, no interrupting. So nothing on the stone stuff, but I saw a book with the Greek symbol thingamajig."

Alex's lips quirked up a bit. "Celtic but go on."

Micheal glared at him but did as instructed. "It was in a different language, so I couldn't read it. I asked Sabine if she could read it, but she said it was a very ancient text that was gifted to her, and she couldn't read it either."

Alex deflated, tapping his foot against one of the support beams on the dock. "Well, I guess we're out of luck trying to figure out what these things are and what they mean."

Micheal smiled brightly. "We'll figure it out.."

Alex wasn't convinced. He wasn't sure if they would be able to get themselves back home. He forced a smile on his face for his friend's sake, not wanting to crush his spirit.

"We will," he vowed despite himself, and it was worth it to see Micheal beam at him. "We should make the most of being here though," Alex said.

Micheal swiftly diverted his head to Alex, astonished by his words. "Alex, you've meticulously planned every aspect of your life out, and now you want to relax in a place that threatens that very plan? What have you done to my Alex?"

Alex narrowed his eyes. "I take offense to that. Just because I have *meticulously* planned everything, as you pointed out, doesn't mean I can't take a vacation."

The brown-haired boy pressed his lips into a thin line to suppress his laughter. "The only reason you aren't panicking is that our hands are currently tied. I personally think we should just stay here for as long as we want. But if you want to go back to being 'Mr. Perfect' in our realm, then oh well."

Alex opened his mouth to offer a rebuttal, then thought better of it. Micheal snorted and fell into a fit of violent giggles and cackles, gripping the sides of his ribcage. He gripped the short support beam to stop himself from falling into the crystal blue water below him.

Alex scooted away in an act of pouting, playing the pity card. "Yeah, laugh it up all you want."

Micheal wiped tears from his eyes. "I don't mean to."

"Yes, you do," Alex declared. Micheal always made fun of his hyper-focus on succeeding in everything in life, and the jump to a different realm didn't change that.

"Oh, come on," Micheal exclaimed. "You have to find it at least a little funny. It's so unlike you."

Alex fought to keep his composure, but even he couldn't

stop Micheal's effect on him. He cracked a smile that turned into a chuckle. "It's a little funny."

As the sun disappeared into the horizon, Alex stood up and kicked Micheal lightly in the back with his foot. "Come on, we should get back before they send a search party after us."

Micheal wrinkled his nose. "Good call."

They trekked back to the village. Everyone seemed to be winding down for the day. The kids were being called in by their parents or older siblings, a handful of them begging for a few more minutes outside. People brought their hunting dogs back in so they wouldn't wander off in the middle of the night.

Just as they were about to walk along the path to Maggie's house, Katelyn appeared on the road. She smiled at them, happier than she was earlier. Calmer.

"How are you two settling in?" she asked in a concerned motherly way, despite being only a couple of years their senior.

Alex returned the smile wholeheartedly. "It's going well. Thank you for everything you've done so far."

She shook her head, waving her hands a few times. "Oh, it's no trouble at all. I will let you continue with your day. We will leave for the Inferno Realm in two days, and then you will be home." A twinge of sadness peeked into her voice that Alex noted in the back of his head.

Micheal nodded. "Thank you. Have a good night, Lady Katelyn."

Katelyn's eyes flicked to him. "Goodnight to you, Micheal and Alex." She continued on her way with a small wave to the boys.

Alex nudged his friend. "Lady huh? Didn't know you were a *gentleman* all of a sudden."

"It's her title is it not? Or close enough." Micheal pushed the door open to Maggie's house.

The woman was bustling around in the kitchen, and she yelled a few words that instructed the boys to sit down.

"You boys haven't eaten a darn thing today, and the gods better help me if I let two growing boys go without food! Sit down, please!"

Alex muffled a chuckle by making it a cough. This woman barely knew them, and she was acting like a mother hen. He did as he was told, not wanting to face the wrath of Maggie. He helped set the table with lightning speed and took his seat..

Twenty minutes later Alex and Micheal had finished with their food along with Maggie. She was staring at them weirdly.

"Y'all are tellin' me that a 'cell phone' can allow you to communicate with someone from another village immediately?"

Alex giggled. "That's the best way I can describe it."

Maggie blew air past her lips. "Your realm is weird."

Micheal raised an eyebrow, leaning back in his seat. "We could say the same thing about your realm. It's different, but it's awesome."

Maggie smiled and took the plates, placing them in a large bucket of soapy water that was her sink. "Well thank you, Micheal, that's very kind of you." She turned around and placed her hands on her hips. "You boys should head up to bed, it's gettin' late."

Micheal groaned but stood up, which left Alex staring in surprise. He turned to tell Maggie, "I have been trying for years to get him to listen to me, and you managed to do it in less than twenty-four hours. What's your secret?"

Maggie laughed wholeheartedly as Micheal scoffed and pushed Alex's head down. "Some friend you are."

Alex chuckled as they climbed up the stairs to their new room for the duration of their stay in Phoenix. He kicked his shoes off, extinguished the candle when it wasn't needed anymore, and climbed under the covers while Micheal just collapsed onto his small bed on the other side of the room. Alex made himself comfortable and fell asleep to the soft sounds of Micheal's breathing and sporadic movement in the depths of sleep.

❧⁓❧⁓❧⁓

Alex knew he was dreaming.

The screaming had started, that god awful sound. Despair hit his ribs like a truck.

He prepared himself for blindness…but it never came. Darkness didn't swarm his vision. He could *see everything*. He could see the sun, such a welcoming sight given his circumstance. However, it made Alex concerned. This wasn't supposed to happen.

He saw fires burning and ravaging a small settlement, the flames as bright as the sun. The screaming was the same, echoing and bouncing all around Alex. Men, women, and children were running as far and fast as they could.

To his left, men and women decked out in dark-plated armor with designs of a dark red or purple attacked with large broadswords. Blood splattered on their armor as they struck down anything that moved.

Awestruck, Alex tried to look around and see everything happening. If he could take in everything he saw, his photographic memory might be able to help him remember it when he woke up. But it was overwhelming.

He was so focused on the fact that he could see that it took a moment for the pain of fire crawling across his skin to reach his pain receptors. Forcing his eyes down, there was no sign of fire. It was as if it was lit within his veins.

Ash and smoke threatened his throat as he inhaled the clouds originating from the destruction. He started coughing, but it didn't get rid of his discomfort. He went

57

down to one knee, and he struggled to stay on his feet. He still wasn't in full control.

He looked up, not wanting to miss anything even if he was coughing up a lung.

A man with the same dark armor and equally dark hair that seemed familiar glared across the wasteland, staring at a large house in the literal center of the village. Alex followed his line of sight.

The house was large enough that could easily house six to eight people comfortably, and it was somehow still standing tall even though the rest of the picturesque setting had crumbled to the ground or had turned into ash and dust. He noted dark shutters and the medieval style. He also recognized that it wasn't burned down, as if the man was preparing to do the deed himself.

Alex couldn't take in any more details because two men came out and raised their hands, halos of deep green and gray light surrounding their hands respectively. They swung their hands in the direction of the first man, and what Alex assumed was their magic came shooting out like lightning bolts but without the crackling or sparks.

If anything were to be magic in this dream, it was definitely what Alex was ogling at now. The magic hit its mark and pierced the man's body, but the man only dropped to one knee and then looked up with a twisted grin.

Alex couldn't keep his posture up anymore. He crumbled fully to the ground with a muted cry of pain, now feeling the smoke spread through his respiratory system. The sensation was the same as his normal torment.

It was the same dream. He was just finally able to *see*. He still couldn't believe it. He'd always wished that he was able to see in his dreams, but he wanted to take that wish back. He watched on as the man with dark armor stood up, giving a flick of his fingers, and the other two men dropped to the ground, gripping their skulls. Red magic hovered around the man's tensed-up fingers.

Alex tried to reach for the two men, to help them in some way, but his body was too tired, too weak. His outstretched hand fell limp to the ground.

Alex's mind was violently brought around to a different scene, one that wasn't supposed to happen. He stumbled and panted a few times, glancing at his surroundings.

Before him was a young girl at least in her middle teens with her arms behind her back, wearing a tattered dress. The walls around her were dark bricks, metal bars partially blocking Alex's view of her. Dried tear tracks faintly painted her face, reflecting in the faint fire light of a torch on the wall.

Her eyes surveyed—more like glared at—someone pacing in front of her in the dark lighting. Alex couldn't see who no matter how hard he tried to crane his neck. Suddenly, the girl's brown eyes laid on Alex in the corner of the room.

Her confusion was plastered on her face, and Alex expertly read it before a ghostly whisper brushed by his ear, "Come find me."

Alex awoke with a start, coughing violently. He could still feel the smoke. His fingers dug into the sheets of the bed, and he fought the urge to claw at his throat.

The springs of the bed frame creaked under someone's added weight. A hand was abruptly on his back, and Alex shifted away from it. The hand didn't return.

Once he was done coughing, he panted as he looked around the room. He was back in Maggie's house, and instead of being in his own bed, Micheal was beside him, hand hovering in the air like he didn't know whether to touch his companion or not.

"Alex, what's wrong? You're freaking me out," the older boy requested to know, worry swimming in his eyes.

Alex waved him off, bracing his hands on either side of

the bed, working on getting his heart to function at a normal rate. He hung his head, chin tapping against his chest as he tried to comprehend what just happened. After years of having the same, horrible nightmare, he'd only just seen something new.

Why now? What am I supposed to do?

He ruffled his hair in a stressed manner, feeling his friend's gaze still on him. "I'm fine, Micheal. Just go back to sleep." His throat finally started functioning again.

Micheal threw his hands out to the side in exasperation. "You are far from fine, Alexander."

Alex knew Micheal was extremely upset with him or scared when he used his full name.

Alex waved his hand again, heart rate back down to a comfortable level. "I'm fine. Just a weird dream."

Micheal's eyes were boring into his soul. "You promise?"

He nodded, giving him a grateful smile, ignoring the guilt gnawing at his heart. "I promise, Mikey."

Micheal's sympathetic look turned into annoyance and playful anger. He climbed back into his bed and pouted. "You know I hate that nickname. 'Mike' is one thing but 'Mikey' is worse."

Alex laid himself back down, pulling the sheets back up to his chin. "That's why I say it, Mikey."

A pillow smacked him in the face. Alex grinned and tossed it back, then shut his eyes.

He woke up in the middle of the night once again a few hours later, absolutely floored by the fact that for the first time in weeks he didn't have any more dreams when he closed his eyes for the second time. Normally, the instant he closed his eyes, he would dream. Not tonight. Nothing happened. He chose to not think about it too much but was grateful for the rest.

Chapter 4

Alex awoke the next morning feeling sluggish but refreshed as he opened his eyes to face an onslaught of sunlight peeking through his window. Turning over to his other side, his body and mind began to operate once again.

His stomach twisted into knots as he remembered his dream last night. The smell of blood and smoke, and the sound of the screams and crackling fires made Alex shudder in horror. It normally never fazed him as the years of experiencing it had become the standard of his nightmare. What he saw last night was different. Different was bad in this case with the dreams.

If it was even possible, he thought that his dream last night was more *real* than any other previous night. He always wanted to examine what was happening in his dreams, but now he hated it. He wanted to be blind once again.

"You okay?" A voice startled him.

He sat up, eyes sporadically looking around the room. Sitting up in his bed with his back against the wall, Micheal's green eyes were staring at him.

Alex shrugged, trying to avoid the fact he'd just acted

like a flailing fish. "I'm fine. Totally. Just dandy."

Micheal raised an eyebrow. "Mhm." Without another word he stood up and put his shoes on.

Not wanting to be alone in the room, Alex followed him by tugging his shoes on and opening the door to their room. The two boys made their way through the small hallway of the second floor and loudly jogged down the stairs. They were unable to contain their excitement about being in a new environment that was drastically different from theirs.

Maggie picked up on their mood and gave a small laugh. "Happy are we?"

Alex struggled to hide his grin. "Maybe a little."

Maggie jerked her head to the main door of the house. "Go have fun, you two. It's early so you two will be able to meet some new people, hopefully."

Alex and Micheal immediately dashed to the door and fumbled to turn the doorknob. As they left the house, they heard one final warning. "Don't you break anythin'!"

"We won't!" Micheal yelled back, then dropped his voice so it stayed between the two of them. "Maybe."

Alex rolled his eyes in good humor. "Alright, what's the plan now?"

Micheal's easy-going smile melted into one of sheepishness. "Didn't think that far, yet. Was there something you wanted to do?"

Alex shook his head. "Nope. We barely know anybody here except the guards and a few others."

The latter bit his lower lip, a familiar habit that Alex chose not to comment on. "Let's just walk around."

Alex didn't object as they sauntered on the gravel, taking in the scenery as the pebbles shifted underneath the soles of their shoes. The trees framing the houses and buildings made the perfect shade over the boys, blocking them from the midday sun.

A woman stepped out of her house, hair in a French braid only to discontinue when it reached her neck, and then her hair was free-flowing in the tame wind. Her eyes widened in surprise when she saw them.

"You must be the boys that arrived yesterday," she said to them, brushing what seemed like flour off her dress. "It's nice to meet you."

Alex smiled at her. "Pleasure to meet you as well."

She gave a teasing smile. "And they have manners as well."

"Mommy!" A little girl called as she ran out of the same house with a boy following. "Can we go play?"

Her mother shook her head with a sad smile. "Not right now, dear. Mommy's busy."

The woman was exhausted, her shoulders slumping forward. Alex nudged Micheal in the arm, hoping he would get the hint to say something to her.

Micheal stepped closer. "We can watch them. If you're okay with that, that is," he added the assurance that they understood the decision to be hers. She looked like she needed a break from her rambunctious kids.

She reeled back a bit. "You would?"

Alex shrugged. "We have no problem watching them for an hour or two. I know we're strangers and you don't want us to nab your kids, so we won't go far."

The woman gratefully exhaled in relief. "If Katelyn trusts you, then I do as well. Thank you, you two. Really." She nudged her two children toward the boys. "Go on. You can play with the new boys."

The kids stared at the newcomers with wonder and giggled, then ran into the large, barren field behind their house.

Micheal and Alex slowly followed, never letting the children get too far out of sight. Alex and Micheal sat themselves down in the middle of the field underneath a tree and watched a few more kids begin to play with the other two, giggling happily and dashing around. The two teens smiled at the sight.

"Pirate would love it here. Kids, lots of room to run, all that jazz," Micheal said.

Alex snorted in agreement. "You're right. Is he going to be okay while we're gone?"

Micheal pulled a face then nodded. "Yeah, Mark won't let him starve. He loves that dog just as much as I do. He just won't admit it."

A peaceful silence settled between them, the giggling and yelling voices of children in the background.

A tap on the shoulder caused Alex to turn his head and found a redheaded girl about the age of seven looking shyly at him, her hands picking at the seams of her dark green dress.

"Hi there," Alex greeted quietly to not startle her. She gave a small wave, her blue eyes glued to the ground while her shoulders sunk inward. "Can I help you with something?"

She peeked up at him, fingers still fidgeting. "Can you braid my hair? My mommy did it, but one of the boys pulled it out." She presented her braided hair that was extremely lopsided and wonky, with large pieces of hair sticking out.

Alex smiled at her and gently directed her to sit in front of his criss crossed legs. After taking her hair out of the plait, he finger-combed her fiery red hair to get the knots out from her time running around.

"It's been a while since I've braided anyone's hair, so mine most likely won't be as good as your mommy's." He leaned around her to look at her face. "How do you want me to do it?"

She wrinkled her nose, her freckles moving with the action. "My mommy starts right here," she said, tapping the frontal region of her head, "and does it to the bottom."

He slowly tilted her head back a bit, guessing that the girl's mother French braided her hair. He took three small pieces and folded them over each other. Once he reached the first piece for a second time, he dragged his finger from her temple to the center of her head, gathering whatever hair he picked up on the way. He did the same thing on the other side, doing his best to not hurt her but making it tight.

"I didn't know you could braid," Micheal said, smiling when the little girl glanced at him out of the corner of her eyes, staying still as a stone.

Alex made an uncommitted noise, focusing on not dropping the strands of hair which would force him to start over. "I had foster sisters when I was younger before I met you. They taught me how to braid. Not very well, but they tried."

Micheal mercifully stopped talking, allowing Alex to focus on finishing braiding the girl's hair.

Alex proudly looked at his creation five minutes later, securing the thin leather strap the girl gave him in place of a hair tie. The girl traced the pattern with her fingertips, and she grinned brightly. "Thank you!" she shouted while hugging the older blond boy, her shy demeanor receding.

Alex smiled at her gesture of gratitude. "You're welcome."

"I'm Gwenivere," she announced confidently, still sitting on the grass.

"Nice to meet you, Gwenivere. I'm Alex," he said back to her.

Micheal butted in. "I'm the more fun one, Micheal."

She giggled at him. "What do you two do for fun?" she asked in a childlike manner.

Alex thought about the question, but he stopped when he realized he didn't really do anything fun. "I like to read when I can, but Micheal thinks that's boring."

She gasped loudly, eyes sparkling with excitement. "I love reading!" She grabbed Alex's hands, and with surprising strength, she forced him to stumble to his feet and follow her.

Alex flailed around to yell at Micheal. "Watch the other kids!"

He let the girl drag him across the road, giving sheepish waves to those who were bewildered as they passed. Gwenivere didn't let up on her pace, moving fast for being so small. She led him into a house that appeared to be along the same structure as Maggie's house but with different style shutters and other minute details. Her dress brushed against the vibrant flowers on the edge of the path leading to the house.

She pushed open the front door with her free hand and yanked him up the stairs. The floorboards creaked under Alex's weight. Gwenivere dragged him to a door at the end of the hallway with a leaf and vine design in the middle of it.

"Is your mother okay with a stranger being in your house?" he asked.

"She won't care. You're nice."

"She might not think that if she finds me in here," Alex muttered under his breath.

The redhead dashed into the room, leaving the door unfastened for Alex. Her room was small but she was young enough that it was sufficient for her. She had a little bed in the corner of the room, covered with a warm-looking blanket. On the floor were a few wooden toys and a few stuffed ones.

However, she went over to a medium-sized bookcase and sat in front of it, already pulling some of the books down. She patted the floor next to her when Alex didn't move fast enough for her liking.

Alex listened to her for an hour as she exploded into an

array of words and eagerness. She went through each one of her books, saying which ones she liked and didn't like, which characters were good and bad, and everything under the sun. He nodded at the right times and answered when she asked questions.

She stood up on her tiptoes at one point, struggling for a moment but retrieved what she was searching for. It was an older hardback book but still held its form within the spine. The cover was a faded blue, discolored by age. It was cradled in her hands like it was the holy grail, a precious object in her mind.

"This is my favorite one," she said, handing it to Alex to look at. Just like all the other books, it was written in a language that he couldn't understand as he flipped through it with care. "It's about two heroes that have to save the kingdom."

Alex smiled softly. "I bet it's wonderful." He handed it back to her delicately. "I wish I was able to read it," he added more softly. "Where did you get it?"

Her eyes practically sparkled. "The crown princess gave it to me! When we lived in Silverbend two years ago, the crown princess and the princes got stuck in a storm trying to get through to go to the palace. We let them stay in our house, and she let me keep one of her books from her carriage."

"The crown princess, huh? She's the heir to a throne?" he asked.

Gwenivere nodded. "The heir to Zalrona. It's our kingdom. Did you not know that?"

Alex felt the embarrassment rise in him. He had only heard the name of the kingdom once from Rex. He was so out of place in this new realm that even a little girl could notice that.

"I'm not from here, Gwenivere. Micheal and I come from a different land, and we don't have many princesses in our...village or kingdom," he fumbled through his explanation.

The girl didn't judge him. "The princess was very pretty. Her crown was too." She methodically stacked her books back on her shelf, putting them in meticulous places up there. "Rex's brother looks like her. Same hair and eyes. They're both nice as well."

Alex bit his tongue to not laugh at the young girl, hurting her feelings would only spark guilt in his heart. "I'm sure if Rex and his brother were related to the princess they wouldn't be living here." She just shrugged her shoulders and continued her task.

They both were led out of the house once the girl was done organizing, Gwenivere holding onto Alex's hand. She continued to babble on about her books and other things that interested her while unceremoniously kicking rocks with her small feet.

Eventually, they crossed paths with Jesse and Micheal walking side by side.

"Making friends, Gwen?" the guard questioned the young girl with a smile.

She hugged Alex's middle, squeezing him tight. "Yes! He's nice!"

Jesse chuckled a warm noise that relaxed Alex. "I know! I met him and Micheal yesterday," he explained, matching her enthusiasm. "I hate to interrupt you two having fun, but I need to borrow Alex from you."

She pouted but nodded, taking two steps backward.

Alex raised an eyebrow at the older man but followed as they trekked away, only after they watched the girl rejoin her friends.

"What did you need us for?" he asked once they were alone.

Jesse had a mischievous smile. "Katelyn figured since the mission for the Inferno Realm is in the process of planning it was a good time to teach you two how to fight."

The blond and brunet glanced at each other and then back at the man in confusion.

"Who are we supposed to fight with?" Alex asked.

As Jesse's smirk grew, Alex's level of serenity plummeted. "Take a guess," the older man said.

Micheal looked at him in horror. "You wouldn't dare."

Jesse chuckled maniacally. "Oh, but we most definitely would." He led them up a short hill where another figure was standing with his arms crossed over his chest, looking out to the horizon. Hunter.

Jesse and Hunter grasped each other's forearms in greeting before slyly looking at the two intimidated boys.

"Here's how this will work," Hunter started. "We come at you, and you do the best to protect yourselves. We're just teaching you how to take a hit. Afterward, we will teach you how to at least not die in a fight."

Alex, the smallest out of the four of them, just stared at the two guards like they were mentally insane. "You'll kill me before you get the chance to."

Jesse and Hunter dominated him in both height and strength. They were extremely built and muscular. Alex could tell even through the armor and leather. He knew which battles to pick, and this was ont one of them.

Hunter unlatched a buckle strap that went around his waist that was holding a sword, then another one that crossed diagonally over his chest and upper back. He let his swords and scabbards fall from his body to the ground with a metallic thud. "I guess you're lucky it's not sword fighting. It's good to get knocked around a few times. No sharp edges."

The temptation to bolt for the hills and never look back was ever-growing. "You're still going to punch me in the face."

The man grinned, showing his teeth in a wolfish way.

"Then I suggest you dodge."

Without warning, the man stepped toward him and kicked the side of his knee, forcing Alex to crumble and sprawl on the ground when his foot made contact. The dirt dug into the palms of his hands as he pushed himself up, glaring at the guard.

Hunter gave an innocent shrug and pulled him upright. And he charged again. Alex dodged to the side, stumbling but staying face-to-face with Hunter. A punch came at him. He lifted his arms to protect his head, feeling his bone throb as he took the brunt of Hunter's punch in his forearm.

"Not bad," Hunter hummed as he kicked Alex in the side.

Alex, still the victim of Hunter's teachings, tried to absorb the blow, but it still stung deep in his lower ribs.

"Haven't you made your point!" Alex yelled in frustration, his tone pitching higher in fear.

Hunter shot him a bored glimpse. "I've only hit you thrice."

"And I understand the message you're trying to get across."

He nearly kicked Micheal in the head in shock when his friend suddenly appeared lying down by his feet, holding his back with one hand. Jesse had knocked him to the ground as well.

"I'm with Alex on that one," Micheal seconded him, raising a limp hand in the air to get Jesse's attention.

Jesse and Hunter shared a look and rapidly started talking in a different language.

Micheal squawked at them. "Hey, that's cheating! No other languages!"

The two went silent once again. Jesse tossed his hand up in annoyance and spoke to Hunter once again, who laughed. Jesse faced the boys.

"Fine, you two win. Micheal, you're with me again.

Alex, you're with Hunter."

Hunter ambled three paces away, giving Jesse and Micheal enough room. Alex reluctantly followed.

"Spread your feet shoulder-width apart." His order was quick and sharp.

Alex did as he was ordered.

"Now stagger your feet into what feels natural for you. Bend your knees a bit and raise your hands into fists."

Hunter adjusted his hand height and placement and pushed him a couple of times to test his stability before he began to teach.

He guided Alex through a few simple but effective defense moves, taking ten minutes each for Alex to mostly master. Due to his good memory, he learned quickly, picking up the moves with little difficulty once he understood what his body was supposed to do.

Alex's shirt was beginning to become wet with sweat under the sun's powerful rays, but he couldn't care less. He was grateful for the guard's detailed instructions and criticisms, and at the end of the crash course of the new fighting moves, he was having as much fun as he possibly could.

"Now it's time to test them," Hunter said. "We'll start slow and get faster later. I'm going to move toward you in different ways, and I want you to do the motion of the techniques you think would be the most effective." The taller man went into a relaxed ready position, waiting for Alex to do the same.

Hunter stepped with light feet, stalking Alex. He stepped to the side and quickly out of sight. When Alex spun his head around, Hunter was right behind him. He bent his arm close to his chest and drove his elbow back, making sure to not actually hit him.

Hunter gave a tilt of his head, not a full nod. "That could work. Again."

He was quicker the next time, and the time after that he was even quicker, forcing Alex's instincts to take hold. Soon they were going as fast as they could without causing damage to one another.

Alex's muscles started to tighten up as they reached the two-hour mark of the session. He got sloppy, and Hunter kicked his legs out, expecting him to dodge. Alex ate grass for the second time that day.

Hunter sucked in a breath in sympathy. He looked over his shoulder to Jesse and saw Micheal was in the same predicament; on the ground and panting. "Maybe that's enough for today?"

Jesse nodded, looking down worriedly at Micheal. "I agree."

Alex slowly got off the ground, body aching from the attacks he received. "Thank you for your careful consideration," he deadpanned as Micheal sluggishly stumbled to him.

"At least you two have something under your belt now," Jesse said, looking on the bright side. "We can keep working tomorrow, and then you'll actually start to spar with us and others. Sword training will possibly come later."

Micheal's eyes widened comically. "Others? Meaning possibly Rex?"

Alex was winding up to tease him, but he remembered that Rex wasn't too fond of him either. He closed his jaw with force.

Hunter nodded once. "Yes, that means Rex. He'll want to see what you two can and can't do, and how much protection you'll need on the journey. We'll be close to dangerous territories."

Alex found his answer vague.

Sharing a grim expression, he and Micheal started walking back into the heart of the village with Hunter and Jesse following. Alex saw the kids still playing, dashing around trees and bushes as their parents would sneak peeks at them to ensure they were safe as they carried out their business.

"Was everyone here born in Phoenix?" he questioned in curiosity. "Everyone seems so close."

Jesse shook his head, wiping his brow with the bits of his shirt on his wrist that poked out from the metal armor. "No, only about half the people are born and raised here. Most people come and go after they have settled for multiple years. It's a fairly new and small village compared to the others in the kingdom. There are a few that have been here for years, like Maggie. Hunter and I are from the same region in the kingdom which is in a different region from Phoenix. His family moved there when I was born, and he and I stayed until we both left for guard training. When we came to Phoenix eight years ago, most of the people were gone."

Alex couldn't understand why that was the case that people were gone.

His confusion must've shown in his body language, because Hunter explained with judgment in his voice, "Most people left after the old lord died. They believed Katelyn was unfit to lead. She was the only heir named by her adoptive father, so it had to be her."

Alex was starting to understand the ways of ruling in the new realm. "So all lords have to have an heir to take their place like a king has an heir. Gwen told me there's a crown princess."

Jesse smiled. "Yes. Of course, they can choose not to, but then it would be up to an election for someone to take up the mantle. This is how it works in other regions in our kingdom. I can't speak for other kingdoms."

"Region," Alex tested the word, "like different sections of this land, and I'm guessing there are multiple regions in each kingdom?" Both guards nodded. Alex knew what that word translated into his realm. "We call those 'states' in our realm. Kingdom would be a 'country.'" He enjoyed sharing pieces of his and Micheal's culture, knowing that the people living in Phoenix were doing the same.

Jesse stared at the sky in thought. "I want to say there are seven regions, but I can't read, so I don't look at maps very often even though they don't require much reading." Alex's eyes widened at the astonishing information about Jesse's reading ability, but he kept his mouth shut.

"There are five in Zalrona," Hunter answered, voice soft but firm as always. "I know of seven in the Kingdom of Crelf which is directly west of our kingdom and a couple of others around the world, but that's it. I never went to school, so my knowledge only comes from other guards who have been in different kingdoms, and also from the limited maps we do have."

"How many *kingdoms* are there?" Micheal asked.

"Eight. Some small, some really big," Jesse said in a bored tone. "Don't ask me about the kingdoms themselves, because that's when I lose interest. I hate it when people start discussing it. They always end up going into politics and that's not really my thing. Luckily out here you don't hear much about other kingdoms unless there's an invasion."

They arrived at Maggie's house, standing on the path and not quite making a move to enter it.

Jesse lightly punched Alex in the shoulder in a friendly way. "Take the rest of the day off. You've got another day of training tomorrow, so be prepared."

Micheal grimaced. "Right. Fun." He kicked lightly at the ground.

Hunter's lips quirked up at the corners of his mouth. "You'll survive."

The two guards stepped away, allowing the boys some peace for the rest of the day.

They left the training grounds. Instead of going into the house, Micheal wandered farther down the path.

"Let's go see Sabine," he suggested. Alex had no objections and followed in his footsteps.

"Don't touch anything that looks fragile. If you break it, you could suffer some type of infection or even die," Sabine warned them as they entered the house. She had begrudgingly let them into the house after they begged for a few minutes.

Micheal gingerly tiptoed around, suddenly aware of his usually heavy footsteps. "Why do you have such dangerous stuff in your house?"

She shrugged. "Because why not? I don't have a cellar to store anything so I just put them on shelves. As I said, don't touch. Books you can knock yourself out with, but you probably won't be able to read them."

Alex went through a stack of books, turning through the old pages. Just like Sabine had said, he couldn't read it. Exactly like he couldn't read Maggie and Gwenivere's books. Though he still took entertainment in some of the drawings in the books and scribbles from Sabine.

Micheal just talked to the woman, which Alex enjoyed because it gave some type of background noise. That was his and Micheal's dynamic. Sometimes Micheal would just talk for hours and Alex would sit silently, listening.

Hours later, Sabine was getting close to kicking them out.

"Don't you two have bedtimes or something?" she asked as she slid a book back into its place in a bookcase embedded in the wall. The two younger men stared at her in disbelief.

"Excuse me," Alex interjected. "That's an outright

insult, thank you very much. I am sixteen years old and do not need a bedtime."

The white-haired woman shifted her weight to one leg sassily. "Then tell me why you were falling asleep earlier."

He had struggled earlier to keep his eyes open in Sabine's presence. "I can neither confirm nor deny that statement," he fired back at her, even though she was right.

The woman theatrically opened the door. "Come on, out you get. You two heathens can come back tomorrow."

Dragging his feet, Alex went out the door with Micheal in toe. Once they were fully outside, Alex was confused. It was certainly late at night, but it was still partially lit like someone was shining a dim flashlight from high up in the atmosphere and it was spilling out across the village. It wasn't difficult to make out the sights of the village when it should've been.

"Why is it so bright out?" he asked, just before Sabine could get the chance to slam the door shut.

She pulled the door back open with bewilderment in her eyes. "Because it is most of the time?"

"Are we close to the poles of the planet?"

Sabine leaned her hand on the door. "I don't know what that means but no. Look up." She pointed up to the ceiling. Alex and Micheal tilted their heads back to look at the sky.

It was a bright array of purples, blues, and reds, painting the sky in sporadic but beautiful ways; as if colors were splattered into the universe with reckless abandon but it still made a work of art. The stars shimmered brightly from their homes in a nebula formation in the heavens. It was the stars that were giving the light.

It stretched on for miles, the brightness never ending. The velvet black sky held so many precious stars, all beautiful and heart-stopping as they twinkled and shined. Magical was the only word this could be labeled as.

Alex was starstruck for a minute. A grin broke out on

his face, eyes scavenging every corner of the sky.

He pulled his eyes away when the shock was gone. "You see stars like these every night?"

The woman bit her lip to hide her laugh. "Yes, Alex. Every night. The stars aren't this bright in your realm, are they?"

Micheal shook his head dumbly, staring at the stars. "Nope. Maybe a couple of hundred years ago, but not in our time."

A small but genuine smile crossed her face, eyes flicking to each of the boys. "Well, I'm glad you got to see it. I'm just surprised you didn't notice last night."

Micheal shook himself out of his trance, lowering his eyes. "We crashed pretty quick at Maggie's. We never thought to look outside."

Even though Alex was fascinated by the stars, he noticed that Sabine seemed conflicted about something, deciding on whether to say the words that were threatening to spill out of her mouth. Her hand ghosted up to brush her fingers over her necklace.

"You better get going, or Maggie will come after me tomorrow," she finally stated, her eyes clearing from thought.

It took both of them seven minutes to get back to the house, moseying along to stare at the sky.

"I bet they have different constellations if the sky is *this* different," Alex excitedly stated.

Micheal shrugged. "I don't know. I'm still confused about how realms work and the 'distance' between realms. Maybe I'll get Sabine to explain it again."

Alex practically vibrated, smiling at the stars. A nudge to his ribs and a soft, gentle laugh made him focus on his friend.

"How are you *this* interested in stars? I mean, they're really cool, but they're just stars aren't they?" Micheal asked.

"Science, Micheal. Science."

"Yes, I'm aware stars are cool to you," Micheal said in a monotone voice.

"It's something different, Micheal. We might never see something like this again. Be excited," Alex ordered with a smile.

Micheal matched his grin, softer than Alex's. "For you, I will be excited about the stars." Alex knocked shoulders with him.

Both of their smiles disappeared when their gaze fell upon a not-so-happy Maggie standing at the front door. She had her hands firmly planted on her hips, disappointment dripping off of her.

"When I told you to go and explore, that didn't mean you couldn't come back at a reasonable time," she said.

Alex shuffled his feet. He never had problems sneaking out or worrying about his adoptive parents because they never cared, but hearing it from Maggie made him feel slightly ashamed.

She ushered them in with a wave of her hand. She grabbed onto Alex's wrist when he went to retreat upstairs.

"Not so fast young man," she chastised. "Both of you eat something."

They each grabbed an apple from her bin of fruit on the wooden counter that was hugging the wall. She watched them eat with hawk-like eyes, and Alex appreciated her concern. It was a welcomed change of pace from Renee and Bradley's parenting.

She sent them upstairs with a shooing motion of her hands when they were done.

The boys settled into bed, unceremoniously tossing their shoes to the side. The soft sound of crickets reached their window as they lay under their blankets. The noise washed a wave of calmness over the room.

For Alex, the calm feeling didn't last long. He was soon

wide awake, his heart pounding in fear at the thought of closing his eyes. He was a prisoner of his own mind. It was a fact. He doubted his suffering would ever end, and that he would be forced to trek through the rest of his life with this shadow looming over top of him. Just because his dreams stopped last night once he fell back asleep didn't mean his sleep would remain dreamless.

"Are you still awake?" Micheal suddenly asked, rupturing Alex's bubble of anxiety and nerves.

"Yes," he whispered back.

"Rex said the Inferno Realm was dangerous. That means people might die."

Alex had known Micheal long enough to read his voice. It was filled with guilt. "I know," he eased him with a soft voice. "People might die just to get us home."

"I don't want that on my conscience."

"I know, Mikey," he repeated, still with patience.

Micheal ignored the nickname and rolled onto his side. There was nothing else Alex could say, so he disappeared into his subconscious prison once again.

The dreams were back.

Chapter 5

Alex let out a pain-filled grunt as his back slammed against the ground, breath evacuating from his chest. He rolled slowly onto his side, trying to get gulps of air back in his lungs.

Jesse chuckled from above him, his laugh colliding with the sound of metal clashing against one another and people sparring with each other hand-to-hand. "You're getting better at least. You lasted longer than the last time." He stuck a hand out for Alex to grab onto.

Alex was pulled up. He brushed the grass off of himself, and he grumbled a few choice words under his breath.

The dark-skinned man clapped him on the forearm giving him a sympathetic look. "I know we keep knocking you onto the ground, but we're trying to help you. This journey is going to be dangerous, and you need to learn to defend yourself," he said bluntly. "Combat is hard to learn in just a few short days, especially when you're going against people like us, who have years of training. Sword fighting is sometimes even harder."

Alex nodded dejectedly. "I get that."

Hunter came up from his left smiling at him. "Wow,

Jesse, you finally have *two* people that you can knock down to the ground. I'm proud. You can't even take down Tucker, and he's small compared to you. So, bravo."

Alex was unaware of who Tucker was, but he knew a backhanded compliment when he heard one. It made him more uneasy about Hunter.

Jesse rolled his eyes and shoved Hunter. "Very funny, Hunter. Hilarious."

Hunter continued to chuckle as the three of them made their way to seek shade under a large tree in the middle of the training ground. "You know I love you, Jess. I'm just messing around with you."

Pouting, Jesse crossed his arms. "Sure."

Alex smiled to himself, not wanting to irritate Jesse even more.

Silence cloaked them as they watched as the other guards continued to train. Somewhere in the middle of the training yard, Micheal got thrown over a woman's shoulder like he weighed nothing, yelping in the process. If Alex cackled like a maniac, the two guards next to him didn't say anything about it.

Alex calmed down from his laughing attack, and he saw that Katelyn and Rex were viciously going at each other with punches and kicks, but neither of them could land any lasting punches because the other would always deflect them. Their eyes shone with fury, kicking and striking with all the strength they had, and their bodies moving with a warrior's expertise. Alex's educated guess that the reason they seemed like they wanted to kill each other had sparked from their disagreement two days ago.

He gestured to them. "What's their backstory? They seem to have a history with each other."

Hunter hummed with a nod, shifting to lean back against the trunk of the tree. "Katelyn and Rex have known each other for many years. Rex was a guard, fresh out of training in their previous village. Katelyn was just a child then. Their village was destroyed. Rex, his little brother, and Katelyn set off on their own, never knowing if anyone survived. You might meet him before you leave. They came here, and Katelyn was adopted by the previous lord of the village as I said before. He passed away about nine years ago, and she became lord when she was eleven."

Alex blinked and looked back and forth between Katelyn and Hunter. "Eleven? Eleven years old? Is that legal here? She was literally a child!"

Hunter and Jesse gave him sad looks. They held the same opinions.

Jesse jumped in. "There were family friends that helped her along the way, and now she's the proud Lord of Phoenix. She's come a long way."

Hunter smirked. "Now Rex, he's still stubborn as a bull even after past attempts to get him to unwind. The only person that seems to somewhat get results is his brother."

Alex acknowledged his statement, slowly understanding the roles of everyone. "So, in theory, Rex is the grumpy old man in the village that never has any fun."

Jesse chuckled. "Exactly. He's the head guard, so it's his job to be particular about the way things run—"

"Jesus! Must you throw me ten feet?!" Micheal abruptly yelled to his sparring partner. He was face down on his stomach and pushing himself up on his hands. He was only five feet away from her, but Micheal Barnes had a flair for dramatics.

The woman just smirked at him, then her brow furrowed. "My name's not Jesus."

Alex shook his head, giggling. Micheal was always there for comedic relief.

Hunter leaned toward Alex. "If you don't mind me asking, how old are you? I've been meaning to ask but never found the right moment."

Alex pointed to himself. "I'm sixteen. Micheal turned seventeen about a week ago."

Jesse's eyes widened. "I thought you were older."

Alex shrugged. "Some people don't look or act like their age where I'm from."

The man fiddled with the latch of his armor on his forearm, tightening it over his leather sleeves. "What do you do in your realm every day? Do you have a job?"

Alex nodded. "I do have a job. I work in a warehouse." He received blank looks. "It's where they keep a lot of stuff for people to buy. I do inventory and load the shipments. That's only four nights a week. Micheal works at an animal shelter. They take care of dogs and cats that don't have owners. During the day we go to school."

Hunter's brown eyes widened in shock. "You go to school? Are your parents important in your village?"

Alex shook his head, not following where he was going with his questions. "Micheal and I both do five days a week. And no, our government pays for public school. If we were in a private school then our parents would have to pay, but my...parents barely have any money to their name."

Hunter narrowed his eyes at Alex in thought. Alex ducked his head.

Jesse tilted his chin up. "Huh. Here, people have to pay. Unless their parents are lords or people of interest and they get a mostly free education. The major cities have more schools and options, but out here in villages like ours kids are raised to find what they're good at and find work. Their education is limited."

Alex nodded along, feeling better about contributing to the conversation. "A lot of people do that in my realm." The word still felt weird in his mouth, foreign. "Kids go to school and realize it's not for them and go down a different path."

Jesse hummed. "Sounds like what I did. My mother sent me to school in our city for a few years but money

83

eventually ran out, and I couldn't go anymore. That wasn't a problem for me, because I couldn't read at all, which was a major problem. The teachers just lost their patience with me. I joined a guard academy near our city and never looked back."

Hunter finally spoke up when no one spoke again for a beat. "You hesitated earlier to say parents. Do you not have parents in the traditional sense?"

The blond bit the inside of his mouth, trying to find a way to avoid the topic at all costs, but Hunter seemed persistent to know. "No, I do, but they're not my birth parents. They adopted me when I was younger."

"You don't seem to think of them as your parents though, even while you live with them." Hunter continued to press.

Alex felt cornered which he didn't appreciate. Aggravation festered in his stomach, bubbling like lava. He knew Hunter was pushing him on purpose to get him to talk. Why was he doing it in the manner that he was? Alex didn't know.

"Does it matter? They're not my real parents."

Hunter stayed quiet for a few seconds, then backed down. "Alright." He maintained his distance, not even looking in Alex's direction.

Jesse scooted to be shoulder-to-shoulder with Alex. "Don't mind him. Hunter is experienced in espionage, and sometimes he forgets he can't use those techniques in daily life." He glared at his friend as the man walked away. "Especially with kids."

"Are you saying I'm fragile because I'm young?" Alex gritted out, his anger taking control.

Jesse remained calm which surprised Alex. "I didn't say that. He shouldn't have interrogated you like that." He looked to observe the training ground once again, watching as others blocked blows. "Do you need to hit something?"

Alex was startled by the question but didn't object. "Yes?"

Jesse embarked toward their previous sparring area. "Then let's go a few more rounds. Just don't think I'll let you make this a habit of taking your anger out in a physical form."

Alex smiled to himself. He raised his fists, about to start toward Jesse but a scream from a long distance away made him stop. It was one that sounded familiar to him.

His mouth went dry, and his windpipe closed. His hands were sweaty as he desperately looked at Jesse. This was too similar to his dream.

No, this isn't happening. He couldn't be sure if he was living his dream-like déjà vu or not. Were his dreams spilling into reality? Did he never wake up and this was actually still a dream?

Jesse finally moved, an expression of confusion crossing over his features. His mouth was forming words, but Alex couldn't understand him to save his life.

Jesse and a few other guards ran over to see the commotion. Alex placed his hands on his knees, trying to get air back into his respiratory system.

"Alex, breathe." Micheal's voice came from his side. The other boy was now closer to him, his usual easy-going smirk gone from his expression. His hands were stuck halfway in the air as if he was tempted to touch Alex.

Alex sucked in a breath, straining his lungs to work properly. He rushed over to the other guards, nearly tripping over his two feet.

Over the hill of the training ground, a group of around thirty people was running into the village with swords and weapons drawn. The guards hurried to act, yelling out to each other about the positions of the hostiles. The sounds of swords locking hilts came about.

Alex could only catch one word from the jumble of

85

concerned shouts. Bandits. He stared out into the distance, captivated by fighting, praying his new acquaintances would make it out unscathed.

"What—" Alex started but cut off his sentence when Micheal pulled him behind one of the trees of the barren plains. His grip was painfully tight on Alex's arms.

"Are you trying to get yourself killed?" Micheal hissed in his ear.

Alex elbowed him in the ribs. "Don't you even."

Hunter ran back up the hill, stabbing a woman in the neck with his sword as he did. Alex gagged at the sight of the blood flooding out of the wound. She collapsed in a heap. The dark-haired guard lifted his sword to block a slash from a bandit. As he crossed swords with the other man, he stared directly at Alex and Micheal, who were now in his sight.

"Hide!" he shouted.

Alex threw his hands up, a gesture showing that they didn't have anywhere to hide. He glanced around, searching for a place where he and Micheal would be safe.

Katelyn's house was the closest to them, but it was also an outlier as it was the only structure that was on a slight incline and obviously the home of a person of power. He would take his chances with being seen.

Grabbing Micheal's hand in a tight clasp, he dashed to the house. A shuffle of Micheal's feet told Alex that he fumbled on the ground as Micheal tried to keep up with him.

They dodged flying projectiles and angry bandits as they ran as fast as their legs would carry them. The house came more into view with every step. Just as they started up the short flight of stairs, a small plea for help stopped Alex and Micheal.

"Help! Somebody!" a young girl yelled. She was cornered, standing against the wall of a house with a large woman standing over her, a bloody sword drawn. The girl's red hair was tangled, and her clothes were dirty which showed she had been in a struggle with her attacker.

"Gwen," Alex muttered.

Micheal ripped his hand out of Alex's grip and started for the little girl. Alex didn't wait long to follow, not knowing what he was going to do to help her, but it was better than doing nothing.

Micheal attacked first from the side, giving a straight kick to the woman's ribs. The shock of someone landing a hit on her and the momentum of the kick pushed her out of line with Gwenivere.

Alex slipped behind her and landed a kick to her head that he knew wouldn't incapacitate her but would be hard enough to rattle her brain. Micheal kicked the sword out of her hand, the blade flying into the grass with a thump, out of her reach.

As Micheal continued to keep the woman's attention, Alex approached Gwenivere. He knelt at her level.

"Hey, remember me?" he asked. She blinked tears out of her blue eyes, and she nodded vigorously. "We have to hide. Come with me." Not giving her a chance to reject him, he clumsily grappled with her hand, pulling her along the stairs.

She screamed when a different bandit, a very large man, came running up the stairs, growling at them. Alex pushed Gwenivere further up the stairs and started to dash up the stairs faster.

"Get in the house, Gwen!" he yelled.

Alex watched as she violently pushed the door open, scurrying into her leader's home, wide eyes trained on him through a small crack in the door. As he reached the door, a stinging pain shot through a small sector of his upper left arm. He hissed in pain, and he turned just in time to see the bandit take an arrow to his chest.

The man jerked and gave a choking sound. His legs buckled underneath him, and he ended up on his back on the stone stairs, taking one last breath before the life left his eyes.

Not having time to find his savior, Alex stumbled into the house, feet catching on hardwood instead of grass.

As he went to close the door, Micheal ran and squeezed through the space left before the door closed, skidding across the floor an inch or two. When he came to a stop, Micheal twisted around and slammed his hands against the door.

Alex joined him, sliding the metal lock in place across the doors. They could still hear the commotion outside, but it was from a distance. No one was near them. No one tried to bust down the door.

Alex took that as a sign that he could step away. He slowly moved his hands off the door, his fingertips being the last thing that touched the smooth wood. He held his hands out in front of his body for a moment of hesitation, preparing to throw his weight onto the door. He tipped his head toward Gwenivere where she sat under the table, hands over her eyes.

"Gwen, you okay?" he asked gently.

The little girl sniffed. "Yeah, I'm fine."

Alex let his hands drop to his side, no longer high-strung about an intruder coming through. "Mikey?"

Micheal glared at him. "Don't call me that. And yes, I'm doing just fantastic." In the span of a few seconds, his irritation became a concern. His green eyes widened. "But you're not! Your arm!"

Taking a second for his brain to catch up, he twisted both of his arms to see what Micheal was talking about. His left tricep had a long but shallow cut going across the length of it, a tear in his shirt revealing it.

"Oh..." he said. Now that he was staring at it, he could

feel the waves of pain rolling through his arm and up to almost his neck. He focused on blood trailing down his arm, disappearing into the sleeves of his shirt. It was disgustingly mesmerizing. The dark blue fabric above his elbow to forearm had faint trails of blood, telling him that his wound had been bleeding for at least a minute. "Ow."

Micheal prodded at his arm, hands making quick movements.

Alex winced in pain and pulled away. "Please, stop. That's not helping." He pushed his sleeve up a bit to press against the bloody gash, biting his lip to stop any whimper or whine to come out from the sting. It would be too mortifying to admit that kind of weakness.

A knock on the door made Alex hit the deck, ducking out of view from the windows. He put a finger to his lips, telling his other companions to keep quiet. The knock became more persistent and the doors rocked as someone pushed on the wood until someone called out.

"Open this door before I break it down, you two," a gruff voice said.

Alex and Micheal relaxed, knowing the owner of the knock and the threat.

Gwenivere sat up straighter. "Rex!"

She got up from her place on the floor and unlocked the door, and she smiled up at the man. Rex surveyed the room with a critical gaze, checking for threats before giving a small smile in return to the girl. She hugged him around the waist.

"Are you alright?" he asked in a parental tone that Alex had never heard from the man before.

"Mhm."

Rex nudged her shoulder to push her out the door. "Your mother is worried about you. Go find her." With that, Gwenivere ran out of the house.

The guard looked at the boys, his amber eyes falling on

Alex's arm. Alex tried to hide it from view. Rex strutted toward him with heavy, powerful steps, but Alex stepped out of the way, giving him a glare of warning. The man stopped.

"Listen, I don't know why you're afraid, but you need to get that patched up by someone. I'm not sure what type of care you receive in your realm, but here that can get infected fast. So it's either me or I drag Katelyn in here." Rex gave him an ultimatum.

Alex didn't do ultimatums.

He stayed silent, keeping steady eye contact with Rex. He hated how stubborn he was acting, but it was just his nature.

Rex shrugged. "Fine. Katelyn it is. Do not leave here, or so help me I *will* track you down." He left the door narrowly ajar in his wake.

Alex considered leaving out the back door he saw when he entered the house, but Micheal directed him to sit down with a wave of his hand. Alex dug his heels into the ground when Micheal forcibly pushed him, but the older boy overpowered him. He always did when it came to brute strength.

Alex huffed in frustration when he was pushed into a chair, waiting for the minutes to tick by until Katelyn came. The stinging sensation was becoming a throbbing one from his injury.

Micheal shuffled into his own chair, kicking his feet up on the table. He pursed his lips. "So that was kinda awkward."

Alex rolled his eyes, staring at his shoes. "Can we not, please?"

"I'm just saying, Alex, it was kinda weird. It's not like Rex is going to hurt you," Micheal said, his voice rising. "I'm worried that—"

"Stop."

"Alexander—"

"Nope."

"Alexander Kennedy O'Connor—"

"Micheal Logan Barnes," Alex interrupted once again, putting as much surliness in his voice as possible. Micheal stared at him. Alex stared back. "I can play the name-game too. Just because my name is a mouthful doesn't mean I can't use yours as well."

A groan sounded from the door hinges. "I've heard many names, but not many quite that long, Alex. Except for royalty." Katelyn brought her appearance to attention, waiting at the door. "It's impressive."

Micheal nodded. "He's got the long name, but I've got the uncommon spelling of my name. I think my parents wanted me to suffer in life by correcting every person I met trying to write out my name."

Katelyn laughed, striding farther into her house and closing the door. She stepped up to a small closet near the stairs, virtually a cabinet, and twisted the knob on the face of it. It opened silently when she pulled it.

"Was there a reason your parents made the spelling differently?" she asked curiously, reaching a hand in. Her hand returned holding a few things. She walked to the table, footsteps deliberately loud so they could follow her just with hearing alone.

Curious as well, Alex looked at Micheal expectantly. Micheal had never gone into detail about it. Alex had grown up learning the spelling of Micheal's first name, taking it as the norm before other Michaels in school had corrected him on the spelling of *their* names.

Micheal hummed in thought. "I think it's because of our heritage or something. But the way they say it is the exact same way it's normally spelled when it's supposed to be pronounced differently. So my theory is that one of them spelled it wrong on my birth certificate and just went with it," he said.

Alex pressed his lips together to hold back a snort of amusement, but his efforts didn't make his smile cease to exist. "I could see your dad doing that."

Katelyn finished setting her belongings on the table. "What's a birth certificate?"

Alex glanced at her collection. There were a few rolls of rough-looking fabric and a jar of some thickened liquid that was murky.

"It's a formal piece of paper you get from the government when you're born. Or country or kingdom in your case, Katelyn. It has your name, your parent's names, where you were born, and all that jazz," he explained, not ignoring the way Katelyn was eyeing his arm.

The young woman shifted her chair closer to Alex, mindfully not getting too close to comfort.

"Can I see your arm?" she asked in a kind voice.

Alex slowly stretched out his arm in her direction, and he watched as Katelyn began her ministrations. She observed the wound, moving his arm in specific directions.

"I have to have more room to work. You can take your shirt off, or I can cut the sleeve off," she said apologetically.

Alex shrugged. "I doubt I would ever wear this shirt ever again, so you can chop away."

She whipped out a knife from a nearly hidden horizontal sheath on her waist, startling Alex with the fast motion. She made her movements slow and precise. He expected her to move fast, but appreciated her awareness of his discomfort and moved slowly to alleviate it. She cut a full circle around the sleeve of his blue long-sleeved shirt and then peeled off the ruined part of the shirt.

She gave a hum to herself and stood up once again, heading for her sink—more like the closest thing to a sink she could have. Grabbing a cloth from the counter, she dipped it in the water and then rung it out. She retook her spot next to Alex and wiped all the bloody parts of his arm the best she could without causing him too much pain. Once the blood was cleaned up, she pressed the cloth fully against his injury.

Alex let out a grunt, and his free hand shot out to grip the table with a tight grasp at the fiery sting. He took a breath and slowly let it out. The pain gradually went away.

Repeating the motion two more times with cleaner parts of the damp object, Katelyn pulled away the now bloody piece of fabric after the third rotation. She turned her upper body and perfectly threw the rag back into the sink from her seat.

While Micheal gawked at her throw, Alex still continually watched her movements. She reached for the jar and twisted the top off. A herbal smell reached his nose. Katelyn gathered a bit of the substance on her fingers.

"This is a salve that will help with the healing. It's going to sting a bit, though, so be warned."

Alex rested his good elbow on the wood table and pillowed his forehead on his hand, eyes tightly shut. Micheal gave a little pat on his head, and Alex reached out to smack him before returning to his position.

Something cold touched his arm. He didn't feel anything bizarre for a moment, but after three seconds, the slash to his skin throbbed excruciatingly.

"Son of a..." he cut himself off, gritting his teeth together. All his muscles tightened in his left arm.

"Language," Micheal unnecessarily warned him with a grin.

Alex couldn't say a rebuttal because he was overcome with the urge to punch Katelyn to get her hands away. If he had thought that the water had stung, he felt like he was now being stabbed repeatedly. He banged his fist on the table three times, hoping that it would somehow release his pain. His whole body tensed from head to toe.

Katleyn's fingers left his arm, and in their place came a feeling of compression. She was wrapping his upper arm with that roll of rough gauze-like material. Going around a few times, Alex started to feel less pain in his arm.

He leaned back in her chair when she was fully done, shooting the Lord of Phoenix an unimpressed look. "A bit, Katelyn? That was more than a bit."

She chuckled, curling a stray piece of hair away from her face and behind her ear. "You wouldn't be saying the same if you dropped dead because you got sick, so I think a 'thank you' is in order." A glimpse of sadness flashed over her brown eyes as if the thought of him dying made her upset, which made Alex narrow his eyes for a moment. He barely knew her. But he huffed a laugh.

"Thank you," he said, "but shouldn't you be helping your people? We only just came to Phoenix, and you're here helping me." He felt like he didn't deserve it. Katelyn had to have priorities for her own people.

Katelyn's eyes flicked to one of her large windows. "No one was critically injured, and there are a handful of people in the village who are capable of handling flesh wounds. This isn't the first time bandits have attacked."

Alex shifted his arm to run his eyes over the dressing Katelyn put on. "How many times has this happened?"

She raised her eyes to the ceiling in thought. "At least three times this year. Larger cities get attacked or looted numerous times a year. Bandits are rebels of the kingdom, acting out against King Malum's rule. They go for any city or village to prove a point that they can be dangerous, but they would never go for Zalrona City itself. It's too heavily fortified with trained guards and assassins. Bandits dominate large sectors of the regions, so they wouldn't ever risk possibly sacrificing their territory or their forces just for an attack on the royal family."

Micheal thrummed his fingers on the table. "What do

they not agree with?"

The woman sighed exasperatedly. "Oh, I couldn't name all of the reasons, but to name a few it would be King Malum is cruel, power-hungry, narcissistic, sociopathic, and so on. Bottom line is that he is unjust with his rule and hasn't addressed a large issue that has been threatening everyone. But I won't bore you with politics."

Alex caught onto the tone of her voice and her secrecy, but the thing that stuck out to him was she seemed confident in her answers like she believed them herself.

"You agree, don't you? That he's an unfit ruler," he said quietly, not commenting on her vague last statement.

Katelyn smirked. "I have no idea what you're talking about." She got up from the table and stored her things back in their homes. "Part of the reason we taught you how to fight was because of a situation just like this. We will likely encounter bandits again on the journey," she said as she crossed the threshold of the front door, ushering them to follow her. "Or other dangers."

Once all three of them were outside, Katelyn shut the door. "While I have you here," she started nervously, "I hope your stay has been somewhat comfortable, and that you haven't been scarred for life by today's events."

Alex shook his head. "Trust me, this has been anything but scarring. Sure, scary people coming at me with swords is terrifying, but other than that, it's been nice. Almost fun."

Micheal nodded, agreeing to his assessment. "The almost dying part gave me a rush, so I've enjoyed it here.

Alex rolled his eyes. "Says the adrenaline junkie. I'll be happy to never have another near-death experience again."

The taller boy tossed his hands into the air. "Now you've jinxed yourself."

Katelyn laughed at their antics, and she looked over the crest of the small hill her house sat upon. Her trained eyes analyzed her people that were now out and about.

"I must leave. I'm glad you boys are okay," she said, smiling at them and swiftly prancing down the stairs, her armor making small metallic clanks as she jogged.

Micheal and Alex retraced her footsteps but at a leisurely pace.

"She has the audacity to call us boys when she's three to four years older than us," Micheal complained.

"Don't whine, Micheal. It's not good on you," Alex quipped.

"Screw off, Alex." Changing the subject, he added, "Let's see if Maggie's alright, and maybe she will give you something to wear that doesn't look like an animal attacked your arm."

Alex grinned. "Something we agree on today."

They soon raced each other to Maggie's house, leaving a trail of dust from the road in their wake.

Chapter 6

It had been four days since the boys arrived in the strange realm, and Jesse and Hunter woke them up at the crack of dawn to go over the basics of sword training. They explained it wasn't completely necessary, but they wanted to stay on the safe side of protecting Alex and Micheal.

Alex regretted getting out of bed, his feet dragging. He didn't know if Jesse and Hunter would see through to their training until they left for the Inferno Realm. Jesse had kept saying that fighting with a sword was difficult, and Alex had a feeling it wasn't going to end well or the two men would give up on teaching them.

The sword had felt unbalanced when Hunter gave it to him, unfamiliar in his hands, but he was grateful that his wound from the day before was on his non-dominant arm. Perhaps he could take most of the sword weight with his right hand and arm. And thankfully, Maggie had given Alex another long-sleeve shirt which allowed him to hide the injury from the two men.

"This will be difficult, so don't be too hard on yourself," Jesse coached as he passed by.

Alex wrinkled his nose at the blade, observing the

metallic shine that reflected in the slowly rising sun. "Isn't this dangerous?"

"They're training swords. Completely dulled down so they don't do any more damage than bruising. You'll live," Hunter quipped back curtly.

Alex messed with the wrapped grip, feeling the torn cloth with his fingertips. *Here goes nothing.*

He had attempted to do the motions that Hunter and Jesse were instructing through with them, but it was too awkward for him. He could understand what his body needed to do, but his limbs would fight against him. It got better as he continued to work on the movements, but he was still sloppy.

"Any suggestions?" Alex asked, feeling slightly defeated after thirty minutes.

"You're faster without a sword. That's just plain obvious. Sword fighting doesn't work for everyone, but you'd also benefit from more practice. However, we don't have time for that," Hunter said, looking at him. He stroked his chin. "A shorter sword might help, but that could also prove to be a problem hypothetically. For now, you'll stick with physical attacks without a sword. Or just stay behind one of us on the journey."

Micheal, however, was fairly decent. He managed to copy the motions that were shown to him as Alex silently cheered him on from the sidelines.

Jesse observed Micheal scrutinizingly after there was a pause in the lesson, weight on one leg with his arms crossed.

"Not great but not terrible. In a dire situation, you'll use a sword. If it comes to that, do your best to block the attacks. You're still an amateur and a sword might not even be enough to protect you. For now, both of you will stay near one of the guards for protection."

"How many guards will there be?" Alex asked, wanting

to know how many people he could choose from if they came across trouble.

"Ten guards, including me, Rex, and Hunter. Katelyn and Sabine will be joining us as well, so fourteen people in total."

"I didn't think Rex would be joining since he wasn't fond of the idea in the first palace," Alex noted.

Jesse laughed. "Rex can't stay away from his duties for long. He's irked about what happened at Sabine's house and Katelyn's decision, but he would rather die than not do his job as a guard."

Hunter focused his eyes on Katelyn's house at a slight distance from the training field. Alex evaluated her home as well, spotting a group of people gathered around. Hunter began to walk, not saying a word to the others.

The three others kept up with him with Jesse taking the lead along with Micheal. Hunter slowed his pace before they reached the group, and he grabbed Alex's shirt to stop him as well. Alex raised an eyebrow.

The guard reached into one of the deep pockets of his leather suit and revealed a six-inch dagger in a short sheath, holding it out to Alex. When Hunter didn't move it away, he slowly moved to grab it. Just as Alex's fingertips touched the material of the cover and straps, Hunter tilted it out of his grasp. Alex gave an annoyed look.

"Do not stab yourself," the older man warned seriously; only then did he let him take the weapon. "Technically, I'm not supposed to be giving this to you since you don't know how to use it. Try not to mention this to anyone else. I'm trusting you know the method behind stabbing someone?"

He swallowed, his stomach twisting at the thought of hurting someone. But then remembered he was out of his league here. It was life or death. He nodded.

"Good," Hunter said. "Don't hesitate. Wrap the straps around your calf to keep it hidden from the others."

Alex nodded firmly. He rolled his pant leg up and attached the dagger to his lower leg, folding his jeans back over it.

They went on their way to Katelyn's house. Alex tried to keep his steps normal with the minuscule amount of weight added to his right leg.

Katelyn was standing in the middle of the huddle with Sabine at her side. She smiled at the boys when they approached. It disappeared as she fastened her figurative mask over her face.

"Sabine has mapped out our journey based on the location she needs to get us to the Inferno Realm. Our goal is to get Alex and Micheal home, but we may come across our adversaries. Keep your guard up. Scouts, fan out around us, just don't stray far. Regroup when we stop for the night."

Sabine cleared her throat. "We'll be heading east for a while before breaking off to go south to have some distance from the coast."

With a few more words passing between everyone, the journey began. The scouts split off, spreading down the tree line facing the east side of the village. Alex knew they would disperse once they were farther in the woods. He looked back at the village of Phoenix. *Do I really want to leave?* He paused. It was a crazy question to ask; there was no way he could stay. But he didn't hate it here even if he hadn't wanted to be in this realm in the first place.

Micheal stepped up to his side, brushing elbows. He didn't pressure Alex to move, something he appreciated. He shook his head, clearing his wandering mind.

I can't stay here. We don't belong. I have a different path set for me.

As he was beginning to walk away, he saw a hooded figure slip out of Katelyn's house and quietly enter the forest along the same path as the scouts. Alex got a quick glimpse of what they were wearing but he didn't see their face which was covered by a thick hood. They quietly entered the forest, along the same path as the scouts.

Alex thought nothing of it, just figuring that Jesse had miscounted or another guard had just recently volunteered to join in. But something in him told him that wasn't the case. He didn't look back as he followed the guards into the forest on the outer edge of the village.

As the journey continued forward, Alex's sadness of leaving Phoenix moved to the back of his mind. He realized that he wanted to go home, but he would miss Realm Six. It had been a short four days, but it had given Alex a moment to breathe. It also reminded him he had to stay focused once he got back to his realm with Micheal.

One thing that did shock him on the way was that Rex had stuck with the group and didn't turn back halfway through the day as Alex had expected. The darker blond had kept his mouth shut most of the time which Alex could tell he wasn't having too much of a hard time with, but the restraint was undoubtedly annoying the older man. Rex had avoided Katelyn most of the trip, obviously still having conflicting feelings about the objective, but he was severely loyal to her; that much was obvious.

Alex was slowly learning the names of the other guards, only picking up a few because they weren't too talkative with him. He kept to himself, watching as the trees changed colors and styles as they went deeper into the thicket of the forest while Micheal, in his true extroverted fashion, talked energetically to the guards flanking them from all angles.

The group made camp thirteen hours after the start of the trek. Alex and Micheal sat shoulder-to-shoulder on the moist ground, backs against a tree, staring into the fire that crackled and popped in front of them; a courtesy of one of the guards.

Alex hissed in pain as he stretched out his legs, muscles cramping and spasming from the very long walk. The other boy beside him hid a giggle with a cough that he still heard.

Alex debated whether he should unwrap the bandages on his arm or not, but he hadn't been in any pain. He was intelligent enough to not test fate unless he strived to face her wrath.

In the seclusion of their own area, the two boys noticed how the guards behaved around each other, including the guards that Alex didn't know well. They dropped their intimidating personas and let some personality show. Laughing, teasing, rough-housing. Even Katelyn seemed to relax, which the boys thought was a miracle. She was always so uptight and serious. It was a nice change of pace when they saw her genuinely have some fun, the tension seeping out of her shoulders.

"I'm calling it now. Jesse's the youngest," Micheal told him in a hushed tone.

Alex chuckled. "What makes you say that?"

"Just the way they act with him. It's the way my brothers used to be with me before they became stuck up. The teasing never stops with Jesse." Micheal's normally cheery voice dropped into something close to sadness.

Alex nodded, able to see the connection he made. "Hunter and Rex are definitely the oldest. Unless they're young and just act old and grumpy."

"Those two are also more reserved and less talkative," Micheal pointed out. "Hunter is good with counterintelligence apparently, so I wouldn't be surprised if he's been hiding his true age and is younger than we initially thought. And I think Rex is just the oldest. He's got that vibe. And he's a decent amount older than Katelyn because he was a guard when she was young. He had to have been at least sixteen years old when they went to

Phoenix."

Alex sighed. "So this is what people watching is like," he stated, embarrassment creeping into his voice.

"Embrace it, Lex. There's no crime in doing so."

"Stalking is a crime."

"Well, good thing it's not stalking."

For the next forty minutes, Alex continued to be reserved just like Rex and Hunter. Micheal continued to jump into a conversation, not waiting for an invitation. He was already being friendly with the scouts who hadn't been around until recently.

Alex didn't mind being in the background; it gave him some peace for a moment.

Once Micheal finally stopped talking for a few minutes, Alex jabbed him in the side. "Look at you making friends," he teased. "A new realm can't even stop that."

Micheal glared coldly at him. "Hey, I can be civil sometimes."

He nodded, unconvinced. "Sure, tell that to Rex."

Micheal glanced nervously at the guard before shifting closer to Alex. As he laughed out loud, Micheal defended himself by saying, "He's still scary, and I am never speaking to him again unless I have to."

Alex snorted, trying to calm down from laughing. "Yeah, sure, like you could stop from running your mouth."

Three scouts came back from rounding the perimeter of the camp one last time, sitting down on the ground, two of them taking the hoods of their cloaks off their heads, revealing a blond man and a black-haired woman. The last guard, who was shorter than the others, kept theirs up, just like the whole time during their trip.

It occurred to Alex that they were trying to hide in the shadows when they were ever close enough to be seen by the main group within the maze of endless trees. It was like they were trying to hide their identity. He recognized the cloth of the guard's hood—it was the same guard who had entered the woods right as they left the village. Alex wasn't sure why the person was being so anti-social. And the mysterious guard sat on the ground in front of Alex.

Not knowing why, Alex's eyes traveled to Rex. Maybe it was because the man was staring at the guard before he pulled his gaze away. Alex observed from afar as Rex's eyes fell on the hooded guard multiple times, body language changing over time, becoming tenser.

Alex tapped Micheal subtly, nodding to Rex and then the person in front of them. Micheal looked confused before reading between the lines. He shifted the two of them away, tugging on Alex's shirt to get him to move. Alex guessed he had a bad feeling.

Tension hung thickly in the air.

Rex crossed over to their area, eyes dark and serious. Just as he was about to pull the person's hood off, his hand was suddenly surrounded by a light gray hew of color and was frozen in mid-air.

Magic? Alex wondered through his shock and worry about the escalating situation.

Rex glared at the guard and growled, "You best let go of my hand, or you'll be in a world of hurt."

Everyone paused. Alex was taken aback that Rex would use that tone or talk that way with anyone. Katelyn frowned from her place of leaning against a tree, but realization was crossing over her face. Alex wasn't getting her train of thought.

The person huffed, sass obvious in their body language, and let the hood fall off their head, revealing a teenaged boy around the age of fifteen with dark hair pooling over his shoulders. He stared up at Rex with a forbearing look. He flicked his fingers, a barely noticeable action, and Rex's hand fell to his side.

Rex crouched down to be at eye level with him. "I

believe I recall ordering you to stay in the village. You have disobeyed my orders. Again."

The young guard rolled his eyes. "My gods, Rex, how many times do I have to prove to you I can take care of myself?" he asked incredulously. Alex couldn't help but be reminded of how Micheal and his brother acted in the presence of each other.

Rex shifted, eyes never straying from the boy's. "You're fifteen and my brother, Tucker. You will never convince me. At least not completely and especially not now. You are so ignorant to come here. You know where we are going, and how much danger you will be in."

The pieces fell into place in Alex's brain, and he bit his lip to conceal a sound. He finally understood Rex's anger.

Tucker's easy-going but annoyed glance became a glare, and he stood up angrily. "I'm very aware of that, thank you very much. It's my choice if I risk my life, not yours."

Rex stood up. The older guard pivoted back around to glare at the others. "Did any of you know about this?"

A handful of people, mainly the scouts, dipped their chins to their chests, escaping eye contact with the angry man. He turned to his lord, brown eyes flashing with anger. Katelyn steadily met his gaze and shook her head.

Rex was about to address his brother once again, but an arrow whizzed past his head. The metal head of it lodged into a tree behind the man. Rex's hand immediately jumped to the sword on his hip, and he shouted, "Dark Knights!"

Alex and Micheal jumped up as they were ushered behind the small wall of guards that materialized around them. Hands grabbed them, shoving and pushing them to keep them in a protective bubble.

Hunter unsheathed his two swords and tossed one to Micheal.

"Knife, Alex. Stay with Micheal," Hunter demanded shortly.

Alex knelt on the ground, fumbling to release his dagger. He held it in his hand, having the pommel facing his chest and the blade outwards. He shifted his hand along the rough exterior of the grip to find something comfortable enough that would allow him to do damage.

"The *what* knights?!" Micheal yelled, holding his sword defensively in front of him but got no response.

Katelyn deflected an arrow with a curse and shouted, "Tucker, Sabine, take Micheal and Alex! We'll catch up!"

Sabine and Tucker appeared next to guards, fighting to grab hold on the two of them. She pushed the boys along, breaking out into a run. The other three followed her lead, weaving in and out of trees, hearing footsteps echoing behind them.

"Duck!" Tucker yelled.

Alex hit the deck, pressing his body against the leaves on the floor of the forest, as Tucker disarmed a man with his sword, slashing him across his deep burgundy armor. The man collapsed to the forest floor. His empty eyes stared into Alex's soul. Alex stayed frozen laying on the ground, heart lumping in his throat.

Tucker raised a hand to another person coming out of the shadows, and his hand glowed gray right before the second man brought down his sword to deliver a blow. Whatever was allowing Tucker's hand to glow, however, held strong and deflected it. He gave a tiny shove with his hand, and the man was thrown up and back against a tree with a sickening thud. The second impact sounded off when he hit the ground.

Alex gaped at Tucker but shut his mouth when a man came toward the other boy when his back was turned. Since Alex was already on the ground and unable to reach for his dagger that had fallen from his hand, he swung a leg out to clip the knight in the back of the knee hard. The knight stumbled, and his defenses lowered.

Sabine's hand now glowed, but it was pink, lighting her determined face. She twisted her wrist, and the enemy was lifted into the air for a moment before she jerked her arm backward and then forward, shoving the man back into a group of enemies, causing them all to tumble to the ground like dominoes.

Alex rolled on the leaves, grasping his dagger once again. He drove it through the cracks of a person's armor who charged him, feeling it split through the layers of skin, embedding the full blade in the shoulder of his victim. He ripped it out, hearing the woman yelp in pain. He stabbed her again and fled. Micheal steadied Alex when he stumbled, and they started running again.

Tucker led them away from the enemy, steering them mindlessly through the dark woods. Sabine took up the rear, shouting directions to him while Alex and Micheal were in the middle.

They ran for what felt like hours before they came across a beach. Sand sprayed in all directions from their running.

Then all four of them collapsed into the sand panting heavily.

Eyes locked on the sand, Alex's lungs burned for oxygen. Even in the darkness of night, Alex could see the spots of the woman's blood staining his hands where they were folding in his laps with his fingers still wrapped around his weapon. He swallowed nausea down and put his dagger to the side. He watched as a drop of blood seeped into the sand.

Sabine rested her hands on her knees and fought to regain her breath. Her eyes took in their location, focusing on the setting sun. "We went west. We'll have to head southeast again in the morning.

Alex sat down and braced his arms behind him, still panting but looking at the two Phoenix village members.

"So...that's what your powers look like?"

Sabine sighed, staring at the forest again. "Yes, that is what they look like for most people. But everyone's magic or powers, whatever you want to call them, are different."

Alex frowned. "How?"

Sabine shook her head. "It's dangerous to talk about magic out in public." Her voice went quiet.

Micheal sat down himself and dusted the sand off his hands, "Why? We talked about it in your house."

Sabine had a distant look in her eye. "Not all lords are as open to talking about magic or even letting their people use it as Katelyn is."

A small group of shouts and war cries from the tree line reached their ears; the enemy was gaining on them despite their efforts. Alex had figured they would lose interest in them and go for Katelyn and the others but he was sadly mistaken as a small squad of them broke through the trees.

He jumped up and took a step back, eyes shooting between the two magic users. "You wanna do something about that?"

Sabine hit Tucker on the arm. "Make a forcefield." She unsheathed a much longer dagger from her waist.

Tucker nodded on instinct but then did a double-take. His jaw dropped in disbelief but then slipped into a protective stance when more Dark Knights popped out of the trees. They gained ground straight toward them, and Alex ducked behind Micheal, feeling more defenseless by the second.

Tucker lifted his sword to defend against a blow from a knight that would have killed him, slicing across his attacker's chest.

"You know I can't do that! At least not one powerful enough to defend us from *everyone* trying to kill us!" he yelled to the women.

Sabine groaned loudly at Tucker's response, shooting an

impatient glance at him. "Do it!"

"HOW?! You do it! This isn't the time for a lesson!" Tucker screamed again.

A Dark Knight tried to hit Micheal in the ribs, but he dodged just in time. He grunted tiredly. "For God's sake, just try!" He yelled, pressing back to back with Tucker.

Tucker shoved a woman off of him and then threw his hands up in the air. A beam of light shot out of his hand and seemed to go on for miles up in the sky. Then a translucent shield quickly surrounded them in a silvery bubble, before the beam of light dissolved into nothingness.

A different light illuminated the darkness around Micheal's arm. Alex noticed it and looked down at his bracelet. It was glowing, a unique color combination of Tucker's gray color and a deep red, before it stopped when Micheal stepped away.

The Dark Knights froze their advances, surprised at the sudden use of magic.

A Dark Knight attempted to stab at the forcefield, and an invisible force thrust the person back twenty feet, over the head of another hooded knight, one they hadn't encountered before.

The Dark Knight had a cloak that brushed against the sand and a hood obscuring the face, and they pushed through the sea of soldiers. The hood wouldn't allow the four others in the forcefield to see their face, similar to how Tucker hid his face. Alex did not like being unable to look their enemy in the eye.

They stopped in front of the forcefield.

Sabine pushed Alex and Micheal behind her. "Whatever you want, it has nothing to do with them. They are innocent."

The person cocked their head to the side like a curious dog. "But they are not." The voice was distorted, but it was definitely a man.

Micheal jerked his chin out. "Hey,*Batman,* we didn't do anything to you. Why don't you and your people just mosey on away."

Alex kept from rolling his eyes. *Not the time for another reference, Micheal.*

The mysterious man's head tilted toward Micheal, and he stared at him for a moment. "Are you sure about that, Micheal Barnes?"

Alex's blood turned to ice. Micheal took a jerky step back, wide eyes staring at the creepy man. Alex grabbed his arm in instinct, trying to pull him behind him like it would conceal him.

"How do you know my name?" Micheal demanded in a hushed tone. "How do you know it?!"

Silence answered him. The Knight did reach out slowly to touch the shield, making it ripple, but he quickly pulled his hand back and sighed. Tucker winced as if the touch to his forcefield was causing him pain. Sabine's eyes darted to the young guard but there wasn't much she could do.

"I know more about you than you know yourself, boy. And you, Alexander O'Connor," The masked man said secretively, cocking his head in Alex's direction now. Alex couldn't respond. His heart was too busy thumping high in his chest and blocking his vocal cords.

The man turned his back on them and started to slink away, but before he reached the end of the beach he looked back. "The young guard wasn't the only one who created that forcefield."

Alex froze, remembering how Micheal's stone had glowed. He knew what the man was alluding to even if Micheal and the others didn't. His own stone became warm against his skin, and he covered it with his sleeve out of fear.

Without a preamble, the man slinked into the trees with his men, and they blended into the shadows, disappearing from sight.

Micheal glared at Sabine. "Who was that?"

Sabine stared blankly at the forests, struggling to find words. She became unsteady in the sand. "It's...no, that's impossible."

Tucker looked at her. "Was that who I think it was? But he's bound to the Inferno Realm."

Alex was getting sick of the secrets between the two of them. Even Katelyn, Rex, and the others kept things from them, not fully explaining enigmas about the magic of their world.

The older magic user shook her head jerkily. Her hands shook. "N-No. He is *not* able to leave his realm. He must've used someone else to do his dirty work—"

Something inside of him snapped, and his hands clenched. "How about instead of trying to hide things, you explain them to us because we almost just died!"

All three of them jumped at him yelling, Tucker and Sabine resembling guilt. Tucker studied the ground and sighed, looking up at Sabine from the corner of his eye.

"They're right."

Sabine gave him a look of betrayal. "But Katelyn and Rex —"

Tucker shook his head, interrupting her by saying, "Rex and Katelyn aren't here. And Alex and Micheal have been openly made targets of the Shadow King."

Alex hunkered down on the sand, dropping his head into his hands, staring at the small grains of sand like they would hold all the secrets he needed. But they didn't, so he bit the bullet and asked his next question.

"What king? And why is he after us? Katelyn said Malum was the king who would want us dead, but she never said he was called the Shadow King."

Tucker looked at Sabine, but she refused to speak, so with a roll of his eyes, he looked down at the other boy. "There's an old legend—well, more fact than legend—about our realm, that the gods appointed Guardians to protect the land against ancient creatures, people using their powers in vain, and enemies from other realms. Not many people know what's real and what's not, but it's been told that someone, the Shadow King of the Inferno Realm, who had equal powers to all the Guardians, had risen hundreds of years ago. Rumor has it that he is the reason the Guardians do not exist anymore; whether he somehow managed to kill them, or they just...faded from existence because of him." He gestured to the forest. "The Dark Knights, the people we fought, are his soldiers."

Micheal held a hand up as he would at school and still proceeded to start talking without being prompted. "Question, so what was so special about the Guardians?"

Tucker balked. "It's...a really long story."

Micheal held his arms out and peered around, seeing the sun barely visible over the calm water. "We've got time."

Tucker nodded reluctantly and looked to Sabine. The young woman had sat herself down as well with her knees curled up to her chest, looking out on the horizon. She sighed heavily and was silent for a few seconds before she softly began to speak.

"The Guardians were the first people who learned how to fully control their powers. They put aside their differences and worked together. There are three branches of magic in our world: protective, mental, and elemental. Those different branches of magic users had a lot of prejudice against one another and were constantly at war; viciously and brutaly for centuries. The three categories are simplicities of our powers. Back then, people only had one of those three powers, and now more variations are possible. More unique."

Alex looked up, thinking of an analogy to help himself understand better. "Like fingerprints."

She nodded and lifted her hand. A small glowing pink

ball made out of pure energy appeared, summoned by her. She rolled it between her fingers. "Everyone's magic is hardwired into them differently. Outwardly, they're different arrays of colors. Mine is pink. Tucker's is a light gray. Some other people's colors may be red or so on."

Alex swallowed uncomfortably, eyes shooting to the other bracelet on Micheal's wrist, the scarlet opal mocking him.

"But that's not really exactly how they are different," Sabine said. "Yes, color plays a part, but magic is a lot like genetics. There are different varieties and endless possibilities of magic. At least now there are. Hundreds of years ago the Guardians were the only ones with slight variations of magic. They were powerful beyond belief."

Alex was silent before he spoke up. "What do the different branches mean?"

Tucker frowned and looked up at the sky in thought. "Well, protective users are basically what they sound like. They protect. That means they can make force fields, and they can have temporary bursts of super strength. Sometimes they specialize in one thing, like how Sabine does barrier magic. Mental is related to picking up objects or living things with your mind, or even controlling memories and the workings of space and time if you're powerful enough. Elemental is when you control one or more elements, like fire or water."

The two foreigners took in the information. Alex could see Micheal's brain was struggling as well to take in the information of magic since the people in their realm only believed in science or religion unless you wanted to be seen as a crazy person.

"Barrier magic?" Micheal questioned.

Sabine lifted her head. "Portals, dimensions, strong but small force fields, keeping people frozen in a certain space permanently unless I say otherwise, etcetera."

Alex nodded, the puzzle pieces clicking together. "That's why you came along. We have to find a portal to get us home."

She smiled to the best of her ability. "Yes. Most people with powers don't know what their powers do specifically until they're around the age of twenty when their powers fully develop. Sometimes people don't even know they have powers until years down the line. Tucker got lucky and found out early." She nudged the boy sitting next to her, teasingly. Tucker forced a smile.

Sabine became serious once again. "There were eight Guardians in total, but one of them died right before the Guardian War started. Three protective users, two elemental, two mental, and one healer."

Alex made a timeout sign with his hands. "Hold up, you didn't say healing was a power."

Sabine nodded. "Because it is very *very* rare, rarer than even having powers to begin with. I've never heard of a healer living in the past three hundred years, the last one being killed in a city raid about three hundred fifty years ago."

Micheal's eyes were filled with wonder. "How long were the Guardians around for?"

Sabine chuckled. "Ages. Centuries. They were around for a long time, but then..." Her face fell. "They were gone. And the Shadow King nearly took over the world until he was permanently banished to the Inferno Realm. No one knows how, but he was and he can never leave. But his soldiers can through magic."

Tucker tilted his head back to look at the stars. "The Shadow King was as powerful as all eight combined. A pseudo-Guardian if you will; that's why it was labeled the Guardian War. And now he's found a way to put his subconscious into another person's body or manipulate them somehow....I don't want to think about what will happen to magic users. He'll either make us his slaves or kill us. And he'll make everyone in every kingdom his servants."

"How do you know it's him?" Alex asked.

Tucker played with the sand in front of him. "It's just a feeling. Earlier it felt like he could tear into my mind just from him being close to me." The horror and fear in his brown eyes was startling. "It's either physically him or he's talking through someone. That is what I believe."

Micheal craned his neck to look at Alex, but Alex didn't let him catch his eyes. Micheal's worry changed into an epiphany and faced the two magic users.

"Wait, aren't we going to Inferno Realm in the first place? Why don't we find a way to kill him?" he asked.

Sabine and Tucker looked at each other, struggling to remain serious before they snorted and broke down into giggles. Micheal stared blankly at them like a confused dog.

"I appreciate the enthusiasm, Micheal," Sabine commended him through fits of laughter. "But you'd have better luck trying to survive a jump off a mountain."

Micheal snapped his fingers with a grin wide on his face. "But it's possible! We just need a plan."

Tucker's demeanor became scared, looking much more like the fifteen-year-old that he was. "Micheal...it's suicide. And I don't know about you, but I don't have a death wish."

Micheal was about to continue, but Alex hit him, not wanting him to upset the younger boy even more. Micheal gave him a sardonic look like he was saying you big softie. He ignored his friend's teasing.

Micheal gave a dramatic sigh, deflating in defeat. "Fine. We stick to the original plan."

Alex smiled exasperatedly for a few seconds before looking to the tree lines. "So now what?"

Sabine laid down on her back, hands folded underneath her head. "Sleep. The barrier will protect us."

Tucker laughed humorlessly. "Until I can't hold it

anymore or either bandits or the Dark Knights come back and slaughter us all."

The woman looked at Tucker weirdly. "You're morbid for a child."

Tucker nodded in agreement with a smile. "That's what happens when your older brother raises you. I'll take first watch," he changed the subject, obviously not wanting to talk about Rex at the moment. He was fearing for his brother.

Alex kept his back to the trees, staring at the ocean. The ocean always calmed him, the congruent oscillations giving him a sense of peace. A connection of sorts.

He was trying to stay awake, but he eventually lost his battle when the adrenaline escaped from his body, and also because Tucker gently recommended that he sleep. He let his eyes slip closed, and he prayed for a decent night's sleep like he blissfully had the other night.

His prayer was not answered. He was back to his normal dream, back at the stage of it where he was on fire. Pressure built up to unbearable pain, but it stopped on a dime when he saw a flash of the brown-haired girl once again.

She was just staring at him straight on with the chains still restraining her. Her raggedy dress was still the same color of purple, and her eyes were filled with tears. The brick background of the cell she was being kept in was flickering back to the large house the two magic users came out of the one he saw in his dream the first night in Phoenix. The confusion was giving him a headache.

Soon, the flickering stopped. The unpleasant, dark cell was gone, and the large house replaced it permanently. It was the same structure with dark wooden shutters and doors.

Alex couldn't understand what was so important about this house, and why he was seeing the girl and the house for the second time. His dreams had always been exact replicas every night, and he needed to know what changed from the time between his realm and when he entered Realm Six.

"Come find me, Alex," the same female voice from before whispered.

Then a man replaced the girl directly in front of Alex, easily a head size taller than her. His hazel gray eyes had tears in them, and his light brown hair was slightly messy. He looked heartbroken.

Suddenly the house burst into flames, the structure beginning to fail. Wood beams fell to the ground, the ceiling caved in, and the house just fell apart. Shouts ran through the house and Alex prayed that whoever was in there escaped before death would claim them.

A different voice, a male one this time, said from Alex's back, "Find them. Find me."

That was when he was back in the fire, feeling his body being burned alive. Alex concentrated and closed off his mind. He was done falling prey to his own torment. He just hoped that his efforts would wake him up.

No, he thought firmly, and the dream shut off like a connection was interrupted.

He sat up in the sand, desperately looking for any enemies. No one was trying to break the barrier that was still up. His breath shuttered in his chest. He rubbed his eyes, pressing so hard he started seeing designs fluttering behind his eyelids, shocked that he was awake of his own free will. He had never been able to do that before. When he opened his eyes, Tucker was staring right at him. The younger boy looked exhausted, but he was still keeping the shield solid.

"I won't pry, but are you alright?"

Alex pulled his gaze away, embarrassment rising in his chest. "Fine," he said in a clipped voice. Tucker nodded. Alex stared at him and was shocked to find no pity in his eyes.

"I understand, you know. Nightmares," he said. "Most of the guards have them, and I'm sure Katelyn has her fair share. They just don't say anything. So you're not alone."

Alex couldn't say anything or his emotions would get the better of him and he would cry. Tucker was the first person to ever say that to him. As Alex lay down, he couldn't be more grateful for his words. No more dreams came to him that night again.

Chapter 7

Alex felt like he had only slept for two hours before being violently shaken awake by someone who had a painfully tight grip on his shoulder. The sun burning his eyes told him he'd slept more than two hours.

"Alex! Get up!" Someone yelled in his ear. His first thought was that it was Micheal, but he was proven wrong when he cracked his eyes open and the slightly blurry form of Tucker kneeling in front of him came into view.

Alex sluggishly got up from the ground, feeling the sand drip off him. He struggled to gain his footing as he was yanked along but eventually was fully sprinting with Sabine, Micheal, and Tucker. He could hear the war cries of someone behind him.

"What happened?!" Alex yelled.

"The shield broke! I couldn't keep it up!" Tucker yelled back. "Then bandits came, and now we're running!"

Sabine was running south and back into the forest, footsteps cracking sticks in half and crunching leaves. Alex didn't look back as his lungs burned in protest of running for so long. He couldn't fathom having to sprint in armor and leather Tucker was, but even then he was faring better than Alex and Micheal.

The trees led to plains, the sun beating down on them. The group crested a hill and looked behind them, seeing a decently sized mob of bandits chasing after them with swords in hand. Alex doubled-over, his hands on his knees desperately trying to catch a few puffs of air.

Sabine looked around the landscape, her eyes narrowed. After a few seconds, they lit up with excitement and smiled.

"I see Katelyn and the others! Down there!" She pointed down the hill. About three-quarters of a mile away were Katelyn, Rex, and the other Phoenix guards.

Tucker looked behind them once more before he sprinted down the hill. Sabine cursed and followed.

Micheal groaned loudly before following, grumbling, "Why does it always have to be bad guys that run fast?"

If the situation were different, Alex would've burst out laughing, but he was being chased by angry people with swords, so he did not.

They reached the others, and Tucker barreled straight into his brother, hugging him tightly. Rex hugged him back with one arm for a split second before pushing him away, so he could grab his sword.

Alex drew his knife and stood side by side with Micheal. His hands shook with adrenaline, but then they shook with fear because behind the bandits were more Dark Knights along with them. Almost an entire army of them, so many more than last night.

Alex was jostled when the guards pushed him and Micheal into the middle of the circle they had formed. Dark Knights and bandits were coming from almost every which way, not leaving much room for an escape.

"The Dark Knights seem to have made some new friends," Hunter announced, flipping the hilt of the sword around in his hand.

Alex saw Katelyn grit her teeth. Rex kept looking to her

for an order, but she never gave one. He patiently waited, but he was undoubtedly itching for a fight.

She finally spoke, her strong voice washing over the group. "Sabine, are these the ruins we need to get to?"

Sabine gulped a breath of air. "Yes."

"Get to them. If they're sacred ruins as you said they are, the Dark Knights won't be able to cross the threshold or any entrance to the ruins."

Alex just noticed the ruins they were talking about; a large church-like building was the closest thing to them. The church was surrounded by other small house ruins that were completely run down and destroyed. Most of them were just chunks of rocks and wood.

"And the bandits?" Tucker asked.

"Fight like hell," Hunter ordered.

Katelyn kept her eyes on the enemy but addressed her men. "I'll buy you some time. Get to the closest part of the ruins...now!"

Everyone started toward the buildings, sporadically stabbing and slashing at bandits and knights, making a mad scramble. Katelyn took up the rear, parrying backward slowly while defending herself against the enemy. She didn't have too many approaching her because the bandits and Dark Knights had started attacking each other. Alex wasn't sure which side started the skirmish, but he wasn't going to complain.

Alex and Micheal crossed the threshold first of one of the ruins and pulled Tucker over as well when a bandit tried to grab at him. Alex hit the woman on the head with the pommel of his dagger and then slashed his knife at her. It clipped her on the arm, producing a deep cut that caused her to retreat. Alex tried to push down the guilt rising inside of him.

She would've killed you if you hadn't done anything. Don't throw yourself a pity party now. He repeated in his head multiple times before it stuck.

Rex and Hunter came carrying Jesse along, holding most of his weight. The guard looked dazed, and his side was dark with what looked like blood.

"Is he okay?" Alex asked, realizing how stupid his question sounded.

"Took a slice to the side," Hunter said, reaching into one of the packs of the other scouts. He pulled out a small, thin blanket and took a knife to cut off a quadrant. He distractedly pressed it against Jesse's side, drawing a yelp out of the other man.

Alex shifted his eyes away to watch with anticipation as Katelyn battled her way toward them, but she was beginning to struggle. A few knights had figured that the Phoenix Lord would give more of an entertaining fight than the bandits would. The Dark Knights ganged up on her.

Rex moved to go help her, but Alex grabbed his arm, tugging him back. The older man glared at him. Alex looked back at Rex with an imploring glance.

"Please, don't. You might get yourself killed."

"And let her die?!"

Alex didn't have a good answer, not one that would satisfy the man.

Rex looked about ready to throttle him, but Tucker stepped up and gave him a teary look that was encouraging him to listen to reason. Rex tried to avoid his little brother's gaze, but it was impossible.

"What have I told you about the eyes?" he complained but stayed put.

Alex put his attention back to the predicament in front of them, eyes following each blow of a sword like a tennis match. It seemed like Katelyn was going to win, seeing as she had the upper hand. Her silver blade hit its mark over and over.

The good feeling was premature. A black shadow

materialized behind Katelyn. The same hooded man from before. The man didn't hesitate to raise his sword and then swing down with a grunt.

The world slowed down to a crawl. Realization passed across the group's faces, all at different times. One of their guards with a bow started to raise it and pull it back, but Alex knew it would be a poor attempt. He felt something beginning to crack inside of him like glass.

The sense of impending doom became heavy inside him, weighing him down, and slowing his heart. Soon, desperation alighted anew. It crackled under his rib cage, powering him. The bleak emptiness was replaced by enlightened fury.

Nothing was heard but the soft buzzing in his ear. A strange numbness moved from his hands to his entire body, all the way to his feet. It felt like a panic attack. He had experienced those many times before, and this was exactly how it felt, but the only thing different about it was that Alex was aware of everything, from Micheal standing next to him, just as scared as he was, to the woman about to be slain in front of him.

All of his emotions bubbled to the surface and flooded his mind. All he could think was *save her, save her.* He'd had this feeling before; the feeling of wanting to do something so desperately. And his childhood therapist told him only one helpful thing: he had to release his feelings out into the world in a non-destructive way like screaming into a pillow. So that was what he did.

He screamed Katelyn's name. Gut-wrenchingly. He would like to think that it was to warn Katelyn, but in reality, it was a way to release everything from his mind. The ground tremored underneath his feet, knocking everyone off balance. Alex subconsciously noted that the bandits began to retreat, and he presumed they were afraid of the power he possessed.

His bracelet *burned* against the skin of his inner wrist. Too busy to react, he focused on the hooded man. The hooded man took a step back from Katelyn, too enamored by Alex. Then, as if a bomb exploded, he and everything around Katelyn was pushed away from her like Alex's scream had a physical force. The Dark Knight's feet left tread marks into the ground, ripping up the bright green grass to expose the dirt below.

The ground stopped shaking, and Alex nearly crumpled to his knees, but Tucker and Sabine heaved him to stay on his feet. He was so weak, knees buckling without command.

The man cocked his head to the side but an arrow grazed by his thigh. He barely flinched. Their archer had released his arrow, and it had missed its mark.

"Katelyn, run!" Rex snapped out of his stupor first, beckoning her toward them. Breaking out of her baffled thoughts, she twisted around and started toward him. The guards made room for her to race across the threshold, but she was suddenly caught in an invisible force field.

Alex frowned, confused as to why Katelyn was standing still until he saw the hooded man with his fist raised, glowing a rich red, darker than the light Micheal's gem had made. A rope-like hew coiled around Katelyn's waist.

She grunted and whipped her head to level her captor a glare. Her sword was useless as it hit the magic, just bouncing back.

Sabine's hand flashed pink, and she shot a ball of her magic at the man. He barely staggered. Then Tucker fired one. Sabine immediately went again. They alternated shots but it wasn't enough to force him to retreat.

Alex saw another archer level an arrow at Katelyn's position. The woman narrowed her eyes in concentration and shifted her hands slightly and let the string of the bow slip past her fingers. The arrow soared swiftly through the air and hit the man's arm that was holding Katelyn in her place, sticking out between the gaps in his armor.

With a pain-filled groan, his magic flickered, and the Phoenix Lord was able to push forward and break free. She crossed into the ruins and glared back at the man. He ripped the arrow out and blood spurted out onto his armor. He gave an angry yell, and then he disappeared before their eyes.

Everyone was silent, and then they turned their eyes to Alex. He was instantly aware of the attention and ducked away.

"What's everyone looking at me for?"

Sabine scoffed and looked at him like he was crazy. "Are you joking? You just caused a quake. That's what we're looking at you for."

Alex shook his head, but it was unconvincing. "That was a crazy coincidence."

A pale Jesse raised a shaky hand. "...perhaps we shouldn't focus on what he did... and on the fact that I am bleeding out."

He paled further, swaying. A few of his comrades rushed to his side and carefully laid him down. Guards swarmed him, some opening their packs to search for something to help staunch the bleeding while others commanded him to keep his eyes open.

Feeling that he was imposing, Alex backtracked further into the ruins. Taking a calming breath, he wandered around, hoping for a distraction. The ruins were mostly stone, crumbling down from time raging a silent war on what the structures used to be.

Alex climbed up a few steps leading to an altar of sorts from a church, fifty feet away from his friends. On the back wall, which was surprisingly still mostly intact, hung a large tapestry that had become faded with time; the colors dull and the fabric worn. In the center was a symbol that Alex was now used to seeing.

It was a triskelion, the exact same one on Alex and Micheal's bracelets. There were multiple colors scattered around, but he couldn't tell what they used to be.

When he caught sight of a smaller triskelion that was on the giant stone slab in front of him, he ogled at it in concentration. He ran his fingers over it, feeling each small little ridge in the rock. It was just like Micheal's; not engraved like Alex's.

He reached for the bracelet on his left wrist and slowly shifted the string to widen it. He slipped it off his wrist and methodically stroked his triskelion with his thumb. Curious to see what would happen, he hovered the two symbols over each other before he started to push the stone down and—

"Alex!"

Alex's head lifted, and he looked to see who called his name. Tucker was waving him over, gesturing to their group. He nodded and looked back at the mural one more time before jogging back. He tried to ignore the stares as he squeezed in, standing next to Micheal. Katelyn and Sabine were quietly conversing.

"What did you do?" Micheal asked out of the corner of his mouth. "Like...what was it?"

Alex mutely shook his head and fumbled for words. "I don't know. I just screamed, and *that* happened. I didn't mean to." He was still trying to wrap his head around it himself. He didn't feel anything when he screamed, only the stone getting hot and burning him. Every frustration became his outpour, the source of whatever that was.

Katelyn turned to address everyone with a schooled expression. "Sabine has a way to get us to the Inferno Realm from this location. We will make camp here for a few hours before entering the Shadows. If any one of you wants to turn back, do it now."

No one moved an inch, not even Jesse who was looking pale and shaky and being supported by his comrades. That

126

made Alex feel warm inside. It surprised him to no end how these people didn't know him well and were still willing to lay down their lives to get them home. Alex, though, wasn't sure he even wanted to go home at this point. He felt too different, too changed to go back. He wanted to find the girl in his dreams but he didn't know where to start.

He sat down on the ground and closed his eyes. He leaned his head back on a few stones that came from the outside wall of a rundown house. Everything was moving too fast. Something was different inside of him and he didn't want it. It wasn't in his nature to accept change so fast.

He opened his eyes when he sensed a presence near him. Micheal was standing in front of him. He had a familiar lost look. Alex wasn't in the mood for it.

He sighed and gazed at Micheal. "I'm not in the mood for a pep talk right now."

Hurt flashed across Micheal's face, but then it was gone in a matter of seconds. He gave a small dip of his head and then turned away.

Alex's eyes fluttered closed in shame, finding comfort in the darkness. He felt horrible for the way he sent his friend away, but he was wallowing in self-pity. He wasn't good at talking when his mind began to spiral with the worst possible thoughts.

The brush of someone sitting down on the ground next to him jostled him gently. He opened his eyes and was thoroughly surprised to see Rex looking at him with a quizzical gaze.

They were silent before Rex broke it. "You look like you're questioning everything you've ever known. It's not a good look on you."

Alex rolled his eyes, unimpressed. "What do you want Rex?"

"To talk," he said with more softness than Alex knew

him to possess. He must've been extremely taken by surprise by what happened to have such a gentle tone.

"About what?" Alex asked.

Rex shrugged. "Anything. What's on your mind?" the older man inquired.

Alex stared straight ahead and fumbled for words for a few seconds before he got a grip. "What I did...it's not normal, is it? Even for people with magic."

Rex bit his lip in thought before his eyes fell on Tucker, Katelyn, and Sabine a little ways away. "I don't exactly know what's normal and what's not, but all I know is that you and Micheal have something different about you."

Alex wasn't completely satisfied with that answer, but oddly enough, it eased his mind a small bit that whatever he did wasn't a figment of his imagination.

Rex hummed. "There was a story that one of the Guardians did that once. Something happened to one of the other Guardians, the one that died before the war started. I believe a mental user, Lloyd Achlys, was the one in danger. Another Guardian noticed Lloyd was in trouble and was emotionally affected by it. He was a mental user as well, and the ground practically split open when he screamed. His powers just shot out of him, pushing everything around him back. No one had ever done that before."

Alex was freaked out. That was not the story he was expecting. It mirrored what Alex did less than twenty minutes ago.

Rex held his hands up in surrender. "Not trying to freak you out or anything, just trying to talk to take your mind off things."

Alex looked up at the sky. He figured Rex would do that. And fail.

"What were the other Guardians' names?" Alex asked. "Sabine never told me."

Rex hissed through his teeth in uncertainty. "I only

know a few. The others were lost in time. One of the protective users was named Cobalt Baron. He was a conjurer. Elizabeth Dalton, elemental lighting. Helena Griffin was an elemental fire user and a conjurer as well. And Lloyd Achlys was a mental magic user as I said before. And he...he could raise the dead. He died before the Guardian War. Those are the only names I know."

Alex blinked. "Raise the dead?"

Rex held a hand up to make him pause. "Not forever. Temporarily. For battle."

The teenager shifted to face Rex better. "So a conjurer could call on something or raise something I'm guessing? Lloyd could literally raise the dead."

Rex nodded, a smile threatening to appear. "You're smart, I'll give you that. Yes, conjurers could *temporarily* call on certain things that were connected to them. Cobalt was fiercely protective of what he called family, and he managed to get a wolf to be tame toward him and the other Guardians. Whenever he was in danger, the wolves seemed to know and provided assistance. He could call on them whenever he wanted." Alex tried to picture such an independent animal protecting humans, but it was hard.

Rex continued. "Helena had a bad childhood of some sort and used her powers for evil or something along those lines. She switched sides and agreed to join the Guardians, so she became known as the phoenix rising from the ashes or just the Phoenix. Lloyd was..." he paused. "He was an interesting case. He was known as the Reaper in many kingdoms. He had been close to death earlier in his life, most likely as a child, and he took that to heart. Then he discovered he could raise the dead with his mental powers."

Alex looked behind Rex to stare at the large triskelion. "How come there are only three spirals and not four? I mean, I know Sabine and Tucker told me that Healers were rare, but it's still a branch of magic, isn't it?"

129

Rex whistled quietly and tapped Alex's head twice. "You've got a lot going on up there to understand that triskelion. Some people still debate it hundreds of years later. Some people think it's because the Guardians were made up of people from three different kingdoms; others think like you and believe it's the branches of magic. We'll never know what that truly means." He jabbed his thumb at the mural. "The theory that seems to be the most accurate is that each spiral is for a magical specialty, and you do have a point. Healing is a type of magic, but it isn't magic that you are born with. Only the gods gift that power to a person. Hence why there would only be three spirals in the triskelion."

Alex returned his eyes to Rex's amber ones. "Have you ever met a healer?"

Rex slowly gave an uncommitted node. "I know of one from a long time ago."

Alex remembered that Sabine had never heard of a healer in the past three hundred years, so he wondered how Rex knew of one, but he didn't pry.

He changed the subject. "How did Tucker discover his powers? Was it random or did it develop over time?" He was asking for the purpose of whether he possibly had powers or not.

It was a crazy theory that he normally wouldn't entertain, but Alex had seen a lot of crazy the past few days, so he was open to anything at this point.

Rex looked at his brother for a moment, who was giggling at something Sabine said, with a soft appearance coming to his eyes like every time he talked about his brother. One of adoration and love.

"Tucker's happened over time." Rex's voice was soft. "I started noticing things first before he knew. He was young, around ten, and I didn't want to scare him, so I didn't say anything. Then some other guards and people in the village started noticing things. I then asked Sabine what to do, and she said I should talk to him about it. He admitted that he had known for a little while, but he was worried that if he told anyone he would be in trouble. She ended up helping him with his powers." Something was off in his voice that Alex couldn't put his finger on, but it sounded like anger.

He had an appalled look on his face. "Why would he be scared of getting in trouble? He was just a kid, still is."

Rex tilted his head in agreement, hand shifting to his sword as if it were an instinct when his anger was rising. "He overheard other kids talking about how their parents visited other villages, and people with magic were not welcomed. He thought Katelyn would kick him out." The older man looked livid.

Alex pulled an uncomfortable face. "Yikes. Luckily Katelyn is cool with powers." His expression changed to one of questioning. "Why *is* Katelyn so welcoming of magic if others aren't?"

Rex seemed to be attempting to gather words, so Alex remained patient, looking at his hands. He fiddled with his nails, and his head snapped up when Rex began to speak again.

"I don't exactly know. Magic hasn't always been kind to Katelyn, but she still knows that other magic users are not at fault."

Alex had a ghost of a smile pulling at his lips. "She is definitely something else."

Rex smiled and nodded. "She's one of the strongest people I know."

Alex nudged him in the side, giving a teasing smile. "So are you two a thing?"

Rex pulled a face and then tilted his head back laughing, which in turn made Alex chuckle as well. The guard grabbed at his sides lightly. "Gods you're funny, Alex. No, Katelyn and I are not together. She's more like my sister.

And I'm too old for her."

Alex smiled. "I'm glad, it's good to have people you're close with."

Rex saw Micheal approaching and clapped Alex on the shoulder, and he stood up. Alex saw him cross over to where his little brother was and stepped up behind him, ruffling his hair and making the waves shift around. Tucker batted his hands away.

Micheal sat down next to Alex but didn't look at him. Alex moved to try and meet his eyes, but the older boy would just move his head away.

"Are you still pouting?" Alex poked him in the side.

No response.

"Mikey, come on," Alex pleaded. He hoped he didn't make his friend too mad.

Micheal just glared at him.

Alex sighed and slowly leaned his head on Micheal's frame, giving him enough time to pull away, but he didn't. "Micheal, I'm sorry. I shouldn't have been mean to you."

A sudden jab between his ribs pulled a gasp from him. He squealed and jumped away. He stared at Micheal, making his eyes show his impressions of betrayal and shock.

Micheal smirked. "Payback is sweet."

Alex gasped and hit him on the head. "You're evil."

Micheal just laughed.

Chapter 8

Sabine observed the sky, eyes guarded and cold, differing from her normally cheerful gaze. Alex wasn't fond of the look on her.

"It is time to go to the Inferno Realm," she announced to everyone. She pulled a knife out from her pant leg and stepped toward the altar of the church, chin titled high in confidence.

Everyone followed her, none overjoyed by the fact that she had a knife in her hand.

She stepped behind it and made a large cut across her entire palm. Alex's nose wrinkled, knowing that cutting herself couldn't have felt good. Micheal nearly gagged and shifted his head away. Alex found it funny that for someone who acted like a tough guy, he didn't handle blood too well.

She looked at the sky and started speaking in a different language. Alex couldn't understand a single word she was saying, but it sounded almost demonic to him. Clouds circled around them, and thunder roared in the distance, creeping closer with each passing second. The wind increased, picking up leaves, and ruffling everyone's clothing.

Alex yelled to Katelyn over the wind. "What's she saying?!"

Katelyn tried to concentrate, but she shook her head in defeat. "It is an old language! I have not heard it in many years!"

Alex kept his eyes on Katelyn, slightly suspicious of her statement. She was holding something back. How long would it be before the people of Phoenix would be straight with him?

The sky was becoming even darker, obscuring Alex's vision to the point where he couldn't see Rex, just four feet to his right. Soon darkness consumed him, and he was blind. The familiar feeling of the ground disappearing and him falling hundreds of feet happened once again.

Screams in surprise rang out at the feeling of their stomachs dropping down to their feet. And Micheal, the psychopath, was laughing wholeheartedly like this was the most fun he had in years.

Alex's feet hit the ground, and his ankles and knees were jarred, a tingling sensation shooting up his legs. He stumbled, falling to his knees for a second. He was sweating buckets as if he had just stepped foot on the equator, the sweat sticking to his shirt.

He wasn't totally off. Around him, there were pits of fire, blowing hot air everywhere. The ground was warm and Alex was honestly worried about his shoes melting.

Sabine recovered the fastest, straightening herself up and looking around. Her bleeding hand left droplets of blood on the ground.

Micheal stood up and panted lightly. "Are we in Dante's Inferno?"

Alex hit him on the back. "I don't know how you know that, but that's enough references out of you."

Jesse looked at him, confusion and amusement rippling in his dark eyes. He filed in behind the others when Sabine began to lead them on, then winced holding his side which was bandaged. Blood splatters poked through the stark white bindings, making Alex's heart clench in fear that something would happen to his friend in his injured state.

"'Dante's Inferno.' Is that another one of your culture's odd forms of entertainment?" Jesse asked.

Alex rocked his hand from side to side. "Eh, some of us like books while others hate them."

Jesse laughed at the face Micheal made. "I'm guessing Micheal is not one of those people?"

"Absolutely not," Micheal grumbled.

Alex fell into step with Jesse as they carefully navigated through the new realm. He watched as Jesse's eyes nervously bounced around, searching for something in the shadows.

"You've been here before, haven't you?" Alex questioned. Rex had mentioned it when Alex had first met him. Jesse's nervousness gave away that he knew what to expect in the realm.

Jesse's eyes darkened. "Yes."

"What happened?" Alex pushed, becoming less confident with his question as Jesse's hand tightened on his sword.

"Nothing good," Jesse said after a long pregnant pause. Alex didn't dare to ask anything else.

They hiked for twenty minutes before Sabine finally led them to an evil-looking castle.

The castle was grand, and it would've been regal in a beautiful manner if it wasn't black as night. The dark stones were tightly packed together, with some sections of the walls more smoothed out while others had divots and slashes. Instead of windows, iron bars had been forced into the openings. There was not a lot of space to act as working windows, but it was enough for archers to fire arrows through or for prisoners to longingly stare out of.

Spires climbed up from the walls, looking like spikes that could impale someone in an instant. The height of each wall, spire, or tower was not symmetrical. The tip of the spires varied in length and width, and not a single pair was identical. The parapet walkways on top of the walls dipped and turned in different directions, making a perimeter around the protective wall. Through the front of the wall, Alex could see the large structure that was in the interior of the castle which had no arrow slits, openings, or any way to see through.

Someone doesn't want anyone to see inside.

"We're going in there?" Katelyn questioned an odd gaze in her eyes. Alex noticed her hand resting on her sword, staring challengingly at Sabine.

Sabine didn't give a verbal answer but nodded once, beginning to walk around the side of the castle.

"This is the Shadow King's castle," Katelyn stated, almost snapping at the older woman. She didn't receive an answer at all this time. Alex swallowed the ever-ascending lump in his throat.

Sabine stopped and looked up the wall, searching for any guards patrolling on top. She stuck her foot in a small hole in the dark bricks and sought for gaps large enough for her hands to grip onto. Then she began to climb. She reached the top, and her head snapped to the side, hearing something.

Her hand was lit with pink, and she silently twisted her fingers, shooting them in the same direction she was facing. After a tense ten seconds, her head popped back over the edge and urgently waved a hand for the others to follow. Katelyn went first, then Alex and Micheal, and soon everyone was on top of the wall.

Sabine grabbed Micheal and Alex by the arm and looked at Katelyn. "We'll get them to the throne room while the others watch our backs and do rounds around the castle."

Alex stopped in pace. "Wait, the throne room. Throne room as in the Shadow King's throne room? The dude that you said could kill us?"

Sabine's dark blue eyes were haunted. "You have to trust me."

Katelyn's brow was furrowed like she was trying to solve an impossible puzzle, but she still gave her orders. "We must get moving."

The guards went in one direction, and Alex, Katelyn, Sabine, and Micheal went in the opposite direction.

They sprinted through corridors, Alex hoping that Sabine would be able to lead them through the mazes of the castle. Sometimes they would have to stop and pause to make sure the castle guards didn't catch sight of them in a junction of the halls. They even saw the mysterious hooded man creeping through the halls silently, his footsteps never making a sound. Alex got the heebie-jeebies thinking about him.

They continued running for what could've been minutes or hours. He stumbled around a bit, dizzy after taking so many turns and stairs. Sabine mumbled words under her breath as they went along, mapping the building out in her head as they moved along.

Alex wasn't sure how she was able to navigate the halls. He couldn't imagine anyone spending enough time in this horrible place and mapping it without getting killed. Her knowledge of the castle was extensive in a worrisome way.

"Stop," Sabine suddenly whispered when they reached another fork in the path, holding a hand behind her. She ducked behind the small threshold of the entrance, pushing Alex to the other side.

He grabbed Micheal on the way. He and Micheal pressed against the wall as tight as they could, bending a bit in the knees, ready to attack if needed. Katelyn stared at the ground, straining her ears.

Then Alex heard it. The sound of footsteps heading toward them and something dragging on the ground. Alex's eyes widened, breath quickening as he silently looked to the older women for answers on what to do.

Katelyn held a finger to her lips, shaking her head in warning to stay still. Impatiently, they all waited, the agonizing steps approaching closer until two Dark Knights stomped right past them, dragging something limp in their arms. Even in the dim hallways, Alex could see blood left on the ground illuminated by the sparse number of torches on the walls.

Were they dragging a body? Alex wasn't sure if he wanted an answer to his mental question.

Alex jumped in hearing a shrieking sound of metal grinding on metal; an ear-splitting noise that created a desire to punch the person causing the disturbance. A thud resonated against the black bricks, and the same scraping sound occurred once more.

After pure silence for thirty seconds, Alex poked his head around the lip of the wall, high-strung until he saw no one. Sabine waved them on, not bothering to look anywhere else but forward.

Alex's curious gaze traveled around. He saw a section of the wall's foundation was torn out and bars replaced it. It was a cell because there was a figure struggling to push itself up. What confuddled Alex was there was no lock of any kind that would allow for entering or exiting. He paused in front of the center.

The person was a man, decently young with olive skin peeking out from his long sleeves. His clothes were dirty and hung loosely on him. His hair was grimy, and blood was caked all over him with slash marks on the fabric of his clothes. Alex winced at the injuries on the man. His eyes latched onto Alex once he was aware of his presence.

"You should leave before you get killed. I don't know

who you are but being here is not worth whatever you're looking for." The man's voice was rough and raspy like he swallowed a box of nails that were grating down his vocal cords.

"Who are you?" Alex managed to get out, trying to keep his voice low.

The man scoffed, pressing a hand to the wound on his shoulder. "Doesn't matter. Just get out."

Alex pointed to his whole body. "You're hurt."

"It's called torture, kid. And this is what will happen to you if you don't listen to me." The man pressed.

Another man in the back corner of the room, curled up on his side, groaned in pain in his sleep. The olive-skinned man lunged forward a step, eyes darting over his body. His shoulders loosened when his cellmate settled down.

"Why are you being tortured?" Alex asked softly

The man rolled his eyes. "Because we royally pissed off the Shadow King on two separate occasions. Happy?"

Sabine snapped her fingers. "Alex," she hissed through her teeth, motioning for him to get a move on.

Alex gripped the bars, knuckles turning white as he debated on what to do. He knew in his heart they didn't have enough time to find a solution to the invisible lock, seeing as they were in enemy territory with people wanting to kill them on sight. He pushed himself back a foot from the bars.

The man was hunched in on himself but steadily met his eyes. There was no hope in his eyes, either locked deep in his heart or it died long ago, extinguished like a candle. He was *expecting* to rot in the cell. To never see the light of day, never see the starry night sky.

"I promise I'll convince them to come back and save you and him," he swore. He wasn't sure why, but he had a feeling that he needed to save the two men in that cell. It was impulsive, but it was what he was going to do.

"Don't make promises you can't keep, kid." The other advised. "And you don't even know me."

Micheal came over and grabbed Alex, prying him away from the man's cell. They turned a corner and the two men were lost from sight.

After navigating for five minutes, Sabine finally led them down a large straight corridor, and Alex's gut was telling him that something was off. She shoved open a large door, and it revealed something he had not expected.

He had anticipated the throne room being empty because he knew Sabine would never put them in danger, that she would've planned to keep them safe.

However, on the far left side of the room, knelt Hunter, Tucker, Rex, and the rest of the guards, their wrists bound by hues of magic and swords held up to their necks, looking pissed off to no end. All of them were disarmed, the weapons abandoned to a remote corner of the room. The only hint of their position was the reflected fire light.

Dark Knights stood tall and still as stone, staring straight ahead behind the Phoenix guards. Their blades never wavered against the necks of Alex's friends.

Sitting on a throne made of dark bones and other unsettling materials in the back of the room was a tall man with shadows hiding most of his body. But even with the cloak of darkness over him, Alex didn't need much introduction because he knew the man that was occupying the throne in front of him, with all his frightening glory, was the Shadow King.

Much couldn't be seen with the darkness of the room but Alex could make out chestnut brown hair and sea-green emerald green eyes. It was familiar.

The hooded man from the previous battle was standing next to him, a sword drawn as well and hands glowing. His magic was holding their friends in place.

"Run!" Jesse yelled out from his place on the floor. The

sword at his throat pressed against the visible skin, threatening to cut. The other guards hissed at him to be quiet, except for Tucker whose eyes were glued to Alex and Micheal.

They didn't wait for another order, making a run for the door.

However, a loud bang startled everyone in the room, and Alex's heart dropped as he watched the throne room door be slammed shut by Knights. Alex felt as if he had been backed into a corner, a predator waiting and ready to pounce on him.

Taking a step backward, he started to speak his concern as he tried to track every movement in the room. "Sabine, That's the king."

Sabine nodded, fear evident in her face. "Yep."

"And he really wants to kill us."

"Yes again."

Alex wanted to hide in a hole for the rest of his life. "Katelyn?" he prompted.

Katelyn's attention wasn't on the Shadow King, however. Her eyes were wide in shock and were locked on the back right corner of the room.

Alex followed the path of her gaze and saw a young girl his age sitting in a cell, her long brown hair cascading past her shoulders and almost reaching her waist. Her purple dress was tattered at the end of the skirt, and her dress sleeves hung loosely around her arms. She had a shard of a deep purple rock hanging over her breastbone that was dull in the dark lighting.

It was the girl from Alex's dreams.

The young girl caught sight of Katelyn, and she braced her hands on the bars. "Sister!" she cried, never breaking eye contact with the lord.

Katelyn glared at the tall man calmly sitting on the throne. "Coward! How could you keep her here?! She is a child!" Stares of everyone passed between the imprisoned girl and the Lord of Phoenix.

Since when does she have a sister? Alex wondered, head still spinning around frequently to keep an eye on everything in the room.

The Shadow King narrowed his eyes. "She is a child that plotted to destroy me. She is anything but innocent."

Katelyn was about to draw her sword when she was thrown against the wall.

Alex jumped backward and out of sight behind a pillar thinking it was the Shadow King or the mysterious man, but when he dared to take a peek, Katelyn was surrounded by pink. Barrier magic.

Sabine's magic.

Alex stared in disbelief, the feeling of ice beginning to attack his heart.

In the group of guards, Rex let out a literal growl. Tucker tilted his head back, staring up at the ceiling in anguish.

Hunter struggled with his bonds. "Traitor!" he yelled in anguish.

She smiled at the guard, an alarming sight. "Sorry, Hunter. This is just the way things happen." Alex had never wanted to hit her so hard before.

Katelyn gave a yell. "I trusted you!" Alex saw Katelyn's eyes flying across the room, desperately trying to find an out. Alex watched the hope leave her eyes.

Sabine's disturbing smile never faded. "I thought you would've learned that lesson by now, Katelyn."

Alex couldn't make eye contact with the woman from his hiding place, so he called out, "Sabine, why?"

Instead of answering, she stepped up to the throne and kneeled. She looked up at the king. "Hello, father."

Uproars came from everyone, mixing to be indistinct.

Alex leaned his head on the wall, feeling his emotions

taking over his brain. He felt around for a dagger that he had hidden in his pant leg and yanked it out of the sheath. He peeked around the corner and flung the knife toward Sabine.

He felt sick to his stomach to do so, but he did what he needed to do to stay alive. A part of him wanted it to bury itself to the hilt in her body. But instead of it hitting her, it hovered in the air before dropping.

"Hello, Alexander. I forgot you were here." The voice came from the hooded man. It wasn't the distorted one from the beach; it was his own voice, deep and rough. The Shadow King's hand glowed.

Alex was lifted off his feet and slammed next to Katelyn with a groan, Sabine and the king's powers combining to hold them. Micheal followed quickly behind.

Katelyn tried to reach for him to somehow let him loose, but she couldn't. She let out a frustrated yell, and a violet color came off her for a moment and then disappeared. Alex let it wash over him. It felt familiar.

He gawked at her. "You have powers."

She opened her mouth to answer, a pang of guilt in her brown eyes, but she was interrupted by the footsteps approaching. The hooded man came up to her and waved his fingers around.

"You know we cannot just take your powers from you or your sister. So, will you give up your powers?"

Katelyn bared her teeth. "Never."

"Then so be it."

The king waved a hand to his knights, and they pulled Tucker out of line. All the guards made sounds of protest, not wanting the youngest of them to be hurt by the king. Tucker struggled and tried to find a way to kick at his captors, but he was dragged in too awkward of a position to do so.

Rex attempted to sever the magic binding his wrists,

eyes never leaving his brother, fear overriding every other emotion.

Tucker's knees roughly hit the ground in front of the king and he glared up at the man. The king rose to his feet and slowly made his way toward the boy. A broadsword of onyx smoke slowly materialized in his hand, the dark metal shining in the torchlight of the room. He lifted Tucker's chin with it.

Tucker evenly met his eyes, trying to be brave but his hands shook where he was trying to break the magic with his fingernails. A desperate plan to free himself. Alex helplessly watched, useless to save him.

"If you lay a hand on him, so help me, I will rip you to shreds." Alex was surprised to hear the words come out of Katelyn's mouth and not Rex's. The rage ignited in her eyes once again.

The king ignored her words, tilting his head as he examined Tucker.

The hooded man spoke once again, "It's him or you. The choice is yours."

"Katrina, don't!" The girl in the cell yelled, white-knuckling the bars. Everyone glanced at her. "He'll use your protective power to break himself free."

Alex's head spun at why the girl called her sister Katrina, but that wasn't the focus of the situation. "No! He'll kill Tucker. He's a protective magic user. It won't matter!"

Katelyn tilted her head, thinking fast for a solution. "Even if he does kill Tucker, his power won't be enough. He needs powers from the Guardians, which he is in short supply of even if I give up my magic. Even then it might not work."

Sabine reached around the back of her neck to release the chain around her neck. On the chain hung that small chunk of swirling gemstone that Alex saw when she first

144

met her. Its blue and red colors were floating around like a galaxy. Alex could feel it beckoning to be released.

"That's where you're wrong, Katelyn. These are Alex and Micheal's powers. They were extracted when they were young. They have the power of the Guardians."

Katelyn's demeanor fell, swallowing heavily as she tipped her head to rest on the wall. She muttered a curse under her breath. All of the fight in her seeped out. She was giving up.

Alex gawked at the woman he thought was on his side. "What in the world are you talking about? Have you lost your mind?! We're not Guardians!"

She looked him up and down with distaste. "You're definitely not *the* Guardians, but you *are* the children of one Guardian, respectively, which means their powers pass down to you."

Alex shook his head in denial. "No," he whispered.

"You are more dangerous than you can ever imagine, Alex," snapped Sabine. "The Guardians' powers are freaks of nature, like Katelyn's. They were never supposed to exist, but fate and the gods decided otherwise. Your powers are just as sacrilegious if not even more."

Alex looked at Micheal, seeing the same confused and shocked expression on his face. He saw it on everyone's faces except Katelyn and the girl in the cell. That didn't make any sense in Micheal's position. His parents were alive and in the military.

Alex had never had his real parents, always bouncing around in foster care until the Johnsons adopted him. His biological parents could possibly be Guardians. But he was astonished at himself that he was starting to believe the psycho in front of him.

"Micheal has parents. He's not the son of a Guardian." Alex denied it, having a feeling his friend wouldn't do it himself.

The king's head snapped to Micheal and before he even said anything Alex connected why the king had looked familiar in his mind. A memory poked him in the back of his head; something from his dream. Alex felt his skin crawl.

The Shadow King was the man in his dream that was leading the attack on the small village, destroying everything in his path. Fire, destruction, and death was his only parting gift. He was the one that could go toe-to-toe with ancient warriors of history. A pseudo-Guardian as Tucker had called him. But that wasn't the only thing that disturbed Alex.

The Shadow King's face looked way too familiar; like he had seen him every day. Alex felt his heart begin to shatter by a revelation he stumbled on.

He turned his head to Micheal, the shock still relevant on his face. Micheal's eyes met his. Alex couldn't bring himself to say anything out loud. All he could do was hold Micheal's gaze and convey his care for his friend.

The king sauntered over in their direction, foot falls reverberating through the room. No one dared to breathe.

"Hello, Alexander. You've grown," he greeted when he stood in front of Alex. Alex narrowed his eyes but didn't speak. "You know it's true, don't you? That your heritage is not what you thought it was."

He wriggled to free himself to no avail. "I know that you're trying to mess with me," Alex said in a tranquil tone.

"Am I?" The king wasn't surprised by his words. "Micheal knows it's true."

Alex turned his attention to the older boy. The brunet shook his head despite the tears in his eyes.

"Stop it," he whispered, squeezing his eyes closed. Micheal understood. It was heartbreaking for Alex to witness.

"Look at me, Micheal!" the king yelled, his loud order

booming through the room. Micheal obeyed him.

Alex wanted to shield his friend from the man but he couldn't do so in his condition, and he couldn't stop the Shadow King from speaking. He could only watch as Micheal's reality came crumbling down in shambles; piece by piece.

"Don't be naive. I'm your father."

Chapter 9

Shock rolled through the room, save for the king's followers, Sabine, the two sisters, and Alex.

Alex had known something was off by the way the Shadow King had been staring at Micheal the entire time and the uncanny physical similarities. No one spoke. All eyes were on Micheal, looking on in fear or astonishment. Micheal's green eyes were wide, and his breathing picked up.

"You're lying," he croaked, shaking his head.

"Your *mortal* parents were never your parents. You have *my* powers, *my* legacy. I have the powers of all the Guardians combined. This still makes me a Guardian, does it not? Even if I was exiled, Katelyn?" The king continued to speak through his monologue.

Alex was confused by his words. It didn't make sense in his head.

Exiled from what and why? Was he a Guardian?

"How about you tell him the truth about what you did?" Katelyn spat out at him. She did not receive a response.

Micheal stared at Alex. Even though he had tears in his eyes, he still managed to get out only for Alex to hear, "Did he just Vader me? I know he didn't just Vader me."

Sabine stepped in front of her father, back turned to him, looking at her now-revealed brother, Alex, and Katelyn.

"Since my father has Alex and Micheal's powers, that means that he only needs someone's powers that are strong enough. Tucker is the strongest protective user I've seen that is not a Guardian or a child of one. He could possibly give my father the power he needs to break free if Katelyn refuses to sacrifice hers."

Still at the throne with a Dark Knight's hand on his shoulder, Tucker shifted around, staring at his hands.

A genuine, reassuring smile crossed Sabine's face, and her hand tightened around the chain of the necklace. Alex's brow twitched, lost by her change of personality.

"Which is why he won't be touching anyone today."

Everything happened in a flash. Sabine launched her magic at her father and threw the necklace down on the ground, shattering the glass.

The Shadow King gave a yell of outrage as Sabine's magic nailed him in the chest. His daughter's actions were not accounted for in the plan. Alex flinched, not expecting him to sound so enraged.

While chaos erupted, the smoky substance from Sabine's necklace traveled to him and Micheal. The two clouds danced with each other, bouncing up and over one another. They were drawn together, never willing to be separated. Until they came into contact with Alex and Micheal.

The magic pierced Alex, a thousand needlepoints digging into his skin as it entered his body. He felt like his insides were burning down to the bone. Excruciating. That was the only word to describe the agonizing pain he was in.

Was this what death felt like? Alex had been sure there wasn't a worse fate than what he suffered in his dreams. He was mistaken.

All he thought was that he wanted to get out of the hold the king was keeping him in and then suddenly he dropped to the ground. It was unforgiving on his hands and knees. He gasped for air, trying to breathe through his pain.

How did I just do that? His eyes locked onto his hands.

Sabine dodged out of her father's reaching grasp and flung a knife at the hooded man to divert him to let go of their friends before staring her father down with a glare. Her magic was summoned to her hands, the orbs of energy illuminating the room.

The masked man's powers faltered, as he was forced to divert his attention to the blade that was directed toward his face. This gave the guards a chance to break free, tackling any Knights near them. They immediately retrieved their weapons and struck down the Knights close to their positions as they made for the door.

Tucker, quick as lightning, aimed a kick at his captors knee, snapping the joint backward with a sickening crack. He handled his sword as it was tossed to him by a guard, stabbing it through the chest of the groaning body at his feet.

The king's lackeys left their positions throughout the room, finally attacking with vigor.

Alex turned to see Katelyn and Micheal still suspended on the wall. He forced his mind to imagine his friends being released of the king's magic just as he did before, and they dropped down next to him.

Without a moment to think, Katelyn made a mad dash for her sister, not caring about anything else. She blasted the bars with her *powers*, and her sister tackled her into a hug, weakly falling into her arms.

Alex dodged a Knight that charged him, and a dark blue color accidentally came from his hand when he automatically brought his hands up to protect his head.

Magic.

The man crumbled like a puppet whose strings had been snipped.

I actually have powers.

He flicked his fingers like he had seen Tucker and Sabine do, and blue vines shot out forcing all the Knights away from him. He didn't know how he knew how to use his powers, but whatever he was doing was working.

Micheal's hands were glowing with fire, the heat warming Alex. He couldn't help but stare in worry because Micheal was extremely upset. The anger was burning in his eyes along with his fists. Micheal summoned a full, menacing fireball in his hand and fired it at his father, forcing him back.

Tucker had been backed into a wall by the tall stature of the king. He ducked as the magic struck the spine of the king.

The king growled, distracted long enough for Tucker to make a break for an escape. Realizing the magic user was no longer at his feet, the Shadow King threw his sword at Tucker in a blind rage.

Alex observed it as it soared through the air. He reached out, willing his powers to protect his friend. Katelyn held a fast hand up in Tucker's direction first, and a small, purple shield stopped the sword from piercing his body. It flicked and died after the blow of the sword. Alex went to his side.

Tucker stared at her briefly as he and Alex engaged more Dark Knights. Alex thanked whatever gods existed that his friend was safe from harm. Mostly.

The fighting spilled out of the throne room, the guards of Phoenix leading the Dark Knights out into the corridors. Alex, Micheal, and Tucker tried to follow but were cut off.

Alex's foot tapped something solid. His dagger lay on the ground, still in perfect condition. He clutched it with a tight grip. It was a lucky find; Alex's new-found powers were becoming less obedient to his wishes.

Eyes searching for his comrades, Alex saw as Katelyn and her sister approached the king with rage boiling in their eyes. Alex attempted to go toward them but Tucker pulled him back by the collar of the shirt to keep him from getting cut down by an enemy sword.

The younger girl's warm brown eyes were faintly glowing a brilliant shade of magenta, menacingly and rotating a purple ball of energy in her hand and between her fingers. Raw power radiated from her.

"You took everything from us," she whispered through gritted teeth.

"Do you see me begging for forgiveness, Amethyst?" The Shadow King placed his arms out to the side. "I'm not. I have no regrets for what I did!"

Alex tried to drown out the king's voice by attacking a Dark Knight before turning his attention back to the fight about to begin.

Amethyst raised her chin. "I'll *make* you regret it," she said simply like she was chastising a child, and she shot her hand out toward him.

The castle erupted with bursts of color like fireworks as Katelyn, her sister, and the Shadow King battled it out. Strikes of magic could be seen from the corridors most likely.

Alex whipped his head around to glare at Sabine, recognizing the traitorous woman next to him.

"Tell us how to get back," he said to her, voice filled with anger.

Sabine grunted as the flat side of a sword hit her in the back. She twirled around and disarmed her attacker. "You never needed me. Your bracelets can take you anywhere you want, but you have to be careful with them," she answered and looked to her father to make sure he was still being engaged and not heading toward her or Alex.

Alex was preparing to yell for Micheal to teleport away, but then he remembered with a jolt that the two men were still in the cells. He regrettably recalled that he had promised to help them, and even if the man he had spoken to didn't believe him, he'd seen a flicker of hope in his eyes. Alex's eyes shot between the fighting and the hallway three times before he pulled Tucker away from the fight once they reached the wide halls.

"I need your help."

Tucker lifted his sword parallel to the throne room floor to block a blow from another sword, protecting Alex in the process. Alex stabbed the Dark Knight through the stomach.

"What could you possibly need in here?" Tucker asked. Then his eyes flickered with disbelief. "You weren't serious back at the cells, right?"

They both hit the deck when a deflected blast of magic came barreling at them. Alex popped up to his feet and held his friend's wrist, tugging him back down through the hall. "Just trust me!"

Relying on his photographic memory, he led the two of them back into the maze of halls, looking for specific details to guide his way such as a brick out of place or certain heights of the torches.

They reached the hallway of the cell, and Alex pressed his hands against the bars.

The olive-skinned man was pacing back and forth in front of the bars as the other man with copper brown hair was awake and sitting, staring through the wall. Both of their heads twisted to the two boys.

"What's going on?" the closest man asked, the same man from their last conversation.

"Two seemingly powerful magic users fighting the Shadow King in the throne room," Alex answered dryly.

The man's eyes had a hint of disbelief. "That's suicide. He's too powerful."

"He's not lying." Tucker defended him. "What did you need me to do?"

Alex knocked on the metal bars with his knuckles. "Can you knock these down?"

Tucker sheathed his sword and called on his powers in both of his hands. Spheres of energy grew bigger.

"Back away," he warned Alex and the men in the cell. He twisted his hands in front of him, and his fingers flexed. His magic shot out to collide with the metal. It didn't bust down as Alex thought, but it rocked the foundation around it, making it weaker. Bits of rock crumbled, falling to the floor. Tucker repeated the same motion two more times until the bars snapped through the middle and tipped down or fell from the ceiling, hitting the ground.

The two men didn't move despite being set free, suspicious of the two boys.

"Come on!" Alex yelled impatiently, waving a hand. The two men staggered after the boys, their injuries still affecting their bodies.

They re-entered the throne room where the battle was still furiously underway. The dark-haired man dodged a knight coming for them. Once he had disarmed the man, he stabbed the knight without mercy with his own sword. He tossed the sword to his cellmate and took a second sword off his victim's body.

Alex went over to Micheal, staying by his side. Those two seemed to be able to handle themselves.

Katelyn and Amethyst were still busy taking their rage out on the king, but Alex yelled over to them, "We have to go!"

Katelyn pulled her sister back. The girl held strong and waved her hand at the ceiling, forcing rubble to fall on the king, submerging him. She gave him one last glare before running over to the others.

Once she was close enough, Alex flipped the stone over

to reveal the triskelion, then forcibly grabbed Micheal's and did the same. They grasped each other's forearms in a tight clasp, connecting the triskelions as they did before in Pennsylvania.

"Think of the ruins," Alex rushed out, closing his eyes and concentrating on taking everyone with them. The Inferno Realm disappeared in a flash of light.

Alex liked to think that he had gotten used to teleportation and that he would feel like he was landing on a pile of pillows. Wrong once again. He hit the ground and it hurt, but he was snobbishly proud that he didn't stumble and that Micheal did. He looked around, and he was oddly calmed by the fact that they were back at the ruins.

They were safe. Just for a little while.

Alex's childish mental victory was pushed aside by his burning, raging anger toward the woman he thought was his friend. He turned to glare at Sabine.

"What was that Sabine?!" he screamed.

No one moved to stop him; they all shuffled away to give them space, even the two men that Alex and Tucker freed.

"So that whole conversation about how dangerous the Shadow King is, was it a warning that you would stab us in the back?"

Sabine opened her mouth to defend herself, but then her lips closed and guilt appeared in her eyes. She looked to Katelyn for help, but she received nothing but a well-placed stare of disappointment.

"You used Tucker as bait! You almost got him killed for nothing!" Alex continued to yell. Whispers traveled around him, but he didn't have the energy to find out what they were saying.

Sabine had a mix of guilt and fear on her face now, and

she held her hands up, showing she was submitting. "Alex... I'm sorry. Please let me explain." She was pleading with him.

Footsteps approached him from behind and a hand pressed on his shoulder. Alex turned to see who was interrupting. Micheal had fear and apprehension in his eyes. Alex was now worried, but his anger was still dominating his brain, unable to let it go.

"Alex, calm down. Let her talk," Micheal whispered and then slowly gestured down to Alex's hands.

He looked down with a frown and saw a blackish-blue color swirling around his fists. He noted that the color was a deeper blue than it was in the Inferno Realm, and he had a feeling it had something to do with his anger. It was like water. Dangerous waters that threatened to sink and destroy anything near it. Alex was afraid of himself now. He forced himself to calm down, and his powers dispersed.

"Please just let me explain," she begged again.

He thought it over for a moment before telling her coldly, "You have two minutes."

She nodded once. "I know I dragged you into the Inferno Realm, saying it was the way to get you home. While that wasn't exactly true, I still helped you. I got you your powers back."

Alex acknowledged her. "Yeah, and how do we have powers? You want to explain that?"

Sabine looked desperate. "I told you! You're children of the Guardians. You, by blood, have their powers. And you could be some of the most dangerous people to ever cross this land. I wasn't lying about that."

Alex gritted his teeth. "You're not explaining why you brought us *right to him*. You didn't know if your plan would work, and you put all of us in danger. And you had our powers to begin with. Why not give it to us with a conversation?"

There was a long pause.

"Good luck getting me to trust you again."

Sabine stepped back, and if Alex focused his eyes hard enough he could see that she was tearing up. "I know, I know what I did, but I didn't know what else to do! I hate my father just as much as you do, please believe that."

Alex wanted to teach her a lesson, hands tightening into fists before Katelyn stepped forward. The young woman laid a heavy hand on his shoulder, giving a light shove to get him to back off. He let himself be directed away from Sabine, unwilling to test Katelyn's patience.

"I think we all need time to think. Sabine, with me. Now." Her hand was firmly attached to her sword, an obvious threat. Rex and Hunter focused their eyes on them as the two women stepped away, Sabine's hands flying with rapid movements as she began defending herself.

Alex turned on his heel and stomped away, feeling his powers wanting to take over. He knew Katelyn would get the full story from the woman. She would be able to decipher what was and wasn't a lie. Sabine seemed genuine with her apology and that she was still on their side. That she was playing the role of a triple agent to her father.

He distantly heard someone following after him, someone whose clothes were long enough to brush against the grass. He let them follow. Walking farther into the ruins, behind the church, he stopped in his tracks.

He had come across a large house that was now rundown, and something seemed familiar. He got closer, and his memory flickered, then he was subconsciously able to see exactly what the building looked like years ago because it was the same house from his dreams. The one where the two magic users came out and attacked the Shadow King. His heart lurched at the small thought that one of those men could've been his father if they were Guardians like he had been questioning. He slowly circled the house, gingerly running his fingers over what was left of the barren structure.

Alex believed that the Guardians would have lived here. It only made the most sense that he kept dreaming of the house, and why the church had the triskelion symbol. His dreams had led him to find the girl, Amethyst, and he didn't know how but his subconscious was telling him that he was standing in the place where the Guardians lived. He didn't have any concrete proof, but it was the best he could come up with. Why would his dream show him these things without a purpose?

His thoughts were interrupted by someone shorter than him with much longer hair standing next to him.

Amethyst was staring up at the ruins and tears steadily filled her eyes. She spoke carefully and ran her fingers over the scorched rocks and wood, touch delicate. "This was once my home, and the Shadow King took it from me."

Chapter 10

Alex swallowed hard, seeing how sad Amethyst was but struggled to understand what she meant.

"This was where the Guardians lived. And no offense but you seem a little young to have lived with the Guardians."

She had a sad smirk. "How do you know the Guardian's lived here, Alex?" Shock was absent from her face and tone.

Alex balked. Now he was going to sound like he was crazy if he said his theory out loud. He scratched the back of his head sheepishly. "I kinda had a...dream about this place. It just makes sense that they would live here."

She raised an eyebrow but other than that her expression hadn't changed. "You dreamed about the Glade." It wasn't a question.

Alex agreed, ignoring the word "Glade" for the time being. "And I saw you in the cell." Amethyst pursed her lips at the reference to the Inferno Realm, a chill seemingly crawling down her spine.

Alex didn't talk for a moment, hoping she would say something. She didn't. Then he asked, "So, you and Katelyn are related. How come she didn't mention you? And why'd you call her Katrina?"

She smiled, but it didn't last long. She twisted a ring on her first finger, the clear gem twinkling. "Before she went by Katelyn, her name was Katrina. I assume she changed it to Katelyn to protect herself. And your other question is related to me living in the same house as the Guardians. What do you think I mean?"

Amethyst was the perfect image of a teacher in Alex's eyes, asking questions that he had to think hard about on purpose to try and trick him for just a bit of amusement.

He racked his brain trying to think about the beginning of the whole journey. Jesse and Hunter said Katelyn became the Lord of Phoenix when she was eleven, which was a little suspicious because of the way they explained it, but then Sabine said that Katelyn had Guardian power.

"Are you two children of the Guardians? Is that why she didn't tell anyone, and why you were captured?" Alex gave an educated guess.

She shook her head, a small smile actually coming to her face. It was a nice sight even though her tears clung to her eyelashes. "Try again."

Alex gave her a non-heated glare but then stared at a rock on the ground, thinking hard. Then it clicked.

"Wait, if you and Katelyn are not *children* of Guardians, but she has Guardian power, does that mean you're actual Guardians?Like *the* Guardians?" Alex stuttered hard.

A smile graced the girl's lips. "You *are* very intelligent, aren't you? Yes, you are correct. I am Amethyst, the Healer."

Alex's eyes widened. "I'd figured that as a healer you would've discovered your powers or gotten them from the gods later since it's such hard magic, but I guess not."

She shook her head ever so slightly. "Katelyn and I discovered our powers around the same time. When she came across hers, the gods gifted me mine without my knowing."

Alex fidgeted with his fingers, a nervous habit that was reappearing. "Amethyst, how are you and Katelyn still alive if you're Guardians?"

The girl frowned. The warm feeling in her eyes was replaced by sadness. "We, the Guardians, never asked the gods how we age. We've been alive for thousands of years while only aging two years more or less. We live a long time, Alex, and that can be a blessing and a curse at the same time. I don't know how Katelyn was able to settle down in a village without raising suspicion, but there are ways to manipulate memories to build her cover."

Alex was beginning to understand what she meant. If he had been made immortal he would watch his friends and family die years later down the line while aging only a few months.

"You watched your friends die." Alex assumed.

She shrugged. "I would've watched more of my friends slowly die if Lloyd hadn't killed them first."

Alex took that information, feeling despair that one of his parents was dead, but then it made his brain spin. "Lloyd Achlys? I thought Lloyd died before the war against the Shadow King and that the king killed the Guardians."

Amethyst looked completely confused, her head tilting to one side. "Who said that?"

Alex pointed to the blond guard that was standing next to Katelyn who was having a conversation with her guard. "Rex, Sabine, and Tucker gave me and Micheal some history lessons. Rex said Lloyd died before the Guardian War."

Understanding crossed her eyes. "I see, I should've guessed they would've told you that. The truth was lost in time or they lied on purpose to protect you."

Alex faced her with a look of confusion in his eyes and faced his palms up. "Why would they tell me that if it's not true? How would that protect me?"

She gently grabbed one of his hands in both of hers. "Because they didn't want you to know that Micheal's father, the Shadow King, was actually a Guardian. The Shadow King *is* Lloyd Achlys. But you would've been able to connect the dots eventually."

Alex felt his silence rock him to his core. Amethyst had said that the king had taken everything from her, and she was quite literal. The king, *Lloyd,* had taken her family, Katelyn and the other Guardians, from her, and she wanted her revenge.

How was he supposed to tell Micheal this?

"Lloyd was the one who killed the Guardians?" Alex asked, choked up. "But why would he kill the people that were his allies?"

Amethyst stared back at the house, a brief gust of wind blowing her hair behind her shoulders. "Killed. I don't even know if that is true anymore. But yes, Lloyd attacked the only people that considered him family just for the purpose of power. Either he had secretly developed a way to learn to use all of our powers or prayed to the gods, but that immense amount of power wasn't enough for him." She sighed. "So he went after us. He took me in hopes that he could learn healing magic. No matter how many times, how many years, I told him my gift is from the gods and can't be learned, he didn't believe me."

Alex had shock written all over his face, he couldn't believe Micheal was related to that monster. The other girl saw his expression and developed a sad smile. Her tears reappeared, but she refused to let them fall.

"Do not mistake me. Lloyd was a good man in the beginning. He had the capacity to feel compassion. I considered him a brother." A hesitant smile crossed her face at the pleasant memories she was recalling that were replaced with horrors. "But then he became power-hungry, and that was eventually his downfall."

He knew Amethyst was trying to make him feel better about the fallen Guardian. It didn't change much, but one part of her words made him slightly nostalgic. Lloyd wanted a son, but he obviously gave him up because he was evil.

But what about Alex's father or mother? Did they even want him? Was he a mistake? He had gone his whole life not knowing if he was wanted or loved by his parents. If he had been given up for a purpose or just because he was too much of a burden. It was a pain that had drilled itself deep into his heart for years, holding on tight.

"Amethyst, who were my parents?" Alex asked in a small voice.

She cleared her throat. "Alex, I don't think it's a good idea. The knowledge could put you in danger. There's a reason my sister did not reveal that information before. We want to protect you. Once you know, things will change."

"Please," his voice cracked with emotion, "I need to know."

Amethyst hesitated before she saw the broken look in his eyes. She sighed in sympathy, but she spoke, "Your father, Paxton Hayes, was a mental user." His father's name sparked something exciting in his heart and mind. "You have inherited most if not all of his power, unlike Micheal who has seemed to inherit bits and pieces of the powers Lloyd has. From what I've briefly seen, Micheal has gained mainly protective and some elemental powers. I would guess a small fraction of Micheal's powers are mental. That means you would be considered a mental user, and Micheal would be protective."

"What was my father like?" He wanted to know. Before, he had lost hope of knowing what his parents were like, but that urge had returned. The discussion of magic could wait.

"When all of us would argue, he was the peacemaker, always looking out for everyone but himself. I see that in you as well." Her lips formed a smile that told Alex she was teasing him. Her eyes got nostalgic once again, but it was happy memories this time. "Pax was always kind. He was the one that convinced me to join the Guardians. I wasn't sure I wanted to leave my sister after the gods gifted my powers to me, but he managed to get both of us to join the others."

Alex stayed silent, trying to push down the lump in his throat.

She wiped a tear with a finger. "He was...a really good person, Alex. He had such a big heart, balancing out all of us. He was one of the strongest people I know and even then he wasn't perfect which he was okay with. There was an incident where Pax needed some space, and he left the Glade—"

Alex interrupted her, "The Glade?" The word had come up a few times before, and he had never addressed it.

Amethyst lifted her arms to gesture around the plane of ruins, her sleeves billowing in the wind. "This is the Glade. Cobalt, Helena, and Katelyn built a protective barrier around our home and the homes of our closest friends to keep us safe from harm, and it would teleport us across the kingdom to keep us hidden. Our people named our home the Glade. But no matter, Pax left for two or three years, and when he came back he had a baby with him. You" A watery smile slid on her face. "Micheal had already been born a few months before you, and Lloyd was the most happy for Pax. All of us were. Pax and Lloyd were always close with each other, both being mental users."

Alex's eyes widened. "Wait, you knew me when I was a baby?"

She smiled brightly, a motherly look in her brown eyes. "Yes, I did. Paxton had named me your acting parental figure if anything happened to him. But I guess that isn't useful now, seeing as you're grown."

Alex smiled back, not expecting that answer, but he was

going to take it. It was information of his past, he received it with a desperation for more. "Who was my mother?"

She shrugged. "He never said. And he never mentioned how you were born. For all I know, the gods could've given you to your father and his partner, whoever it was."

Alex blinked, his brain not totally able to wrap around that concept. "Gods can do that? Just give a newborn baby to someone?"

She giggled at his shocked reaction and nodded. "Yes, the gods can do that."

"I don't know if my God can do that," Alex said softly after a moment, getting another laugh and smile out of Amethyst.

Her eyes sparkled with joy as her lips turned upward. It was as if she was falling back into her normal rhythm of life. Alex was the first person to make her smile and laugh after her imprisonment and he would do it again. But he still had one more question.

"How am I still here eight hundred years later?"

Amethyst's face dropped immediately and looked back at the house, and then at the surrounding ruins. Alex looked at her hands closely, and he could see they were starting to glow from her fingertips. Her emotions were triggering her magic.

"We made a deal with the gods eight hundred years ago. We approached them after Lloyd exposed his true intentions. You were about four years old." Her voice was clipped and tight, which shocked Alex, able to read the anger in her voice because of years of decrypting the tones of others.

"What was the deal?" he couldn't help but ask. Based on her subtle cringe it was unpleasant.

Amethyst refused to meet his eyes. "If we let you two be taken away from your fathers, from *us*, they would trap Lloyd in a new realm that wasn't inhabited. We had no choice but to do so...or we would all die. The gods upheld their promise, but not before Lloyd blasted a powerful blow of magic I have never seen before. My family disappeared except for me and Katelyn, and even then she couldn't protect me from his clutches."

Alex felt somber. He understood why the Guardians paid that price, but it didn't stop the hurt from stabbing him in the heart. He would've never had a normal childhood—not with a Guardian for a father—but his chances had been squandered before he got the chance to try. He had been sent away for the good of humanity. And *God*, that stung in his chest. For just a moment, he wished that he had a higher priority than humanity in his father's eyes when the Guardians made the deal.

His heart also broke for Amethyst and the amount of pain she went through for being so young. Well, young-ish. The only family she had left had been torn asunder, fractured from the inside out. And being held captive for hundreds of years wasn't healthy for the psyche.

"Pax wanted to keep you, he truly did, but he knew Lloyd would use you and Micheal against us." Amethyst wiped another tear of guilt away. "So we sent you two through a portal with your memories wiped along with any possible powers, never knowing if we would see you again." The girl finished, her voice still harsh. She added after a moment of thought, "As for the time difference, the portal may have kept you in limbo for hundreds of years, or you have just been aging slowly over time. I do not know."

"It's the former," Alex muttered.

He looked over his shoulder, and his eyes fell on Micheal's far away form. His best friend was sitting next to Tucker, in careful conversation, opening up to the younger boy. Even if he wasn't showing it, the Shadow King being revealed as his father was killing him inside. Alex had been able to read the pages of his mind since they were nine years old.

"You were to be separated under the gods' orders. Never to know of one another." Amethyst whispered, placing a hand on his shoulder but pulling it back quickly. "How in the world did you find each other again?"

Alex huffed, tiredly rubbing his face. His eyes were glued to Micheal. "We met years ago. It was just...a coincidence I guess."

Micheal's upper body slouched inward as Tucker's attention was directed somewhere else. Melancholy descended into his eyes, the light in them threatening to burn out.

"Is there a way to bring Lloyd back?" Alex asked. He would do everything he could if it meant Micheal got his father back. "Anything?"

Amethyst's face was sorrowful. "No. We tried for years, begging for him to see the damage he had done, but he would not listen. Lloyd is gone. Dead. There is no bringing him back."

"Is *my* dad dead?" he asked in a voice nearly impossible to hear, but Amethyst's keen ears had picked it up.

"Have faith you'll see him again," she answered cryptically.

Alex stopped breathing. The answer hadn't been expected. He turned to face her and asked again. "Is he dead?"

Her eyes traveled behind his head, landing on something, and then flicked back to him. "The ones we love have a way of finding us again. But do not get your hopes up, Alex."

Alex hung his head, ruffling his hair with one hand like he did when he was stressed, still trying to figure out if Amethyst was giving him a hint or not.

"Thank you for telling me," he said sincerely.

Amethyst bowed her head. "It was my pleasure. I...just

hope you understand why we sent both of you away." She shifted with unease.

Alex's eyes softened, catching onto her nervousness. "I do. It was a tough decision to make." Misplaced anger and resentment wouldn't get them anywhere.

Amethyst shakily sighed, turning her back to him once again. Alex swore he saw her shoulders begin to shake. Seeking to give her privacy, he backtracked away from the ruins, leaving Amethyst to her sorrowful thoughts and memories.

He looked at what Amethyst was previously glancing at behind him, and his eyes fell on the church. Odd. He ignored it for now.

Once he reached the group, he made himself comfortable next to Micheal who was staring at Tucker, wide-eyed.

Alex lifted his chin. "Why does he look like he saw a ghost, Tucker?"

Micheal's head spun to place his gaze on Alex, playful anger dancing in his green eyes. "He just said that Katelyn was a Guardian. And the little brat knew it the whole time!"

Alex's jaw dropped as well. "What?! I am wounded, Tucker. You couldn't have given me a hint *beforehand*?"

Micheal's eyes shot to him once again. "You knew?!"

Alex shook his head, thrusting a hand out to point at Amethyst's small form near the ruins. "She just told me!"

They both narrowed their eyes at the Phoenix guard.

The youngest boy crossed his arms, blowing a bloody piece of hair out of his face. "You're at most two years older than me, Micheal. I'm hardly little compared to you."

Micheal raised an eyebrow. "Really? That comment was the one that you had problems with?"

Tucker sighed and raked a hand through his hair to keep it from continuously falling in front of his face. "Yes, I knew Katelyn was a Guardian. Rex had met her years ago in our village, and they became close friends. I was little. Then our village was attacked. Katelyn accidentally used her powers, and she had no choice but to explain to Rex. Then we moved around the region and found Phoenix. It was secluded enough that no one would find her unless she wanted them to, and she used a potion to change the memories of everyone to make it seem like we had been there since birth, but we weren't."

The young guard frowned to himself and saw that his older brother and Katelyn were staring at them. They were close enough to overhear their conversation.

Tucker hissed quietly. "In hindsight, I don't think I was supposed to tell you that."

Alex and Micheal broke out in laughter, knowing that it wasn't a good idea to make those two mad. Tucker was being summoned by his brother, and he looked at Micheal with pleading eyes. Micheal shook his head and pushed Tucker up from the ground and toward his brother.

Once Tucker was gone, Micheal turned to Alex, smiling softly. But it was still off.

"Your father loved you," Alex blurted out quietly, seeing the confusion flash across his friend's face before it melted into sadness. "He was a Guardian. Lloyd Achlys. He was a mental user. And he loved you."

Micheal glared at him. "My *father* is a sociopathic murderer that just tried to kill us. Don't ever try to tell me that he loved me."

Alex grabbed his arm, keeping him facing him head-on. "I didn't say the Shadow King. I said Lloyd. Lloyd who was a good man that *was* your father. The Shadow King isn't your father, not really." Micheal's eyes were shining with tears, but they formed a pleading look, begging for him to stop. Alex tugged on his arm once. "I wouldn't lie to you about this."

Micheal thought it over before shakily nodding.

"Micheal, Alex," Katelyn suddenly called them over.

They both frowned at each other but stood up and approached the Guardian without a fight. Rex was still standing next to her and Amethyst. Alex kindly didn't mention the tear tracks still visible on her face as she stuck to her sister's side. Sabine had her arms crossed defensively over her chest, not making eye contact with Alex.

Katelyn studied both of them. "You have a choice in front of you now that you know the truth behind your heritage. You can leave and be safe, or you can stay. The choice is yours. But it is dangerous here for you, now more than ever."

Micheal cleared his throat. "What happens if we leave? We've been gone for almost a week from our world. Could that have consequences like it's-really-been-a-year in our world?"

Amethyst stared at the ground. "We do not know. I have no idea how time works in your realm compared to ours."

Alex shrugged. "The only problem would be if our teachers reported us missing. No one else would."

Rex reared back a slight bit. "If you were missing, wouldn't your parents look for you?"

Alex laughed venomously. "Yeah right. My adoptive parents want nothing to do with me. Micheal's...his parents and one of his brothers are in the military, and his other brother isn't the best caretaker either." Alex had stumbled on the word "parents" because he didn't know if Micheal still felt the same way about them.

Given the stormy look on his face, Alex guessed he was still thinking through some things.

Micheal suddenly spoke. "Let's stay."

Alex's head craned around to stare at him. "Seriously? I thought you wanted to go home."

Micheal denied it with a shake of his head. "No, this might be the last time we step foot here. Our normal lives can wait a few more days."

"I don't have a problem with that." Alex dipped his chin in a slow nod, attempting to read Micheal's tone, but he couldn't tell if he was upset, angry, or a mixture of these emotions. Fighting with Micheal on their possibly dangerous decision needed to come later.

His train of thought was cut off when a group of people just appeared right in front of their very eyes. Shadows casted onto Alex as human forms came into sight. They created a circle around their group of him, Micheal, Tucker, Rex, Sabine, and the two Guardians. Alex immediately felt fear grip his heart as he bent his knees to get into a defensive position.

Their forms were practically glowing, making Alex squint. The glow died down. Obscured faces hidden by hoods and cloaks stared around, the sunlight barely enough to reveal part of their faces. Alex didn't recognize them.

Rex went for his sword, but Katelyn held a hand up to get him to stop and gestured for her other guards from multiple feet away to do the same thing. Still paranoid by the surprise appearances, their swords were not returned to their scabbards but clutched in a docile manner at their sides.

The fact that the people were freakishly tall and emitted intimidation was the first thing that clicked in Alex's thoughts. The armor that was partially concealed by their cloaks had foreign symbols and words that Alex didn't recognize, similar to the ones in Sabine's books.

His second realization was that these people seemed like they could do a lot of damage if their weapons were any hint of that.

His third and final was that they had magic. *Powerful* magic. No other explanation existed for their sudden presence.

"You have broken a deal, Ms. Grey," one of the men

said, glaring at Katelyn.

Grey must be her and Amethyst's last name, Alex noted.

Katelyn glared right back at him, raising her chin. "And what specific deal is that, Rudnos?"

Everyone in the group of new arrivals tightened their grip on their weapons: bows, knives, daggers, swords.

The dark man's eyes leveled in a glare at Alex and Micheal. "The deal that these two would never set foot on this land for the rest of time."

Alex gasped quietly, remembering that the Guardians had made a deal with the gods; these people must've been them. It was the only explanation for why they had surrounded Alex and Micheal. The way they glared at the boys like they were nothing but small insects that could be squashed made Alex fear them.

Amethyst took a step forward and pushed the two boys between her and Katelyn, her smaller stature dwarfed by the gods but she did not falter. "We do not know how they have reached the realm. We did not break the realm barrier to do so. We have followed your rules."

"The deal still has been broken. And now you will pay for it." A woman all but hissed at them. Her daggers gleamed in her hands.

The group of newcomers raised their hands and started chanting in the same language, or a similar one, that Sabine had done when she teleported them to the Inferno Realm. Alex had picked out a few words that the woman had said.

Alex felt something shift inside of him like his brain was flashing danger signs at him. He gasped and gripped his chest, stumbling into Rex. The older man held his arm to keep him from tipping over, grip almost bruising to hold onto him. Something was seriously wrong.

"Katelyn, what's happening?" Micheal asked, nervousness seeping into his voice, the heel of his palm rubbing his chest.

She was staring wide-eyed at the men and women surrounding them. She started to tremble. "No...they wouldn't."

Amethyst seemed to disagree. "I think they are!"

Alex felt weak in the knees, still leaning against the broad Phoenix guard. "Doing what?!"

"Releasing the Shadow King," they replied at the same time.

Micheal stared at the god closest to him. "Are you crazy?! Do you know what he would do to everyone?!"

The god stuck out a hand, and Micheal was rendered mute, unable to make a single sound. He loosely wrapped his hands around his throat, opening his mouth but nothing came out. Terror filled his eyes.

"Do not speak of what you do not understand, boy. The fault lies with you and the other child for coming here. The blame is on you."

The gods stopped chanting and simultaneously looked back at the two girls.

A stern-looking woman stepped forward, sizing up the Lord of Phoenix. "Do well to not break another deal. Or you will deeply regret it."

Then all but one of them disappeared. The last goddess with ashen white hair snapped her fingers, and the world flashed.

Suddenly everyone was teleported to a different location. Alex didn't feel a thing. He hadn't even known that his location had changed until he looked around.

They were surrounded by tall trees, the ground painted with leaves. Alex scanned their new location for a sight of the ruins but didn't find them.

Katelyn went on high alert for a few seconds before she

paused and took a deep breath. "We're back on the outskirts of one of the villages nearby Phoenix."

Micheal balked, his voice returning, "Like our village, Phoenix? Which was at least a hundred miles away?"

Katelyn just nodded.

Alex's hands shook and he looked over at her. "Is he truly back?"

Katelyn watched the horizon like she could see the king rising from his dimension. The wind began to blow, ruffling her hair.

"Yes, he is."

Alex kept looking around at everyone, seeing varying degrees of concern and heart-stopping fear in the guards' eyes; Katelyn, Amethyst, and Sabine just looked furious.

The two men from the king's castle were having a hushed conversation, looking stressed. The copper-haired man was still favoring his side, a protective hand pressed to his ribs. He looked tempted to lean into the other man's space.

Alex addressed all of them. "How are you five not freaking out? You realize Lloyd will go after all of you. He'll kill you."

The two men didn't respond, barely glancing at Alex before returning to their rapid, soft conversation.

Katelyn leveled him a knowing look to keep him quiet. "Alex, I have been alive long enough to know that when it's your time to die, you can't stop it. If I die, I'll die knowing that I did my job as a Guardian."

Tears welled up in his eyes at her statement. "You can't be serious?" he asked softly. Death should never have been the answer.

Her firm expression transformed into a more reassuring one. "Luckily, I do not plan on dying today or anytime soon. But there's no way we can defeat him. Not with his army and definitely not with his powers. He'll be out of practice with battle, but we have no idea what he's been doing in the Inferno Realm."

Micheal's brow furrowed, now a common expression for him. "Well, then, what do you suggest we do?"

Amethyst looked at Rex and then peeked at Tucker. "It would be different if the other Guardians were here, but they aren't. We're on our own. We need to call upon our allies, and we'll need a lot of magic users to have a fighting chance."

Rex glowered at Amethyst, unsatisfied at what she was insinuating about Tucker fighting.

Katelyn caught that and stood next to Tucker. "You have seen his powers. He knows how to control them."

"He's fifteen. He'll be made a target. An *easy* target," Rex replied, his frustration obvious.

The other guards around him seemed to agree, not wanting one of their own to be in even more danger. Tucker's eyes darted to all of them, face bleak as he soaked in their concerned faces.

The copper-haired newcomer stepped forward, leaning his weight on one leg. "He's good at what he does. He's powerful and in control, for now at least." His companion was in his shadow, eyes stormy as they bounced between the other man and Rex.

Rex blinked at him in anger and confusion. "I don't know who you are but stay out of this."

The man smirked and tossed his hands in the air, turning his back to the guard. His prison-mate seemed to chastise him as they walked away.

Alex bit his lip in apprehension. He could step in and defend Tucker's skills, defend Rex, or just stay out of it. He saw Micheal shake his head out of the corner of his eyes, telling him to leave it alone, but Alex was never one to *not* argue.

He crossed over to stand next to Tucker's free side and

ignored the huff of disapproval from Micheal.

"Rex, he's already been made a target. I get he's your brother, but you have to let him make his own decisions. It's his life." Alex kept his voice soft but determined against the stubborn man.

Rex looked like he was about to explode, and Alex flinched slightly, bracing for Rex to start yelling but it never came. He peeked an eye open and saw that Rex was staring quizzically at his little brother.

"Are you sure?" he asked Tucker. The man's voice had never sounded so tense, so fearful for his brother.

Tucker nodded. "I might as well go down fighting."

Hunter and Jesse winced, glaring at the young boy. Jesse stepped up and shoved his shoulder.

"Don't joke like that."

Tucker just chuckled to mask the fear coursing through his body. Visible shakes in his hands sold him out to Alex's keen eyes. Alex nudged arms with him in solidarity, waiting for Tucker to give him a curt nod before he gave him space.

Hunter went to Katelyn's side. "I can send word out to our allies. Silverbend will get here first, most likely, and then the others will follow. We need a plan of attack if it comes to that."

Katelyn nodded, anger flashing across her face. So much power radiated around her that Alex could feel it sweep over their group.

"The gods better hope no one dies because of it."

Chapter 11

Their return to Phoenix was unforeseen to the people of the village. Instead of their lord and guards returning absent of the two foreigners, Alex and Micheal were still present and the village had gained two more strays. It made the citizens uneasy. The only person that was ecstatic of the boys' prolonged presence was the little red haired girl, Gwenivere.

And not to mention the threat of war made them terrified. Katelyn had taken it upon herself to notify her people, Rex stuck to her side.

Preparations were already beginning to unfold but Alex chose not to be present, needing to have a long conversation with Micheal about a multitude of topics.

It had gone better than Alex had expected, with Micheal soaking in the information with menial comments. He seemed almost relieved to learn the information but he was mainly shocked.

A few hours later, Alex went searching for Amethyst, wanting to know more about the Guardians. He had brought Micheal up to speed on the information that Amethyst had shared.

What she had told him should've been enough, but his

urge for knowledge was too great, so he had pulled himself out of his bed to reach Katelyn's house, slipping past Micheal and Maggie.

She and the boys had a tearful reunion as the long-lasting adrenaline had died down, and the impact of the journey had settled in. She had ordered them to get some rest in their room, foreboding them from discussing battle plans with Katelyn and the others.

It's not like we'd be of any help in the first place, Alex had wanted to say to her but had bit his tongue. He defended his choice of sneaking out by convincing himself that he would limit his questions to Amethyst to strictly be about Guardian business.

He did not speak to anyone on the way. He did not wish to possibly be interrogated regarding the news of their journey in relation to his revealed heritage. He was unsure if the news had gotten out, and he was not willing to risk it.

Alex frowned as he heard loud voices coming from the crack underneath the main door of Katelyn's place. He pushed on the door and peeked his head in.

"Gods Rex, why do you have to be so—" Tucker was in the middle of yelling, hands animatedly in the air, and paused when his friend popped his head into the doorway. Rex also turned his attention to the door, and he shook his head to himself. His glare on his brother did not waver, however.

Alex stood there awkwardly for a few seconds, shuffling his feet. "I can come back," he offered nonchalantly. Amethyst's wearabouts could be put on hold for a while. It had only been a guess that she was in Katelyn's house.

Rex waved a hand. "No, it's fine." He pointed a finger at Tucker and then said something to him in a different language that Alex didn't understand but he didn't need to. He got the gist of the words; Rex was irritated at Tucker. The eldest guard took the back door, leaving the two teenagers to their own devices.

Tucker slumped into a seat, dropping his forehead into his hands while bracing his elbows on the table. His long hair made a curtain around his face, the waves giving him a perfect chance to hide.

Alex winced, cursing himself that he threw himself into this situation. Closing the door, he crossed the wood floors to reach the table. He grabbed a chair for himself and spun it around so he could lean forward onto the back of it.

"What was that about?" he asked curiously.

Tucker sighed and folded his arms on the table. His posture exposed how drained he was.

"He was chewing me out about the whole 'sneaking out of the village' thing. And then common disobedience came up. Then the powers. He's just so frustrating sometimes," he explained with a slight, childish whine to his voice. Alex had a feeling the boy wasn't allowed to be a kid a lot, having an immense amount of pressure on his shoulders.

"Yeah, brothers are jerks like that sometimes." Alex sympathized with him.

Tucker finally faced him fully, eyes swimming with innocent wonder. "Do you have siblings?"

Alex shrugged. "I guess? I've had foster brothers and sisters, but I didn't know them well because I haven't seen them since I was young. Micheal has two brothers, and they're pains sometimes. So I get it." He didn't want to talk about his adoptive family, steering away from the topic. "Honestly, Micheal is practically my brother as it is, and you see how he irritates me sometimes. I'm sure Rex is the same way. You still love him, don't you?"

Tucker thought but nodded, light brown eyes pointed downward again. "You're right."

Alex smiled. "I know I am. I'm the smart one. But Rex does seem a little uptight. Does he get that from your parents?" He immediately knew that was the wrong thing to ask because his normal bubbly personality dropped to zero.

"I...I wouldn't know." His voice was so small Alex wanted to stab himself in the heart for making him upset. "Our parents were killed when I was very young," he continued slowly and softly. "I don't remember them well or their mannerisms. There's just nothing there. Rex is eleven years older than me and was fourteen when they died, so he raised me most of my life. He told me what he could about our parents, but I just don't remember them."

Alex tsked. "I'm sorry. I shouldn't have asked."

Tucker grimaced but shook his head. "No, it's fine. No one ever knows until they ask."

Alex bit his lip. The last thing he wanted to do was tell Tucker about his family, but if it would make him feel less alone, he would tell them.

"I was told my parents were dead or just disappeared. I wasn't given anything about them. I didn't know their age, the year they possibly died, or their appearance. All I had was my first name. There was no record of my last name, so I was given the last name of my first foster parents. Foster parents are normally temporary, but their name stuck with me. I haven't changed it since," he explained.

Tucker paused, staring at Alex with a newfound impression. The tilt of his chin impelled him to keep going.

He gave the other boy a weak smile. "I got landed into a couple of foster homes apparently. I don't remember a lot, nothing worth remembering really. I eventually got adopted by a couple that had lost their son in an accident. They were nice at first..." Alex trailed off.

"Then what?" Tucker prompted gently.

Alex huffed humorlessly and started playing with his fingers. "Then they started to become alcoholics. Turns out they just wanted a blond kid with blue eyes to replace their son. And when I wasn't him...they hated me."

The dark-haired boy gasped softly and covered his

mouth with his fingers. "Alex, I'm so sorry."

He sighed but didn't allow Tucker's apology to continue. "It's okay. Part of it is my fault." He picked at a loose splinter in the wood. "I suck at making relationships and have problems connecting with parental figures, so I push them away. It's also part of the reason why I'm so quick to act on my emotions. Maggie's the first adult that I've ever felt cared about me."

Tucker's honey eyes were filled with sympathy, and Alex hated it. He despised making people feel bad for him.

"I've learned to deal with and live with it," he said, wanting to get the conversation over with. "I know I shouldn't, but I feel bad for them. They just don't want to say goodbye to their son. I can't forgive them for the way they have treated me, but I don't hate them. Not really."

Tucker let his hand fall into his lap. "You're a good person Alex," he suddenly announced, completely genuine.

Alex smiled through the mistiness in his eyes. "Thanks, Tuck."

Tucker let out an elongated sigh, a smile coming back. "So how does it feel?"

The older boy stared at the guard for a long moment, and the protective user motioned to his hands. Alex finally deciphered the question.

"Oh! The power thing." He flexed his fingers, able to hold back the surge of his powers through his veins that wanted to come out. "It's....I don't know how to describe it."

Tucker brought his own protective powers to his hands just enough for a soft glow. "I guess it's different for everyone. Before I developed my powers, I felt like something was missing. Like a piece of me." He methodically stared at his hands, even as the light went back inside of him.

"I just feel normal," Alex said, breaking the silence. Tucker turned his eyes to Alex, giving him his undivided attention. "I mean...." Alex fumbled with his words. "When I first used my powers in the Inferno Realm, it wasn't hard. It came like second nature. I don't know if that's good or not."

The dark-haired boy nodded along. "You're special, Alex."

The statement made his nose wrinkle in distaste. "Special isn't the word I would use."

Tucker broke down into laughter, such a bright sound. He hit the table a few times. "Oh gods, I need that." He giggled after a moment, failing to contain the last bits of his amusement.

Perplexed, Alex gawked at him. "What's so funny?"

Tucker shot him a mocking expression. "Don't be dense. One of your parents is a legend. Literally. For hundreds of years, children grew up with the stories of the Guardians. Of how they saved lives, fought for peace, and were the right hands of the gods themselves. Of how powerful they were. By proxy, you and Micheal are just as powerful."

As he laid his head on the table, Tucker chuckled again. "It's such a cliche though," Alex complained.

Tucker held his hands up. "It's the truth. You're different, and it's good to be different sometimes."

"Is controlling your powers hard for you?" Alex questioned.

He gave a so-so hand gesture. "In the beginning it was. I was a hothead at times." That wasn't an image that matched in Alex's head. In the short time he'd known the young guard, he was one of the sweetest people he had met, and he couldn't imagine Tucker being quick to anger. "In a way," Tucker continued, "my powers made me stop having such a quick temper. I could hurt someone if I get angry enough. That thought alone terrifies me."

Alex patted his head. "Good thing you learned control then. Or else I could be talking to a very different person."

He was met with a grateful look and a sigh.

"I'm supposed to be on patrol, and now I'm late," the younger boy stated as he stood up, sheathing his sword that was leaning on the table. "Hope you are happy." Alex's blond hair got ruffled by Tucker, an action Alex typically did to him. He ducked away.

"You're welcome."

Just as Tucker touched the handle of the door, someone began to yell, "You absolute bit–" The curse was never finished.

Alex jumped. He wasn't aware there was another person in the house. Tucker was shocked as well, hand on his weapon. It was coming from the basement of the house. Alex stood up, swinging his leg over the chair to get away from it.

"What was that?" Alex asked.

"I don't know. I know Amethyst was down there with the two people from the Inferno Realm," Tucker said.

They ran down the stone stairs to go assist the person but skidded to a stop.

The two prisoners of the Shadow King were present, both sitting on a spare bed tucked in the back corner. The one with the copper-colored hair was bare-chested, showing brutal scars and bloody wounds littered across his body. The scar tissue was extensive, the network of marks never ending. The pink tissue was raised on his skin. The intense wounds he had received never healed properly.

Amethyst was standing with her powers glowing in her hands, hovering them over a painful-looking stab wound to his shoulder. Blood was trickling out of it, streaming down his pale skin. The man had his eyes tightly shut, hand gripping his companions tightly.

"Everything okay?" Tucker asked slowly, uncomfortable.

Amethyst nodded sadly, barely acknowledging their presence, continuing her work on the injured individual. He gave a groan of pain, leaning further into the man next to him.

"You're fine," the other man whispered, the statement more gentle than hostile.

Alex waited in silence for a minute, unable to drag himself back up the stairs. The miracle occuring before his eyes had his entire attention. The girl dropped her hands to her side. The wound was completely healed. Laurence slumped, unable to hold his body up. The other man wrestled him to lean against the wall.

"Is it always like that? The healing?" Tucker questioned in a quiet tone.

The Guardian had a crestfallen expression. "Yes. That's the price. It takes time, I cannot do it with just a wave of my hand. I can heal anyone that wishes to be healed, but it causes them an extraordinary amount of pain."

Laurence gave another groan, a testament to her statement. His body quivered in pain as he slowly began to hold his own weight.

"We can take a break. I'll be back down in a few minutes." Amethyst reassured him. Pressure lifted off his shoulders, taking deep breaths. She padded back up the stairs but not before brushing Alex's hair momentarily in a motherly way.

Alex looked at the olive-skinned man. "While I'm here I wanted to thank both of you."

His face remained emotionless. "For what?"

Laurence straightened up but didn't move out of the man's space.

"You fought off Dark Knights in the throne room, and you didn't kill us the moment you got a weapon."

"Listen, Max and I are not good people, kid," Laurence spoke, and Alex was able to hear his voice this time without him cursing. "Don't try to make an image that we are. All we did was take the opportunity to escape."

Tucker was physically taken aback with his venomous tone while Alex schooled his body language and face.

"I don't know who you are or what you have done, but you helped us stay alive in some way. I'm thanking you for that alone and not anything else." Alex kept his voice firm.

"Then you won't have a problem with us disappearing tonight," Max stated as if it were a final decision.

"We could use your help, though," Tucker objected. "We don't know if or when the Shadow King will come."

"Not our problem. You and your friends are the ones that tested his patience. We're not looking for that kind of heat," Laurence explained.

"Fine," Alex spat out. "Run away."

Max sat up straighter. Alex noted how the man was just as built as Rex, meaning he could do damage if he wished.

"Don't make the error of mistaking us for cowards." Max's voice was hard as stone. "We've had enough torture done by him for decades. We will not risk being held captive again."

"What did you do to make him imprison you?" Alex couldn't stop the questions from coming out, not having a filter.

"We screwed his right-hand man's plans up big time on two separate occasions. Virgil Crassus—he's the king's commander. The Shadow King allowed us to be tortured for information on his orders. Don't underestimate either of them. They both lead the army."

Tucker was lost. "Right-hand man? The one with the hood and magic?"

Laurence nodded, wincing when he pressed a hand to his ribs. "Yes. The king was the only one that was barred to the realm, never able to leave. Virgil and the rest of the Dark Knights are not. The king has the Commander do his bidding, and he can speak through him at moments because they're both mental users."

Alex subconsciously flexed his fingers. "Mental users can do that?"

Max shrugged which made his and Laurence's shoulders brush. "Don't ask me. I'm not a mental magic user. It's only what I have been told. Mental users have a certain connection on a nonverbal level. It makes them very dangerous people."

Tucker awkwardly pulled his eyes away to the wall. Alex clenched his hands into fists by his thighs. Shame and worry spread through his body, heat rising in his face. Laurence and Max perceived Alex with sharp gazes.

Max's lip quirked up. "You're one of them, aren't you?"

Alex stepped back an inch and swallowed the lump in his throat. His vocal cords wouldn't work, so he gave a tense nod.

"There was a special unit of Dark Knights," Laurence casually said, eyes stuck to the ceiling. "They had magic and were assassins for most of the Shadow King's agenda. While bandits are too afraid to make attempts on royal lives, this unit would do its best to make sure its targets would end up six feet under, including nobles and royals. Mental users are always higher in the chain of command. They always make the most dangerous and capable people."

Alex kept hearing his friends say that magic was powerful and came with responsibilities. Responsibilities that were thrown onto him without preamble. Losing control was a possibility. He did not want that on his shoulders. He wasn't prepared.

"A word of advice? Find an anchor or you'll never be safe to be around," the man warned.

Amethyst's soft footsteps entered the room. Her fingers laced together in front of her dress as she tiptoed, her old one had been traded out for a newer, darker purple that Alex only just noticed. It most likely came from her sister. She still had her necklace on.

"Would you like to continue?"

Laurence said a few choice words under his breath but nodded, jaw set tightly.

Alex and Tucker exited the room and headed back to the main floor, giving the men some privacy. The blond stared at his hands. He wanted to bring his powers out, but he was too afraid. Afraid of himself once again.

Tucker reached forward and grabbed Alex's hands, closing them. "Stop," he ordered as his normally soft voice was hard. "Don't freak yourself out. You're in control. He's just trying to screw with you."

"I wasn't in control when I pushed Virgil back when I screamed," Alex whispered, tears stinging at the back of his throat. "And Laurence is right."

"No one's perfect." Tucker softened his eyes. He had no idea how hard his words hit Alex in the gut like a sucker punch. Alex was supposed to be perfect. He *had* to be. "Not even you, Alex. I trust you. Rex trusts you. Katelyn trusts you. You don't have to go through this alone. We care."

Alex blew a breath out, blinking furiously to get rid of the tears. He let go of the other boy's hands, crossing his arms over his chest in a defensive manner. Emotions were swirling around in his head about his newly discovered powers and having people that care about him other than Micheal. As Tucker led him out the door for some fresh air, Alex had an epiphany that there was nowhere else he would rather be.

Chapter 12

Alex sat on the windowsill in his room, staring out the glass pane. They had been back in Phoenix for the past few days, and things were quiet. Katelyn and Amethyst had continued to keep their secret about being Guardians from the people. They didn't want to reveal that part of themselves unless necessary.

Allies were called upon, and the few villages that had already arrived had made camp around Phoenix. Alex wasn't bothered to attend the other meetings of alliances. He'd been present at the first two and then he stopped showing up, going behind Maggie's back to do so.

And true to their word, Laurence and Max had disappeared into the night once they were healed and rested. Alex hadn't been surprised that they kept their promise to leave.

Alex had holed himself in his and Micheal's room in Maggie's house most days, not wanting to come down. His brain hurt as he thought about everything that had happened in the past week or so. When Tucker had left him after their chat with Laurence and Max, his mood had done a spin toward feeling moody and anxious.

The realm seemed to pick up on the dark cloud looming over everyone's lives. The wind had picked up at a constant rate, making the air more chilly. The leaves had lost their vibrant colors, becoming dull. Everything looked dark and gloomy. As if nature was aware of the threat that was upon them.

There was a knock on the door. Alex sighed and didn't look toward the door when he said, "It's open."

Someone stepped up behind him and put a warm hand on his spine. It wasn't Micheal because the person's hand was too small, so that left one other person in the house.

"Why don't you come downstairs, Alex?" Maggie suggested, being motherly as ever.

Alex didn't move. The woman sighed and tugged him up from his spot and started dragging him back down the stairs. The boy grumbled but let her direct him.

She sat him down at the dining table, holding him down for a few seconds to make sure he stayed in his seat before retreating into the small kitchen. Alex laid his head down on the table and groaned insignificantly in frustration. He wasn't exactly sure what he was angry about, but he was a teenager and that was kind of normal for him.

Maggie came back and put a cup of water in front of him and put her hands on her hips. "Now, what's got your feelings all in a bundle?"

Alex sipped on the water, avoiding her eyes. "Things don't make sense."

She chuckled. "Well, hon, that's how life works sometimes. I know it sucks, but you've gotta find a way to push it away for now. We've got big issues."

Alex looked out the window again and nodded grimly. "Thanks, Maggie," he told her, finally looking into her eyes.

She stroked a hand through his hair. "You're welcome, sweetheart. Now, go out and find Micheal. He's been worried about ya."

Alex stood up, the back of his knees pushing the chair away from him. He pushed the door open, the wind smacking him lightly in the face. He shivered slightly and started the walk to Katelyn's house where he knew Micheal was.

He passed little kids on the path, and as they waved to him, he gave a small wave back, finding it nice that they were kind to him without them knowing him well. Gwenivere had even come up and hugged him as tight as she could with a toothy smile.

He turned the old-fashioned doorknob to open the door; as soon as he crossed the threshold, he had multiple swords being held to his neck. He immediately threw his hands up in a submissive manner and turned to the men that were holding the swords to his throat.

"It's just me!" he shouted.

The Phoenix guards relaxed and all gave him apologetic smiles that he nodded to. He looked around and saw multiple maps scattered around a table. Three swords lay abandoned on the wood to hold the maps down. Amethyst and Katelyn briefly looked up at him before the younger girl waved him over.

Alex took his place beside Micheal and stared at the maps. "Do we have a plan yet?" he asked quietly, noticing how all eyes were on him. He did his best to ignore the attention.

Amethyst huffed and shook her head, making her long, soft beach curls move. "No. We have reached a dead end. We're calling a meeting with the other lords soon to see what we can come up with. For now, there's no way we can defeat the king and his army at the same time. Most of our allies have banded together with us but our forces will not be enough when they arrive if he continues to raise the dead. He has unlimited range of the realm now and could attack at any moment."

Alex held a hand up, not understanding. "Wait a minute. You're telling me that his army is made up of zombies?"

She nodded, amusement dancing in her eyes. "Very intelligent zombies. Most of them have the ability to think for themselves, and they still follow his orders. The more powerful Dark Knights are even more independent. Rex did tell you he could raise the dead. That's how he makes his army. People die, and he brings them back to life in the Inferno Realm."

Micheal shivered next to Alex, crossing his arms. "Just when I thought he couldn't get any more freaky."

Alex leaned his hands on the table, observing heavily marked-up maps, looking for just a single loophole that would give them a chance. He had left his room twice, and both times were to see how the battle strategy meetings were going before he had spiraled into his sour mood. The planning hadn't gone great the previous times he had been present.

"Well, there's one way isn't there? The Guardians." He'd been doing some piecing together in the hours locked up in his room.

Whispers sounded through the room. Amethyst's brown eyes dropped to the floor, as did Katelyn's. The lord put a hand on his back.

"Alex, there's no way—"

Alex gave Katelyn's sister a cold glare. "You said it yourself. If the other Guardians were here, we could beat him. Amethyst said they aren't dead."

Amethyst's eyes widened in shock at the conviction in his voice. "Alex, I have no idea where they are—"

Alex slammed his hands down on the table, making it and other objects around it rattle. Micheal jumped back. "I think you do! You kept eyeing the church ruins when we were talking about the Guardians. Why?"

Amethyst's eyes darted to her sister before settling back on Alex. "I have my suspicions about their location, but I do not know how to reach them. Lloyd wasn't sure if his magic had truly killed them as he intended or if he just merely locked them away. He was obsessed with us in his hellish prison and always let me overhear how he would eventually kill my family if they were still alive. He said he could still feel one of them, which was your father, Alex. They are locked away. I have no idea where they are, and I have no idea how to release them."

Alex gritted his teeth together, trying not to explode at the girl, but he was just so angry.

Micheal raised a hand, hesitating to touch him. He swallowed a lump in his throat. "Alex, you need to chill out." The younger boy didn't care, his hands forming into fists. Micheal shook him desperately. "Dude, you're glowing."

Alex thrusted his anger-filled thoughts out of his mind and looked down at his body. His hands were surrounded by the blue aura of his powers, almost like water. The scary part was the swords that had been strewn across the wood table were levitating about six inches in the air. He ripped his hands away from the table as if he were burned and stepped away from his starting position. He looked back down at his hands to see his powers had been sucked back into him. The swords clattered back on the table. He flexed his fingers.

"I'm sorry," he apologized, voice deadly quiet, staring at the swords that had clattered back down to the table. "I'm sorry," he repeated.

Katelyn looked concerningly at him. "Your emotions are heightened. It's common with mental users when they discover their powers," she explained and not just to Alex but to everyone in the room as well who was looking at him

192

like they were afraid of him.

He tried to pay attention to words bouncing back and forth between the two girls and the others in the room, but he was too focused on Micheal's fidgeting. He was able to just see his fingers out of the corner of his eyes. It was irritating the heck out of him, but he couldn't snap at Micheal to stop it because he couldn't control it; he hadn't had access to his medication for multiple days. That wouldn't be fair to Micheal.

Alex then decided to space out of the conversation, eyes locked on the swords. It was absurd how such a thin blade of metal could cause so much damage.

"Alex," something whispered in his ear.

He looked out of the corner of his eyes for the source, but he couldn't find it at first. Then his breathing caught short in his throat. In front of him was a large gray wolf, nearly as large as the table in front of it. Its yellow-golden eyes appeared to glow in the early sunset peaking through the gaps of the closed shutters. They had been closed for the past few days. The wolf was staring straight at Alex. The boy looked around to see if anyone else saw what he was seeing, but they didn't stray from their conversation.

The wolf lightly trotted to the door and pushed it open with its paw. It stepped out of the door and before the door closed the wolf looked back with an inviting gaze.

Can wolves even do that? Alex could feel himself start to breathe faster from anxiety and he could practically feel his blood start pumping through his veins. He stepped to the door and Tucker grabbed his arm gently.

"What's wrong?" he asked, his brown doe eyes tracing Alex's form with worry. His soft statement caused everyone to turn to Alex.

Alex looked at the others in the room, but he pulled out of Tucker's grasp and pushed open the door. Tucker tried to speak to him, but he was too focused on looking for the large furry beast. He looked high and low, and then he barely caught sight of it on the edge of the woods on the very far east side of the village's perimeter, the opposite direction of the ocean.

Just as he was about to follow it, he heard something that made his blood run cold. A few screams echoed through the woods, and Alex's breathing picked up even more as his heart dropped to his stomach. It was the screaming from his dreams.

Wake up, Alex. Wake up, he told himself, trembling severely in fear, eyes shut tightly. *This is just a dream. Just a dream.*

When he didn't wake up and the screaming didn't stop, his eyes flew open.

Hands suddenly wrapped around his wrist, a firm pressure that grounded him. He jumped, but he let the person continue to hold him.

"Alex, you look like you're freaking out. What's wrong?" asked Micheal.

This frustrated Alex because people were in trouble and Micheal and Tucker were in the way of him helping them.

Alex gazed at him like he was crazy. "You're seriously telling me you don't hear that?" Another scream rang out.

Micheal huffed in annoyance, but the concern shined in his eyes. "Alex! Nothing is happening! What in the world are you talking about?"

Amethyst stepped forward and appeared in Alex's peripheral vision. Alex kept his eyes forward, not wanting to lose sight of the wolf.

It's trying to lead me into the woods.

"Something is affecting Alex and his powers. I don't think he can distinguish reality right now," she said, failing to mask the fear in her voice.

Tucker played with his hands. "What does that mean?"

Amethyst was going to answer, but Alex suddenly broke

out of Micheal's grasp and started to walk to the woods. He could hear the others following behind him, awkwardly shuffling.

Micheal was getting frustrated, and he roughly pulled Alex back. "Alex, you're going to get yourself killed if you go in there. You're defenseless!"

Alex glared hard at him, and a deep blue glow began to emanate from him. "We have powers now—"

"That you don't know how to use!" Micheal shook him by the biceps. "I'm not going to let you get yourself killed by Dark Knights or bandits! There is *nothing* in those woods."

"Are you sure about that?" Alex asked rhetorically, lifting his fingers to force Micheal off of him. Just the tips of his fingers glowed when they touched the brunet, who shook his head as if something entered his body and crawled up to his head.

Micheal paused, shook his head, and opened his mouth to yell at Alex before he stopped suddenly. He turned as if something had caught his eye. His eyes narrowed, and when he saw the gray wolf, he jerked back.

"What...what is that?" He pointed to it with a shaking finger.

Alex's brow furrowed. "You can see it?"

A faint line of his magic floated over to the Lord of Phoenix. Katelyn blinked a few times. She stepped past both of them and focused her eyes on the forest in front of them. She stood there for a long moment until she reeled back. "How can that be?"

Micheal shook his head again and pivoted away from Alex. "Alexander, whatever you're doing right now, stop it."

Alex tossed his hands into the air in front of himself. "Micheal, I'm not doing anything. I don't know how to use my powers fully, and you know that!" His friend was right before, no matter how much he wanted to deny it. He didn't understand his magic.

Micheal continued to argue with him until Katelyn put a visibly shaking hand on his shoulder. "Micheal, this is not Alex's doing. He wouldn't use his powers against you on purpose."

Micheal quickly shut his mouth and tore his gaze away from his friend. Alex was made aware of the quiet screams pounding in his skulls and from the thick trees, and he started toward the woods again. This time, Katelyn followed him for a few seconds to get sight of the wolf.

The wolf turned and dashed into the forest. Alex broke out into a sprint, trying to keep up. Micheal cursed.

Crunching from behind reached his ears, the tell-tale sign of footsteps pursuing after him.

Alex weaved in and out of the trees, ducking under low-hanging branches, and jumping over rocks. Everything was going great until Alex's arm was grazed by a flying projectile coming from the depths of the darkness. An arrow. Alex gave a short hiss at the sting and threw himself behind a tree, falling dead silent. Micheal did the same a few paces away.

The arrow had clipped him directly above the wound on his left arm where a sword had cut him days before. He shifted the bandage to cover the new bleeding injury.

Micheal was glaring at Alex. He was not happy with this predicament because they were both very unarmed with powers that they didn't understand despite any argument Alex tried to make earlier about having them.

A twig snapped, and both of them froze, with only the sound of his heartbeat flooding Alex's ears. He clenched his eyes closed for a few seconds before reopening them.

A foot appeared next to a tree, and Alex made the quick, slightly irrational decision to tackle him. He used a maneuver Hunter had taught him in his combat crash course a week ago, albeit sloppily, but it worked to get their enemy down to the ground with Alex on top.

The person who had fired the arrow was unsurprisingly a Dark Knight of the Shadow King. Alex continued to grapple with him, the armor on the other man making it harder for him. He distantly heard the sound of a dagger being ripped out of its sheath. He turned his head and saw that the man on the ground had wrestled his dagger out and was aiming to bury it between Alex's ribs from behind.

He was preparing for death when something with incredibly large jaws bit his attacker's arm.

He quickly got off the man as the wolf attacked the knight. The knife was dropped and the animal sunk its teeth into the knight's neck, shaking his head like a rag doll. Once the beast had done what he needed to do, he went a few steps away and barked at Alex.

Alex jumped back toward Micheal, not expecting it. "C-Can wolves bark?"

Micheal stood next to him and stared down at the creature. "I don't see why not. Living proof is right in front of us."

The animal gave a smaller bark and grumbled as it silently walked away. Its head kept swiveling back at the two and would walk a few steps before repeating the same action.

Alex tugged on Micheal's hand, urging him to follow. The taller boy made a noise of dissatisfaction but allowed himself to be pulled along.

The darkness made it difficult for Alex to keep his eyes on the large creature, but the one thing that helped him was the wolf's yellow eyes. Alex continued to hold Micheal's hand, not wanting him to get nabbed by anyone even if they now had a magnificent wolf guarding and protecting them.

Alex and Micheal came to a stop when a large wall of vines appeared in their path; the wolf, however, continued. Just as they thought it would slam into a wall of rocks, the animal passed right through as if it were stepping through water.

Micheal frowned and stuck his arm through to see if the same thing would happen. He pulled his hand back and observed it.

"Huh," Micheal said, amazed. "The wall Rapunzeled us." He smiled at Alex. "Get it? Because her tower was hidden by a wall of vines in the movie?"

Alex rolled his eyes so hard that they almost got stuck in the back of his head. "What did I say about pop culture references?" Micheal just gave him a dazzling smile.

Micheal took the lead in parting the vines, and Alex followed him through. The wolf was just sitting there with a tilt to its head, and then it approached Micheal. It lightly clamped down on Micheal's pant leg with its front teeth and tugged. Micheal let out a laugh and obliged the wolf, who was becoming more amusing. Alex snorted too and patted its head sweetly.

Soon they broke through the trees and were met with the last sight they would expect to see. It was the ruins from days ago. Alex stepped forward and stared down at the wolf, who, if it could have an innocent expression, was wearing it now.

"How..." he looked back at the ruins and was lost for words.

"Didn't it take us days to reach the ruins?" Micheal asked.

Alex nodded. "Amethyst told me that this was the home of the Guardians called the Glade. She said that the protective users made a barrier around the Glade that would teleport around the kingdom. Maybe we just got lucky."

The wolf huffed and started trotting again.

Alex looked to Micheal, the silent question of whether they should follow it passing between them. The other shrugged, not objecting to it, and they both walked side by side.

The wolf seemed to be enjoying itself, running around, climbing up stones, and jumping off. It made Alex smile softly. Micheal bit his lip and nudged Alex's hand with his. His companion gave him attention, still mindlessly following their new friend.

"I'm sorry I accused you of using your powers against me. I shouldn't have done that," he admitted, eyes guilty.

Alex pulled his eyes away, fidgeting with his fingers. "But I did. When I touched you, it did something like you could see what I was—" He stopped short with his words and his steps.

Micheal paused as well, looking around for a threat but didn't find one. He grabbed Alex's arm. "What is it?"

Alex had a lost look in his eyes.

"I hear it again." The screams and cries of despair constructed a longing to curl in a ball on the ground.

Beginning to shuffle toward, he migrated close to the wolf. Its ears were pulled back, and it was whimpering—a pitiful sound to be heard.

Alex patted its head. "You hear it too, don't you?" he asked rhetorically, very aware that animals don't speak English. He closed his eyes and strained his hearing to find the source of it. He started toward the sound. Soon it was almost unbearably loud to the point where he wanted to cover his ears. He opened his blue eyes and saw he was in front of the altar in the church. He reached his fingers out and as soon as the tips of his fingers touched the cool stone, the sound stopped.

The silence was deafening.

He saw the triskelion raised in the stone, congruent to the one on his and Micheal's bracelets, and he looked at his wrist. He nearly forgot about the bracelet. He slipped it off and hovered his indented triskelion over the other symbol, hypothesizing that the two shapes were the same size and fit perfectly together. He had nearly done it the last time he was in this position but had been interrupted.

Just as he was about to connect them, Micheal grabbed his wrist in a vice grip. Alex was stopped once again.

"Alex, think about this. Magic exists in our lives now. This might do something bad. We don't know what this is going to do," Micheal tried to reason.

Alex shook his head, ever stubborn. "I do." He really didn't know what was going to happen to be honest. It was just a hunch. And with that, the two symbols collided. He felt pressure start to push on his head like a migraine waiting to happen. He put a hand on his head and slumped in the knees, groaning in pain.

Micheal kept him upright while muttering, "I told you so."

His face dropped as he looked at Alex, looking oddly in the direction of his eyes, and Alex guessed they were glowing or doing something odd. Rocks and minerals crumbled and quivered around them, a strange sight to behold. The two of them glanced around to find the source. They couldn't see anything clearly because the back of the church still had some structure left, the tall walls blocking their view.

The wolf's ears perked straight up, and then it tore off running. The boys heard what sounded like other animals making sounds and small yelps. They both simultaneously rushed to make sure their new companion was okay, and Alex had to hold back a noise of surprise.

Four other wolves were running around and playing with each other, including the one that found Alex and Micheal. There were two with pure white coats, one with jet-black coloring, and another with a mixture of brown and black.

Micheal's eyes widened in surprise, but he nodded, understanding. "Cool. I'm going to avoid that reunion. I'm still confused about what happened and where those wolves came from."

Alex nodded, agreeing with him, but when he turned around his heart suddenly stopped.

The ruins had changed. Dramatically. The houses were rebuilt, and the window panes shined in the sunset. The structures were similar but also equally different from the houses in Phoenix. And Amethyst and Katelyn's old home, the Guardians' house, was magically restored to its former glory like in his dreams.

His eyes had to be playing tricks on him.

People inside the house must've become aware of the commotion because shadows danced across the windows. The door swung open with a mighty creak.

A young woman in her early twenties, around the same age as Katelyn, stepped out, picking up her ground-length dress so she wouldn't trip on it when she went down the few steps. She was about to interrupt the wrestling that was occurring, but she stopped, confusion replacing her annoyance.

She put her hands on her hips and called out, "Titan!"

The wolves paused and one of them, the biggest and the one that guided the boys, dashed to her. It grinded to a halt at her foot, looking up at her. Her mouth was agape in shock until she ran back into the house and yelled through the doorway. "Cobalt, Titan's here!"

Alex and Micheal were frozen, mostly hidden behind the church. Alex had never seen that woman before, but he had definitely heard the name Cobalt before.

Alex rapidly hit Micheal's arm and then his chest. "Oh my God...I know who she is."

Micheal looked the woman up and down. "Seriously? Who?"

"One of the Guardians," he whispered. "Either Elizabeth Dalton, Helena Griffin, or another Guardian."

Micheal gasped. "You're actually serious, aren't you?

You're talking about the Guardians that are supposedly dead or no longer in this realm?"

Alex was breathless. "Yes."

A tall, muscular man stepped out of the house, eyes rapidly traveling across the green grass. An older woman around the age of thirty, with marginally darker skin than the first girl and coiled hair piled on top of her head, followed him. The man's pale brown eyes, almost amber like the wolf's, landed on the creature, and his face broke into a grin. He pointed to the ground near his feet. The wolf sprinted to him and then sat at his feet. The man patted his head, kneeling down on the ground, holding the wolf's head in his hands.

"How are you here?"

Micheal smacked his lips in apprehensiveness. "Um, I don't know if that's a good idea. That's a full-grown wolf."

Alex smiled a bit and shook his head to defuse his concern. "Cobalt was, well I guess *is*, a summoner. He could summon them to him momentarily, and he managed to tame one. I guess he tamed four others. I told you this."

Micheal sighed. "You're the one with the good memory, not me."

Titan looked back, and his eyes flashed at the boys. Alex gulped, not knowing what that meant.

The air crackled with static electricity, making a few pieces of Alex and Micheal's hair stand up. The younger woman had followed Titan's gaze and laid eyes on the two teenagers standing suspiciously behind the church.

"Well, it looks like we've got some visitors," she said in a low tone, her eyes as well as her hands sparkling like lightning. Elemental magic.

"So that's Elizabeth," Alex squeaked out. "Good to know."

Everyone else pivoted toward the boys, and they pulled out weapons or brought their magic out. Alex threw his hands up in the air, as did Micheal, to convey that they were not a threat. He took a small step toward them.

"We're not here to attack you."

Micheal nodded with him. "Even if you were, you could easily beat us."

Cobalt growled low in his throat. "You feel dark, boy. How did you get here?"

Alex and Micheal shared a nervous look at the comment about Cobalt thinking he was dark. He could feel Lloyd's powers in Micheal.

The sound of someone landing on the ground behind them made them jump. They turned, and an Asian man was crouched low on the ground. He stood up and reached toward his back to grip onto two swords that could easily filet them in half with one arching swing.

Alex backtracked slowly but remembered that the same threat was behind him. "Let us explain—"

"Pax, get out here!" the other woman, most likely Helena, yelled.

Alex's words died off at the sound of his father's name. His heart started pounding, pumping adrenaline through his body that made his hands shake and stutter. He stood rigid and frozen.

Footsteps sounded through the halls, and he saw a figure walk out of the house. It was the same man from his dream. He was taller than Alex, his hair was a bit darker, and his eyes were a slightly different color, more gray than blue, but he was undoubtedly and unquestionably Alex's father. He couldn't explain it, he just...knew. Like a tug on his soul.

Micheal nudged him and whispered. "Lex, is that your...?"

Alex tried to nod. He didn't know how to feel. He always wanted to know who his parents were, but he was never given an answer until Amethyst. Nothing—no name, no age, no pictures. And now that Paxton Hayes was standing in front of his very eyes, he was a mess of emotions.

Paxton cocked his head to the side, critically looking the boys over while stepping down the stairs, cautiously joining his companions' side. "You two are definitely a long way from home. How did you get here? No one has been able to break the realm barrier keeping us here."

Alex stared at him for a few seconds before he slowly pulled his sleeve up and showed him the stone. He didn't know if that would ease his mind, but he was counting on his lucky stars that it would do something to keep them from attacking them. Everyone's eyes fell on it, and their weapons slowly dipped down into a less defensive position.

"How did they...?" Helena started to speak but then closed her mouth when the man nearly stumbled forward. Her hand nearly darted out to steady him.

Paxton, now only a few feet in front of the boys, switched glances between the boys, and his gaze changed into one of surprise. Alex was pretty sure he saw dire hope and a few tears beginning to form.

Alex, not being good with words, said the first thing that came to his mind, "Hi, Dad." He gave him a shaky, sad smile.

Paxton took a step forward, eye wide. "Alexander?" he whispered desperately.

Alex bit his lip, hating that he could feel his own tears start to fall. "Yeah. I go by Alex, now—"

Paxton rushed forward and hugged him tightly, strong arms surrounding him. Alex gladly hugged him back. He hoped no one else saw his tears. There was nothing else he could do at that moment. He saw Micheal out of the corner of his eye turn his back, giving them a moment of privacy, but a small smile came to him. Micheal knew how much it meant to Alex to meet his parents, at least one of them, so

Alex expected nothing less of his friend turning away.

He just wished Micheal would've been able to have a moment like this with one of his birth parents, but Alex was aware he still loved his parents in their realm and didn't wish to break that bond.

The other Guardians put their weapons away entirely, staring at the two boys with wonder. Looking over his father's shoulder, Alex watched as Elizabeth's lightning died down, as did the flickering in her eyes. She calmly folded her hands in front of her, eyes wide. She was blinking at him like he was a ghost.

Paxton looked at Micheal quizzically over Alex. Micheal gave an awkward smile. Neither of the boys knew where he stood being the son of the man that imprisoned the Guardians, but Alex would defend him to his last breath.

Paxton pulled away from his son and addressed the other teenager, "And you must be Micheal." He got a nod. The Guardian gave him a short hug as well and put his hands on the teen's shoulders to look him over. A nostalgic look came upon him. "You look just like your father."

Micheal looked down at the ground. "I don't know how to take that. He's a psycho."

The man lifted his chin with a smile. "I meant it as a good thing. I'm talking about Lloyd. Not the Shadow King." The boy nodded finally, and the older man patted his head.

Alex came up behind him and budged in. "I know you all are probably confused, but we need to go, right now."

Paxton radiated confusion. "Why? And how exactly did you get to our realm? We sent you away."

Alex huffed a smile. "I'll be happy to explain everything to you after we defeat the King."

Elizabeth looked highly confused and had a hard time looking the boys in the eye. "What does Lloyd have to do with this? We locked him away in a deal with the gods. You two were the price right before Lloyd got the last word and locked us in here before the gods stepped in." The Guardians shared her confusion.

Alex shuffled his feet. "The gods released him because we are back here."

Paxton's eyes flashed turquoise, and he started to say things loudly in a language neither Micheal nor Alex understood, but they could get the gist that he was angry. Elizabeth nervously bit her lip as Helena expertly moved out of his line of fire. Once he expelled everything from his system, he looked at the other Guardians to see their input.

Cobalt crossed his arms again, looking stormy. "I hate to be the one to say this, but we can't beat him without Katrina and Amethyst. We know the gods would never take his powers, and we're down by two. Even if the 'miracle children' have powers, he'll be able to beat us again."

Alex took offense to the nickname.

"They're both alive. Amethyst was imprisoned, and Katelyn managed to stay out of Lloyd's grasp. We have been staying with the two of them," Micheal said. "And before you insult us, remember we're the ones trying to help you escape," he snapped.

"Ryder?" Cobalt questioned, ignoring Micheal and Alex.

Alex could barely hear him when Ryder grumbled, "Seems like a bad idea. How do we know this isn't a trick?"

"I'm asking you to trust us," Alex said. "We have no other plan that won't end in hundreds dead when Lloyd takes over. He will stop at anything to destroy everything to get what he wants. We need you."

"And how do you plan on getting us out of here, kiddos?" Cobalt clearly dug at Alex and Micheal again. His smirk was sharp.

Alex lifted his left hand up, showing his sapphire stone once more. "You recognized this earlier. These teleport you to different realms or whatever; who says they can't do the same here? I mean, we got here with them."

Helena raised an eyebrow. "Lloyd used everything in his power to lock us away when the gods went to put *him* away. He'd been planning it for years, and he gathered enough strength and knowledge to be able to do it. His attack...it was meant to kill us, but he faltered, and it only enclosed us in this place."

"What you're dealing with is powerful barrier magic. The bracelets might not be enough to get us *out*," Elizabeth added, her tone more gentle than her comrade's.

"Just get over here please?" Alex begged, getting fed up.

Paxton took the first movement to him. "I trust you," he whispered, and Alex wanted to embrace him once again.

Alex grabbed Micheal's hand, ignoring the surprised looks on everyone's faces. "We have to *go*."

Alex ordered everyone to stand around the two of them. The others reluctantly came close, and the wolves sat patiently next to Cobalt when he stood next to the two women.

The boys flipped their stones over, connected the triskelion symbols, and grasped each other's forearms. Alex and Micheal both knew to picture Phoenix as a white flash flooded their vision.

Chapter 13

This time, neither of the boys stumbled. The Guardians stood as if nothing had happened, used to teleportation in some way. The wolves immediately started to scamper around, happy to be in a different place. Another single pulse of light came from the bracelets, shooting out in all directions for miles.

"What was that?" Alex asked.

"The realm barrier of our prison breaking. It would seem Lloyd didn't account for the stones being out into the open and didn't add certain protections to keep this situation from happening. They would be the only possible option to break a barrier," Ryder said, but he was distracted by looking around the area. "The gods took the stones back from us years before Lloyd turned on us, so he must've forgotten about them."

"Unless that's what he *wants* us to think," Cobalt grumbled. No one responded.

The small village of Phoenix hadn't been burned down when Alex glanced for himself, so he sighed in relief. He looked up at Katelyn's house, surprised to find the shutters open. He saw the guards milling around in the living room, probably waiting for them to get back. Katelyn and Amethyst stood side by side at the head of the table that he knew was littered with maps and plans. People Alex didn't recognize were present as well.

Other lords most likely.

The Guardians were glancing around, needing to adjust for a moment, so Alex tugged Micheal away.

"What do we tell the others?" his friend asked.

Alex shrugged. "The truth. They're the Guardians. It would be kind of hard to hide it."

His ears caught the sound of a door creaking open toward Katelyn's home. Tucker stepped out, appearing bothered as he moped down a set of stairs to reach the path. Pacing slowly, distress painted his face.

Titan bounded over to the boy, circling him. The young guard immediately froze and stuck his hands out in front of him.

"Oh...hi! Please don't eat me," Tucker pleaded with him as the other wolves came as well, happy to see another person.

"Does he have protective magic?" Cobalt suddenly asked from over Alex's left side.

Alex nodded but then did a double-take, staring up at the man. "How did you know that?"

He chuckled. "The wolves wouldn't react like that unless he was a protective user. They can sense powers like that, among other things. And I can sense his power."

Micheal shivered in fear. "Remind me to not piss your dogs off, ever." Cobalt clapped him on the back.

Tucker pulled his gaze up, and they landed on the other two teenagers. His eyes ignited with happiness and relief. He dashed to them, and he threw himself at Alex. Alex hugged him for a few seconds, and then he was suddenly on his back. Tucker was glaring at him with his arms crossed. He had kicked Alex's legs out from under him and shoved him to the ground.

"Don't ever do that again. You scared me!" Tucker exclaimed.

The three boys laughed, and Alex got back to his feet. Paxton was hovering behind him, notably nervous that another boy had just knocked his son onto the ground in a matter of a few seconds, but Alex gave him a reassuring smile as he stood back up.

Tucker lifted his chin toward the five people behind his friends, apprehensive. "Who are they?"

"The Guardians," Micheal answered nonchalantly.

Tucker just blinked at him and the other people, stunned into silence, jaw unhinged. He sighed and put his hands on his hips, looking up to the sky. "What did I do to deserve this chaos?"

Micheal forced back a laugh. Alex wanted to chuckle as well.

"Welcome to the club, Tuck," Micheal said.

The young guard began to lead the group back up to the house, still in slight shock over the revelation of the warriors, taking them in visibly as if they would disappear into thin air. Alex stuck by his side, making his apology silent for running into the woods. Tucker opened the door without a preamble.

All eyes turned to them, some relieved, some unemotional. Jesse and a few others smiled in relief while Hunter and Rex's hands drifted to their weapons at the sight of the strangers in the doorway. Katelyn and Amethyst paused their conversation, ignoring the others in the room, zeroing in on the door.

"Gods, Alex! Don't ever run off like that—" Katelyn had started, stepping around a short man Alex didn't recollect ever seeing before to walk toward him and Micheal, but her words died off. She was staring at her old family with wonder, crystal tears making her hazel brown eyes sparkle.

Amethyst made the first move, not afraid to show her child-like happiness by practically tackling the three men into a hug while Katelyn moved like molasses to them. Elizabeth embraced the Phoenix Lord with gentle arms, crying herself.

"We thought you were both dead," the lightning user whispered to her. Katelyn tightened her arms. She couldn't answer.

Alex smiled at the reunited group and stepped toward Rex. The man was fixing a glare at him along with the other Phoenix guards in the room that had been on their journey to the Inferno Realm. He gulped and asked, "Did we do something?"

Rex stared at him with an astonished expression. "Are you serious?"

Hunter smacked Alex on the head. As he squawked, the older man chastised the pair. "First Alex starts acting weird and leaves the house. Then you two start fighting. And finally, you both run off into the forest. Yes, you did something very wrong."

They simultaneously rubbed the back of their heads sheepishly, not making eye contact with any of the guards. Tucker bit his lip forcibly to not laugh out loud and stuck close to his brother's side. His smirk was one of satisfaction that he wasn't on the receiving end of his brother's tongue lashing.

Sabine was tucked into a corner of the room, eyes stormy, staring at the Guardians with an almost fearful look. Alex nudged Micheal with his arm to get his attention and gestured to Sabine. Micheal took one look at her and then looked away.

"Not my problem."

The shorter boy huffed at him. "Whether you want to admit it or not, she's your sister. Now, go be a good brother and talk to her."

Micheal glared at him but slowly made his way over to the magic user. Sabine turned her head away from Micheal, frustration dripping into her posture. Alex couldn't hear them but saw Micheal begin to talk softly, forcing himself to stay calm as he talked.

A small smile played on Alex's lips. Micheal was always loud and excited and happy, and it was different to see him so quiet as he talked to Sabine.

"We will continue tomorrow." Katelyn dismissed the other lords and guards of other villages. Her firm voice had returned even if she was emotional. "Planning will have to wait until the next few days when hopefully the guards and lords of Henix and Fifan arrive."

Katelyn and Amethyst engaged in a conversation with the two other women as the guards carefully regarded Cobalt and Ryder. His shoulders brushed against someone as they stepped up behind him, and he knew it was his father.

He smiled brightly to himself, feeling something different flutter in his chest. He had never had a parental bond with Renee and Bradley, mainly because he never wanted to after a few years passed with him in their home. Paxton was like a breath of fresh air. It was as if his father had a sense of gravity, drawing Alex toward him.

"Alex, how did you get here to this realm?" Paxton asked softly and curiously.

The boy sighed, racking his brain for exactly what happened. "Micheal and I were walking home from school, and we came across a new opening in the path in the woods close to where we live. Micheal wanted to explore it, so of course, I got dragged along."

Paxton chuckled quietly, a deep sound resonating from chest, as the story continued.

Alex's smile fell to a degree. "Then we started walking and we saw some weird things. The trees had dark blue leaves, which is not a kind of tree we have in our realm. I continued on, and we found this eerie highway where all the cars were frozen."

Paxton frowned and played with the word that Alex had said. "Car. What's a car?"

Alex balked, and then he answered to the best of his ability. "It's like a carriage but without the horses, and it has a battery and a lot of mechanical work, but these were old cars. Great invention, nonetheless. All of them were run down, and that area was not marked on any map I have seen of my town. Micheal found a creepy doll and tried to scare me with it. He found the bracelets on the doll." He held up his wrist.

Paxton gingerly grabbed his son's wrist and traced the stone with his thumb.

Alex didn't pull away but asked, "What are they?"

Paxton nodded, still holding Alex's hand. "When we were first brought together, there were many attacks around all of the regions, kingdoms, and even other realms. We were the first line of defense against people who abused their magic or threatened the lives of our people. It would take days upon days to reach our destination, and we couldn't reach other realms, so eventually, we came up with the idea of teleportation. The gods gifted us these and the ability to teleport." He tapped the sapphire.

The teenager blinked in shock. "Wait, this was yours over eight hundred years ago?"

His father chuckled, making Alex feel warm inside. "Yes, Alex, this was mine hundreds of years ago. I assume Micheal has his father's. Eventually, we were so used to teleportation that we no longer needed the stones. We gave them back to the gods. It would seem that one of the gods wanted you to come here and they sent them to your realm."

"Why?" Alex questioned. "Why give us these if they

were going to release Lloyd as a punishment when we got here?"

Paxton shrugged, the motion trying to ease Alex's frustration. "I do not pretend to know the gods' motives. They always disagree on things, but they believe in majority rule. If most of them agreed to let Lloyd free, then that's what they would do."

Alex gawked at him. "That makes no sense."

Paxton sighed. "I know it doesn't. I believe the reason they made us bargain eight hundred years ago in the first place was to punish me. We were forbidden to have families other than the ones around us. And when I had you, the gods were not happy. First, they were mad that Lloyd had Micheal, but I was the final straw. That's why the gods made us give you both up to lock Lloyd away. They wanted you gone so bad. However, they knew I would never let you go unless drastic measures were taken. They knew exactly what they were doing when they said we had to sacrifice something close to us."

Alex understood, but it was highly unfair in his racing mind. The gods could've done the dirty work themselves, but they made the Guardians do it for them.

"Why didn't they let you have kids?"

"The gods liked to control us like dogs." The Guardian grimaced. "They chose where we went and which people we saved. At least in the beginning that was how it was. As years passed, they loosened the leashes and we had more leeway, but we were still ordered to never have children or family of any kind. You would be a distraction."

"Do you think I'm a distraction?" Alex asked. He thought about how revealing himself to his father could blindside the man into ignoring his duties as a warrior.

"No," was Paxton's simple answer.

"Why not?" He couldn't push down his fear of abandonment, and he couldn't comprehend how he *wasn't* a distraction. Paxton had him even though he knew it was forbidden, which got him in trouble in the long run.

The man frowned, puzzled, and leaned closer to him. "You're my child; not some play toy that they think you are. I will do everything to keep you safe." He held Alex's shoulders straight. "If that's you being a distraction, then so be it, but I will not see harm come to you."

Alex swallowed, staring at his father in a stunned fashion. He slid the emotions away from his face, not wanting everyone else in the room to possibly see how Paxton's words moved him.

Paxton developed a nostalgic look again, resting his weight on one leg. "But I did miss you growing up." The guilt and regret in his voice was astounding to Alex. "I understand if you wish for me to keep my distance."

Alex felt shocked, and hugged his father once more, soaking up the time he had with him. Something in his heart told him their time together wouldn't last long. "I don't blame you."

Paxton sighed once again, his years weighing heavy on his posture. The teenager wrapped his arms around him tighter, trying to convey to him that everything was fine.

"However, I don't want to impose on your life, Alexander," his father admitted, holding the back of his head. "I haven't been there for you, and I know nothing about you. I let them take you away without much of a fight. I don't even know how old you are."

"I don't care about that, and it wasn't your fault." Alex didn't move out of his arms. "You're here now and we've already made a connection within the first few minutes. That's more than what my adoptive parents have done for me."

His father pulled him back, taking in every detail of his son. "If you're sure, Alex."

He nodded. "I'm sure, Dad."

215

Paxton gave Alex some space, looking more relaxed than he was before. "I'll do my best to do good for you. It has been many years since I have been your father."

"We both have things to learn," Alex quietly said. He debated telling him about his previous relationships with his adoptive parents, and the reason why that relationship failed.

"You can tell me anything," Paxton whispered just as gently with no pressure to his words, his eyes so open and ready to listen.

"I'm not good with parental figures so, I may come off as confrontational," he explained slowly. He didn't know how he expected his father to react. People normally stared blankly at him or gave him weird looks if he accidentally mentioned his abandonment issues and bad connection skills. But Paxton didn't do either.

"I understand what you mean. We'll both be patient with each other." Paxton offered the middle ground to him.

He smiled. "I would like that."

Chapter 14

Alex dragged a lazy finger across the crystal blue water, seeing how it rippled out into the small oscillations of the soft waves of the bay. He could hear the faint sound of the water lapping against the shore, just a small sound. He reached over the edge of the short dock to repeat the motion.

The wood creaked under the weight of another person joining. When Alex turned he discovered it was two people, not one.

"Hey," he greeted softly with a polite smile.

Katelyn returned the smile as Sabine messed with the end of one of the small braids she had recently placed in her hair. She didn't look up from the wood at her feet.

"We saw you leave and figured you could use some company," Katelyn said as she settled herself next to Alex, legs perpendicular to his feet that were pulled up.

"You sure you're not checking up on me to make sure I wouldn't wander off again?" he asked with no heat behind his words, leaning back against the support beams of the end of the dock.

Katelyn huffed a laugh. "Okay, fine, that's the other

reason." Turning her head and looking at Sabine, she patted the space beside her.

The ivory-skinned girl hesitated and then stiffly sat down. Alex watched as the Lord of Phoenix let her eyes fall to the horizon. Alex knew she wasn't speaking to fill the silence like she normally would; she was giving him a chance to talk.

"Why didn't you tell me about my powers or Paxton?" he asked, surprising himself by not sounding angry. Normally, if he found out someone was lying to him, it would make ire boil in his blood. Katelyn gave him a grin that wasn't pitiful like he expected.

"Took you long enough to ask." She had a knowing gleam in her dark eyes. "I didn't tell you about your heritage because I, myself, wasn't quite sure if you were Paxton's son. The notion seemed too far-fetched for me to accept or believe. It had been hundreds of years since we sent you through the portal, and I was so sure you had grown up and had passed on.

"Even when we fought in the Glade ruins before the Inferno Realm and your powers reacted to your emotions, I still couldn't believe that you were the little boy we sent away. No matter how similar that show of power was to that of your father, I didn't have it in my heart to admit it."

Alex shook his head a few times like it would make everything click inside of his head. "What do you mean by similar to my father?"

"Paxton is a reactive person just like you, Alex. He's just better at hiding it." Katelyn sighed, pushing her braided hair from her shoulder. "There have been times when he has gotten so upset or afraid that his powers would defend him in order to protect him by trying to destroy everything near him. Lloyd had been in trouble once before, and Pax's powers shot out and killed the person that was attacking Lloyd. He leveled everything in a seventy-foot radius."

"Powers aren't sentient beings," Alex whispered his declaration, but even he had to admit that he wasn't confident with his answer. He remembered that story of Paxton and Lloyd being told to him by Rex in the ruins.

Katelyn tipped her head to the side. "In normal circumstances, yes; powers do not have minds of their own, but ours are different. They can break the basic laws of magic, which means they can take over if they want to. They weren't meant to exist," the lord carefully said.

Alex jutted his chin to the silent woman next to her. "She said that before. What did you mean, Sabine?"

Sabine was startled at being addressed but clumsily explained. "I mean, it's what they are. The Guardians' powers were rare cases of power that have never been seen before. Their magic is too powerful for any person to possess. Whether the gods gave them or not, they're too dangerous."

The information he was receiving was making his head hurt. He'd thought Sabine had been dramatic about her statement in the Inferno Realm to make her father think she was on his side, but what she said contradicted that thought.

With his head in his hands massaging his temples, he asked, "Then how have I not been burned to a crisp or have something drastically bad happen to me? You told me that Micheal's magic—and mine—and could potentially be more dangerous."

"If Paxton had you with a woman, it could've been a risk because he had no idea if the state of his powers would harm you when you came into the world."

"But you don't know if that was the case, right? Because the gods could've given me to him?" Alex responded for clarification since Paxton never explicitly stated how Alex was born. He still didn't understand why the gods would give Paxton a baby if they hated the thought of the

Guardians having children.

Katelyn bobbed her head up and down. "Correct. And the fact that Micheal had been born first helped ease our minds since he was a healthy little boy and his powers never made an appearance. I don't want to say he was a test to see if we could have children, but it crossed my mind a few times."

"Why did you never ask them which case it was for us?" Alex questioned, implying he was asking about Lloyd and his father.

"It wasn't my place to ask. Lloyd never spoke about a specific partner when he had Micheal, but I do know that Micheal had another parent. I didn't think it would be fair of me to question his or Paxton's judgment about their own children."

Alex accepted that, but he had one question still nagging in the back of his head. "Did my dad ever mention anyone? A woman, a man, anything?" He knew how desperate he sounded, but he was trying to learn anything he could.

Katelyn shook her head. "He never mentioned anything about romantic partners. He was always private about that. Her hand fell to his arm, giving a squeeze. "If you have more questions, I think you should ask your father."

"If it helps," Sabine spoke up, "my father never mentioned Paxton having anyone that he knew of. And he knew a lot of details about him that he wouldn't shut up about."

Alex knew she was trying to help, but there wasn't much he could do with that information other than be more creeped out by Lloyd. "Good to know, but I've been meaning to ask both of you a question, sort of related to your father, Sabine."

"Go for it," Sabine said, as she leaned back on her hands.

"You both knew that the ruins were the Glade, right?"

Katelyn shot him an offended glare. "Of course I did. I *lived* there."

The barrier magic user nodded, ignoring her friend's comment. "Yes. My father told me how to find it since the whole teleporting-across-the-kingdom thing was a problem. He had me memorize the pattern and track where it would be. I obviously couldn't take the shortcut that I'm guessing you and Micheal used, about half a mile away with the vine wall, because then everyone would be suspicious of how I found such a convenient path for the journey."

Alex leaned his chin on his fist, scooting closer. "How do they work?"

"By impressive barrier magic. I've read a few books talking about the Glade, but it was all speculation from witnesses when the Guardians were still active. They never explained the magic behind it." Sabine laid her head on Katelyn's shoulder with a pleading pout. "But if a certain someone would happily explain, my questions would be answered."

"Nope," Katelyn popped the *p*. "I can't give you all of our secrets."

"Rude."

"Deal with it."

Alex snickered at the two women. It was nice to see them fall back into their normal rhythm of life given the circumstances that opposed them. He could see that they cared about each other even if Sabine had gone behind their backs. However, he was still apprehensive about her intentions. His heart skipped a beat and his throat tightened when he started to open his mouth to say something, but he pushed through.

He stared at her sadly. "Why Sabine? Why not tell us your plan from the start?"

Sabine looked down in shame, biting her lip. Katelyn

scooted back, not wanting to be in the middle of the conversation. Alex only had his eyes on Sabine.

"It had to be real," she whispered, "or he would know."

Alex frowned in thought. "How would he know, Sabine? Something could've happened and we all would've been killed."

She glared at him lightly with tears in her eyes. "Because my father has the ability to poke around in people's heads, ripping out every piece of information he wants. So, yes, it had to be real."

Alex gaped like a fish out of water. There was nothing he could say to that as the woman wiped her eyes except for a quiet, "I'm sorry." She ducked her head and didn't look up again.

Feeling that eyes were upon him, Alex spun around. In the distance, standing in the grass near the transition of the green foliage into sand, were Paxton, Ryder, Cobalt, and Micheal. He raised an eyebrow even if they couldn't see that far.

"That would be them wanting you, I would presume," Katelyn announced, giving a shove to Alex's body.

He grumbled but stood up, grateful for an escape from the awkward situation he created. "Are you going to tell me why?"

"No, I will not." She just smiled at him. "I'll stay with Sabine."

"You're impossible," he mumbled.

Alex strided to the three men and his friend, smiling at a tired-looking Micheal. "Hey sleeping beauty," he greeted.

Micheal stuck his tongue out at him. "Just because I don't wake up at the crack of dawn doesn't mean I'm lazy."

"Your words not mine, Mikey."

The taller boy moved to smack the sandy-haired boy, but Alex dodged out of the way, seeking cover from his father's larger form. When Micheal halted his advances, only then did Alex move away.

"What are we doing?" he asked when they started moving.

"We're teaching you how to use your powers. Amethyst gave us the details that you two do indeed have powers that you don't know how to use," Ryder stated, eyes facing forward.

Alex sheepishly looked to the ground, watching as the grains of sand in the grass decreased the more steps they took. "Great."

Cobalt nudged him with a sinister smirk. "No time for a pity party."

Ryder led them up to the familiar stretch of empty land a safe distance away from the rest of the village except for a few large trees that towered high in the sky.

"I'm really starting to hate this training ground," Micheal murmured under his breath, meticulously stretching his back and arms.

Alex quirked an eyebrow up. "You gettin' old?"

Micheal deflated and gave him a deadpan look as Alex snickered. "Oh, you hush it."

"Micheal," Ryder called from multiple feet away. "Come with me."

Alex said a brief goodbye as Micheal left him, and he glanced at Paxton and Cobalt. Cobalt followed Ryder after looking Alex up and down, obviously having no confidence in him. He left Alex and Paxton alone, and Alex's father gestured for the boy to follow him. They stopped walking when there was enough distance between them and the other pair.

Alex laid eyes on an object that he hadn't seen before in the training ground. It was a boulder that had a decent length and width to it; he could sit on it and still have room around him.

"This wasn't here before," he pointed out.

The man smiled. "You're right. It wasn't."

"So what's it for?" Alex was confused.

"How many times have you used your powers?" Paxton deflected, not answering.

"Technically four times." He scratched the back of his neck and then started counting on his fingers. "My magic shot out of me when Katelyn was in danger. I used them in the Inferno Realm. I made swords lift in the air without notice. I touched Micheal and my powers went into him and Katelyn somehow, made them see something that I was only seeing," Alex finished truthfully.

"Were you wanting to use them? Did you consciously know what you were doing?" The man kept his face passive.

"No. In the Inferno Realm maybe, but it started with me not bringing them out on purpose." Alex hesitated to say the facts, not wanting to admit how many times he could've hurt someone, but he told Paxton anyway.

Paxton thought for a moment, not looking at Alex. "Here's what we're going to do. I don't want you using your powers at all unless absolutely necessary. That means you have to stay calm or else your body will react to your emotions. Your body is new to your powers since they were taken from you as a child."

"Why were they taken from us?" He poked his question into the conversation. "What was the purpose of that?"

Paxton sighed heavily, exhaling in a bored way. "The gods knew they would send you to a non-magical world. To keep you safe from possible persecution from your realm's laws, they took any possible power from you. At least that's what they wanted us to believe. They just didn't want you to grow up with them so you wouldn't get powerful. You both were too young to show signs of having any, but the gods chose to proceed with the extraction. Even if their decision was for their own paranoid protection, it turns out they made the right call."

Alex nodded along with his words "And that's part of the reason why I lose it because my body is trying to catch up to my magic being put back into me."

"Correct."

Alex did a sigh of his own. "Magic is complicated."

"It most definitely is, but you'll get used to it," the Guardian sympathetically agreed. "Now, I want you to do something." He reached into one of his pockets and pulled out a coin. "Lift this with your powers."

"How?" Alex asked.

"Do what feels natural to you for now."

Alex cocked his head to the side in an unassertive way. He took a few steps back and stared so hard at the coin in his father's hand that he thought he would burn holes into it. He moved his fingers around slowly, bending them and tensing them as Amethyst and Sabine did with their powers.

He found a position with his hands that was somewhat normal even though he felt ridiculous, and he urged his powers to the coin. A faint glow wrapped around the coin. He slowly lifted his hand, and the piece of metal trembled, but it didn't budge up into the air. He dropped his hand.

"Keep trying, Alex."

The encouragement made him zero in on the coin once again, and he gave a more violent twist of his fingers. It fell again. It took him two more times to get the coin to follow the path of his fingers, and it hovered out of Paxton's hand.

His face broke out into a smile. "I did it!"

His father laughed. "Yes, you did. Now try it with that." He pointed behind him to the boulder.

Alex flinched, and then he gawked at Paxton. The challenge just went from one to one hundred times harder. "Are you serious? I couldn't even lift that physically."

"You lifted the coin," he said, tossing it in the air and catching it. "You know the motions that you need, and what you need to imagine in your head. Yes, it will take more effort, but you can do it. So do it. Don't be afraid of failure."

Alex gave him pleading eyes, but his father's resolve did not crack, and he pointed firmly to the stationary rock. Alex couldn't fight his way out of this one.

Chapter 15

Alex panted heavily once he let the rock fall to the ground. He'd only lifted it one foot up in the air. He placed his hands on his knees, the sun beating down on him. He'd been trying for two days.

"Why is it so hard to lift a stupid rock?" he asked rhetorically. Cobalt snorted in amusement from his place under a tree nearby, protected by the shade. His favorite pastime was to throw passive-aggressive sounds or comments Alex's way.

"It's not easy, Alex." Paxton coached, ignoring the other man's sound of entertainment.

"But I've been trying, and it's not working."

"Try *again*. Picture it in your head, Lex." His father had picked up on the nickname, and Alex hated it.

He slipped his eyes closed. He saw in his mind the small boulder lift itself into the air. He recalled the feeling of his powers and how he lifted the coin a few days ago. Opening his eyes, he reached a hand out, straining his fingers as his magic surged through him. It shot out to wrap around the rock. He moved his hand up slowly in the air, willing the object to follow his movement. It quivered and lifted off the ground. His muscles tensed as he moved it further into the air. It climbed up further than last time, reaching two feet, then three feet. Once it reached four feet his magic faltered, and the stone came crashing down into the dirt.

Cobalt cackled at him, which was an odd sight for the normally impassive man. Alex glared at him, full of disdain.

Paxton sighed heavily and shot his fellow Guardian a bored stare. "Cobalt, go be useful for once today and help Ryder with Micheal."

The protective user grumbled and groaned as he got up from his spot on another boulder.

"And don't antagonize him!" Paxton shouted over his shoulder. Cobalt ignored him.

Alex pouted to his father, feeling defeated. He wasn't used to failing at something he tried hard to succeed at. His body and his mind were equally exhausted.

"It will take time, Alex. What you told me you did in the Inferno Realm was you acting off of adrenaline, emotions, and your body reacting to your powers being reintroduced to you as we talked about before. Controlling your power is a different level than just acting mindlessly with it." Paxton attempted to ease his mind. Alex guessed his father could see the stress hiding in his eyes because the older man started pulling him towards the sidelines of the training ground, giving him a merciful break.

Jesse was animatedly discussing a topic with Rex under one of the other out-of-place trees in the area, and the other guard was respectfully listening. Jesse stopped when Alex tiredly went to his side. The teenager groaned in a childlike way to show his frustration. Normally, he'd never be caught dead complaining like a kid, but he couldn't muster any self-control not to.

Rex smirked. "Not going well?" he asked cheekily.

Alex shoved his shoulder in retaliation, but it didn't do much since he didn't move very far.

"That was pathetic," the guard added.

Rolling his eyes, Alex sat on the ground. "For your information, no, it's not going well."

Instead of teasing him again as he expected, Rex replied, "You'll get it in time. You're too stubborn not to. Micheal's still shaky as well."

Alex peered on the other side of the field, seeing Cobalt and Ryder throwing small pebbles at Micheal at low speeds to get him to shield against them. It didn't work most of the time. They would hit Micheal's skin when he failed to summon his powers, and it would make him hiss in slight pain.

Alex wrinkled his nose in sympathy. *That can't feel good.*

"Silverbend and Nodium settled in two days ago, but I assume you all knew that," Jesse announced. "Henix and Fifan have confirmed they are coming and will arrive by sundown at the latest. We're waiting for word back from Ruddox City. They would provide us with the most soldiers."

"Will it be enough?" Alex asked, eyes never straying from Micheal's moving form.

"It'll have to be, or we're all dead," Paxton stated darkly, shadows creeping across his face from the tree. "Do they have any magic users?" He directed the question to the two guards.

"A handful in each city or village. If everyone comes to aid, it'll turn out to be around twenty to twenty-five in total." Rex's voice said it all. That didn't leave them with a lot of options. Silence stretched on for minutes, and Alex spaced out while staring at the dirt.

He didn't like the odds of the possible battle. A lot of people were going to die, and for what? It was his and Micheal's fault for coming to this realm in the first place, and they were the reason behind Lloydbeing released from his fiery punishment. They weren't even sure Lloyd was

229

going to make a war effort toward them. Things had been quiet. Alex figured if Lloyd wanted the Guardians slaughtered that he would've done it already.

A shadow rippled over the grass, blocking the sun. Alex's head snapped up, and he was faced with a flying projectile coming straight at him and the other three men surrounding him. Jesse and Rex scrambled out of the way while Paxton just stared at it. His hands twitched as if he was about to lift his arms, but Alex beat him to it by accident.

Alex threw his hands out, sending only ocean-blue beams out of his fingers to meet the flying projectile. With the smallest flick and change of direction with his hands, he sent the offending object flying in the other direction. The boulder rolled to a stop.

Alex's breathing was labored, hands still out in the air as they became heavy, and then ultimately sank to his side. His vision went blurry for a few moments before his eyes focused. Right in front of him was Cobalt with his own hands faintly glowing. He was the one that had sent the boulder in their direction by blasting it with his powers.

"What was that?!" Alex screamed at him to get his point across. "You could've killed us!"

Cobalt just cynically grinned at him, coming closer. "But I didn't. I just forced your hand. And your father never would've let you get hurt."

"You didn't know if it would work!" As he continued to yell, he was reminded of the memory of him reprimanding Sabine in such a familiar way. He was sick of repeating that sentence.

"Whether you believe it or not, I know you, kid. You're just like Pax; you need a reason to act. Your powers are no different. You can't be scared to use them."

"I'm not scared," Alex said as his heart fluttered at the thought of his magic sending that rock into a living person if he had pushed too hard in a different direction.

"I'm not convinced."

"I don't care if you are. You don't even know me. And that doesn't mean you can just career a rock toward us!"

Cobalt rolled his eyes so hard that Alex thought they would end up permanently in his head. "Gods, you're just as stubborn as you were when you were four years old. Don't try to argue with me. We won't be able to hold your hand forever."

Alex glared in his direction as he turned his back, his hands shaking with unhinged resentment. A few words of someone's voice speaking to another passed by him, too quiet for him to hear. A hand touched his shoulder.

"Let's take a walk," his best friend ordered rather than offered.

Alex hugged himself.

"I hate that he's right," he said through gritted teeth when he and Micheal were out of earshot.

Micheal swiped a hand through the air. "Eh, you're both right in a way. They're more experienced with magic and training, but they don't know us. We're different from the little kids they knew hundreds of years ago."

Alex hummed dejectedly.

The brunet stuffed his hands into his pockets, taking in a breath of air. "It's so weird that they knew us when we were kids. The way Tucker and the others described the Guardians, it was like they were gods. And your father is one of them."

"So was yours," Alex pointed out, messing with his thumbnail.

"My father was lost in time. No one remembers him like the others. Most of them think he died." The taller boy was trying to hide the pain behind a mask, but Alex was able to see past it.

"You don't know that. We have only been to one village,

and we can't even read the language here. People might *worship* him; you never know." Alex changed his tone of voice to sound more lighthearted. "And he was still active with the other Guardians for *years* before he was presumed dead. People most definitely thought of him as a god as well."

Micheal smirked minutely. "I guess."

"Alex!" a shriek resonated throughout the village. A quick, small form barreled into Alex's stomach, knocking the wind out of him. He groaned in pain as a tiny human dug into his hip.

"Hey, Gwen," he greeted when he caught sight of fiery red hair.

"Hi!" she exclaimed, and Alex swore it blew out his eardrum. "I'm happy."

The two teens laughed.

"We can see that. Why are you happy?" Micheal asked.

She bounced on her toes, playing with the end of her ponytails. "There are new people! I love new people!" She went into a rapid mess of words about the new people she met from the other villages.

"She's a mini you, Micheal," Alex teased under his breath. Micheal stuck his tongue out and failed to defend his case.

"I saw the two men leave a couple of days ago. I wanted to follow them into the woods, but they wouldn't let me," she stated cryptically, randomly bringing it up.

"Two men, huh? Did one have dark hair and the other brownish-red hair?"

"Mhm." she bobbed her head up and down.

"That was Max and Laurence," Alex explained. "We helped them, but they had to leave."

She stuck her lower lip out, plucked a flower out of the ground, and picked the petals. "Why?"

Alex struggled to find the words he wanted.

"They had been kept in a bad place for a long time," Micheal said, saving him. "They aren't very trusting of people, and they wanted some peace."

When the little girl didn't respond, Micheal shot a desperate look over her head to Alex. Alex's eyes widened and he shrugged, not knowing if she would understand.

The girl had a stormy and serious face, making her lips turn down into a frown. Alex braced for her confusion and sadness but was pleasantly surprised when her face broke into a smile.

"Okay!" she cheered, satisfied with the vague answer. With that easing her mind, she started skipping down the gravel path, leaving her older friends in the dust.

Alex snorted quietly. "I think you're rubbing off on her."

Micheal grumbled under his breath.

"I still can't believe Max and Laurence just left like that," Alex said.

"Well," Micheal shrugged, "they were secretive. I tried making small talk with them on the day of the Inferno Realm situation, and they wouldn't say anything. They're kind of weird."

"Don't call people weird, Micheal Barnes; it's rude," Alex chastised.

"Fine, fine, they're not weird, but there's something they were hiding."

"Mikey, they were held captive for years, give them a break."

"Don't call me Mikey."

"I'll call you whatever I want."

"Jerk. I so wish I could curse you out in another language."

"You wouldn't dare."

As the pair went back and forth, bickering like there was no tomorrow, Alex couldn't help but admit to himself that there was no one else he'd rather be within a new realm.

Micheal made his life more full and kept him from being alone. Alex only hoped he could return the favor if the battle was to happen.

The Shadow King had to die, and he prayed Micheal wouldn't get cold feet and back out.

Chapter 16

The villages of Henix and Fifan crossed the threshold of Phoenix the following morning after Alex stormed away during training. Alex had watched in the window in his hideout—his room, hiding from a certain protective user. He had been avoiding Cobalt at all costs, not wanting to see his smug face after Cobalt got under his skin. However, he did go to meet the other village lords and their guards and soldiers. Unfortunately, Cobalt was present, so it was an unavoidable proximity between him and the other man.

A day later, Micheal burst into their room. "Lex, Ruddox's here. Come on, let's go," he said, shaking Alex's bed.

Alex sat up, blinking his eyes to wake himself up. It was still early in the morning.

"What?" He yawned. "I thought we haven't heard from them yet?"

"So did I, but the scouts confirmed it was them. Your dad and the others are talking to the lord now." The brunet's eyes were sparkling with curiosity, and Alex internally groaned. Micheal was never so excited in the morning, which meant he was going to be insufferable the remaining hours of the day.

The taller boy stepped closer and yanked Alex out of bed. Alex swatted at his hands as his body and mind adjusted to being awake.

He couldn't be too excited about the arrival of Ruddox because something else was occupying his mind. His dreams hadn't come back, and he didn't know if that was a good thing or not. If he was being honest with himself, it put him on edge. The dreams had been the exact same for years, and then they suddenly stopped once they had freed Amethyst and she had enlightened him about the history of his and Micheal's heritage.

Every night for years, he mentally prepared for the onslaught of images and pain, but now that it was gone, he didn't know how to feel. He wouldn't say he missed it, but he wasn't reassured by how abruptly they stopped after years of them attacking his sleep. Ironically, not having the dreams was more strange than experiencing them.

Micheal glanced at Alex as they left the house. "You good there? You looked stressed."

"Just thinking," Alex mumbled.

They looked around the land of the village, searching for their friends. The village was buzzing with nervous energy; the guards paced around with stressed out expressions, the villagers kept their eyes on the horizon just waiting with bated breath for danger to appear, and even the children stayed close to their homes.

Alex caught sight of a mass of people near the edge of the village with Katelyn and the Guardians included. He nudged Micheal in the side and gestured toward them, beginning to swiftly walk.

As they approached, they took in the sight of the impressive-looking people. The armor, weapons, and the sizes of the newcomers were enough to give Alex that assessment of them. Ruddox was a powerhouse city.

Titan was perched at Cobalt's feet, and he nudged Alex's thigh with his nose when he got close. The boy patted his furry head.

A woman in dark, mainly leather armor was standing in front of Katelyn, conversing with her with a slight smile. Next to the new woman was a man that was about five years older than Rex (Alex guessed he was thirty-one years old) with a jagged scar that ran from his eye to his cheek, but that was the only flaw Alex could see.

"Even with the scar he's easy on the eyes," Micheal leaned in to mutter to him, holding a mischievous smile.

"He's at least thirteen years older than you," Alex gasped, sounding appalled. "Do not get any ideas."

"I didn't say anything to suggest otherwise. Just making an observation." Micheal grinned.

Alex rolled his eyes and focused on the woman who he guessed was the lord of Ruddox City. That would be the only reason she was addressing Katelyn first.

The woman's eyes landed on Alex and then Micheal, her grin widening by a small fraction. "So you two are the infamous realm crashers."

Alex chuckled nervously. "You've heard of us?"

"Word travels fast. Just be lucky that the Zalrona City hasn't received word, or you would have an entire army after both of you by orders of King Malum."

He looked to the Guardians on instinct, mainly his father, and he was met with a reassuring smile from Paxton. He remembered how Paxton had promised to protect him from anything, and that would include King Malum's army.

"King Malum is going to find out though," Alex mused.

She nodded, looking grim. "Yes, eventually he will. Hopefully, you find a way home before that. Now, another rumor has popped up about a realm barrier that has been broken nearby. You want to explain that, Lord Katelyn?" The woman gave a teasing smile, obviously skeptical and unbelieving of the rumor. Chuckles filtered through her ranks.

That was the beam of light we saw after the teleportation ended, Alex recalled.

Katelyn nodded once, not matching her smile. "You would assume correctly. A realm barrier has broken that was imprisoning five of the Guardians for eight hundred years. The 'realm crashers' you speak of are the two children of the Guardians Lloyd Achlys and Paxton Hayes."

The other lord and her guard reeled back as did Alex. She was exposing them to people whose intentions were unknown.

"That's not possible," the woman whispered.

"You're lying," the scarred man said from her side, shaking his head.

Titan bared his teeth and growled lowly in warning but stayed sitting next to his master's feet. Cobalt didn't say anything, but the wolf stopped growling while the man put a hand on his head for a few seconds.

"You sure about that?" Rex said, sizing the other guard up. For once, Alex was thankful for Rex's protective nature. The scarred man took a step, straightening his back.

"Prove it," another guard from Ruddox's group requested aggressively.

Katelyn narrowed her eyes but ripped a knife out of her baldric. She brought the blade down across the skin of her palm, crimson liquid streaming out of the open wound.

"God, Katelyn!" Micheal exclaimed.

The woman held her hand out to Amethyst, blankly looking at her as blood dripped off of the side of her hand and into the grass.

Her sister gave her a displeased look but grabbed her hand nonetheless.

Amethyst brought her powers out and waved her fingers across Katelyn's wound a few times as Katelyn hissed in pain, standing still as a statue. After ten seconds, there was no evidence of the knife cut except for the blood staining her skin.

"Satisfied?" She held her hands out to the side, sarcasm in her tone. "My sister is Amethyst Grey the Healer, and you are in the presence of the Guardians," she said as she looked at the people behind her. "I am one myself. I am Katrina Grey."

As she finished, the Ruddox people were still suspicious of the others behind her. There was no proof from them.

Elizabeth started to bring a hand up but gazed back to Paxton. He gave her a nod.

Elizabeth's hand crackled and buzzed with her powers, chin tilted up in a sign of confidence. Helena held a ball of fire that made her dark skin glow. Ryder and Cobalt let their hands start to glow, fingers and hands stationary. Paxton slowly made movements with his fingers to maintain the energy he was holding at the tips of his fingers. They seemed bored with the demonstration.

The Ruddox people stared at the young Healer, and then at the others. They spontaneously dropped to their knees.

Amethyst cringed and spun the ring on her finger. "Oh, please stand up!" She begged. "You don't need to do that."

Alex stared blankly at the kneeling people, not knowing what to think.

"I hate it when they do that," Ryder said to himself, but it wasn't quiet enough to not travel to Alex.

As everyone went back to a standing position, Alex asked him, "Is that a common reaction?"

The man nodded. "Sometimes. Half of the regions and kingdoms treat us like gods. We hate it."

Alex snorted a laugh. He wondered just how many people would bow down to the Guardians. And what positions of power they could hold.

Cobalt stepped up, eyeing the scarred Ruddox guard, and then looked to Katelyn and Ryder. "Now that the last of our allies have arrived, I recommend we make a barrier. Just as a precaution in case the Shadow King and his Dark Knights do indeed stage an attack."

Alex knew Katelyn would agree. They were exposed here.

"I still have scouts doubling back for reconnaissance. They should be back within the hour," the Lord of Ruddox stated.

Katelyn gave her a nod. "Understood. Ryder and Cobalt meet back here in an hour. Until then, assist in helping everyone settle in." Cobalt gave her a look, but she held up one finger to stop any protests that could come from him. "My village, my rules. Go."

Alex had to turn his head to not laugh at the protective user's irritated face. When Alex turned back, Katelyn gave him a wink. He grinned at her. It was satisfying to see Cobalt get knocked down a few pegs.

Alex hated sword fighting with a passion, and the reason was not that he was bad at it. Totally not.

The flat side of a practice sword hit him in the back, making him stumble. He panted in exhaustion, giving Jesse, who was the one that hit him in the back, a defeated look.

"I told you," Jesse said in a sing-song voice. "Sword fighting is hard, Lex. Would it make you feel better if I told you that you're improving?"

Alex did his best not to pout. "Maybe. I still feel like I'm being used as a punching bag."

"Sometimes the best way to learn is to get knocked around." Jesse wasn't being as sympathetic as Alex would've hoped but he knew it was for the best. He couldn't be coddled.

He sighed. "I thought Hunter said I wasn't a great fit for sword fighting, so why am I still training?"

Jesse put a hand on his hip. "Because the Dark Knights will stab you to death like they almost did last time. Things have changed. Dark Knights weren't anticipated last time. You can't use your powers fully, so you need a backup plan. That would be sword fighting."

Alex suffered for another thirty minutes. Every time he dodged, parried, and slashed, he became more battered, and he felt like he had cracked a few ribs. Time had passed, and Jesse took mercy on him and told him they were done for a moment, instructing him to relax if he could even do that in his current mental state.

Alex dragged his feet as he prowled down the hill to reach Maggie's. He didn't know if he had ever felt so tired.

"You look like you went a couple of rounds with a rabid dog," an unfamiliar voice called out.

He whipped his head around like it was on a swivel. He caught sight of an unfamiliar and pretty girl with strikingly blonde hair, even more blonde than Alex's, standing in the shadow of a house. The glimpse of her armor gave away that she was from another village. Alex learned that armor had different defining symbols or styles of the villages and cities, a coat of arms of sorts.

"I feel like it," he responded with a tired grin.

She snickered. "Yeah, I bet. My sisters and brothers would smack me around when they taught me how to fight when I was younger. Not that they don't anymore, but at least I'm able to hit them back."

Alex laughed, taking a few steps closer to her. "One day I'll be able to hit them back just as hard, but today is not that day." He sized her up before sticking a hand out. "I'm Alex O'Connor."

"So I have heard." She shook his hand. "I'm Dakota

Whitlock. I'm from Ruddox City."

Alex smiled. "I'd tell you where I'm from but you wouldn't know where it is."

"Fair. And if you needed much time to try and explain it, I wouldn't be free for long. I got thrown on babysitting duty somehow," she grumbled. "The mother looked frazzled and I offered to help. Then more kids joined the group. And I'm regretting my choices right now. They never stop wandering off."

He grinned, seeing the children running through the field again, tackling each other. "Yeah, I got roped into that a few times. Good luck."

"Thanks." She smiled at him as he walked away.

As he persisted down the path, he didn't stop to talk to anyone, needing to collapse on something soft. The promising relief of a couch that would cradle his tired bones and muscles kept him on his feet.

Alex entered Maggie's house, smiling at Micheal who was lying on the rickety couch in the small living room.

"Relaxing?" he asked.

Micheal exhaled with a smile on his face. "Yes, I am, indeed. Hunter cut me some slack since I've been doing good with training. How is your *attempt* at sword fighting going?"

Alex wrinkled his nose and pushed Micheal's feet off the edge of the couch, sitting there in place of them. He sighed in relief, the fatigue catching up with him. "Funny, Micheal, real funny."

"I'm just happy I'm finally beating you at something."

"Relish in it because it won't happen again, even if you are the athletic one," Alex warned him. The two of them had always been competitive, and it didn't matter what it was about. Alex reclined further into the couch, relaxing his sore muscles. "I'm just happy we don't have to watch any kids today. Some girl, Dakota, got stuck doing it."

"Yeah, I briefly met her when Gwen tried to run away from her." Micheal pointed out the window with a limp hand.

Alex snickered. "Poor girl. That had to sting just a bit."

Micheal shrugged. "Dakota didn't seem to care. I think she was just irritated that she let one slip away."

Silence fell upon them, and Alex felt his friend's eyes burning into him. He looked at Micheal with an eyebrow raised as Micheal just stared at him.

"Can I help you?"

"You're still hiding, aren't you? From Cobalt?" Micheal had a knowing smile.

"I'm insulted that you think I'm hiding." Alex stuck his chin out.

"But you totally are."

"Am not."

Micheal gave him an incredulous look. "Alexander, if you weren't hiding as you say, you'd be with your father who has not been in your life for sixteen years. You are hiding."

Alex crossed his arms in defeat, turning his head away. "Fine. Cobalt is intimidating, so I'm hiding."

Micheal snorted. "You big baby."

Alex shoved him and the brunet hit the floor. They both laughed, basking in the normalcy, knowing that chaos was coming for them.

Chapter 17

Alex and Micheal stepped through Katelyn's doorway, animatedly talking about what they were going to do when they got back to their realm. They had no idea how time would pass in Realm Six in comparison to their realm, but Sabine had a theory that it was borderline the same even with the distance between the two realms. Alex had pointed out they would need to figure out a lie when they got back, but Micheal was fighting him on it.

"Come on, Lex. It's not that big of a deal if two teenagers go missing for a week or two. No one's probably going to notice." Micheal brushed off his concern, waving at Katelyn who was sitting with a cup in front of her with the other Guardians around the table.

"Hey, Katelyn." Alex nodded to Katelyn. He went back to his conversation with Micheal without another look at anyone else in the room. "Really, Micheal? Remember the teachers that we see five days a week? And remember how your brother and my parents don't know where we are, so they wouldn't be able to make an excuse for us?"

"Gosh, you're a habitual worrier." Micheal rolled his eyes, plopping himself down on the couch next to Tucker who Alex just noticed. Dakota was on a couch opposite that, and Alex took a seat next to her.

"I can't help it, and you know that," he said, crossing his arms over his chest.

Katelyn gave a loud slurp of her drink, looking at all the people piled into her house. "I have lost all control," she stated matter-of-factly.

"Have fun trying to get rid of us." Tucker smiled sweetly at her.

She narrowed her eyes. "Shouldn't you be patrolling or something?"

He shook his head. "Nope. Jesse took over for me."

"Meaning he did it out of the goodness of his heart or did you bribe him?" She set her gaze firmly.

Tucker looked away with a happy grin. "Whatever helps you sleep at night."

Amethyst and Elizabeth snickered.

Katelyn looked at Paxton and Cobalt with a deadpan expression. "Do you see the amount of disrespect I receive from him? No manners."

The young guard gave a barking laugh. "Like you expected me to have manners? Have you forgotten who I live with?"

Katelyn dropped the subject with a shake of her hand and a giggle.

Alex, however, was not ready to drop his concern with his and Micheal's situation. He compelled Micheal mentally to look back at him and continue their conversation. It worked and the older teen did a double-take when he saw Alex's expression.

"Oh, don't you give me the kicked puppy look, Alexander. It only worked when we were eight, and it won't work now. Stop worrying about it," Micheal scoffed.

Alex dragged a lazy finger across his jeans, still going with his facade. "I don't push away your feelings when your problems are bothering you."

Exasperatedly, Micheal tossed a hand up in annoyance. "Really, the guilt trip? Isn't this a job for your therapist, to get you to stop worrying?"

"I hate him, I haven't gone in years," Alex said defensively. "I'm just wanting to share my struggles with you like I allow you to do with me."

Dakota's eyes flicked back and forth between the two of her new acquaintances. "I'm very lost."

Alex just looked at her blankly, realizing that the Ruddox girl was indeed sitting next to him. Last time he checked, he and Micheal weren't close with the girl, so he was slightly confused as to why she was in Katelyn's abode. "No offense, but why are you here?"

"Tucker brought me. My lord ordered me to 'make friends with other people here as if I can't make friends on my own. But keep going, I'm interested." She rested her chin in the palm of her hand that was propped on her knee with a grin.

He returned his eyes to Micheal's. "Mikey, the police could be on a manhunt for us because someone probably reported us missing."

Micheal leaned forward. "First of all, don't 'Mikey' me. Secondly, we live outside of Troy, Pennsylvania, aka the middle of nowhere. No one is going to be searching the entire country for us. It'll be okay, Lex."

The blond let out an elongated sigh. "I hate feeling unprepared."

Micheal laughed with a teasing smile. "Welcome to reality, Alex. Not everything in life can be planned."

"I hate you."

"No, you just hate that I'm right."

"Dad, back me up!" Alex called to his father, sitting up straight. He had to hold in a smirk at the Guardian's lost and worried look. It was entertaining to see him scramble for an answer.

"Um...can't help you with this one, Alex." Paxton gave him a sympathetic and tense smile.

Alex dramatically sunk into the couch. "Left to fend for myself by my own father."

Tucker and Dakota broke into laughter at Micheal's face, which was screwed up in a dumbfounded look. "And people say I'm the melodramatic one. If only they could see you now."

"What's a therapist? Sounds weird," Helena said, apparently still caught up on the word from the previous conversation.

Alex glanced at her, still leaning back. "You don't have those here? It's like a doctor but for your head, I guess? They're supposed to help you if you have emotional trauma or disorders. I don't know how to describe it. I didn't go for long. Didn't need to."

She wrinkled her nose. "Odd."

"We had something similar in my kingdom," Ryder softly stated. "Except they would take parts of your brain out like it would fix your problems. Most of the patients died or had lasting side effects, so the doctors stopped using that method."

Tucker gagged, hunching over. "Gross! Why would they think that would work?!"

Ryder shrugged, unbothered by it. "I don't know."

Micheal grimaced. "Yeah, we would call that a medieval method."

"So you *are* from a different kingdom." Dakota jumped in, clapping her hands once. Her focus was on Ryder. "It was always assumed, but no one had concrete evidence."

The Guardian gave a curt nod. "Yes, I am from the Nimita Kingdom, Helena is from Thora, and everyone else is from Zalrona."

Helena thrummed her fingers against the table. "I used

to be the heir to that throne. But then I ran away."

Alex straightened up, recalling Rex's comment days ago in the Glade about Helena destructively using her powers. He wondered if that was why. "You're a princess? Why'd you leave?"

Flames flickered in her eyes, literally and figuratively. "My parents made me use my powers for their twisted ways. Thora and Zalrona had been at war centuries ago. I had gotten fed up with them quickly and moved to Zalrona when I was twenty-two. Ten years later I met these unstable people and became a Guardian."

Elizabeth took a sip of her drink. "Rude," she mumbled.

"Could you take the throne and make the kingdom better?" Alex asked. He thought about the King of Zalrona and how he was a tyrant. If Helena could possibly take her position as queen hundreds of years later, her army could...

He chastised himself in his head. *Don't be stupid, Alex.*

The woman snorted sardonically. "Even if I wasn't killed on the spot for desertion from years ago, I was cut out of the family. It's in literal stone that I am no longer an heiress. I now have no right to the throne."

Alex steadily met her gaze. "You wouldn't go back anyway, would you? You wouldn't be able to stand being in the same home that destroyed you."

Helena had a stoic look on her face while everyone shot Alex odd looks. Alex flushed a bit under the attention, feeling that he had blurted out his words without thinking.

"Sounds like you're speaking from experience," she said gently.

Alex coughed awkwardly, wanting to flee from the situation. "You could say that." He could feel Micheal's sympathetic gaze, and the sharp eyes of his father on him. It made him flush even more as he peeked a look at his friends. Only Tucker's eyes were traveling across the floor, politely ignoring the graceless statement from Alex.

Dakota gave him a sad smile. "I second that statement. It's why I left my old kingdom and went to Ruddox. So don't feel weird."

Alex bobbed his head, grateful for her words to distract and divert everyone's attention to her and away from him.

Katelyn abruptly stood up, her chair screeching against the floor. "Alright, everyone out or go to the basement. I have lord business to attend to and no, you may not listen in. Go."

Outstretching her arm fully, she pointed to the door.

A few of the Guardians started to protest her instructions, but by Paxton's reaffirmation that Katelyn had her own responsibilities, they stopped.

Alex shuffled out of the house, and he was soon standing outside with Micheal, Tucker, and Dakota.

"She kicked us out real quick," Dakota muttered, rubbing her thumb over her right eyebrow. "What's next on the list?"

Tucker put his head to the side. "We could just walk around, but we can't go far or we'll run into the shield. Unless your lord doesn't want you gone long, Dakota."

She raised an eyebrow with a smirk. "As long as I'm not lazy, Lord Ophelia doesn't care what I do. I personally wouldn't consider walking to be a lazy act. Got anything fun to do here?"

Tucker snorted. "In Phoenix? No, not really. Unless you consider farming fun. You've got the bay and ocean close by, but that's it. Walking just seems like the best idea, that way no one can yell at us for causing problems."

Alex laughed. "People do that?" He couldn't imagine the reasoning behind Tucker's statement. Everyone was so nice in the village.

Tucker nodded. "Mostly just the other guards annoying me. I would like to avoid that at all costs because then they tell my brother that I'm messing around. They're just joking, but I'd still like to stay clear of them."

Dakota kicked a rock with her boot, beginning to walk slowly and aimlessly. Alex and the two others quickened their steps to catch up with her.

"Most of the guards in Ruddox are jerks, so I don't really talk to them," Dakota said.

Micheal nudged her shoulder. "Why?"

The girl shrugged. "I've tried to bond with them, but they get on my case a lot. They say they're trying to help me, but I think they don't trust me to handle myself. I don't want to say it's because I'm a girl, but that's what it seems like. They're all decent enough, it's just little things."

Alex grimaced. He couldn't say that he had been in that position before, but he still had sympathy for her. "That doesn't sound fun. Is that why your lord sent you to make friends with people from Phoenix?"

Dakota's tan skin developed a blush, creeping up her neck to her cheeks. "Yes. And you seemed nice from what I saw."

Teasingly, he smiled at her and chuckled. "Were you spying on us, Dakota?" He put an arm around her shoulders

Her eyes widened, and she shook her head rapidly. "I did not say that." She hit his arm off as he laughed once more.

"Well, if it means anything, I think you're nice too," Alex said. Dakota ducked her head, but he caught the sight of a grin.

The group ended up on the path that led to the water, and Alex didn't mind. He liked being close to water. Micheal was walking in front of Tucker, and Alex could see how he was meticulously moving his feet a certain way to shoot sand up from the ground and behind him, the grains landing on Tucker's leather boots.

"If you kick sand up on me one more time, Micheal, I swear I will hurt you with no mercy," Tucker threatened.

Micheal craned his neck to stare at Tucker over his

shoulder and squinted at him. "Huh?"

Tucker scoffed and kicked sand at Micheal in retaliation. "Don't play dumb with me."

Micheal assessed the sand on his shoes with a newfound expression of offense. "I don't know what you're talking about."

Alex clicked his tongue in disapproval. "If you had Pinocchio's nose, it'd be growing right about now." Tucker and Dakota scrutinized them, confused. Alex had forgotten for the umptieth time that their realm did not have the same forms of entertainment as his and Micheal's. "It's an old fairytale."

Dakota closed her eyes and shook her head to clear her thoughts and then opened them again. "Good to know, I guess?"

The quartet sat on the sand right before the dock. Alex was grateful for his long jeans, hating the feeling of sand on his skin.

"How are the magic lessons going?" Tucker asked out of the blue, a smirk forming.

Alex raked his nails through his hair and blew a long exhale. "Not great. It's hard."

Micheal shrugged, grimacing. "Same. Cobalt is a tough man to please. Ryder's nice, but he's quiet."

"I just suck at controlling my magic," said Alex dejectedly. "Which is not a good thing."

Tucker's grin of satisfaction transformed into one that was more gentle. He pressed his hands behind himself, his palms digging into the sand. "I don't really remember Sabine training me with my powers, but I do recall that it was difficult. It's a bit of a blur."

Dakota waved her hands through the air, a jerky movement that got everybody to stop talking. "All three of you have magic?" Her eyes were wide.

Alex nodded, looking at the others as he explained. "Yes.

Tucker has protective powers, Micheal has mainly protective but also elemental, and I have mental. Why do you ask?"

She maintained eye contact with him and cleared her throat. "Nothing. Just never had friends that have magic."

Alex had to give it to her; she was a decent liar. But she wasn't good enough. Alex had been lying for far too long in his life to not miss the signs from their new friend. The way she cleared her throat, how she stared straight at him to show innocence, and he had seen her fingers twitching, urging to fidget, but she couldn't find anything. He chose not to say anything.

He had secrets of his own. A hypocrite, is what he would be if he ratted her out.

Micheal was staring off into the distance of the small bay, distracted. "Why are the terms powers and magic interchangeable here?"

Alex rolled his eyes fondly. "Because they just are. Just like Katleyn is 'lord' and not 'lady'. Right?"

Tucker nodded. "They mean the same thing. Magic is typically used in this kingdom, but it doesn't matter. Alex is right."

Dakota took a knife from her left calf-high boot and flipped it in the air before catching the hilt in the palm of her hand. She tossed it forward, and the blade of the dagger hit the wood of the supports of the dock. It rattled back and forth as Alex stared at it.

"Was that necessary?" he asked.

She smiled, showing her teeth. "Nope but it's fun."

Micheal ripped it out of the wood, studying it. He moved his hand up and down with the knife in his palm to test the weight. "It's heavier than I thought it would be." He sounded almost disappointed.

Chuckling in shock, Alex held a hand up, facing the inside of his hand to the sky in exasperation. "It's *metal*,

Micheal. I don't know what you expected. My dagger has a decent amount of weight, but it's still light."

Micheal scoffed. "Don't talk to me like I'm a child. How was I supposed to know?"

"Logic maybe?" He shrugged. "You do have a brain, don't you?"

"Well, excuse me, Mr. Academically Inclined," Micheal sneered at him. He began to sulk and started carving something into the wood with the dagger. After a moment he pulled away, brushing his fingers over whatever he had left behind.

Alex lifted his chin. "What'd you do?"

"Just marked my initials," said Micheal. Alex scooted over and he did see the letters MB engraved on the dock. "Figured we could leave something behind," the brunet continued.

Alex nibbled on his lip in thought before plucking Dakota's weapon from his hands. He held it in a backward grip and started dragging the tip through the dry lumber.

He formed the A with little difficulty. As he went to carve the O, he quickly realized he would have trouble making a perfect circle so he made it boxy. He stared triumphantly at his masterpiece, and he changed his hand position so his fingers were holding the cold blade with the handle stretched out to the Phoenix guard. Tucker raised an eyebrow.

Alex straightened his arm out even further. "Come on, we'll be the magic trio with Dakota being an honorary member if she so wishes to be."

Tucker sighed heavily but grasped the offered tool. He moved closer, kicking sand on Micheal in the process. Micheal sputtered. Tucker and Alex shared a cruel and delighted smile.

Soon, Tucker was done, and Alex looked over the letters but realized it was different lettering than he expected. It was in Standard.

"I never asked," Alex began, hands digging into the sand, "what is your last name, Tuck? Because I can't read that."

"Lennox," Tucker said. "What's yours and Micheal's?"

"Mine's O'Connor and his is Barnes. Why?" he asked.

Tucker started writing again but underneath Alex and Micheal's initials. When he pulled away, he handed the knife back to Alex.

"I put your initials in our language," the guard explained.

Alex moved to kneel in the sand and returned the favor, putting TL into the wood. He brushed any stray pieces of wood off of the support beam. He gave the sharp weapon back to Dakota.

"How does Standard work?" Alex asked Tucker.

"There are twenty-six letters in our alphabet. We take the letters to form words. I don't know how else to explain it." Tucker shrugged. "From what I can tell your language is similar to ours since we can understand each other."

Alex nodded. "It would seem so. Ours is like how you explained Standard, but our letters look different. I think that's the only thing."

Tucker smoothed out a patch of sand in front of him with his hand. "Let's test it. Tell me the number of each letter in your name. Like the first letter is the fourth letter in the alphabet. And then I'll say the letter in Standard to see if they match up. A little experiment."

Alex said the alphabet in his head, only going with his nickname and not "Alexander" which would take too long for him. "First, twelfth, fifth, and twenty-fourth."

Tucker took a minute to write down what he needed and looked it over with scrutiny in his eyes. "A-L-E-X? That's how we spelled your name here."

Alex nodded. "That's how I spell it. Seems like the

letters are indeed the same, just written differently."

Dakota squinted at the two of them. "Couldn't you just sound it out? Was it really necessary to write it out? That's how I would spell his name in Standard. Both languages only have twenty-six letters and we say the same words. The characters are just different. It should not be this hard."

Tucker shushed her, putting a hand up. "Let us have our fun, Dakota." The girl threw her hands up.

"My name is weird in our realm," Micheal blurted out. "Two letters are switched around."

Dakota glanced up at the sky in thought. "Well, now that Tucker and Alex came to the *quick* conclusion that our alphabets are the same, I can tell you that we typically spell it M-I-C-H-E-A-L."

Alex was taken aback by shock. He had not expected Dakota to give the exact spelling of Micheal's name. Everywhere in their realm, people spelled it with the A and the E flipped. He took a gander at his friend and Alex saw the same surprise in Micheal's green eyes.

"That's how I spell it but no one else does. That's the norm here?" Micheal asked, words fast.

Tucker nodded slowly, looking a little concerned about the speed of Micheal's speech.

Alex had a thought come to him. He recollected that Paxton was the one to name him. His name had been his own since the moment he was born. Who said the same couldn't be said for Lloyd naming Micheal?

"Think about it, Micheal. You said that your parents spelled your name weirdly on purpose, but it's supposed to be pronounced differently. Lloyd must've named you, and your parents just didn't change it when they adopted you. That's why you've always been confused about your name."

The sound of his father's name made Micheal stare out into the distance. Alex winced to himself, knowing that he shouldn't have brought it up.

Dakota and Tucker picked up on the tense change in the air because Tucker's eyes were dancing back and forth between the two, trying to have a silent conversation with Alex. Alex stared at the sand. He didn't know what to say to Micheal so he stayed silent.

No one broke the silence, much to Alex's dismay. He had hoped that Micheal would be more open to talking about his unique situation with his newly-revealed adoptive parents and Lloyd but for the first time in his life, Micheal wasn't open to talking.

Footsteps sounded softly in the sand, nearly silent. A Phoenix guard approached them, his face grave. Tucker lifted his chin as his comrade.

"Is something wrong?" Tucker inquired.

The man nodded. "Dark Knights have been spotted by the scouts. You and Dakota are being ordered to patrol the perimeter."

Alex tried to regulate his emotions but he couldn't pause the fear coursing through his body.

Chapter 18

Alex hiked side by side with Dakota, who was sticking close to his right side. They were patrolling the perimeter of the village barrier, looking for any signs of Dark Knights or Lloyd. Katelyn and Paxton had specifically instructed Alex to stay far away from the barrier, but Alex wasn't about to let Dakota go on her own regardless if the others would be mad.

Ever since the sign of Dark Knights two days ago, nothing had happened. It had put everyone on edge.

He trained his eyes on the forest to their right. The protective shield had just reached a foot or two past the beginning of the tree line. The birds that normally perched high in the trees throughout the day had disappeared.

"It's quiet today," Alex said to her halfway through their walk. "Nature has seemed to disappear from Phoenix."

Dakota hummed. She had pulled her long hair back into an elaborate braid, and it whipped around when she turned her head to the woods. "Your assumption would be correct. It's almost *too* quiet."

Alex nudged her. "I didn't peg you for being a pessimist." Within the days of getting to know her, Dakota was an optimist at heart, so her suggesting that danger was near them was out of character.

Dakota shoved him. "Oh, you—"

A branch cracked, the sound cascading through the air. Alex was startled, and in a flash, Dakota nocked an arrow on her bow and drew the string back to her chin. Her hands were steady. Another snap came, and then another after that in closer proximity. Alex bared his dagger, holding it in a defensive stance in front of him.

A shadow rippled on the ground, back and forth between trees. Like a game.

"They're toying with us," Alex whispered.

A figure stepped forward from behind one of the large trees with dark hair and green eyes.

"You *are* smart, Alexander." Lloyd drawled in a bored voice. His eyes were gleaming with berserk excitement.

Alex gritted his teeth and shifted to stand partially in front of Dakota.

"Go tell Katelyn we have a guest," he told her in a hushed tone, his eyes never leaving Lloyd's form. The last thing he wanted to do was to turn his back to the man staring at him.

Dakota reluctantly and slowly lowered her bow, glaring at Lloyd. Alex pushed her shoulder desperately, willing her to move faster. He had no idea if the barrier would do anything against the onslaught of magic Lloyd could use. She began to run.

"How cute," Lloyd said with a cynical smile. He took a labored step forward, his grin never dropping. Alex couldn't help but take a half-step back. Lloyd stopped his advance to chuckle, a low tone that slithered up his spine like a snake preparing to inject its venom in his veins.

"Oh, little Alexander. Are you afraid? You never used to be afraid of me when you were little," Lloyd continued to talk, a false pout pulling at his lips.

"You don't know me," said Alex, quiet but firm. He wasn't going to let the monster in front of him try to manipulate him.

The Shadow King waved a finger, shortening the distance between him and Alex. "I do. I knew you for many years after Paxton had you. You were never scared of me or the other Guardians, and now you are? Just because Katrina and your father told you that you should be?"

Alex shook his head. "I'm old enough to make my own decisions regardless of what I've been told. You sent Dark Knights to try and kill us and my friends." He stood up directly to the shield, close enough that his breath could touch the barrier. He could see the visible but faint lines of magic.

"Who said I tried to kill you?" Lloyd asked, hands folded neatly in front of him. "Hasn't it crossed your mind that I just wanted to see my son?"

He shut his eyes in frustration. "You wanted to use us to get Katelyn to the Inferno Realm. You wanted to take my friends' powers to free yourself. I also saw what you did to Max and Laurence."

Lloyd broke out into harsh laughter, making Alex feel even more uneasy. He leaned over to press his hand against his knees. Alex was beginning to see why Micheal concluded that the king was not right in the head.

Once the Shadow King recovered from his fit of maniacal laughter, he pursed his lips to give Alex a pitiful gaze. "So you're the one that let them out. I'm assuming you had help from someone because you could not break those bars yourself. It was that young guard, wasn't it? Tucker. But, by the gods, you are more naive than I thought —"

"What's that supposed to mean?" Alex interrupted loudly.

"I'll let you figure that one out for yourself if you live to tell the tale to another soul."

Alex narrowed his eyes, feeling caught off guard. He knew Lloyd was very powerful. He had attacked the Glade, hundreds of years ago, and he must've been the one to break the protection around it. He didn't know why Lloyd hadn't done the same to the one thing separating him and Alex.

"Why haven't you killed me yet?" he asked. "You've had long enough to do so."

"You're the reason I'm free, Alex," Lloyd said simply. "Consider it a thank you." Fire flickered in his eyes as he stared into Alex's soul. "However, I will not hesitate to kill you if you get in my way. So, if you would, please start running, or this will end with your rotting corpse six feet in the ground."

Alex frowned, not comprehending what Lloyd was saying until Dark Knights came out of nowhere like moths to a flame.

They surrounded the barrier as far as Alex could see, just staring at him. One of the knights stepped forward, hood covering his face. *Virgil.*

Lloyd's hands began to glow, his dark crimson powers spreading up the length of his forearms to his elbows. Alex cautiously moved backward, wanting to make sure no one was bluffing.

Lloyd put his hands on the barrier and pushed once. This action caused the shield to warp and oscillations were visible when Alex looked up. The Dark Knights started getting antsy, shifting their weight as they muttered amongst themselves.

Alex broke out into a run, the wind blocking his hearing. His heart sped up with both fear and physical exhaustion. He willed his legs to move faster. Out of the corner of his eye, what looked like the horizon was flashing between violet, jade green, and charcoal gray, spreading up to a single point in the sky. The shield was coming down.

He barreled past people and broke through a group staring up at the sky. Three tried to stop him to plead with him to tell them what was happening, but he couldn't.

He reached Katelyn's house and started banging on the door. He remembered that she rarely locked the door during the day and opened the door himself.

As he burst into the room, he caught sight of Rex, Jesse, Hunter, and Tucker standing to one side of the main room, weapons drawn at the sound of Alex violently opening the door. The Guardians were in another corner, staring worriedly at him. Paxton stepped forward.

"Alex?"

Before Alex even got a word out, the ground shook and everything was no longer fine.

Alex rushed to the window as did a few others. He squinted, straining to see what had caused the rumbling.

On the edge of the village, the Dark Knight mob was gradually moving toward the village. But they stopped not too far from their position in the woods, just glaring into the village.

Alex's hands shook as he stumbled back from the window. "They're here." Everyone straightened up. "Where's Katelyn and Dakota?" he rasped out.

"Here, Alex."

He spun around and Katelyn and Dakota were standing close to the back door of the house, the door wide open. Katelyn gestured for everyone to step outside. Alex re-entered the outdoors, eyes whipping around. Cobalt's wolves slowly moved out from the shade of one of the houses, growling in the direction of the strange people.

People in the village were panicking, understanding the danger they were in. Most of them had gathered in front of their lord's home in a mass, hoping she would tell them what to do; others fled in different directions.

Gwenivere was among the mass at Katelyn's front door, her eyes wide with terror. She went to Alex's side and attached her arms around his waist.

"All of those who are not warriors, run into the forest! Keep running and don't stop!" Katelyn yelled. The villagers of Phoenix were very good at following that order, sprinting for the tree line that didn't contain any enemies that would kill them. The protective Guardian pointed to the trees, making eye contact with two white wolves that were closest to her.

"Go protect them. Lead them somewhere safe, anywhere."

The wolves followed her order. They bounded into the forest, just blurring streaks of color.

Gwenivere tugged on his shirt. He went down on his knees and tried to push her away gently. "Gwen, you have to run," he told her, holding her shoulders.

Tears fell from her eyes and her lip trembled. She threw her arms around his neck. He hugged her back but tilted his head to observe the Dark Knights who were still at a standstill hundreds of feet away.

The girl pulled away. "Be careful. Don't die, please?"

Alex laughed sadly. "I'll try not to."

"Gwenivere!" a woman screamed. Gwen turned her head and took off running toward the woman. They had the same red hair and blue eyes. Alex knew she would be safe with her mother.

Alex and Micheal observed the allies' soldiers and guards that had meshed with Phoenix's. They had all gathered, seeing the threat before them.

Lord Ophelia of Ruddox stood next to the other village and city leaders of Fifan, Henix, and Silverbend. It was a large number of soldiers, but it might not be enough to defeat the king and his army combined.

"This is actually happening. Why did he take so long to

attack, and why is he just standing there?" he asked, dumbfounded.

"Mind games most likely. Lloyd was always good at that," Cobalt tensely answered.

"What do we do? Sure, we have attack plans but..." Alex asked and trailed off, voice trembling with panic.

Paxton tightened his grip on his sword. "We kill him."

The other Guardians shot weird and concerned looks at Paxton.

Amethyst played with her ring once again as she spoke, "Pax, there's no going back if we do that."

Paxton turned to her, face blank. "Lloyd is too far gone. He's as good as dead."

Elizabeth blew a stray strand of dirty blonde hair out of her eyes. "Well, I agree with Paxton. This has to end one way or another. It's us or Lloyd. I, for one, would like to live."

"We need every magic user we have to beat him or else we won't stand a chance. We didn't get a chance to discuss that actual plan for the death of the king with magic users." Ryder pointed out.

"Ryder has a point," Helena agreed. "All magic users step forward."

Twenty people besides the Guardians, Tucker, Sabine, Alex, and Micheal, stepped forward. Paxton and Cobalt conversed quietly, hand movements getting slightly erratic. They came to a consensus about something and pulled away with grim looks.

"Spread out but stay as close to us as possible. We'll need to surround him and attack him all at once if our efforts begin to fail. He won't be able to fight all of us," Cobalt ordered. He turned to Sabine. "Please, tell us you have something up your sleeve."

The white-haired woman shakily smiled. "I've got something."

Helena lifted a hand and played with her fire magic; the flames crackled in her eyes as well. "Well, this should be fun. I've been waiting for the chance to punch him in the face." Her voice was filled with venom and a smirk was imprinted on her lips.

Alex's heart was in his throat as they marched down the hill that Katelyn's house was perched on, knowing he was about to stare death in the face once again.

Every step towards the opposing forces felt like a step closer to death.

Someone brushed knuckles with him. It was Hunter.

The guard had moved his shorter sword from its normal place on his back down to his hip with his longer weapon, probably for more convenient draw time. In one of his hands was the three-foot sword similar to the practice sword that Alex had been training with for the past few days.

Alex gave him a miserable look, knowing that his taking the sword would make it real. A beat went by and Hunter extended his arm out even more. Alex reluctantly wrapped his fingers around it and took it.

Hunter clapped him on the back, his smile not reaching his eyes. "Don't die," he repeated what Gwenivere had asked of him.

Alex tried to chuckle, but it sounded like he was choking on his fear. "Thanks, Hunter."

He looked at his best friend and wasn't shocked when he saw the terrified look on the boy's face, but he couldn't say anything to bring him comfort.

A tap on his shoulder startled him. His brain entered fight-or-flight and went to jab the person with his elbow when Paxton held his hands up as high as he could while holding an intimidating sword.

He must've slipped away from the others.

"God, you scared me," he said, pressing a hand to his chest.

"Alexander, listen to me very carefully." Paxton's voice was more stern than usual which made Alex worried.

"What is it?" A weary feeling filled him.

"If things go bad, I want you to take Micheal and leave our realm."

Alex glanced between his father and the Dark Knights that were coming closer into view with every step. "What? I'm not leaving everyone like this." He didn't know how to take his father's statement.

"Yes, you will," the man ordered. "I am not letting either of you two die. You *will* leave if it means you get to live. I refuse to let Lloyd take your lives from both of you."

Alex wanted to continue fighting with his father, but their time to speak was over. They were standing right in front of the Shadow King.

The armor he wore closely resembled his knights' armor, just darker if that was even possible. Certain cracks covered the armor, which was filled with the same purple and red color that glowed even in the sunlight. Alex hadn't noticed minutes before. Next to him stood Virgil with a sword in hand with his signature hood still covering his face.

"Hello, old friends," Lloyd greeted the Guardians, but his green eyes were fixed on Paxton and no one else.

"It's been many years since we were considered such a thing," Paxton commented, eyes never leaving him.

Lloyd smiled and slowly raised one hand to gesture to the group. "When has that ever changed?"

Paxton's lips pulled down into a sneer. "The moment you betrayed us," he growled.

"Betrayed you?" Lloyd asked as if surprised by the statement. He stared at them silently, only to laugh maniacally a second later. As he finished, he looked at them again and placed a hand over his heart. "As I recall, it was all of *you* who betrayed me! You turned against *me*; threw me away like I meant *nothing*."

"You did mean something to us once," Paxton protested.

Elizabeth stepped forward, face set in a determined expression. "It was because of what you were doing, Lloyd!" she shouted. "You were trying to take over the realm! Not just ours but all of them! We couldn't stand by and watch the realms fall into chaos!"

"I was trying to make things better!" Lloyd tried to explain, emerald eyes flashing with frustration. "I wanted us to have the power! Not the lords, the kings or queens, and not even the damn *gods* themselves! Just us! Imagine it!"

Paxton shook his head, hand tightening on his sword. "That's where you were wrong, Lloyd." Alex could see the tremors in his hands "It was never our responsibility to lead. We are protectors. If you give power to the wrong person, they use it to their own advantage and delusions. If we were to lead, we would end up as tyrants and that's exactly what you are."

"Don't lecture me, Paxton." Lloyd sneered, gesturing to him with his sword. "You're no saint either. You dragged two teenagers into our lives, putting them in danger from the moment we met them."

When Amethyst and Katelyn simultaneously raised their chins at his words, Alex knew Lloyd wasn't talking about him and Micheal.

"Says the man that kidnapped a girl for hundreds of years," Paxton shot back at him.

Lloyd cocked his head to the side. "You'd do well to remember, Pax, that *I* was the one to tell you how valuable Amethyst was, but you didn't want to listen to me. So technically it's your fault that I took her. You enabled my ability to take her. I locked all of you away and the opportunity was right there. I tried to take her *precious* sister as well, but of course, Katelyn, ever the intelligent one, slipped from my fingers. If you hadn't brought them into our lives, she never would've been in that position in the first place."

Alex felt very uncomfortable, feeling that he was listening to a private conversation he had no business knowing, even though he knew about most of the bad blood between the group. He also had the sudden urge to punch the man in the face. The result would've been satisfying but would've ended in a painful death.

Amethyst's hands started glowing as well as her eyes. "You sick, ruthless"

"Tell me I'm wrong, Amethyst," Lloyd interrupted, a sinister grin on his face. "Deny the fact that if Paxton hadn't brought you and Katelyn to the Glade, you would have been in the Inferno Realm for hundreds of years."

Next to Paxton, Cobalt was getting fidgety with his multitude of weapons attached to his armor. "Can we skip the heart-to-heart and kill him already?" the protective user asked.

"Always the instigator. Never thinking with your head; just jumping at the first chance to kill something that moves." Lloyd dug into him.

There was a sound of an object whizzing through the air, and a Dark Knight twitched and jerked. He collapsed to the ground with an arrow embedded in the gaps of their armor, blood slowly dripping out of the wound.

Everything instantly erupted into violent, confusing, and absolutely destructive chaos.

As the battle began, Alex turned around to find who had fired the arrow, and it ended up being Dakota, her bow still raised as she fired another shot. He stared at her. She locked eyes with him and gave a shrug, and she flipped a grown man over her shoulder.

"What? No one else was going to."

Alex would've laughed if he wasn't so pumped full of adrenaline and terror.

Swords clashed. Magic sent enemies flying. Screams flooded the air. It was like another nightmare that Alex couldn't escape.

He ducked underneath an arrow that was coming toward his head. A Dark Knight tackled him to the ground. The grass wasn't soft at all. It knocked all the air out of his lungs.

Alex desperately started to kick the man and grappled with him. He grunted as a foot cracked him in the spine, making his lungs struggle for air for a second time.

You have a sword. Use it, genius.

Overtaken by rage, Alex frantically slashed his sword at him, and soon the man went limp. He scrambled to his feet and leveled his sword. Another man closing in on him growled like an animal at him, but it was cut off by another sword stabbing him from behind. He fell to the ground and choked on his own blood. From behind the dead man stood Cobalt. Cobalt gave him a wolfish smile and then left to fight off more knights.

Alex huffed softly, then he turned and ran to join Tucker, Micheal, and Dakota toward the back of the fight. He ducked around enemies, doing his best to not use his sword or his powers to the extent that was possible in the middle of chaos. He tried to keep mental tabs on friends but bodies were starting to blur and mix together.

"Catapult!" One of the allied soldiers shouted, pointing up at the sky.

Alex let out a string of curses as he ran for cover, blindly running. Tucker grabbed him out of nowhere and threw his hands up to form a shield. A light gray bubble formed around anyone near their position.

Tucker struggled with maintaining it, screwing his eyes

shut as the flaming mass hit the shield. He waited until it rolled off the magic bubble, and then he released it.

"Thanks, Tucker," Alex said, taking a breath of relief, but his heart stopped as he saw that Katelyn and Paxton were engaged in a skirmish with Dark Knights that were starting to overwhelm them.

Katelyn locked hilts with her sword in one hand while the other was shooting magic at as many Dark Knights as she could. Paxton was relying on mostly his sword. They were both losing ground. To make things worse, the catapult had just released another projectile.

Alex had no time to think. He just sprinted toward them.

"Alex!" Tucker screamed his name in worry, realizing what he was trying to do.

"Alexander!" Micheal called as well, using his full name once again.

The recklessness inside of him made him ignore his friends, charging toward the two that were in even more danger than they were aware of. Once he was close enough, he imagined the fiery ball of tar and rock being suspended in the air, just like the coin his father had trained him with. His hands adopted a glow, and his magic shifted inside of him. It rushed through his veins.

He tossed his hands in the air, and the rock stopped on a dime. Alex felt like his knees were going to buckle underneath him. With great effort, Alex tossed the rock to the side with his mind, and he promptly fell to his knees. His muscles screamed and burned, and he felt a migraine pressing at his temples. Why were his ears ringing?

He slowly pulled his eyes to survey the destruction around him. Bodies were hitting the ground dead faster than Alex had ever seen before. Screams rang through his skull as his hands gripped the grass as if it was his lifeline. It would be so easy to just let everything go and disappear into unconsciousness. Maybe Lloyd would make his death quick.

"Get up!" Someone shouted at him from far away, but he couldn't tell who. The clipped tone forced his body to follow the order that was yelled, but it got him nowhere.

It was overwhelming. His head was pounding, his vision was fluttering in and out. A cold object tapped him on the chin. Alex squinted up and gasped.

The King of the Inferno Realm was staring down at him with a dark look emanating from his eyes. Alex scrambled back, crawling backward on his hands, his vision spinning.

"I warned you, boy," Lloyd sneered, prowling toward him. "And now my eyes will be the last thing you ever see!"

With a grunt, he lifted an arm to slice Alex in half. Alex strained to lift anything around him to help protect him, but his fingers just fumbled around the grass. He held his arms up in the last attempt to protect himself.

The pain never came. Alex slowly opened his eyes and found that Lloyd's sword was stopped by another blade crossing it perpendicularly.

"Do not touch him," Paxton stated calmly. The king bared his teeth at his old friend and attacked him in a fit of fury. Paxton forced Lloyd to back away by shoving all his weight with his sword against Lloyd's.

Alex's head was spinning so much that he couldn't differentiate who was a Dark Knight and who was a friend of his.

A person in a dark shirt and black jeans wasn't too far away from him. It took him a while to recognize the clothing, but when he recognized that person as Micheal, he stood up and stumbled over to him. He soundlessly gripped Micheal's arm to steady himself. Micheal's brows pinched.

"What's wrong with him?" a voice asked.

Another voice spoke, "It's his powers. He used too much at one time, and he doesn't fully understand his limits."

He was pushed to be back-to-back with someone. A sword was pressed to his hand, and he recognized the grip as his sword. He gripped it more tightly, feeling the rough fabric of the hilt under his hand. He was forced to walk a farther distance away, the sounds of the battle getting fainter. Micheal was leading him to the back end of the fight.

"When I tell you to swing, swing," Micheal spoke to him through the fog.

Alex panted a few times and couldn't give a verbal answer, but he did nod. His blurry vision was disappearing gradually, but it wasn't fast enough for Alex's impatience or anticipation.

"Incoming Alex," was the warning he received.

Something hit his sword, and he tightened all the muscles in his arm to make sure he kept a hold of his weapon. He went on the defense, blocking blows and jabs through his still-blurry vision. He jumped back a few times, pushing Micheal forward, relying on his instincts to keep him alive.

He made contact with the person's flesh and didn't hesitate to strike for the knight's arm. His blade sunk into skin, going deep. Blood splashed on his hands and arms. He swung again and he watched as the knight's arm was almost completely severed. With one more hard hack, the dismembered arm fell to the ground and the man collapsed to the bloody soil, screaming. Alex put him out of his misery.

The rest of the battle was a blur for Alex. He had battled many knights and taken many beatings. He felt the stinging sensation in his superficial injuries and the blood dripping to the ground.

He had regained his strength from that burst of his powers, but he knew better than to use them unless he wanted to pass out in the middle of the battlefield. Regardless of if he still felt drained of energy, his fight-or-flight instincts kept him afloat.

Three sharp whistles rang from nearby. Alex shifted toward the direction of origin and saw Cobalt had done the whistling.

"I think he wants us closer. Let's go," Alex ordered Micheal and Tucker who were around him.

The trio dashed over to the Guardian, dodging and sliding out of the way of arrows or swords or flying projectiles.

"We're getting crushed out here," Tucker announced as he expertly flipped a man onto his back and stuck his sword into his chest.

"It's now or never," the older man announced. "Katelyn and Amethyst are pinned down. Helena is taking on Lloyd's second-in-command with Elizabeth. Paxton and Ryder are doing their best to handle the king, but they're losing ground."

Just as he finished that thought, Lloyd growled, waving his hand. Ryder was grabbed by an invisible force and was thrown roughly forty feet from his original position. Cobalt flicked his fingers. Ryder didn't make contact with the ground as a dark gray hue shielded him from the impact.

He blinked and then looked up at his friend. "Thanks."

Cobalt pursed his lips disapprovingly. "Mhm, just don't get thrown again."

Ryder rolled his eyes.

Up ahead Alex saw that Paxton had no choice but to engage Lloyd head-on alone. *Reckless*, Alex thought but quickly dismissed it because that was exactly what he did earlier.

The group started migrating over to the king. Alex saw other magic users doing the same, giving them a minuscule nod of confirmation. Lloyd and Paxton were circling each other, their weapons missing from their hands. Lloyd chuckled.

"You can't win, Paxton! I know you too well."

The other man didn't say anything, just glaring at him. The dark mental user slowly moved his fingers, making his powers dance on his fingertips, blood-red like Micheal's.

"I know you, Pax, whether you want to admit it or not." His voice was filled with venom.

A string of red shot out and hit Paxton. Alex's heart jumped thinking his father was going to meet his end, but he just winced, never falling.

"You had so many chances to kill me, but you just couldn't do it." Lloyd was taunting him now, that much was obvious.

Paxton's eyes flashed an aqua blue, and his hands clenched. "I have no issue killing you now." His hand twisted, and a ball of energy shot out to meet Lloyd's.

Lloyd returned it with a blow of his own and Paxton was forced to go down on one knee to regain his strength.

Alex got close to his father while fighting his own battles and out of the corner of his eye, he saw Sabine creeping up behind her father with something gleaming in her hand. It was one of her daggers; the tip covered in some kind of viscous substance that slowly trailed down the face of the sharp blade. Without warning, she swiped in a downward arch and embedded the blade in her father's shoulder, aiming for the exposed flesh.

Lloyd screamed in pain and reacted rather violently, now on the defensive. He lashed his hands around, desperately trying to protect himself and to fend Sabine off. However, his magic never sparked to life in his hands.

Lloyd tried again, then stepped back and stared at his hands. He flexed his fingers in a pitiful attempt to regain strength. It didn't work. His powers were no longer flowing through his hands.

"His powers are weakened!" Sabine shouted, meeting eyes with Alex.

The king turned to his wayward daughter, enraged by her newest betrayal.

"Ancient witch magic," Lloyd hissed, seething with anger. "Really, Sabine?" He didn't pay any mind to the steel sticking out of his shoulder. "Of course, my daughter, ever the scholar she is, is still planning to thwart me."

Sabine fled as he started toward her. Paxton got into his space, glaring at Lloyd. Lloyd met his gaze steadily as he extracted the blade from his shoulder. He flipped it over his fingers with precision.

"Just because I don't have my magic doesn't mean I can't kill you." With that, Lloyd launched forward, initiating hand-to-hand combat with Paxton. He continued to fight with Paxton with his bare hands, but the non-weakened mental Guardian had the upper hand and kept pushing Lloyd back. The dagger was lost to the grass.

Tucker appeared out of nowhere and pulled Alex out of the line of fire. The other Guardians were gathering around, all looking battered but ready for another rematch with their perennial archenemy.

"Tell me, Paxton," Lloyd requested as he landed a lucky punch on the warrior's ribs, "did you ever care?" Paxton didn't answer him. "Was everything you said to me a lie?! *Was it?!*"

Alex watched with a tense gaze as Lloyd and Paxton continued to exchange blows.

"Answer me!" Lloyd screamed at him.

"We were your family, and you threw it away Lloyd!" Paxton screamed, fed up with fighting without words. "I meant everything! Everything I said to you was true! That you weren't a monster! Just because you became one doesn't mean I wasn't telling the truth!

"You plotted against me! You betrayed me! All of you

did!" The king shouted back. He looked Paxton dead in the eye, green eyes so cold and promised violence. "You wanted to kill me from the moment you met me."

Alex killed another adversary and stared at the two warriors, not understanding what he was talking about.

Paxton had tears in the corners of his eyes, never allowing them to fall. "You know that's not true. You plotted against humanity! I couldn't stand by and watch you kill everyone unless they groveled at your feet!"

Lloyd gave a yell of frustration. "You took my son away from me." He launched arms with Paxton and they began to grapple.

Paxton released an audible sound of aggravation as well, leveling his knee in Lloyd's side, effectively forcing him to stumble and release him. He blocked a punch once Lloyd recovered.

"Can you tell me you wouldn't have used him for your twisted plans?" the Guardian asked.

Lloyd raised his eyebrows in a challenging way, sweeping a leg out. "Correct me if I'm wrong, but *you* bargained *your own son—*"

Alex gritted his teeth together and shot a ball of his magic at the king's back, making him stumble. "I don't blame him. You're a monster." He shouldn't have jumped into the fight, but he did anyway.

"Stay out of this boy! You know *nothing* of the things your father has done." It was blatant that he was losing his patience with the boy.

Alex tossed his hands in the air to block a blow of a Dark Knight. "At least he isn't trying to kill everyone! The only person who has done that is you!"

Paxton hunched over to grasp Sabine's dagger from the grass and stabbed Lloyd again, this time in the front of his shoulder, near his chest, between his armor and leather suit. Lloyd roared in pain, one of his tan hands with split knuckles surging up to jab at Paxton's throat. Paxton stumbled back.

In a fit of fury, the king ripped the knife out of his body. He flipped the knife in his hand, the steel patterns on the handle glinting in the sunlight, and chucked it at Alex. The boy saw the desperate attempt to end his life coming and sidestepped out of the way.

Micheal came to his side, hands alit with fiery red magic. The other wielders of magic came around inconspicuously as possible. Cobalt's signal had been given.

No one moved in their radius of the battle, vigilante to any schemes or secret maneuvers.

Lloyd held his hands out to the side, staring at Micheal for a long time."Are you really going to help kill me, Micheal? Your own father?"

Micheal didn't speak. His father continued to look at him. And that's when Lloyd struck.

He lunged at Paxton, a dagger shining in his hand that had been hidden away in his armor. Paxton tried to parry around him, but Lloyd feinted, catching him off guard. The knife plunged into the weak spot of his armor on his side.

Alex's heart crashed and thump in his ribcage as his father sunk to the ground. He tackled Lloyd, only making him budge away from his father. The Shadow King's armor was tough as he slammed into him. He faced Lloyd as Paxton tried to gather his strength where he lay on the ground.

Regaining strength and vigor, the Dark Knights launched more violent attacks, drawing the magic users away, including the Guardians. Alex was alone...so alone.

Lloyd pitched forward with the intent to kill Alex. Alex held his hands up, zeroing in on the blade curving toward his neck. He rolled his fingers, using his magic to stop Lloyd's attack. One of Lloyd's hands was frozen in Alex's magic. This, unfortunately, left Alex open for an attack which is exactly what he did.

A punch found its way into his ribs. Alex dropped one hand to protect his chest in vain, gasping for breath. Willing his magic to spread, Lloyd's whole arm became immobilized.

A kick connected with his shin, making his leg buckle but he fought to stay standing.

No matter how many times he was hit, punched, and kicked he wouldn't stop until Paxton was safe. But his magic was beginning to fail and Paxton's still form remained on the ground. Lloyd was pressing the weapon closer to him with a smirk.

"You're out of tricks, young one." He was putting all his strength into driving the knife into him. His magic slammed into Alex.

A terrible pain erupted in Alex's head, nearly making him crumble to the ground. He yelled in frustration. Just as he thought his magic had been depleted, an odd sound of armor bending and breaking took Alex's focus. He looked down just in time to see the tip of a sword was sticking out from Lloyd's stomach, crippling the armor.

Lloyd's eyes widened in shock, trembling hands going to the gushing blood. Crimson blood pooled in his mouth, trailing past his lips.

The sword was ripped out, causing more blood to flow and flood the ground. Alex released Lloyd in surprise.

The man gave a sound of pain and weakly turned around. Alex stepped to see who incapacitated the Shadow King. He was expecting Cobalt or Ryder or even Katelyn but no.

It was Micheal. Micheal who looked like he wanted to drive that sword through his own chest now, eyes blown with shock.

Instead of shouting curses and yelling as he did with Sabine, Lloyd just looked at him, tilting his head, eyes intensely staring at Micheal. Blood slipped between his fingers, his armored chest beginning to tremble.

"Micheal, keep him down!" Cobalt called to him from thirty feet away as the king was straightening up once more. Cobalt was too occupied fighting knights to do so himself, but Lloyd's forces were rapidly depleting.

Alex doubted the Shadow King was going to attack again even with his attempts of standing up. He was swaying too much.

Micheal had a blank look in his light eyes. The sword trembled in his hand before it slipped out of his grasp. He didn't move an inch to follow Cobalt's order, hands trembling.

Ryder approached him and directed his powers at Lloyd. His powers made rope-like bonds around Lloyd's entire body, surrounding him. The Shadow King was still putting up a battle even as he was losing blood fast. He took a feeble step.

"Micheal." Ryder's voice raised in pitch, pushing him to help, stepping as close to Lloyd as possible without the risk of getting his ankles taken out. Ryder strained his arms to combat Lloyd's strength.

Micheal only raised a hand, red magic contrasting with Ryder's jade green.

In his weakened state and with the added magic from his son, Lloyd was forced to his knees. He tried to fight the magic off, but he kept collapsing back to the ground. He stared up at Micheal, unable to fight all the energy being shot at him. Alex wanted to stab him as he saw it. He was striving to non-verbally manipulate Micheal into saving him.

Alex caught Micheal's gaze and silently pleaded with him to go through with it. They both understood that this was going to kill his father, but Alex couldn't let him continue to threaten humankind. He just hoped Micheal's rampted thoughts were a mirror of Alex's.

Alex kept his guard up while he helped his father stand. Paxton had a hand against his wound, but he was making his way to his feet with assistance from Alex. Lloyd's dagger had landed in a vital place.

Lloyd went limp on the ground, glaring up at the other Guardian.

Ryder slowly lowered his hands, magic disappearing. Lloyd struggled one last time to push himself up but his arms collapsed again. Whatever Sabine had stabbed him with was still affecting him along with the immense amount of magic that was just blasted at him and the wound inflicted by Micheal.

Alex stepped up with Paxton, waiting to see what he would do. To him, it didn't seem like the King of the Inferno Realm was going anywhere.

Cobalt sidestepped toward Paxton, blood splattered on his face and armor. "The wound is fatal, but I don't want to give him or Virgil a chance to do something funny while we wait for him to die." Cobalt held out Paxton's sword to him. "Do it. Or I will."

Paxton stayed deathly still for a beat. His fingers nudged against Cobalt's as he took the hilt of the sword. He stepped up to his former friend and stared at the man, then his weapon.

"Last chance to kill me. *Relish* in it," the weak king muttered, maneuvering himself onto his knees. "Or will you give that honor to my son?"

"I'm not going to make your son the murderer of his own father." Paxton was clear with his words.

Alex would've killed Lloyd himself as well before he would put Micheal into that position.

Paxton leveled the blade to Lloyd's chest, placing it in a vulnerable place. He tightly closed his eyes as he drove the tip of his sword into Lloyd's chest. The squelching sounds of the sword entering his body and the man's screams of pain were enough to turn anyone's stomach.

Alex refused to look at the blood streaking the end of the sword poking from the other side of the man's chest, and he especially didn't look when his father ripped his sword out.

Lloyd ultimately crumbled to the ground, revealing the devastated, broken look on Paxton's face. At his feet, Lloyd wheezed, limp, and his breathing shallow. He pressed a futile hand to the gaping wound in his chest.

None of the Dark Knights around even bothered to try and save their master, just stationary with shock.

"Fall back!" Virgil shouted to his men, only just noticing the fate of his master. Many did not bother to stop them as they ran for the hills, however a few swords clashed until the battlefield only held Phoenix and allied soldiers.

Everyone stepped back except for Paxton, who continued to stare at Lloyd's dying form.

Micheal went down on his knees, covering his mouth with his hand, trembling as his empty eyes stared at his father. Alex rushed to him and put a shaking but supportive hand on the side of his shoulder.

Amethyst looked indifferently at Lloyd. Cobalt growled and took a step forward, seemingly ready to wring Lloyd's neck, but Amethyst stopped him. The young girl pointed to Paxton, silently telling Cobalt to let him deal with Lloyd.

Alex had a feeling Amethyst wasn't lying when she said that Paxton and Lloyd were close. His father needed a minute as Alex gathered up Micheal and directed him farther away. He couldn't help but keep his eyes on the scene in front of him.

Katelyn limped over with Elizabeth supporting her, both women sporting injuries. The dirty blonde woman had tears falling from her brilliant crystal blue eyes. Alex shot her a small smile and then redirected his attention to his father.

Paxton kneeled beside Lloyd and lifted his head gingerly, demonstrating kindness that Alex knew Lloyd didn't deserve.

Gasping for air, the Shadow King cracked a smirk. "So this is how it ends."

Paxton nodded once, and his eyes filled with tears. "You left me no choice," he whispered, gravely quiet and voice trembling. "I hope you know that. Please."

"You were always the hero in our story," Lloyd responded, his voice strangely not filled with anger.

Paxton held him tighter, not looking away until Lloyd's body went limp. Once it did, Paxton closed his own eyes and sucked in a breath. His limbs shook minutely. The other Guardians went down on their knees as well, heads dipping to their chests. It shouldn't have come to this even after they had hundreds of years of fighting and hating him. They did truly care for Lloyd. And now he was gone, and grief hung heavy in the air.

"Amethyst!" Someone screamed bloody murder. It jarred Alex out of his state of mind. Scrambling, his gaze found a stressed Tucker with tears streaming down his face and a person at his feet. Alex dashed toward him.

He skidded to a stop when he saw a familiar and wounded figure near his friend's now kneeling frame. There was a knife embedded in the person's abdomen. Alex recognized the knife itself, the familiar pattern of vines crawling against the silver metal. It was Sabine's knife that she had stabbed Lloyd with and that Lloyd had thrown at Alex. It had landed its mark, but it wasn't Alex. It was Lloyd's own daughter.

Sabine's white hair was dirtied up with soot and dirt, but the same braid crown still held up throughout the battle. Her chest was heaving with labored breathing as her hands and someone else's were putting pressure on her wound.

Her face was pinched in agony, a furrow in her brow. Ivory skin now pale as snow as the blood proceeded to flow.

Tucker was the one trying in vain to help her, but the crimson liquid was slipping fast through his fingers and Sabine's blouse.

"Alex, help!" he cried desperately to his friend, eyes wide with anxiety and fear.

Alex went down on his knees next to Tucker, Micheal on her other side. Alex quickly observed Sabine's wound, trying to find a way to stop the bleeding. He was about to turn to Hunter, Jesse, or *someone* for help, but a cold hand gripped him, making him jump. He looked back down, tears blurring his vision.

Sabine's shaking hands were the ones that covered his, and she shook her head slightly.

"Stop. It's no use," she whispered weakly, the words cracking in her throat.

Alex swallowed back tears. "I can't let you die," he whispered. He refused to let this happen. He'd been through enough pain in his life, and he wasn't going to allow Sabine's death to be marked on the list as well.

Sabine smiled despite everything, a warm action during such a tragedy. "Yes, you can. It's okay."

Micheal let a tear fall as he knelt on Sabine's other side. "Amethyst can help you."

Alex turned to the mentioned Guardian, just remembering she was a healer. "Do something," he commanded, trying to sound strong, but his voice broke.

The girl observed the daughter of Lloyd with regret deep in her brown eyes. "I cannot. She no longer has the will to live. There's...nothing I can do."

Tucker let out a whimper and turned away, not ready to see his friend die. His hands stirred with shakes on top of her abdomen. Rex knelt next to him and gently pulled him away. The boy tried to fight his brother, but Alex gave a gentle push to his back as well.

When Alex looked back, Micheal was holding both of his sister's hands, staring into her eyes.

She smiled up at him, the grin happy given the circumstance. "I'm glad I got to meet you," she whispered. "Even if it wasn't under better circumstances."

Micheal shook his head. "Sabine, I need you."

She continued to smile, unshed tears settling in her dark blue eyes. "It's okay. You have Alex. You never needed me. You'll do great things, Micheal."

Micheal shook his head desperately, knuckles white from his grip on her hands. She tried to squeeze back, a futile attempt.

"Promise me you'll be good," she breathed gently in a motherly tone. She had some humor in her smile, one last venture to bring her brother a bit of joy.

Micheal shut his eyes, swallowing to clear his throat. "I promise."

Sabine opened her mouth to utter a few more wounds but her voice was too fragile. Her hands clutched Micheal's once more with a final surge of strength. Soon her breathing gently stopped and her eyes fluttered closed. Her final, delicate breath brushed against Alex's skin.

A sob built up in his throat, but he shoved it down. But the tears couldn't be contained.

Tucker couldn't wrangle his emotions and let out a wounded and strangled cry, but no one moved to comfort him.

Sabine was dead. There was no bringing her back.

Micheal looked down at her pale, bloodied hands. "It's not fair," he whispered.

A raindrop landed on her pale hands, and then another, and more after that. The slight drizzle recreated the exact emotion Alex felt. Lloyd had been defeated, but at what cost? How many people had they lost?

The sound of long clothes ruffling pulled Alex's attention upward. He scrambled up when he saw who it was.

The gods were back and staring at the scene and destruction around them. Smoke billowed high in the air, bodies laid strewn across the battlefield, and blood tainted the ground as far as Alex could see. It was gruesome. But their faces were bored underneath their hoods.

Paxton lunged in front of Alex, blocking him from the gods with his broad frame. Cobalt wrestled Micheal away from Sabine and stood protectively in front of him as well. Micheal still tried to grasp for Sabine, but Cobalt's vice grip anchored Micheal behind the man.

From every corner of the chaotic setting, soldiers' faces expressed a jumble of confusion, wonder, and fear. But Alex and his close group of friends understood. The gods were present for a purpose known only to them.

Everyone didn't speak for a while. Finally, one of the women did.

"You have disobeyed many of our ancient laws, children." Her tone was sharp and disapproving.

Alex wanted to jump at the woman. They were the reason Sabine was dead. Their decisions had led to this. Alex tensed his muscles, ready to jump, but Paxton held him back. Alex bit his tongue, so he wouldn't get himself zapped out of existence by an angry god.

A different woman went down on her knees and stared at Sabine with motherly eyes. The other gods around her rolled their eyes.

"What are you doing? We must deal with Lloyd so no one can use his body," one of them said. A man that Alex recognized from the ruins, one that Katelyn had called Rudnos. "Virgil has slipped away, and I don't feel like dealing with him resurrecting Lloyd."

She glared at her comrade as she pushed her hood down

to reveal skin that was darker than Helena, but she had a similar style of tightly coiled hair. "Her life was taken by her father, a person she swore to destroy for humanity. Have a soul for once."

She dragged a slow hand over the girl's form, and her hands glowed. Sabine's body started to glow golden. The light reflected brightly, and Alex gasped in amazement.

Sabine's body hovered in the air, and she disappeared in a golden glow that reminded Alex of pixie dust. The material shot up into the sky, and the stars twinkled and sparkled even in the gloomy daylight.

"She will watch over all of you now." She gave a smile, which they guessed was a rarity for her.

With the impatience of small children, the gods stepped around Lloyd's body and ushered the woman to do the same. They whispered amongst themselves as Alex hugged Micheal gently and put a hand on Tucker's shoulder as well, whose eyes were locked where Sabine's body had previously lied.

Rudnos marched away from the goddess, head held high with dignity. He towered over Lloyd's mangled and lifeless form. Giving a sharp wave of his fingers, the smell of fire and smoke attacked Alex. Embers could be heard crackling. He turned Micheal's head away, having a feeling that he knew what he was doing with the Shadow King's body.

The crackling flames of the fires made Alex's skin crawl, but eventually, they dissipated after an uncounted length of minutes. The god turned to Alex and Micheal and gave them a dirty look.

"I suppose the intruders may stay, given they behave themselves."

Everyone glared at him but didn't say anything. He seemed to have the gods' respect or their fear. Both were powerful in the right hands.

All the gods disappeared except for one; the woman that

had made Sabine's body disappear.

She tilted her chin down to Alex's hand. "Keep good care of the stones. Wouldn't want you to get stranded away from your family, now, would we?" She winked at them and followed her comrades with their flair for dramatic exits.

The teen looked at his father. "Huh, was she the one that sent the stones to our world?"

Paxton thought for a moment before shrugging while nodding. "I guess so. She was always the nice one."

Cobalt stood next to his brother-in-arms. "We should gather the wounded."

Paxton dismissed him with a nod. "Agreed."

Alex wasn't looking forward to seeing the guts, blood, dismembered limbs, and dead bodies that plagued the battlefield. He prayed that the allied soldiers didn't ask too many questions.

Chapter 19

Alex had to push down nausea climbing up his throat as he assisted in dragging bodies, dead or alive, away from the battlefield. He struggled with a particularly heavy woman larger than him that couldn't walk. He tried dragging her, but he just ended up causing her more pain.

"Sorry, sorry," he apologized.

A person with tan skin and blonde hair unexpectedly lifted her legs, as Alex held her under her arms.

"Hiya, Alex." Dakota smiled at him.

"Hi, Dakota. Thanks." Alex still struggled, but it was much easier with another person.

They helped the woman to the triage set-up in the center of the village, seeing Amethyst and a few other medical-knowledgeable people patching up wounds, Maggie included.

The older woman nearly burst into tears when she saw him, pulling him into a hug after he and Dakota put the woman on a cot.

"Oh gods, Alex. Are you alright?" She brushed his blond hair from his eyes.

"I'm fine, Maggie but what are you doing here? Katelyn

told everyone to run."

Maggie scoffed at him. "I wasn't gonna leave my boys. I knew I could be of some help after. I just hid until the fighting was over. Now, you're sure you're okay?"

"Just peachy, Maggie." He smiled weakly. "Have you seen Micheal?"

She tsked and looked around. "No hon, sorry. I'm sure you'll find him."

Alex strolled around, only speaking a few words to Dakota.

In the empty field, he saw his father staring up at the cloudy sky with tear tracks still on his face. His side was bandaged, but he knew his father wasn't showing his emotions because of physical pain. He left his dad to his sorrows.

"Come on, Micheal. Where are you?" Alex mused to himself pointlessly.

He searched high and low for him until a revelation smacked him in the face. He sprinted to the beach. Sand kicked up from under his feet as he jogged to the dock.

Micheal was indeed there, sitting at the very end, hunched over with the side of his head resting on his knees. Alex sighed as he sat down next to him.

"Fancy meeting you here again." He tried to lighten the mood.

It failed when Micheal turned his head to lay his other temple on his knee, staring at Alex with broken, bloodshot eyes.

"Please, don't," he begged.

Alex moved closer and nodded, pulling Micheal into a side hug. He kept his mouth shut, not wanting to upset him somehow.

"I hate karma," Micheal said quietly.

"What do you mean?" Alex looked down at him.

"Just when I accepted her as my sister, she gets killed by

our father. All because I dragged us into the forest."

Alex sighed. "If it wasn't for you 'dragging us into the forest', I wouldn't have met my father, and we wouldn't have come here in the first place. And we wouldn't have known where we came from even if you thought you did. There is some bad but also some good in this."

Micheal sniffed, wiping his eyes with the sleeves of his shirt. The dark gray fabric was stained with burgundy red. "I guess..."

The air around them went silent other than the sound of the water slowly moving in the bay. The wildlife around them sang and chirped delicately. Alex was happy to have some peace and quiet, but he knew better than to hope it would last long.

"I want to go back," Micheal said, breaking the silence.

Alex couldn't form words for a moment. He turned his head. "What?"

"Home, I want to go home."

Alex felt his blood rushing through his veins and the unconscious irritation with it. "Micheal...you were the one saying that we should stay."

"And I'm changing my mind," Micheal's voice was unusually firm. It made Alex nervous. "It isn't always about you, Alex, even if everyone thinks you're the golden child."

He narrowed. "Are you kidding me? Are you trying to blame me for something? Because whatever you want to say, just spit it out already."

Micheal just scoffed.

Alex chuckled humorlessly. "Oh, that's *so* you, just running away from your problems." He hated when they argued like this. He rivaled Micheal on the basis of impulsiveness; he wasn't able to shut his mouth when he was mad.

"You're the one that continues to live in an abusive household and is in denial about it. Don't talk to me about running from my problems. You do it every day." Micheal fired back, scowling.

Alex slammed his hands down on the wood underneath him. "*You* are always the one to tell me to get away from Renee and Bradley, and now you want me to go back to them? I get that they aren't the best people, I realize that. I finally have people that care about me other than you, and now you want to take that away from me." He glared at him and shook his head. "Go away."

Micheal didn't move.

"Get away from me. Maggie's worried about you. Go see her and stay away from me for a while." The blond nudged him unkindly.

The other boy shoved himself up, looking like he wanted to kick him into the water but decided not to. Micheal stalked up the sand, leaving him alone.

As Alex stared across the water, he wondered how in the world his life ended up like this. His life had been planned out from the age of eleven, and he had never deviated from it. But that plan went right down the drain when Micheal took him into that forest.

He tried to force himself to understand his friend's feelings about their realm and that he was grieving the loss of his sister. Alex wouldn't be able to understand how that felt. And while he wanted to stay, he still had a life to get back to in his realm. He groaned to himself and dropped his chin to his chest.

"Alexander, is everything alright?" a man's voice from behind him startled him.

He spun around to face the person who scared him, and his heartbeat slowed down when it was just his father. "Jeez, you scared me. Again"

Paxton waved him off, sitting down next to him. "Sorry about that, but is everything okay?"

Alex kept his distance. He rubbed his eyes, trying to get

rid of the tears that had appeared while he was stuck in thought. "No, not really. Things are just so different now, and I don't know how to accept that." His father was just so open and welcoming that the words just came tumbling off his tongue regardless if he truly wanted to.

"Change can be scary, especially when you don't know where it's going to lead," Paxton said wisely. "It can be good, though, Alex."

The teenager nodded, not making eye contact with him. "I know." He crossed his arms over his knees. Alex felt his father move to put a hand on his shoulder but stopped, fingers barely brushing his shirt. Paxton pulled his hand away.

"That's not all that's bothering you, is it?"

Alex hesitated, the words stuck in his throat before they finally came spewing out. "I just blew up at Micheal. He wants to go back to our realm, and I don't. But one of us can't leave without the other because the stones need two people. So I just had a spat with him. But that's not it. Not exactly." He felt as if he was rambling, so he got to the point. "I was so angry at Sabine for what she did. She had my trust, and I thought she broke it right in front of me in the Inferno Realm."

The Guardian furrowed his brow. "What do you mean?"

Alex looked at his father. "You don't know what happened? Amethyst and Katelyn didn't tell you everything?" He got a shake of the head as an answer.

"Only that you got most of your powers back in the Inferno Realm. What else happened?"

"She was working with her father secretly to get me and Micheal to the Inferno Realm because Katelyn would follow us to protect us. Lloyd needed her power to be free along with ours which Sabine had in a necklace. However, she was against him the whole time and broke the necklace which gave us our powers back. But I was so mad at her

291

afterward." He bit his lower lip to stop it from trembling at the memory of him blaming her for putting everyone in danger, the simmering rage that had exploded.

"She died because she went against her father to get us our powers back and keep us safe. That was eventually her downfall. She had no obligation to us, but she did it anyway." The tears began to fall, cascading down his face. He felt numb. "And now she's dead."

"It wasn't your fault." Paxton reminded him gently. "It wasn't Micheal's either. She made her choice. But that doesn't mean you can't grieve her death, Alex."

His head shot up, turning to his father with bloodshot eyes. "How? How can you spend thousands of years watching the people you love die?"

His father looked into his eyes for a long moment, his hazel gray irises holding compassion. "I knew that was the deal when I became a Guardian and the gods manipulated the way we age. That I would watch hundreds fall and leave this world. At first, it was very hard to move on from the deaths of friends or even family, but as time passed, I found ways to remember them or honor them. I have to believe that I will see them again one day in whatever afterlife there is."

The blond wiped away his tears, sighing. "Will I have to take up your mantle if you die in my lifetime? Isn't that how it works here—people of power have heirs to take their place?" He couldn't bear it if he had to watch his new friends and family die while he had to move on from them. The responsibility would likely end up making him dead inside, an empty shell of the person he used to be.

Paxton shook his head, brow pinching as if the thought caused him physical pain. "That will be up to you. No one will force you to be a Guardian unless that is what you wish."

He messed with his shoelace. "Do you want me to?" he

292

asked quietly.

Hands moved his shoulders to face Paxton. Blue eyes met gray.

"I want you to make your own decisions. Don't let anyone ever tell you what choice you have to make. I'll be happy if you're happy."

Alex gave a watery chuckle. "You're pretty good at this parenting thing for not doing it for long. That's probably one of the sappiest things you've said so far." He changed the subject so that he wouldn't start crying again.

The man laughed. "Glad you think so. But what happened with you and Micheal? You said you got upset with him, and he seemed angry when I walked past him."

Alex grumbled, "I told you. He wants to go back. I don't."

He got closer to Alex. "Why don't you want to?"

Alex gawked at him. "Didn't we have this conversation? You're my dad, I want to stay with you. I've been just going through the motions in my realm, and now that I'm here...I don't want to give this up. I'm finally happy, but he's not."

Paxton had a knowing smile, but it was off. "And you're still going to go with him if he wants to."

Alex laid back on the dock, staring up at the sky. "I don't know. I could refuse to go back, and he'll be stuck here with me, but he'll hate me for it. We have our spats, but he's really mad this time. He might learn to live here but he'll never forgive me."

Hands dragged him up, and he tried to go deadweight on his father as the man pulled him into a sitting position.

"Have you tried using your words?" Paxton asked in a teasing way.

He groaned in a childlike manner. "Yes, I have, thank you very much. Micheal's just stubborn."

"And you aren't?" Paxton challenged. "If you're any child of mine, you have my bullheadedness."

"You win, you win. I'll talk to him." Alex settled. Paxton was giving him a firm glance as Alex looked back at the water. When Alex raised an eyebrow, Paxton jerked his head up the beach.

"Now? Like right now?"

"Yes, Alexander, go." His father shooed him.

Alex's shoes slowly pooled with white sand as he treaded up the short stretch of deep dunes and onto the grass. He found his way to the path and took the walk back to the village, for once ignoring the scenery around him.

The village was still in shambles, but it was better than it was a few hours ago. Rex was assisting a Henix guard with getting debris away from the houses, putting it in a pile to decide what to do with it later.

"You look like crap, kid," Rex said when he saw the blond.

"Speak for yourself," Alex shot back. He was right; the guard had gash marks marring his armor and his skin alike, mainly on his hands and inner forearm where his vambraces and leather didn't have much surface area.

"So what did you do to Micheal?" Rex brushed off his comment, getting back to work.

"Was he pouting or something?" Alex asked.

"He looked like a mad, kicked puppy, so something must've happened between you to make him mad." The older man had a dry smile. "Only a type of mad that a sibling or someone close to that title could achieve."

Alex ran his eyes through the village but couldn't catch sight of his friend. "Where is he anyway?"

Rex sighed in thought. "I think he's with Tucker and that girl. Don't know where they are though. Good luck."

Alex grimaced. "Thanks, I guess." Then he set off for his mini-mission of searching for and finding his friends. He asked around a few more times, and he eventually got pointed in the right direction.

Dakota, Tucker, and Micheal were helping clear the rubble as well. Micheal froze when he saw Alex. Tucker and Dakota went awkwardly silent.

Alex switched eye contact with Tucker and Dakota. "Can we have a minute?"

Tucker looked between the two of them before nodding. He pulled Dakota away as she hissed in protest.

Alex crossed his arms over his chest. Micheal did the same, digging his shoe into the loose dirt underneath him.

Alex cleared his throat. "I understand you want to go back. I do. I know we have lives to go back to. But I also need you to understand that I have a father who I want to see. You were robbed of that opportunity, I know that." Micheal nodded along but didn't speak. He was letting Alex finish. "I will go back with you, but I need you to promise that you will let me come back once and a while."

Micheal sighed heavily, leaning his head on the side of a house. "It's not that I don't want to come back ever, Lex. I just need time. And I need to talk to my parents."

He nodded. He could live with that. "Alright. Then we have a deal."

Micheal gave a weak smile.

Tucker and Dakota came back after two minutes and they began working immediately. Alex stayed to help. He noted how Micheal stayed silent for the rest of the time with him, Tucker, and Dakota.

There wasn't much Alex could say to fix his friend's broken heart.

Alex and Micheal shoved open the door to the house at dusk, looking around. They hadn't been in the house since the night before and weren't shocked to see some damage that had been caused by the battle and blasts of magic.

They lit the candles that were scattered through the ground floor to protect them from the throes of darkness that would soon be upon them.

Micheal took the responsibility of putting the furniture back in place, while Alex returned a few nicknacks to their proper home and replaced the books on the small bookshelf. They didn't want to make Maggie do it herself once she was done patching everyone's wounds.

Alex began to move upstairs. Opening the door to their room, he was surprised by the amount of natural light coming from inside the room. He looked up and stared up at the roof—or lack thereof. Instead of the wooden beams and panels, there was a giant hole right in the middle of the room.

Only bits and pieces of debris were sprinkled around the room—an easy clean up compared to the destruction outside.

"Huh," he mused while tilting his head to the sky again, "you don't see that every day." He went to the banister of the stairway and yelled down, "Micheal, come take a look at this."

Micheal sighed, dragging his feet up the stairs. "A 'you better take a look at this' cliche, Alex? Really? You're better than this."

Alex poked his head. "Don't sass me."

His friend stepped into the room, his previous smile turning into a look of bemusement and wonder mixed together. "Interesting."

"That's a word for it." Alex laughed. "Guess we're stargazing tonight." He threw his pillow on his bed which was slightly crispy from burn marks, but it was still functional. He brushed the ash from his sheets and laid down. His only hope was that they wouldn't get rained on.

Dusk turned into night, and the stars shined a little less bright this night even if they were more vibrant than their realm. Alex noticed the dull tone of the normally bright starlight that he had adjusted to the past week as he stared through the blasted ceiling.

"Even the stars are sad," he mindlessly whispered. It struck his mind that Micheal had had a very rough day with the death of his biological father and his sister, and Alex didn't want to tip-toe around the subject any longer. "How are you feeling?" He felt awkward asking; Alex wasn't the best with emotions.

"Fine," Micheal whispered back, so opposite from his normally loud and cheerful voice.

"Do you want to talk about it?" He turned over on his side in his bed, pillowing his head on his palm.

"No," Micheal didn't tear his eyes away from the stars.

Alex swallowed, not knowing what to say or do. He didn't know if a hug would be appropriate at the moment coming from Alex. He strained his brain for something to say that wouldn't sound stupid or insensitive, but he was blanking. But then he remembered the words of a shrink that his parents had made him see when he was younger.

"It's okay to feel, Mikey," he said gently, biting his lip in apprehension, not knowing if that was a proper thing to say.

The boy sniffed. "I know, Lex. Thank you."

And if Micheal cried quietly in the safety of their room for most of the night, Alex didn't say anything.

Chapter 20

The sun shined brightly on top of Alex, whose hands were braced against the railing of Katelyn's balcony. His eyes were pointed downward, refusing to look up at the happy sight of the people rejoicing after the past few days' events. A war between good and evil was finally won, even if it didn't feel like it to Alex.

The losses weighed heavily on his shoulders. He still didn't know how his father and the Guardians were able to deal with the death of their friends throughout the years, even the deaths of village members they didn't know well. Alex was still stuck on the deaths of the Ruddox, Henix, Nodium, and Silverbend soldiers.

Titan's wolf buddies had shown up the day before with the people of Phoenix. They had been upset about the destruction of their homes, but they were thankful for the Shadow King being defeated.

After hundreds of years of torment from Dark Knights, there was no one else to resurrect them which meant they would eventually all get killed off and would go extinct just as long as another conjurer doesn't dare to raise the dead. But Alex didn't want to entertain that possibility.

A person stepped up behind him, and on instinct, Alex's hand shot down to his waist where a dagger was hidden in his pocket.

"Just me," a youthful voice said from behind him.

The blond relaxed, and his hand went limp as he put it back on the rail. He had no need to turn, he knew who it was.

"Hey, Tucker. Sorry about that," he apologized.

Tucker stepped up next to him, leaning his cheek on his fist. He tapped his friend's skull with his free hand. "You're thinking awful heavily in there."

Alex stared at him for a few seconds. Tucker had a small smile on his face, but it was forced. His posture showed he hadn't slept well in multiple days. Grief ran deep in his honey-brown eyes.

"You're not okay either, are you?" he asked in a gentle voice.

The younger boy's face fell, and he broke eye contact, tapping the rail nervously with his fingernail. "I was mad at her. But I didn't want her to die."

Alex huffed and crossed his arms over his chest. "I understand. She was your friend. You didn't expect her to betray you, but it still hurt when she died. It wasn't your fault."

Tucker's lips twisted into a forced smile for a short while but it was more of a grimace. "You should listen to your own advice sometimes."

Alex smacked him on the head with a scoff. "Respect your elders, child."

The guard pouted at him. "You're barely older than me, that's not fair."

The two boys laughed as they continued to play-shove as they smack talked to each other. The two eventually stopped, and Tucker became more reserved.

"You're leaving, aren't you?" he asked with a depressed

voice.

The older boy responded with a nod, being honest with him. "Yeah...but we'll come back."

Tucker bit his lip. "You can't promise that."

Alex gave him a quick hug, tugging him close. Tucker held him back and then let himself be pulled away.

"We'll see you again, Tuck. Don't worry. And no pouting," Alex teased, tugging on a lock of his hair. Tucker batted at his hand but smiled.

They walked through Katelyn's house, and Alex took it all in. The moment he left the village, his and Micheal's lives would never be the same. The peace this realm contained even through war—it would be mourned the most.

They exited the house and started walking to the dock. The path soon turned into grains of sand, a good amount of it seeping into Alex's shoes.

The soft sound of the water lapping against the shore relaxed Alex, and they headed over to where a group of their friends was gathered and talking softly, with Micheal staring off into the ocean.

Once they reached them, Micheal pulled Alex aside. Alex gazed at him patiently. He could see his friend was struggling for words, and he granted him a few moments.

"I don't want to make you go if you don't want to." Micheal finally settled for. "I know that your life can be so much better here without your parents or bouncing around between realms or whatever. All I'm trying to say is, are you sure you want to do this?"

Alex shook his head. "You're my best friend Micheal. You aren't getting rid of me that easily. If you need a few years to say goodbye to your family, I'll deal with mine for a few years. I'm also not quite ready to leave everything else behind. But I have to talk to Amethyst before we leave."

Micheal glanced at the brown-haired girl and then

nodded.

Alex caught the healer's eye and jerked his head, asking for an audience with her. She cocked her head to the side but strolled with him.

"I probably should've told you this a while ago, but I just couldn't do it. I think my dad would freak out if I told him and would demand that I stay here," he opened with, as he moved sand with his foot.

"What is it?" Amethyst held his hands out, a gesture that told him she was ready to listen.

"Before I came here, *years* before, I started having this dream." He saw her face become concerned and pale. It wasn't giving him much encouragement to continue. "It was always the same. It was Lloyd attacking the Glade. But I was there. I could feel and hear everything and was aware of it. When we came here, it changed. I saw you in the Inferno Realm and someone asked me to find 'her'. To find *you*. And then it changed to my dad." Alex's eyes strayed to his father. "And now the dreams are gone. I don't know why."

The brown-haired girl's face was pinched in confusion and thought. "I don't know what it means, Alex," she admitted after being silent. "Dreams are dangerous. Especially since you're mainly a mental user. I can see if I can find anything." She kept her tone patient, her warm brown eyes soft as she smiled at him.

Alex hugged her, and she turned to walk away. Alex blinked as she went to rejoin the others. "Wait, what do you mean mainly a mental user?"

She didn't answer as she walked away. Alex would bring it up the next time he saw her.

When Alex went back to Micheal's side, Maggie rushed to hug the boys. "You two better come back." They hugged her back and then slipped away from her.

The two sons of Guardians stood side by side with each other, facing their new family. The Guardians were bunched together, the warriors looking at the two boys with varying degrees of worry and reluctance to let them go. Ryder and Cobalt stuck to the back of the group, the most unsentimental out of everyone. Elizabeth and Helena stood behind Paxton, Katelyn, and Amethyst. Alex and Paxton's eyes met and the boy hated the amount of fear and worry in them.

Next to him, Rex had his arm around Tucker's shoulders, keeping him in place, with Hunter and Jesse adjacent to them. Maggie had her hands folded in front of her, giving them a teary gaze. The people of Phoenix all looked sad to see them go, but they respected their choice to go back to their world. It wasn't like they could stop them.

"We'll be back. Promise," Alex offered, aiming to ease their minds.

Micheal hummed in agreement, slinging an arm around Alex's neck. "We just have to make sure no one thinks we're dead and develop a cover story to use whenever we come here and go back."

Alex's father stepped forward, looking him in the eye. "Alex, it is very hard to balance two lives."

Alex leveled a calm gaze at his father, and then glanced at everyone behind the man. "It's worth it for family."

Paxton kept pushing, tone rising. "Alexander, you could be in danger in your realm now that your powers are no longer dormant. We have no idea what is in your realm. *I* don't know how to protect you. People could come after you. Virgil is on the loose, we don't know what he's—"

Alex did the only thing he could to ease his father's panic. He hugged him, cutting his words off. "Good thing I have a father that can protect me when I come back," he whispered, only for him to hear.

Words were building back in the man's chest, but they stopped. He hugged Alex back for a few seconds, relishing the moment, and then letting him escape his grasp. Alex squeezed his father's hand once.

He stepped up to Micheal and showed him his wrist. "Are you ready to go?"

Micheal looked around one last time. "Let's go home."

It's not 'home'. Not anymore.

Alex connected their wrists, and the realm they had come to love disappeared from beneath their feet.

Chapter 21

Alex's feet touched the ground, softer than the previous times with no dizziness. *I guess I'm getting used to this.*

When the light died down, he was met with blue leaves on the ground, trees climbing high in the sky, and the old cars still stationary. Micheal turned and his knee slammed against the side panels of the cars. He went off in a frenzy of curses.

Alex muffled his laugh with his hand and turned his head. His shoulder still heaved with silent chuckles. While Micheal continued to be in pain, Alex scavenged for the belongings that they had left behind.

The ground was damp under his feet, insinuating it had rained or drizzled recently. Black caught his attention when he panned his eyes around. Their backpacks were left exactly where they had dropped them.

Alex rushed to them, scrambling to grab his phone. He needed to know how much time had passed. He needed to know that he would be about to see his friends and father again and that time didn't change drastically in certain realms.

"Micheal, what day did we leave?" Alex desperately

asked, still looking for his phone. Micheal started searching through his own backpack. He never got the chance to answer because Alex remembered the date himself. "November 7th," Alex said under his breath. He finally found his device and pressed the power button, praying he still had battery.

His phone came to life and he quickly read the date. November 18th. Only eleven days since they had left. Alex let the phone fall back into the bag.

"We're good," he said at Micheal's awaiting glance.

Micheal deflated as well, putting his bag on his back. "Time to face the music. Let's start walking."

Alex grabbed his bag and followed Micheal's footsteps. As they stepped out of the clearing, the trees swayed in the breeze and covered the entryway. Alex had a feeling they wouldn't be seeing the frozen highway ever again.

The walk back took less time than Alex recalled. Micheal was smart this time and used his phone to direct them out of the forest. It led them to the main highway. They walked silently, taking the same path they do after school, feeling the sense of normal coming back to him. Somberness and gloom invaded Alex's heart.

They reached their neighborhood and prayed the neighbors wouldn't see them. They reached Alex's house first, and he felt around for the key in his backpack.

Before he opened the door, he leaned his head against the cool steel and said, "We need a lie."

Micheal nodded slowly. "I have an uncle in New York. We went to stay with him for a few days because we both got upset about something. Yours can be academic pressure, and mine will be my worry for my military parents. Cops will feel bad because of the sob story and tell us not to do it again if they get involved. No one will suspect anything." His confidence was comforting.

Alex took a few breaths, running the scenario through

his head. It could work. "That's what we'll go with. Good luck." While Mark appeared to not care about Micheal, he was still his older brother. That protective urge would never dissipate. And Mark was vocal with his feelings.

Micheal looked to the door behind him. "You need it more than I do." He moped to his own house.

Alex waited for Micheal to open his door before entering his own house. He quietly pushed the door open, staying in the threshold. He paused for a beat and then took three steps. Silence greeted him. No one said anything. There was no movement. He sidled carefully through, closing the door with a quiet click.

Instead of going up the stairs, he felt compelled to check around the house. He checked the guest room and dining room to find nothing. When he went to the kitchen, he swallowed.

Renee looked up from the counter, just like she did almost two weeks ago when she was asking for money, but this time she was absent a bottle in her hand and the askew papers had been cleaned up. She stared at him, and Alex just stared back.

"I covered for you," she said finally. She wasn't angry. She was...calm.

Alex couldn't believe his ears. "You did?"

She nodded. "I nearly reported you missing, but I didn't want to deal with the cops. Your friend's brother came knocking on the door and asked if I had seen either of you. I told him no but guessed you two went somewhere for the heck of it. I got the school off your back as well."

Alex didn't know exactly how to feel. For all she knew, he could've been kidnapped and didn't tell any of the authorities, but what she *had* was the most she had done in a long time.

"Thank you," he said awkwardly.

She nodded. "You've been taking mental health days.

The school bought it. You probably don't have many left at this point." She went about her business, leaving Alex alone with his shock.

Alex's feet didn't move until he forced them to, still surprised at his adoptive mother's actions. The stair creaked under his weight, and he mindlessly entered his room. He kicked the door shut but didn't move to lock it. He didn't feel the need to.

He gave a call to Micheal but it went to voicemail after a few rings.

Mark must be giving him an earful.

He went through the endless texts and voicemails from his friends, all of them having the same worried tone that progressed with each message. Once all of them were vaguely answered, he lay on his bed, processing. His memories of his adventure in Realm Six made him tired and his eyelids fell closed. He was swept into darkness.

Until he wasn't.

He was standing still, his bare feet on the ground. It was pitch black. This wasn't just him dreaming. Something was wrong because he could *move*. He took a cautious step, and then another one, and then another.

He carefully turned around, and a sliver of light was on the floor, like light spilling out from underneath a door. And it actually was a door, he realized as his eyes adjusted.

He approached it. He stretched a hand out. His hand touched wood. Reaching for the doorknob or handle, he felt almost hot.

He found a knob and twisted, opening the door. He stepped into the room, his feet feeling wood and he cringed as light attacked his eyes.

Rays of sun came from a window to his left. He shielded his eyes with a hand until his eyes adjusted. Glancing around, the room had wood flooring, some dusty furniture, and a fireplace, but it wasn't lit. It seemed to be abandoned.

There was nothing indicating any signs of life.

Why am I so hot? A layer of sweat glistened in the sunbeams.

The door slammed shut behind him. Alex jumped and glanced around, feeling the presence of someone else in the room.

"Did you really think you could just get rid of me?" a man whispered from behind him.

A hand closed around Alex's throat, cutting off his airway. Alex struggled, trying to pry the hand off of him to no avail. He switched to kicking but he was pushed against the wall.

Alex felt himself losing consciousness after a minute of struggling. Before he felt like he was going to pass out, he saw a pair of piercing green eyes, and then he was back in his room.

He jerked up in his bed one hand tightly wrapped around his neck where the ghostly presence of another hand remained. He coughed a few times. The sound of panting filled the silence in the air.

Once the feeling left him, Alex slowly loosened his grip and stared down at the bed. His dreams were back, but it was different now. The rules had changed, and Alex didn't know why. He didn't *understand.*

Alex held his head in his hands, his breathing not slowing. He had recognized the person that was strangling him. He couldn't forget those eyes.

Lloyd.

The journey will continue...

Nicole Cavey is the author of the exhilarating fantasy series Realms Crashers. She was born and raised in Ellicott City, Maryland. She began to place her thoughts on paper in the seventh grade but never planned for something greater. She has always had a love for the fantasy worlds that she read about and decided to begin her own in 2021 at the age of 15. In college, she will pursue a career in criminal forensics but will continue her passion for reading and writing. Nicole currently lives in Maryland with her family and four-legged animals, plays travel softball and rides dirtbikes.

CPSIA information can be obtained
at www.ICGtesting.com
Printed in the USA
BVHW041159210423
662798BV00007B/421